"By all means, my dear!"
~Dorian Lord

THE BILLIONAIRE'S FAKE FIANCÉE

ANNIKA MARTIN

Chapter One

Tabitha

REX'S angry baritone voice rumbles through the polished wood door that separates his majestic office from the lowly world of normal people.

I wince inwardly. You can only make out random words, but it's clear that he's both stunned and enraged at the incompetence of the mere mortals who surround him.

Amanda's eyes widen. "Maybe today's a bad day to bring me in there?" she squeaks.

I try for a breezy smile. "It'll be fine," I say. "Everybody annoys and upsets Rex. Once you get to know him, you'll see it's just how he is."

More yelling.

Amanda looks like she wants to melt into the wall. She tightens her grip on the handle of my rolling salon case, sparkly pink with polished silver hinges and hardware. I've been letting her wheel it into my clients' offices as a visual aid to help prepare them for my absence, a way of passing my mobile stylist torch. Just for a few weeks, anyway.

Hopefully just a few weeks.

More angry rumbles.

I smile like it's so amusing. "Oh, *Rex*!" I whisper.

She searches my face. Am I joking?

I was hoping she could have an okay interaction with him before being exposed to his terrifying, god-throwing-thunderbolts management style.

Too late now.

I pull her farther to the side just in time for a trio of men in suits to burst out and head down the lavishly carpeted hallway, down past the rows of offices—little glass boxes where Rex keeps his assistants. Most of the offices are darkened now, being that it's eight on a Friday night.

We watch them head down the hall toward the empty area where more of Rex's assistants toil each day.

They keep going, picking up speed as they enter the area where the assistants to Rex's assistants toil. There's probably a dungeon somewhere beyond that where those assistants' assistants' assistants work, and below that, a torture chamber would not be a shocker.

More grumbling from inside.

"He's not a bad person," I whisper. "It's just his style." Rex O'Rourke is an achingly gorgeous man with a large frame and sooty eyelashes, but he's definitely scary—in a sort of gothic way, I like to think. He's some kind of financial powerbroker, the head of Rex O'Rourke Capital.

"Erp," she says, unconvinced.

My smile does not waver. No way will I let her wiggle out of this.

I employ two stylists, and Amanda's my best. I need my best for Rex because there are very specific ways to shape his short beard and cut his hair, and I don't like to think of somebody getting it wrong. You have to appreciate the handsome shape of his face; you also have to account for his habit of shoving his hands through his hair when he's irritated, which is always, and which results in a dramatically swept-back style.

I kind of love when he does the irritated hands-through-his-hair thing. And his beautiful lips go frowny, and his hard energy fills the room, and people literally scurry for the hills like ocelots sensing a coming tidal wave.

And I'll be busily setting up my mobile salon, and I know I shouldn't find that amusing, and I definitely shouldn't imagine pressing my hands against the velvet-smooth scruff on Rex's cheeks and kissing his big frown.

Nevertheless.

I guess I've always had a bit of a crush on him. More than a crush. Rex loves to act like I'm the most annoying person in the universe, but the heart wants what it wants.

In spite of Rex's seeming annoyance with me, I do feel we have a certain connection—that we're *simpatico*—not that he'd ever acknowledge it any more than a roaring, angry lion would acknowledge that a little breeze feels nice.

No, Rex exists in a rarified realm of celebrities and billionaires, a sparkling stratosphere where you never have to wait in post office lines or claw price tags off of things and your quest for world domination might actually work.

I've been cutting his hair every Friday night at ten minutes after eight, which is when aftermarket trading closes, whatever that is. He can't be bothered prior to that. If there's one thing I've learned about him, it's that world domination is the only thing he cares about.

More yelling. Another suit, a woman this time, bursts out of the office. A man follows her, then another, moving quickly. Something must've happened because usually it's quieter at this time of night. I like to think of it as our time, stupid as that may sound.

3

My gaze drops to Amanda's white-knuckled grip. If her hands are shaking, she'll screw up Rex's haircut for sure.

I'd be the one to cut his hair this evening, but my wrist is immobilized in a brace thanks to a repetitive stress injury that's on track to destroy my life. I'm supposed to take six weeks off. If it's not better by then, another six. I don't know how I'll pay rent. I barely have rent for this month.

I can't think about that.

Amanda stiffens as Rex's growl sounds through the now-partially-open door. Growling his words. Another unfortunate underling is still in there.

"The trick with Rex is to relate to him with a sense of fun," I whisper. "Fun is your suit of armor. And never let him see you sweat. Never let him smell blood in the water."

She grips the case harder. "Oh-kay."

"Seriously, no matter what, always show that you're having fun," I say.

"But I'm not naturally fun like you are," she says.

I want to tell her that I'm not naturally fun, either, but she wouldn't believe it. I've learned to be fun. Being the funnest person ever and never letting people see me sweat is my life strategy, and it's served me well. Especially with Rex.

Rex is an investment guy. Maybe hedge funds—I'm never really clear. He's some kind of celebrity in the business world. They put his picture on the front of magazines a lot. Not any kind of magazine I'd ever buy, but the Patek Philippe watch bros seem to grab up anything with his picture on it like the last Doritos at a party full of stoners.

And sometimes when you go to news websites to get the latest on the royal babies, there'll be a sidebar with other news stories to click on and you'll see his name alongside blurbs about what stocks he's buying and selling, what he thinks about this or that market. People always seem to be reacting to what he says, whether it's to agree or disagree. Basically, any statement that comes out of Rex O'Rourke's mouth is a *thing*.

When you're walking around in his posh, eco-friendly headquarters—a converted warehouse complex—you see his signature on signage everywhere. His signature is the literal logo of Rex O'Rourke Capital, as though it's his promise. Rex O'Rourke is a monster, but if you sign on the dotted line, he'll be your monster.

"Just walk in there with your head held high and find the fun," I say. "You're having fun, and he's all hatey, and that's on him. It's the only way to deal with somebody like Rex."

"Okay." She nervously bites her lip.

"It's true. Surly men like Rex always have a dark and painful secret and zero fun in their lives."

"How do you know?" Amanda narrows her eyes. "Did you get that from your soap opera?"

"Well...yeah," I admit. "But that doesn't make it less true."

I have a soap-opera themed Instagram account. I find soap operas incredibly soothing. Sometimes when I can't go to sleep at night, I think about my favorite characters. I've been doing a lot of that lately, needless to say. A wrist injury is a scary thing when you're a hairdresser.

"The only way to deal with a man like Rex is to put on a smile, lace up your sparkly boots, and ignore his growls. Think of him as a lion with a thorn in his paw. It's not about you. He just has a big ol' thorn in his paw," I say.

The way Amanda stares at me, you'd think I'd grown my own lion's paws, and maybe even a big, fluffy mane.

I do feel that Rex carries a kind of dark weight—it's something that I keep in mind when he acts like he hates my jokes or makes frustrated sounds when I stroll in wearing my awesome outfits. Personally, I think it's good for him to be exposed to somebody who is an imaginative dresser. The man seriously lives the life of a gothic villain in a lonely castle, though his gruff style of human interaction doesn't seem to hurt him in the womanizing department at all, if gossip sites are anything to go by.

I sometimes examine the pictures of him that appear online, partly to see how the style holds up in the wild, though I can't help but notice that the rail-thin models and socialites he appears with dress in a completely boring way. A lot of earth tones—mostly black. Totally funereal. Like they think fun colors might hurt his eyes or something.

According to reports, Rex O'Rourke never sleeps with the same woman twice. Even so, women line up around the block for a crack at him. A recent Sunday feature paints him as quite the Casanova. Is he amazing and dramatic in bed with all of these women? Is that what's going on?

More grumbled words.

"I don't think I can do it," Amanda whispers.

"I wouldn't have brought you to take my place with him if I didn't think you could do it," I say, taking a firmer tone now. "You got this."

"It's kind of amazing that he likes you," she whispers. "It seems like he wouldn't like somebody with a fun attitude."

"Likes me? Are you kidding? He hates *me*, too. It's possible he hates me even more than he hates everyone else."

"What?" Amanda is freaking now. It's eight after. Two minutes to haircut time. "He hates you?"

"I completely annoy him. He's an utter asshole to me. I don't let him get to me, but yeah, he is not a fan."

She gapes at me. "Why do you put up with him? Tabitha, you have a massive waiting list. Guys dying for *you specifically* to be their stylist."

I shrug.

"Is it possible you're a masochist?" she asks. "I think you are."

Rex's red-headed right-hand man, Clark, slips out the door just then. "Hey, Tabitha!"

"Hiya, Clark!" I say.

Clark's eyes fall to the brace on my wrist. Quickly I cross my arms, hoping he didn't really notice. I don't want Rex to know why I'm taking time off. I introduce Clark to Amanda and explain she's taking my clients temporarily. Clark winces at the closed door. "Possibly not the best day for a change."

"Gulp," I say brightly. "It can't be helped. If he's upset, I'll amaze him with my favorite Stefano-faking-his-own-death storyline from *Days of Our Lives*," I joke.

Clark snorts. "Somebody has a death wish." With that he heads off.

"Rex O'Rourke likes to hear about soap operas?" Amanda asks.

"Oh my god, no, he hates to hear about soap operas," I say, rolling my sleeve over my injured wrist. "Few things agitate him more. Rex hates anything that is pleasurable or relaxing. When you give him a scalp massage, you have to pretend that it's the only way his hair follicles will lie naturally. That's what I told him—if he doesn't let me do it, the haircut won't lie right."

"Why not just skip the head massage?" she asks. "I mean, if he hates it…"

"Just because," I say.

Because of all the people in the world, he needs it the most. The man literally has no pleasure in his life.

As if on cue, Rex yells at somebody—every other word is a number; that's Rex's thing when he's yelling. My phone pings that it's ten after.

"Go time," I say.

Amanda swallows with seeming difficulty. I knock on Rex's door.

A grumble from inside. "What?"

"Haircut."

A grunt.

"That means 'come on in.'" I grab my Hello Kitty shoulder bag and lead Amanda into his grand office where every surface is cold and flat and the view of the harbor is breathtaking.

And at the center of it is Rex in all his glowering glory.

His beauty stops my heart for a second, like it always does. His gray eyes glitter, and his skin glows with annoyance, and even the shiny parts of his hair seem to brighten with aggravation.

"What is this?" he grunts, meaning, *why is a strange woman with you?*

"This is Amanda Barnes. She's taking over my clients for the next six weeks."

Amanda smiles uncertainly. "Nice to meet you, Mr. O'Rourke."

"Six weeks? Where the hell are *you* going?"

"Vacation." I motion for Amanda to start setting up the mobile station. She opens the case, pulls out the tarp, and unfolds the collapsible stool.

I can feel Rex's gaze on me.

"Amanda's amazing," I say. "And don't worry, your front office did the whole background check on her, and everything's okay. No trails of dead bodies or lamps made of human skin." You have to have a background check before you get within a hundred feet of Rex's office.

"Is okay with my front office the same as okay with me?" he says.

"Amanda is amazing," I repeat brightly. "Ready?"

He stalks over, managing to express annoyance in every fiber of his muscular frame, and sits himself down on the stool.

I nod to Amanda, who puts the cape around his shoulders, willing her not to shake too hard. I give her a reassuring smile upon her successful completion of the cape-snapping process.

So far so good.

Amanda begins to comb his hair. I stand where Rex can't see me, smiling and nodding encouragement, breathing in Rex's hard, spicy scent. She puts down the comb and places her hands on his scalp for the massage.

"No, no, no." Rex shakes her off. "Fuck off with that. Cut it and be done."

Amanda looks at me for help.

"Very well, she'll skip that part," I say brightly. I turn to Amanda. "Right here." I smooth up the back of his neck with my good hand. "Just a very clean fade up the back and sides."

"Why can't you do it this one last time and she can watch?" Rex asks.

"Because this is better," I say.

Amanda pulls out the electric razor and the mobile power station.

"So what the hell?" Rex rumbles. "Did you wake up one day and decide it was a good time to take a six-week vacation?"

I go around to face Rex, arms crossed. Our eyes meet, and my belly flip-flops. It's so rare that I speak to him face to face. Usually I'm behind him or at his side, focused on his hair. His beautiful eyes glitter. It's unnerving.

I keep my bad wrist hidden under my left arm, even though I have my sleeve all the way down. I don't want him to even notice the outline of the brace. I told all my other clients about my repetitive stress injury, but Rex is different. Rex is different in every way.

"People do take vacations," I say.

"A six-week vacation? Did you wake up one day and say to yourself, 'I've built this business and now I'm going to abandon it for six weeks because, *why not*'?"

I smile. "So weird. That is exactly what I woke up one day and said to myself!"

"A six-week vacation," he growls.

The buzz of the razor starts up. "Okay, you have to stay still," I say.

"You know who takes six-week vacations? Losers."

I stifle a grin. It's such a Rex thing to say. "Maybe I'm finally taking that romantic vacation to the Hello Kitty amusement park in Tokyo that I've been dreaming about." Rex hates my Hello Kitty thing. I have a tattoo of Hello Kitty on my ankle that I once took perverse glee in showing him.

Rex narrows his eyes, face lit with ire. It does something very wrong to my belly. "Romantic vacation? Is your boyfriend an axe murderer? Is that it?"

"How do you know I'm not going on my own steam? Maybe it's romantic because of my love for Hello Kitty."

"No way would you be able to go to Tokyo on your own steam," he says. "You're a wage slave in Manhattan. I don't know or care what you charge, but you work by the hour, which means you're doomed always to have roommates, never to have a retirement savings, and to eventually be a sixty-year-old ward of the welfare state being supported by people like me. Best case."

"Rex O'Rourke." I smile at him sweetly. "Do I need to put a relaxing jasmine-scented towel over your face?"

He glares.

Amanda looks like she's going to have a coronary event.

"Maybe my axe-murdering boyfriend will be enjoying my jasmine-scented towel in Tokyo," I tease.

Rex's expression changes right then, and I don't know what to make of it. There's this beat where everything's weirder than usual. Did I just cross a line? Everything is awkward. I go over to where Amanda is nervously perfecting his fade.

"Nice," I say. "This is an amazing job she's doing."

I can feel the darkness rolling off Rex.

She puts aside the razor and takes up the shears, fluffing his hair with her left hand.

"Here's where I kind of start…" I indicate the shape that works best with Rex. "See how…" I show her where I let the length come in.

"Right," she says. "Got it."

A top stylist like Amanda can tell a lot from the week-old haircut—enough that most mobile stylists might just send a substitute in their place without training them on the specific cuts, but I've been personally introducing her and giving her the lowdown on each person. I act like I'm all fun and games but I'm dead serious about quality. I don't think my clients are even aware of it, but I am, and that's what counts. So even though Amanda could probably get the cuts ninety percent right, I want my people to have a hundred percent with zero trial and error. I want my clients to experience seamless top quality. Especially Rex.

Half the battle of cutting hair is assessing somebody's personality and what they want to project to the world and then making them look even more like that. Rex was easy. His message to the world is, *I have this under control, so screw off!* Brutal perfection wrapped in barbed wire. Keep out!

Not that he needs a haircut for that. I could do a clown bowl cut on him, and he'd still manage to project brutal perfection wrapped in barbed wire.

But I'd never give him a bowl cut. Rex gets this awesome long-on-top 1920s cut that looks as amazing when it's perfectly combed back as when he's all worked up and doing his hands-in-hair thing.

"I don't have all day," Rex barks.

Amanda stiffens. I don't like him focusing so much on her.

Silently I indicate the other angle I want her to see. "So, in other news, remember how Stefano helped EJ kidnap Sami's husband and put a lookalike in his place?"

"Did I just see that rewatch recap on your Instagram?" Amanda says.

"Wait, what?" Rex bellows. "Jesus Christ, it's not enough of a waste of time to watch soap operas in the first place? You're recapping old episodes on social media?"

"I certainly am!" I say brightly.

That's one of the things I do with him—when he says something mean, I act like I think it's a compliment. You can't let a man like Rex see weakness.

"Soap operas provide amazing life lessons," I add with a wink at Amanda. The menacing sound from Rex is beyond priceless. I can't see his face, but I can practically feel his glower radiate through me.

Eventually it's time for the beard trimmer. When I first came to Rex, whoever was cutting his hair was doing his beard in a full shape—so wrong! Shaping the beard is really shaping the face. Rex's face is roughly sculptural, and the close way I do his beard enhances his looks.

"Amanda," I say, "if you go slightly concave here, do you see the line that you create?" I indicate the sweep of the beard edge down from his cheekbones, hoping she sees it, how extra gorgeous he looks with the tight beard shape.

Amanda nods, but I think she really doesn't see. People don't really see him.

Doing facial hair is a very personal thing. Rex might not realize the magic that I work on him, but that's okay.

Rex is an asshole who won't miss me at all, but I'll miss him.

"The line is here." I slide my left hand down the side of his face, smoothing a swath from just below his cheekbone straight down to his jawline. That's my absolute favorite part of his beard.

If my wrist doesn't heal, I might never see him—let alone *touch* him—ever again.

Chapter Two

Rex

IT'S MONDAY NIGHT, or actually just before three in the morning on Tuesday. The Shanghai stock exchange is about to close and I'm with my team on the quant floor—we're huddled around a table filled with to-go containers in front of a wall of monitors. Our eyes are on a pair of charts at the center— diverging lines that say our new strategy has killed it.

The algorithm we developed based on our new strategy moves the dial just a fraction of a fraction of a point, but when you deal with the numbers we deal with, it's enough to make or break a small economy, and the trend is holding for the sixth day straight when tested live, which means I'll be giving each of them the kind of bonus they could retire on.

The trend holds. And holds. I can feel their excitement building. The clock turns over.

Somebody behind me sucks in a breath. That's the only sound I hear. The dozen of them will hoot and dance and hug as soon as I'm safely out of earshot, but for now, there's silence. Large displays of emotion annoy the shit out of me.

"There it is," I say. "Nice job. Keep it up." Without another word, I get out of there.

Up in my office, I grab a quick nap, and then I wake up just after six for premarket trading and new initiatives with London.

Clark walks into my office at around nine, coffee in hand. "Did you just get here or did you never go home?" he asks.

"Stayed with the quants."

He stops in front of me, watching my face, assessing my mood. He's been with me from the start, and he can read me like nobody else.

"What?" I say, taking the cup.

"It's Driscoll."

"What *about* Driscoll?" I ask.

Driscoll is a family of brands that controls a huge portfolio of funds, including some massive private pension funds and investment funds that I've been working tirelessly to get my hands on.

We have a small part of their business, and we've given them an incredible return. I feel like I'm on the verge of getting all of their assets under management. If I could do that, I wouldn't just be playing the markets; I'd be controlling the markets.

"I spoke with Gail," Clark says.

"Good." Gail is Gail Driscoll, matriarch of the Driscoll family of brands. "Is she ready?" Meaning, ready to give it all to me.

Silence.

"What?" I bark.

"She's considering other suitors."

"What?"

"Her board's involved, and they're conducting some sort of review now. It's between you and Wydover."

I nearly spit out my coffee. "You're joking." But his expression is wooden. He wouldn't joke like that. Not to me, anyway. "This is coming from Gail?"

Clark nods.

"Has she lost her mind?"

No reply.

Gail's known for good decisions; she's a seventy-something woman with a sharp intellect and a spine of steel. Shrewd and tough in business, she comes out of a central Texas ranching family. I've always respected her, in spite of her ridiculously puritanical ways.

Then it comes to me. "Jesus Christ. Is it that Sunday feature article?"

Clark raises his eyebrows above his gold wire-rimmed glasses. He doesn't have to say it. He thinks it could be.

"Did she specifically say it was the article?"

"She didn't have to," Clark says. "Everybody thinks you're some kind of sex-addled emperor now. You're Caligula up here, having orgies and bathing in the tears of virgins. Gail can't be loving that image. You know how she is about image. She's careful about who she ties her brand up with."

The Sunday feature article from a few weeks ago was so far from the truth it's crazy. Yes, I never sleep with the same woman twice. But I'm always up front about who I am—I'm the asshole who won't call or text or come around for a second date. Ever. I go to great lengths to make that plain right up front with women.

"Such bullshit," I growl. "And with this new algo, I've barely left this office for two months straight. Now I'm Caligula?"

Clark sips his coffee.

I want to kill somebody. I employed a team of people

whose specific job it was to keep a lid on articles like that. Needless to say, I fired them when the article hit the presses.

"Making us compete against Wydover," I say. "What is she thinking?"

Clark waits.

Pete Wydover of Wydover Asset Management is our biggest competitor. He's a cheater and a liar, but unlike me, he comes from old money, which seems to buy him a squeaky-clean image no matter what he does.

Clark sits and crosses his legs. He has short, coiled hair and a coiled runner's body. He's smart, intuitive, and clients love him. "Ready for the good news? I took Gail to breakfast."

"Good." Clark is good with Gail. He's good with all of the clients. "And?"

"I told her about the new algorithm. She's very interested. Very positive." He pauses then, and there's something about the pause I don't like.

"What?"

"I told her how eager you are to discuss it with her. On the yacht next week."

I turn to face him. "What?"

"You know you have to say yes this year," he says. "If you want her business."

He's talking about a two-week megayacht trip I always get invited to. A yearly Driscoll affair with extended family, friends, and business movers and shakers. I've turned down the invitation for the past three years. It's a megayacht that's longer than a football field and full of shuffleboard courts, cabanas, games, musical shows. A little slice of hell, basically.

"Anything but that."

"Rex. If you want Driscoll—all of Driscoll—then you will put on a sailor hat, and you will get on that yacht, and you will show her somebody who fits in over there. You will correct the impression that the article made."

I groan.

"I'm sure the thing has business services," he says. "You can work while you're there."

"On what planet do I take two weeks out of my schedule—"

"You want Driscoll?" he asks.

I sigh. "Is Wydover going to be on board?"

"No, but he was at her New Year's ranch gala. Maybe that's how he wheedled into the running."

The Driscoll ranch gala. Another invitation I blew off.

"You take that vacation," Clark says. "Somebody else has her ear, and they're talking up Wydover. And now the article? You need to get in there and do some personal damage control. Show Gail that the guy who gets her the best return is also the Driscoll family kind of people."

I'm not the Driscoll family kind of people. I grew up in South Boston, living in the back of my father's bar, working after school from the age of ten. To read that article, however, you'd think I spent my youth brawling in gutters and snatching old ladies' purses when the truth is, I did everything I could do to keep my nose clean. What's more, the article made my rise look like it was all about luck. Sure, I was lucky—I made my luck by being the best at what I do. Working twice as hard as Pete Wydover.

"You think Wydover had a hand in that article?" I ask Clark.

"Hard to say," Clark says. "The point is, you have to go. This is the price of admission for her account. I'll be there. She invited me, too."

I stare up at the ceiling. Clark's right. This is the price of admission. Except I hate boats. I hate events. I hate forced socializing.

But I love the idea of the Driscoll account.

Having all of Driscoll's assets under management will give

me more financial power than most governments, but it's about more than that—there are only a few accounts of that size in the world. Landing one has always symbolized something ineffable to me. Strength. Freedom. Untouchability. But more, somehow—something I can't put my finger on.

"I guess I can work in my room," I say.

Clark is watching me. Monitoring my expression in a way that makes me nervous.

"What?" I ask.

"There's more," Clark says.

"What more could there be?"

"This Rex in the article, it's not reality. We know that."

"Right," I say.

"I told her how upset you are about what they wrote. How untrue it is, especially that bit about a different girl every night. And…" He pauses ominously, then, "Your fiancée is even more upset."

I nearly spit out my coffee. "My fiancée?"

Clark winces.

"You didn't really say that," I try.

"I panicked. She was unhappy about that article, and she had that Gail Driscoll stare—she needed to hear something that showed they got you wrong, and I just blurted it out."

I suck in a breath. "Me with a *fiancée*? Who would buy that?"

"Gail did. She was happy to hear it. She likes you, Rex, and she needed to hear something like that. She wants to believe in you."

"But it's not true," I say. "I don't have a fiancée, and I never would."

"I know. I shouldn't have said it, but I needed to come up with something," he continues. "And then once I said it, I had to go with it. So, you're engaged. Deeply in love. You can't wait to start a family. You're keeping it under wraps for now.

Shielding your fiancée from the media and all of that. You're very protective of her because she's not the kind of girl you usually go for. She's changed your world, and it's been amazing to see. Gail ate it up."

I gape at him. "You know Gail hates any kind of dishonesty." It's one of the few things Gail Driscoll and I have in common.

"I know," Clark says. "But you should've seen how she lit up."

"You couldn't have explained the exaggerations in the piece?"

"She needed something positive. I went with my intuition."

"So you made up a fiancée of all things? Hey, why stop there?" I bite out. "You should also let her know I've been fashioning tiny mobility-assistive devices for underprivileged three-legged kittens. I mean, a fiancée?"

Clark has good instincts about people, but I don't like this. I'm upfront with what I am. In business, I'm the asshole who gets results. In romance, I'm the asshole who'll show you a good time. Nothing more.

That's always been good enough.

I go to the window. Clark knows I want that account with every fiber of my being.

"You've had no public dinners or pictures with a woman since Thanksgiving weekend. And now it's almost March," he says. "It's perfect. You met somebody in early December. She's different. Hates the public eye and all that."

I watch the snow clouds roll in off the water, thinking miserably of being away from my operations and my team for two weeks.

"You've been eating and sleeping this algorithm lately," he continues. "The timeline works perfectly."

"Fine. I'll go on the yacht. Work remotely. Put in a few hours on deck chairs. Show up for dinners and whatever bullshit they've got planned. Maybe in a few months we put out a press release where my fiancée broke it off."

Clark sucks in a deep breath. "So…right. That was my original thought."

Was his original thought? I turn to find him regarding me warily. "What?"

"Gail invited your fiancée," he says.

"Excuse me?"

"She wants your fiancée to come," he says.

I blink, disbelieving. "Did you tell her *my fiancée* is busy?"

"Well." Again he winces. "I felt like she'd smell the lie if I said that. So I told her I'd check, but I thought she'd be excited."

"Are you shitting me?"

Clark shakes his head. "You really have to bring her."

"Who? She doesn't exist!" I say. "What have you done?"

"It's fine," he says. "We'll find you a fiancée."

"Find me a fiancée," I say, disbelieving.

He winces. "Sorry."

Anybody else who pulled this kind of thing, I'd fire them so fast. But not Clark. It's not just that he's been with me since the beginning. He's a loyal friend. And brilliant with clients. Usually.

"She won't figure it out," he adds. "People bring fake dates to weddings all the time. This is a step up from that. We'll find you an actress to play the part. Tell her not to bother you while you're working."

"And what happens when Gail goes to the next Broadway show or goes on Netflix and sees the fiancée I briefly had and then broke up with starring in something? Gail's not an idiot."

"A model, then."

My mind reels with the insanity of it all. "I thought we were going for a camera-shy fiancée," I say.

"Right," he says.

"Okay, we'll figure it out. We'll put her in another cabin."

"She can't be in a different cabin. She's your fiancée."

"I won't be in the same cabin with a beautiful woman throwing herself at me. I don't like the odds of me resisting that for two weeks. And then I'm stuck in a tiny space with somebody I've slept with and don't want a relationship with? I'd rather be trapped in a *Sound of Music* sing-a-long."

Clark nods. He knows that I don't do sleepovers, I don't do the same woman twice, and I would never actually bring a woman home. "Maybe if you request a two-room suite, and one side is the office and you sleep in the office…" he says.

"The small-space problem remains," I say. "Jesus."

"How about a woman you find annoying?" he tries. "And she stays locked in the bedroom?"

Something in me perks up at that. "That might work. An annoying nobody with the qualities I hate."

"Though an annoying nobody with the qualities you hate is ninety-nine percent of the human population. We'd have to narrow it down."

"A female," I say. "Reasonably hot, but somebody whose personality irritates me so much, I wouldn't want to touch her with a ten-foot pole."

Clark's smirking. "Hot with the qualities you hate. Maybe more specific?"

"You need a list? Give me your go-folder."

He holds up the brown leather folder he brings everywhere. I snatch it and take it to my desk, grabbing a sheet of paper. I clip it to the top inside of his folder. At the top I write "REX HATES:" with a bold underline. Then another bold underline for good measure.

I pause.

"You hate perky, bubbly people," Clark reminds me. "You're always saying that."

"True," I say. "A bubbly attitude annoys me." I write the numeral *one* and "bubbly personality."

"Maybe we find some low-level model who is perky and bubbly," Clark says. "And it would have to be somebody into soap operas. You hate when people are into soap operas. And that can be what she watches when she's shut up in her room."

"That's the perfect number two item," I say. "Because it shows the woman is an imbecile who I have nothing in common with." I write the numeral two and "thinks soap operas are profound." I tap the pen on the smooth mahogany surface of my desk, trying to imagine the most annoying fiancée to take on this trip.

It's almost too bad Tabitha is probably halfway around the world in Japan by now. But then, I want a plausible fake fiancée. Nobody in their right mind would buy me marrying somebody like that.

"Number three," I say. "Impoverished. Impoverished people are easier to control."

"Impoverished meaning what? How impoverished?"

"Pathetically impoverished. Hourly worker. Takes public transportation. You know, impoverished. Number four, laughs at anything. Number five, stupidly positive attitude." I'm writing it all down.

"Wanted, one soap-opera-obsessed, pathetically impoverished woman with good looks and a stupidly positive attitude. Are you imagining this as text for a Craigslist ad?" Clark asks.

I ignore him, adding "colorful hair streaks, sparkles, etc." as item six.

Clark nods. "Don't forget Hello Kitty stuff. You hate when people have a Hello Kitty obsession."

"How do you know?" I ask, surprised.

"The ten times you told me," he says.

"Huh. Well, I do hate it." I jot it down. "And seven, narrates her expressions and reactions to things. As in, *sad face.*

22

Heart eyes. Sigh. Gulp. Eight, turns popular songs into songs about her pet and thinks other people might actually find that amusing. Nine, feisty with an athletic build. That is the opposite of my type." The women I usually go for are waifish, both in build and personality.

"So, this is getting to be a really specific list," Clark says. "Are you sure you don't have anybody in mind…"

"I'm giving you a gestalt," I say. "An overall picture of a type."

"I think I know what a gestalt is," Clark says.

"Good. I don't need her to embody every one of these traits, just get close and you'll have the precise opposite of my type. She'll need to dress acceptably for the trip. Get a personal stylist involved." I hand the go-folder back to Clark.

He looks at the list strangely. The paper is thick, linen, embossed with my name. A gift from the sultan of Brunei, another client.

"Ask around discreetly," I tell him. "Ask the assistants to reach out to their network of friends. Pay half up front and a nice bonus for afterwards. We need a contract, but don't run it through legal. Call Ivan and explain it to him. He'll draw it up." Ivan's an old friend who came up with me in South Boston. "And for crissake, have him draw up an iron-clad NDA. I mean iron-clad. If our fake fiancée whispers one peep about what we're doing, she needs to know we'll be turning her firstborn baby into a taxidermy toothpick dispenser."

"You want that in there specifically?" he asks.

"Very funny." Though if anybody would do it, it's Ivan.

"Do you want final say? Any kind of sign-off on the woman?" he asks.

"While I compress three weeks of work into one? I should also get involved in this ridiculous search? No. You go figure it out," I say. "You're the one who got me into this dumpster fire."

Chapter Three

Tabitha

REX'S LIEUTENANT, Clark, leans against our closed door, arms crossed, next to the Hello Kitty bowl where we keep our keys. The smooth fabric of his suit contrasts with the mottled white surface of the door whose paint covers decades of cracking and peeling. And though he's of average height, he seems somehow extra large and unreal among our vintage and secondhand things.

But what's most unreal is the check that he just handed me. I stare at it, feeling excited and happy and a little bit wary.

"What do you think?" he asks.

I think it can't be true.

I think that five minutes ago, I was running doom-and-gloom scenarios about what will happen if my wrist doesn't heal. Namely: I lose my clients for good. And then what? How does a person even make a living without the use of her right wrist and hand? You need both hands for work in restaurants, salons, and most tipped gigs. And those arc thc ones that pay the best hourly.

No way can my roommate, Jada, afford to float me the rent. She can barely afford to pay her half. I'd be evicted. Separated from my friends.

My mom is too out of it to help, and Dad would never let me move in to his place—I'd cramp his bachelor style. He barely wanted me in his place while he had custody of me as a child—except when I was guaranteed to bring fun and help land him dates.

I'd be out on the street, clutching my hamster, Seymour.

But now I'm holding a check that would cover rent for an entire year. It's so much money!

But that's not the most surprising thing. The real shocker is that Clark wants to hire me to play Rex O'Rourke's fiancée. For two weeks. On a yacht. Not just any yacht, but a Flying Fox megayacht, he told me, which is bigger than a super-yacht.

I'd only be playing the part in public spaces, he was quick to add. Not behind closed doors. As if I couldn't figure that part out.

He made me sign a document of secrecy, standing right there, just to hear the offer. I kind of want to scream and hug him, but he's from Rex's world, where hugging and screaming is the devil.

"Questions?" he says.

"It's a lot to…take in."

"What part is unclear? Should I go over it again?"

"No," I say. "You explained it really well."

"Well, then?"

"I guess I'm wondering, why me?" Because nobody ever picks me for things.

Clark gets this funny look on his face, and then he covers it with a smile. "You're perfect for the part. You meet Rex's criteria perfectly."

"But Rex doesn't even like me. I kind of think I bug him."
He might even hate me, but I don't say that.

"I assume you're free…" His gaze falls to my wrist brace.
Did he put it together that I'm not going somewhere fun for a
vacation? "But above all, you're perfect for the part," he says
once again.

"But isn't he usually with models and socialites and you
know…"

Clark shrugs. "Maybe those aren't the kinds of girls he
marries," he says mysteriously.

"And I am? Are you sure this isn't some sort of elaborate
joke?" Visions of the movie *Carrie* run through my mind.
Nobody picked Carrie for anything, either, and then her mean
classmates elected her homecoming queen, and she was so
happy—until they dumped blood on her.

"How long have you been cutting Rex's hair?" Clark asks.

"Two years and four months?" I say.

"And in that time, did you ever get the feeling that Rex
enjoys jokes?"

I snort. "Point taken!" Jokes would definitely make Rex
mad. Even positive sayings seem to make Rex mad.

"It's just a part," Clark says. "We just need you to play the
part of fiancée in public spaces on the yacht. You'd also be
agreeing not to date anybody else publicly for three months
until we release the news of your *breakup*." This he embellishes
with quote fingers.

It's still hard to believe that Rex thought I'd be perfect for
this—that Rex, sleek and powerful lion of Wall Street, would
pick *me* over all of those willowy blondes. I'm more sturdy than
willowy. More of a workhorse than a prancing palomino.

Rex O'Rourke with his billions and his beautiful sweep of
hair coming off his forehead like a dark flame burning out of
his annoyed mind. He picked me.

My pulse races as I think of all of those Friday nights, just us at the top of his building overlooking the twinkling lights of Wall Street. The way his shoulders relax a notch whenever I do the head massage. The sexy scowl he gets when I regale him with soap news, or tease him about his grumpiness. The feel of his short, glossy beard. The smooth warmth of the back of his neck under my thumb as I perfect his fade. I doubt he feels anything for me, not like I feel for him, but it means something that he thinks I'd be a good partner for this mission.

It means a lot, actually, and it's more than the money.

"And you know I'm not an actress," I say.

Jada bursts out from her bedroom door. "Tabitha, if you don't want it, I'll do it. I'm Jada Herberger, professional actress. What does it pay? I can do fake fiancée for Captain—I mean, Rex O'Rourke."

Clark frowns. "I didn't realize we had an audience."

"Well…" I hold out my hands as if to say, *you're in a Manhattan walk-up!*

Jada plucks the check from my hand and gawks at it. "Oh my god! Tabitha!" She looks back up at me with a mixture of horror and shock. "Oh my *god*!"

Personally, I'm just glad she didn't call him Captain Sternpants in front of Clark. Because we discuss Rex frequently, and that's our name for him. We have elaborate theories about his sex life and his level of sternness in bed. Spoiler alert: it's a hot level of sternness.

"Tabitha!" she exclaims again.

I pluck it back. "He offered it to me." And in fact, I feel that I'd be brilliant at it.

Through gritted teeth, she says, "Yet somehow you are managing to sound like you don't want it." She widens her eyes at the check that is now in my impoverished little fingers, like maybe I didn't see the number of zeroes. Like maybe I didn't notice that and I should look again.

ANNIKA MARTIN

"Well, maybe I'm kicking the tires," I answer through gritted teeth.

"Well..." she says, again through gritted teeth. Again she widens her eyes. She has sparkly eye shadow on. Sparkliness is something we bond over. "Maybe don't kick a dent in the car itself?"

Clark clears his throat. "And now I'm going to have to ask you to sign that NDA, too, Jada," he says. And then he gives me a hard look, like it's my fault I share a tiny apartment with my galpal whose room is five feet away.

I say, "It's cone of silence here, you don't have to worry."

"Cone of silence!" Jada says. "The total cone is all around us."

"I'm afraid the cone of silence doesn't hold up in a court of law," he says. "So we're gonna go with an NDA." He whips another sheet of paper out and hands it to Jada, along with a pen. I turn so she can use my back to sign it.

"I need you both to honor this," he warns.

"Cone of silence is more powerful than your court of law, buddy," Jada says. "Either way, you can trust us."

"I'm sorry, I swear...we're both very trustworthy." I do a hasty sign of the cross, or at least what I remember of it from movies. "I'm very serious about secrets. I always keep my clients' things confidential. I have clients with nose hair and ear hair and weaves and all that. I never talk about it." *Except right now.* "Not that I'm saying for sure that I have clients with nose hair or ear hair or weaves. Um...come sit." I can't ruin this. I really need the money.

I lead him to our tiny living room and clear some pillows and our bedazzling stuff off the couch.

Jada makes another face at me. Because, that check!

Clark sits down, managing to make our sweet little red couch look somehow shabby, and tells me the terms. The length of time requested is sixteen days—two days for travel on either side, fourteen for the yacht itself.

"Okay, objection." Jada puts up her hands. "Are we clear this is platonic? Because my galpal's sexual favors would cost way more than this."

"Let's be clear here," I say. "No check is enough for this galpal's sexual favors. I would never do that."

"Well," Jada says. "I mean, five million dollars? Maybe?"

I lower my voice. "He's not asking for sexual favors."

"But like...five mil."

"Ladies, this is absolutely not about sexual favors," Clark says.

Jada and I exchange glances. *Ladies*. The 1950s called. They want their term for *women* back.

"This is, in actuality, a very boring assignment," Clark continues. "You'll have a suite with Rex, it's true, but there will be a bedroom that will be all yours. And you'll make occasional on-deck appearances with him for dinner and other obligatory upper-deck activities, and otherwise you will promise to spend your time in that room where you're free to watch TV and read or whatever you like. And you are specifically forbidden to speak with Rex or interact with him in any way when not playing the role in public."

"Forbidden to speak with him?" I ask, incredulously.

"Forbidden—I really can't stress that enough. He has very important work to accomplish on the ship, and he is not to be bothered. You're to deal with me for needs and questions. Think of us as co-workers, you and I, working together to create the illusion of Rex settling down with a woman who's very different from his usual type. He wants to show this client the image of a family man. The marrying kind of man."

"Oh, I get it," I say, as it all becomes clear. "This is about the article. Repairing his image."

"That would be part of the goal, yes," Clark says. "The

article was in no way accurate, and you'll be helping to portray that."

I experience this stupid level of relief to hear Clark say that. Rex is a gruff person with commitment issues, yes, but he's the kind of guy who owns what he is—that's something I appreciate about him, whereas the article made him out to be some kind of cruel, power-drunk playboy. So wrong. And he thinks I can help him with that.

Well, he's right. I can!

"That article was a real hatchet job," Jada says sympathetically. "Someone has it out for Captain Sternpants, huh?"

Clark's lip quirks. "Excuse me?"

I stare at Jada. Like, *did you really just say that?*

"I mean…Rex. O'Rourke. What?" Jada grabs my sleeve. "And you're the commoner. You're Matt Damon's waitress."

"Okay, my roommate is done joking around," I say to Clark. "I feel like this can really work."

"And you're not involved with anybody at the moment? The team didn't find anything on your social media account to suggest romantic involvement over the past winter, but there was a Clayton Rice and then Bernard Reston and…" Clark goes on to name a few guy friends, one of them a former "friends with benefits." I tend to prefer the friends-with-benefits style of dating. "Are any of them still in the picture?" he asks.

Jada snorts. "Not to worry."

I give her a hard look. "I'm not dating at the moment. Those are really just friends. I really think I can pull this off."

"We can't have pictures surfacing of you with other guys while you're supposedly engaged to Rex. No drama or smitten suitors."

"There won't be," I say.

"Definitely not." Jada bites back a smile. "Tabitha is not one for romance drama."

"Absolutely not," I tell Clark. "You guys have made an amazing choice for fake fiancée. Like a stroke of genius." I smile and hold up my hands as if to frame a picture. "One, I get along with anybody. Two, I deal with people from all walks of life, and the whole fake fiancée trope?" I'm thinking of my years of soap opera watching here. It's like I've been training for this! "Let's just say, you guys are going to be *very* pleased with my level of expertise."

"Excellent," Clark says, shuffling papers.

"Picking me was a stroke of brilliance," I add, because I want him to get it. Rex may not like me on a romantic level, but I'm going to do an amazing job for him. I can't think of anybody who's more suited for a fake relationship than I am.

Clark pulls out the contract, which is ridiculously long, and starts explaining the different clauses.

Still, it's strange. Did Rex pick me because I'm like the girl next door? Because he knows how good I am with people? Rex really is a challenging person. Maybe he gets that I can hang in there with him better than most. Maybe deep down he feels our strange connection.

Either way, I so need this. I wait, eager now to sign on the bottom line.

Clark wants to go over everything—every detail. I'm actually supposed to initial the part where Rex is to be allowed complete peace and quiet whenever we're not on deck because of his time-sensitive project. I jot down TE.

This is really happening. I'm getting excited to be the official owner of that check.

"Who goes on a Caribbean cruise on a gorgeous yacht and spends all their time working?" Jada asks.

"Rex O'Rourke," Clark and I say in unison.

Jada snorts.

I rub my hands, following along and nodding, trying to show him how chill I am about the whole thing.

A private jet to Miami where we meet the yacht of some rich family? Pleasant smile.

Motoring around the Caribbean? Polite yawn.

Another NDA to cover everything that happens on the yacht and a bonus structure that has my heart pounding a million miles a minute? Shrug.

A massive winning-the-account bonus if we're successful? A personal shopper who will be setting me up with a wardrobe that I get to keep? Gah!

But I keep calm. I don't even mind the rule that I have to take out my pretty blue and purple hair streaks.

Whenever Clark is busy riffling around the papers, I make OMG faces at Jada, and she makes OMG faces back at me. I almost have to stop looking at her after a while, but OMG.

So I'm trying to act serious and natural. Because I have this feeling that at any minute, Clark will stand up and go, *record scratch*! Why are we giving this girl all this money and a free yacht trip where she gets to sit in her room and watch streaming content? And then he takes the check with all the zeroes and rips it all up and I'm out on the street with Seymour.

I cannot allow that to happen.

And I try not to let it mean anything that he picked me. I remind myself that guys are like dogs in that they have lots of instincts. Somehow, deep down, Rex knew I'd kick ass as a fake fiancée. I know when I'm a transaction, when somebody wants me for a specific reason that has nothing to do with caring about me.

So I smile, expertly putting Clark at his ease, demonstrating an important quality in a fake fiancée.

Eventually the contract is signed. And the check is in my hands. And I'm closing the door behind him.

I spin around and put my finger to my lips.

Jada grabs my arms and we wait for the elevator bell. And

then a few more seconds for the thump of the elevator doors, and then we scream and dance and go change into cocktails-out outfits.

～

THE FIRST TIME I went to cut Rex's hair, I was really scared to meet the boogeyman of the financial district, really scared I'd screw it up. After the stories I'd heard about him from his previous stylist, who'd moved out to L.A., I was shaking in my pink boots.

I'd arrived early and an assistant with a cute bob and a hard stare led me through a maze of gatekeepers past floor-to-ceiling arched windows, flashing monitors, and brightly colored workstations. Finally we headed down his hall of toiling minions and arrived at his office.

The assistant pushed open the door and there he was, tie loose, shirtsleeves rolled up, surrounded by broker-type bros and techie-looking people. They were all staring at a monitor with total intensity, but none with the intensity of Rex O'Rourke. It was like he wanted to melt the monitor with the power of his mind.

Then something seemed to happen on the screen, and they all leaned in, and Rex placed his meaty fists onto the table. Like he wanted to shove the table into the ground *and* melt the monitor.

"Friday haircut's here," the assistant called across to them. "I'll have her set up."

Right then, Rex glanced over.

And our eyes met. Something about him struck me deeply in a way that I can't explain. His sooty hair twinkled; his lashes glowed black as night. And god, that stare.

He seemed so totally powerful, yet fiercely isolated. A man

alone in a group. A man with his very own container, a titanium turtle shell.

And then somebody said something, and his attention was back down, glued to that monitor, shutting out the whole world.

I unpacked my stuff in the far corner of the office that the cute-bob assistant indicated I was to inhabit, arranging my things on a towel, quietly watching Rex scowl. And then something important seemed to happen on the computer, and Rex's minions straightened, like invisible marionette operators suddenly pulled their strings tight.

Except Rex. He was still bent in, knuckles on wood, metal-melting stare. "There it is," he growled.

Then some bell rang, and they all relaxed. And the people all left, except for my guide. Rex eventually stormed over, and she introduced me as Tabitha, the new stylist.

"Hello, Mr. O'Rourke," I said.

"Haircut," he said, seeming displeased. That was his hello. He sat on my mobile stool, and he barked an order, and the woman started reciting numbers off a pad like a strange alien communication.

"Excuse me, I'm gonna have you tilt your head back, and I'm going to put this relaxing, warm jasmine-scented cloth over your face for a moment," I said.

The cloth-over-the-face thing is something I do to make my clients feel pampered and special.

Rex fixed me with a hard look. "If you put that thing on my face," he growled, "I'll rip it up and throw it out the door, and you along with it."

The assistant stiffened and regarded me nervously, like maybe I'd freak out and run away.

I just smiled, because *OMG, seriously? Who is so extreme? Rex is so extreme!!*

But of course I didn't say that.

"We'll skip the cloth," I said. Though I didn't like it. This was part of my thing, and Rex was ruining it. Who doesn't enjoy relaxation? He nearly lost his mind a minute later when I tried to do my special Tabitha Evans scalp-relaxing massage.

"Hey!" He pulled away and twisted around. "What are you doing?"

"A scalp-relaxing massage?" I said.

"No massages!" he snarled. "No. Massages. Ever. Got it?" This he snarled with extra *rawr*.

And I don't know what rose up in me—some innate sense that he needed some pushback. Without even thinking, I looked him in the eyes and I smiled, and I whispered, "*Rawr!*" But my own fun version.

I could feel the assistant stiffen even more.

And Rex's glower brightened like when you blow on hot coals. My heart pounded like crazy, but sometimes you have to meet people where they are. I knew he could fire me, but I always go with my gut when it comes to people.

"What was that?" he snarled.

He was challenging me to repeat the fun *rawr*, but I knew that would be too far. I'm good at finding people's edges. I may not be brilliant or beautiful or fit and trim, but I'm good at people.

"Your scalp is too tense," I told him. "I cannot work on such a tense scalp. The haircut won't be right."

Though honest, I'd never met a person who needed a scalp massage more than Rex. He needed a full body and attitude massage. It was too perfect he hates massages. Of all the details about him, that was my favorite.

"I meant the other thing," he said.

"Oh, *that*," I whispered.

His scowl intensified. Maybe I should've been scared, but I felt this strange happiness inside me when he did his turbocharged scowl.

"Make that sound again and you're out," he said. And then he waved two fingers. "Just get on with it."

I got on with it. I did the massage. I cut his hair so beautifully, I wanted to kill myself. It lay perfectly on his crazy angry beautiful head. And I shortened and shaped his beard in a way that perfectly intensified his dark elegance.

I grabbed the mirror, excited for him to see, but the assistant caught my arm. "He doesn't do…" She shook her head.

Doesn't do mirrors? *No vampire jokes. No vampire jokes,* I chanted to myself.

However, I wasn't going to let the cut go unacknowledged, so I went around in front of him and made a little square with my fingers, which is something my galpals and I do when we see something frame-worthy. "So good," I said. "Thumbs up!"

He gave me a glower and that was that.

Afterwards I went online and read about him. You can't even find a photograph where he's smiling. Even in groups where everybody else is smiling, Rex always looks so serious— part of the crowd, yet apart from it somehow, a glowering presence among the polished elite, a man with a shell of ice around his heart.

And he chose me out of all of the possible fake fiancées. He picked me.

～

JADA and I head out for a night of dancing with the goal of consuming our weight in tapas and Bellini spritzers.

"I can't believe it's happening," Jada says. "Does Captain Sternpants even have the skills to act like a doting fiancé? Do you think he can pull it off?"

"Oh, I doubt it," I say. "Maybe that's why he needs me,

The Billionaire's Fake Fiancée

because I smooth over his total assholishness with a bright gloss of fun."

"I don't know how you tolerate him."

"Jerks are my jam," I say, cocky from my third drink.

Jada goes at her alcohol-soaked orange slice, ripping at it with her teeth like a pretty little mongoose.

"I really think my luck is changing," I add.

Jada gives me a serious look. "Just be careful." *With my heart*, she means.

"Dude," I gust out. "Please. You're telling *me* to be careful with a guy?"

"I am," she says. "You've always had such a crush on him."

"Have you forgotten who you're talking to? I could write a book on the shittiness of guys. I could do a ten-part webinar on it. The shittiness of guys and how not to get sucked in. I think I'll call my course, 'Don't Fall for Him, Sister!'"

She looks at me sadly. Thinking about my past. I make a funny face, and then my phone pings. It's a message from Clark with an attachment—a schedule for me with two appointments with the personal shopper, the pickup time for when the car will take me to a private airport, plus the tracking code for the designer luggage that will be delivered to me.

We look up the luggage on Amazon. A supposedly tasteful set. Brown and tan. The opposite of my style, but what do I care?

One drink later, the questionnaire comes through.

"Wow, they're covering everything," she says.

But then we open it up and read it, and we're just laughing. There are questions about employment history, school history and dates of graduation, where I've lived, place of birth.

"This is hilarious," Jada says. "Are they repurposing a rental application as a fake fiancée questionnaire?"

"Where's the space for date of last tetanus shot?" I joke.

Jada stirs her drink. "This is what you call a fake fiancée scheme concocted by two dudes."

We snigger some more about the questionnaire. You know Clark wrote it. Rex wouldn't involve himself in this level of detail. Or would he?

"Oh my god," I say, pointing to an item that says, simply, "family of origin." "What is that even supposed to mean? Asking me to do this was a cry for help," I say. "I'm making my own damn questionnaire. For both of us to answer."

"Let's do it! Let's do it right now!" she practically screams.

We order another round and start putting questions down. First thing: pets! Then name of favorite childhood pet. Favorite food. Foods you hate. Siblings. Briefs or boxers or boxer briefs. Top gross-out thing. Top bucket list stuff. Side of bed. Favorite music, favorite movies, favorite books.

Making a fake fiancée questionnaire is surprisingly fun, and I'm definitely unleashing every bit of nosiness that I ever had about Rex.

"Night owl or morning person?" Jada asks.

"Rex is neither a morning nor night person. He has one setting, and that's grouchy." But I put it down, because he needs to know that I'm a morning person.

"You know what you also need? A getting-together story," Jada says. "How did you go from stylist and client to romance of the century?"

"Totally," I say. "It's the first thing people would wonder."

"Did he just ask you to dinner one day? You're cutting his hair and he wants to know, what are you doing this Saturday?"

"Too boring," I say.

"Sometimes boring is believable."

"Yeah, but Rex is not boring. I think Rex saw me out somewhere after a month of my cutting his hair. I was out for tapas on a Tinder date, and he found himself burning up with jealousy. It was then he realized he had to have me, and that's when he asked me out."

"Burning up with jealousy behind a fern," Jada says. "You want to get in the little details."

"Okay, he was behind a fern, but not hiding. Rex wouldn't hide. It's just where his table happened to be."

"And he didn't realize what a high point of his week your haircuts were until he saw you with another man. And he was wining and dining an important client from Tagastan. And then he came up to you and asked you out."

"Tagastan," I say. "Perfect."

She shrugs.

"But here's the thing—Rex would never hit on a woman who's out with another man," I say. "He's an asshole, but not a douche. Rex has a code—a very old-fashioned code."

"I like that," Jada says.

"A dark emotion must compel him," I say.

"Okay," Jada says, "how's this—the Tinder date was going poorly. The guy was drunk. And Rex had been watching you from afar, burning up with jealousy behind his fern. And then the guy gets handsy, and you push him away but he won't get the message and lay off, and suddenly Rex was there."

I sit up. "And Rex clamps his muscular hand on the guy's shoulder, and he growls—literally growls like an animal. And in a low and menacing voice, he says, 'walk away.'"

"Don't you want him to say something more dramatic?" Jada asks. "Like, 'touch her again, and I will rearrange your face like a *marble cake*.'"

"Would a man say that to another man, though? Rearrange your face like a marble cake?"

"Why not?" Jada says. "A marble cake is kind of swirly, you know?"

"Rex is more of a 'talk softly and carry a big stick' guy. He goes understated. Like, he has this insane control over himself, but inside he's a raging volcano."

"Really?"

"Yes," I say. "Growling is like half of his communication. That's what he'd do. A growl and a simple command."

Jada lowers her voice to a loud whisper. "You think he growls during sex?"

"Yes," I say without hesitation.

"I'm getting goose bumps," Jada says. "So we've established that he growls. A simple command and a growl."

"True enough," I say. "And my sniveling Tinder date is immediately alarmed—he is alarmed on a primal level, deep in his lizard brain. He senses danger. Yet he's a douche, so still he has to impress me, and he's all, 'what the F?'"

Jada snorts out her drink. "Tabitha, you definitely have to have the Tinder date say 'what the F.' That is too priceless."

"Done!" I scream, but it might be the Bellini screaming. "Why did I say yes to this Tinder douche? I don't even know! And then Rex is like, 'if you touch her again without her express permission...'" I'm pointing at Jada, doing the Rex growl.

Jada grabs my finger. "I will rearrange your face like a freaking marble cake!"

"Okay!" I say. "Why not? I'll run it by Rex. If nothing else, it'll spur him to say what he'd really say in that kind of circumstance. It's a way to start collaborating."

"And then you'll immediately text me," Jada says.

"I will let you know his answer at my earliest convenience," I assure her.

"And the Tinder douche runs off. And you're sitting there, trembling."

"And Rex comes to me, and he cups my cheeks in his confident hands. His touch is kind of harsh, yet gentle. He's being as gentle as he can possibly be while trembling with dark and explosive angst."

"He's like King Kong," Jada says, "so hot and powerful and overcome with emotion that he's frightened he'll hurt you, but he can't resist kissing you. He takes your lips in his. It's a trembling and forceful kiss, my friend, and you're on a high barstool. And he moves in on you and you wrap your legs around him and feel his shaft. Like steel!"

"Okay, that part might not go in our couples origin story," I say. "I'm gonna stay with just the first part."

We go on to concoct our first date (at Primo's in Tribeca) and our first kiss (at the Central Park Pinetum). By the time we go home, Rex and I have a full-blown imaginary relationship.

~

IT'S INCREDIBLY HARD to not tell my girlfriends about my fake fiancée gig, because they've all been incredibly worried about my wrist and my livelihood. My solution is to totally avoid them, but it's not easy.

I run into Noelle from down the hall, just getting back from her mail route, looking cute in her blue jacket. She makes me wait while she quick changes and drags me out to the Cookie Madness down the street for coffee and cookies. She peppers me with questions about my wrist, and suggests remedies that her fellow mail carriers swear by. "And if worse comes to worst, we won't let you be homeless," she says, meaning the gang in the building. "We'll figure something out."

It means everything.

"Unless we're all homeless," she adds unhelpfully. She updates me on the rumors of the new owner of the building kicking us all out. She insinuates he's been corresponding with the zoning office.

"I'm not going to ask how you know that," I say, biting into a National Pig Day cookie.

She shrugs. "Best that you don't." Noelle's a shy small-town girl but she's all alone in the world—our building is her only family. "And I'll tell you this—if he decides to tear it down, I will be flipping a few tables at Malcolm Blackberg's office!"

I smile. She's such a waifish little pixie—I love to imagine her flipping tables.

~

MIA FROM UPSTAIRS has her yearly clothes swap on Saturday —it's a fun party where we lug bags of unwanted shoes and clothes to her place—stuff that either no longer fits or stuff that falls into the *WTF was I thinking?* category—and we swap them around.

So we're all sitting around with our drinks and piles of clothes. Our friend Lizzie is holding up a vintage maxi sundress with giant red flowers. "It's so beautiful, in a kind of throwback Sonny and Cher way, but seriously? The halter-style top with my weird shoulders? Just say *god, no*. But if anyone needs something for a glam occasion…"

And Jada, who has consumed twice as much pink bubbly as the rest of us, screams, "Tabitha! Cocktail hour on the Flying Fox megayacht!"

And all eyes turn to me. Because *cocktail hour on the Flying Fox megayacht* is not a phrase that would generally appear in a sentence with my name.

I feel my jaw unhinge. "Uhhh."

Jada claps her palm over her mouth, eyes wide. "Shit!" Needless to say, this does not dampen interest. Nor does the fact that she screams, "Forget I ever said that!" when she removes said palm.

"You're going on a megayacht?" Vicky asks. "What?"

Vicky has Smuckers on her lap, and she's petting him into oblivion, but even Smuckers looks interested in the megayacht news. His little tail is going a million miles an hour.

"I can't tell," I say. "I've signed something, and so has Jada." I give Jada a hard look.

"We signed something," Jada confirms.

"Is that a yes? To the megayacht?" Mia asks.

"Look, I sooo wish I could tell you guys, but we both signed such serious NDAs, both Jada and I. And if it gets out, we are so screwed. Forget you heard it."

Vicky frowns. "Are you cutting hair?"

"I really can't tell you?" I wince. "But I swear it's not a sex thing."

"Cone of silence," Jada says.

"I assumed you were visiting your mom," Lizzie says.

Jada shakes her head with major drama. I grab a tank top nobody wants and throw it over her head. "Stop emoting!"

"I'm sorry!" Jada says from under the shirt.

"You guys," Lizzie's sister-in-law, Willow, says, "a nondisclosure agreement is a really serious thing. These two could get in trouble for revealing even this much." She looks around with a dark expression. "We must completely forget that our Tabitha is going on a Flying Fox MEGAYACHT!" She pumps her fist in the air. "Woo-hoo!"

Everybody is laughing.

Vicky throws the maxi dress at me. "Try it on!"

I go in Mia's bedroom to try it on. I'm kind of glad they know. Everybody just assumed the two weeks was about visiting Mom in her sad assisted-living facility up north. I hated the dishonesty—my girlfriends are everything to me. Living in this place near this clan of women is more important to me than any of them knows. They just have no idea.

I come out in the dress and do a Spanish dancer pose, and everybody's clapping. No way can I wear it, though. Rex's personal shopper took me out this week and fixed me up with a new wardrobe composed entirely of brown, black, and white garments, with zero fun patterns unless you count stripes, which I don't.

Mia gives me tips on what silverware to use when—she was just in a *Downton Abbey* sort of play where she had to learn it all.

Jada feels awful she told. She's making all seven women do a cone of silence oath that they won't tell. "It's really important that this doesn't leave this room," she says over and over.

Vicky goes in her case and pulls out a *Smuck U* pendant where Smuckers is wearing a sailor cap and blue bow tie. Smuck U is her fun line of jewelry with animal faces that's going for top dollar in the hippest stores. "I knew I made a Smuckers sailor dog one for a reason. I want you to have it."

"I get to bring Smuckers!" I say, so touched and grateful. I can tuck it inside my outfits, a way to bring my girlfriends along. And with Rex's check, I won't have to move away from them. Unless the place gets torn down, that is.

"I'm sending a box of megayacht cookies to share," Lizzie says. "Maybe I'll try to find a picture of the actual Flying Fox brand of yacht and make cookies to match. They are gonna be completely cute."

I press my hand to my pounding heart, feeling like I have a team of fairy godmothers on my side.

Chapter Four

Rex

CLARK WALKS up to where I'm standing at the foot of the air stairs, just outside the hangar. It's a cool, crisp, sunny day. Perfect for a flight to Miami, which is where we'll board Gail's yacht.

"Everything's loaded in," he says.

"Where's my fiancée?" I ask.

He glances at his phone, then pockets it. "Near."

"She hits the items on my list?" I ask.

"Definitely." He regards me nervously. "Maybe you should've signed off."

"I hardly have time to sign off on every random person who takes a minor role in my organization. My fiancée is nothing more than a paid prop. This trip is already wasting enough of my time."

"She'll be portraying your romantic partner," he says. "It's not so minor. In terms of a role."

"She'll be my partner for all of the two minutes I plan to be on deck per day."

Just then, a black car comes into view. The car pulls into the hangar and up behind the car we arrived in. The driver goes around and opens the door.

And Tabitha steps out.

I straighten. Blink.

"Wait a minute," I say, unable to comprehend what I'm seeing. "Hold on a moment. What?"

Tabitha waves at us from across the tarmac.

I suck in a breath as she approaches. My mind reels at her transformation. She's in a brown jacket and skirt set. Her thick, dark curls are tamed with clips, smooth and sleek, and her tan high heels make her legs look…very long.

"No," I say.

"She fits the list," Clark says. "Perfectly."

"*Tabitha*. The *hair*dresser. Is the lynchpin to rescuing our billion-dollar account?"

Clark frowns. "She'll do a good job. Gail will love her. You know she will. You said somebody who irritates you. She irritates you."

"What were you thinking?" I gust out. "Jesus Christ."

"Don't Jesus Christ me," Clark says under his breath. "She hit every item on your list."

"Maybe so," I say, trying to process all of this. "But I didn't mean…to actually hire *Tabitha*."

"Why the hell not?" Clark asks.

I don't know why the hell not. The truth is, she's convincing when you get her out of her boots and bangles and Hello Kitty T-shirts.

Beyond convincing.

She's more of a handsome girl than a classically pretty one, with strong features and a sturdy build. But all put together like this, she looks…convincing. Possibly even compelling. Or something.

"Picking her was a stroke of brilliance, and you know it," Clark says.

"I thought she was going to Japan," I mumble.

When she's a few yards away from us, she puts down her small suitcase and her purse, plants one hand on her hip, and flings the other up into the air. And there she stands, beaming at us, all dimples and sparkling brown eyes. "So we're doing this!"

Clark laughs. Something churns in my gut. Of course he'd find her amusing.

"Hilarious," I mumble under my breath.

She picks up her stuff and comes up to join us.

"Hey, Tabitha," Clark says when she reaches us.

"Hey, Clark," she says, smiling conspiratorially, and then she turns to me. "Hello, fiancé!" she says. "We need nicknames. Like, babe or something. But not babe, because that's totally unimaginative."

"You call me Rex," I say.

"You can call me kitten."

I give her a hard look. "I'll be calling you Tabitha." She's the kind of woman who'll take the wheel if you don't stop her.

She sighs. "Okay…*Rrrex*."

Clark snorts and takes her small suitcase, which matches the very giant one that my driver is extracting from the trunk of the town car.

She beams at Clark. "Thanks."

"Wait a minute," I say, aggravated already.

They both turn.

I yank the case out of Clark's hand. "She's *my* fiancée," I say in a low voice, "not yours. Let's try to be in character here, huh? The help needs to buy our engagement. And *you*…" I say to her, pulse racing.

Her pretty brows furrow. "What?"

"Just…" I don't know what I want to say. *Behave, act normal.*

"I got this, Rex," she says in a way that makes my blood churn. I wave her up the stairs in front of me and go up behind her, feeling agitated at the way her skirt cups and shapes the curves of her ass.

I remind myself that it's good I have this agitated reaction to her. There will be no temptation, no distraction, no sex— and therefore no emotional demands. No morning-after obligations. No scenes when I tell her to leave me alone. No being trapped in a confined space with somebody I don't want to be with.

I didn't make a billion dollars just to end up as one-half of a miserable couple hemmed in by four walls and tearful demands. I worked like a dog to have the precise *opposite* of that.

She pauses at the top of the air steps. I set my hand on the small of her back, conscious of the sensation of her under my touch. Is she wearing some extra-soft fabric? I never think about fabric. The women I touch are usually naked for me already. I like them to undress themselves for me. I like my things unwrapped.

"Showtime," I mumble under my breath, guiding her into the main cabin.

"Wow," she says, looking around, impressed, eyes like saucers. She's already screwing up her role.

I lean in. "Try not to look like a fucking extra from *Oliver Twist* gaping at a loaf of bread. As my fiancée, you're used to this kind of luxury."

"But I've never ridden in your plane," she whispers playfully, with a little tilt of the head. "I'm impressed." She straightens as the pilot approaches. "You always do have such excellent taste, *Rex.*"

I need to tell her not to say my name like that. It's

distracting.

"So true," Clark says, catching up to us. "After all, he picked *you*."

She beams at him.

I introduce her as my fiancée to the pilot and the crew. They're shocked at the news of my engagement, but try not to show it. "Congratulations," says Cassie, my head attendant. "I didn't know…" She looks at me, bewildered.

"It's not public yet," I say. "We've been keeping a low profile. We expect absolute discretion."

She nods. "Of course."

I don't like misleading the people who've been with me forever, but we can't go back now. It's not as if we can tell them it's just a ploy; people gossip, and a pretend engagement would be more gossip-worthy than an actual engagement.

"It's my fault he couldn't tell," Tabitha says, sliding her hand into mine like it's the most natural thing in the world.

I swallow, stunned by the feel of her fingers sliding so intimately between my fingers. I need to tell her not to do that. The whole point is for me not to be distracted.

"I just prefer it under wraps for now," she continues, "and Rex has been so cool about it. With all of the negative publicity about his supposed peccadillos, and my grandmother so injured, I think she'd keel over if she learned of this engagement. She would see those articles about Rex—and, well, she's old, and things upset her."

"I get it. I'm so sorry," Cassie says.

"She'll be fine," Tabitha says.

"Well, congratulations." She looks between me and Tabitha. "I'm really happy for you."

Does Tabitha truly have an injured grandmother? Clark said something about some backgrounder he filled out on my behalf, and she must've filled one out too. I recall something in my inbox. I should've looked at it.

I realize I'm staring at her. Does a fiancé say something at this juncture? "How is she today?"

"As good as can be expected." She squeezes my hand.

I nod.

"Let me show you the ropes," Cassie says, thankfully ending this conversation. "This plane is a Versace 1120-E. We like you to take the forward upright seating during takeoff. Stan and I have the front row for proximity to the kitchen." She leads her to the work seats, waving her hand. "Mr. O'Rourke likes to use this area as an office." Cassie shows her the Wi-Fi and safety stuff, brings her through to the next section, the rear lounge area.

At one point, Tabitha looks back at me, pointing at something and mouthing something behind Cassie's back.

"What now?" I grumble.

"The couch," Clark whispers from behind me.

I head back to the bar to get a drink while Cassie shows her the bedroom and bathroom. "What," I say. "It's a fucking couch."

"Give her a break. It's a couch on a *plane*," Clark says. "You were probably impressed the first time you saw a couch on a plane, too."

I frown. To be honest, I can barely remember. I was so caught up in a haze of anger and distress. Buying luxury things back then, it was just about punching my way out of the dark hole I grew up in, a fuck-you to the world for busting my balls nonstop. I never really enjoyed the stuff.

The staff goes back to their posts, and Tabitha and I take our seats across the table from Clark in the forward section, ready for takeoff.

Tabitha stares at me like she has an important communication.

"What?" I say.

She looks over to make sure Cassie isn't near, and then she

circles her pointer fingers around, indicating the plane, I suppose. She makes a face of shock, eyes and mouth open wide. When I don't react, she opens her mouth even wider and jiggles her head around.

I simply stare. I refuse to reward her drama with a reply.

"Excited face," she says.

"Could you not narrate your faces?"

"Fine," she says. "A-plus. Is that better? Your plane gets an A-plus. It's amazing, Rex."

"I'm so relieved," I say.

She buckles in as we taxi to the runway, not catching my sarcasm, or maybe ignoring it. "Here we go," she says.

"Indeed," I grumble, casting through Google trends.

"Don't your electronics need to be in airplane mode?" she asks nervously. "We're about to take off."

I give her a look. "It's my plane."

"But I thought it interfered with piloting communications."

"Nope," I say.

Clark leans forward. "The airplane mode rule is just an FCC thing to protect against radio interference to networks on the ground. A lot of people flying over cell towers with their phones on might crowd the networks."

"What? All this time I thought it was a matter of life and death!"

"Myth."

"Okay." The plane picks up speed. With trembling hands she pulls out a bright pink packet. "You guys want some gum? It's watermelon."

Neither of us wants watermelon gum. She stuffs three pieces into her mouth, then clutches the hand rests. I study her polished hairdo, tucked into hairclips that match her brown suit, looking for signs of the purple and blue streaks that are usually in there.

"You want a drink?" Clark asks.

"Cassie already offered. But, no," she whispers.

"This plane is very safe," I inform her.

"I know. More likely to die in a car and all that. Still. I'm a nervous flyer." She looks up at me with those sparkling brown eyes, wide-set, like her cheekbones. "I don't fly a ton," she confesses.

"My pilot did five tours in Iraq and Afghanistan," I tell her, and then I fix my gaze firmly back onto my computer screen, a hint that it's time to leave me alone.

"Yeah," she says. "But you know…"

I look over when she doesn't finish the sentence. She narrows her eyes and pulls her lips to the right, her expression for when she's about to say something I might not like, though knowing I might not like something is never quite enough to keep her from saying it. "I'm a nervous flyer, and it didn't help that Cassie told me that this plane was made by *Versace*."

"So?" I say.

"Versace." She tilts her head and squinches one eye shut, her signature *huh?* face. I'm surprised she doesn't come right out and say, *huh-face!* But apparently some faces are to be made, and others narrated.

I look over at Clark. Have Versace jets been crashing in the news?

Clark shrugs.

When we don't exhibit the reaction she seems to expect, she leans in and says, "Do you know what Versace is really good at? Evening bags. Structured blazers. Stitching together bits of fabric and leather in a really pretty way—with a needle and *thread*. You have to ask yourself, is that really the kind of company you want making your plane?" She pauses for effect. "You know what Versace is not known for?" she continues. "Jet engine construction."

"It's an excellent plane," I inform her.

Clark grins. "Versace simply means it's a luxury brand of

jet," he says. "It's not like Versace's people made this plane in the Versace garment factory."

"Well, here's hoping," she says brightly.

"I promise," Clark says.

She nods, but you only have to look at her hands gripping the armrest to know that she's white-knuckling it. I'm guessing she underplayed her fear of flying. Though to be fair, she's hanging in there like a trooper, not that I'm paying attention. I have things to deal with—like the London Stock Exchange sliding into a shaky close.

She relaxes when we get to cruising altitude. Finally I can get something done. My plan is for her to watch movies in the lounge at the back of the plane. "Come on," I say, getting up and leading her to the back.

Clark comes, too.

"So this is more of the talking area back here," I say. "This pocket door closes it off from the quiet area where we work up front." I slide it closed. "Soundproof. You can lounge on the couch and watch shows and take what you want from the bar."

"You'll be up there working this whole trip while I'm back here?"

"This whole trip, yes. I have a lot to do, and when I'm at my computer up there, it's dead serious work time." I want her to get that right away.

"Got it," she says. "Business in the front, party in the back. Like a mullet. You should name this plane the Versace Mullet."

Clark is suppressing a smile. "There you go, Rex. I always told you the plane needs a name. The Versace Mullet."

I give him a look. He doesn't need to be encouraging Tabitha. "Clark has a file full of names and photographs for you to study," I say. "So that you know who's on that boat. Who we care about and all that."

"Good. And when should we go over our questionnaires?" she asks.

"I don't think we really need to go over them. It's in my email…" I turn to Clark. "Right?" Clark nods. "I'll review it before we land."

"You haven't even read it?" she says.

"I'll review it later. It's not as if somebody's going to be grilling us."

"You'll *review* it," she says. As though there's something wrong with that.

"I can assimilate large amounts of information quickly," I say. "It's kind of my thing."

"Did you get the questions I sent you?" she asks.

She sent questions? I look at Clark.

"I forwarded her questions to you," Clark says.

"Okay, I'll find them and review them," I say. "For now I need to get to work."

"Okay, hold up." She makes a little motion—two fingers pointed upward. Tabitha's fingers talk as much as her mouth does. "I'm here to help you pull this off, right? And I need you to know that I'm going to do such an amazing job." She lowers her voice to a whisper. "But I do have a few concerns."

Clark touches her arm. "The pocket door is soundproof. The crew can't hear us. You don't have to whisper."

"Okay, a few concerns," she says more loudly.

I roll my eyes. "We heard you the first time. What?"

She swallows. "So I'm all in on following your instructions perfectly, but there are some things fiancés know about each other. Things that will help us pull this off. If the yacht is full of, like, oil sheiks from the Mideast who don't speak English, I'd say we don't need to really know that much about each other. And your"—here she makes quote fingers—"*questionnaire* would be fine in that case."

Clark frowns. "Are you putting quotation marks around my questionnaire?"

"Kind of. Because here's the thing—your personal shopper

had me picking out cocktail party outfits. What that says to me is *interaction*. And if the person you're trying to fool is a woman? And we're socializing with her?" She shakes her head. "You guys. Just tell me it won't be a woman who's been around the block a few times."

"I'm a private person," I say. "I don't share, and you don't either. You're a prop on my arm. And there are a hundred guests on the yacht."

Tabitha isn't satisfied. "But who are we trying to fool? Is it a woman? And does she have half a brain? Because when I said that thing about my grandmother in front of Cassie? You were like, *oh really*? You had an *oh really* face."

"I did not have an *oh really* face," I grumble.

Clark clears his throat. "You *did* appear to be a little surprised about the grandmother detail."

I give him a scowl. The last thing I want to do is to go over his questionnaire, and I definitely don't want to answer whatever extra questions Tabitha has cooked up.

Tabitha smiles. "My grandmother's gonna be fine, by the way. She was hit by a car. Crossing a street in her little town up in Maine. She's very feisty, but she's in a cast that goes practically over her hip."

"Oh," I say. "I'm sorry."

"Dude, it's all made up, but do you see how knowing those details would've helped with Cassie? You could've chimed in like, 'She's a fighter.' And then you would beam at me and say, 'Just like this one.'"

"Not a thing I'd say."

"Well, you could growl about distracted drivers. A few color details will go a long way."

I have to admit, there's something to getting our stories straight. I don't typically know the details of the women I'm with—the fewer details the better. But I'd know more about a fiancée.

"Fine. Ten minutes," I say. I storm to the front and get my tablet, and then I go back and refresh my drink. There's nothing I hate more than talking about myself. Unless it's talking about my past.

Clark smirks and heads to the front. "I'll be doing some work."

My mood is dark as he closes the pocket door. This is exactly the opposite of how I envisioned this trip—it was supposed to be me on the quiet side doing work and Clark dealing with all of this. This fiancée thing was *his* plan, after all.

"What happened to Japan?" I ask.

"The Japan thing was a joke," she says, focusing on her tablet. "I never actually said I was going."

"So, why the vacation?" Was she taking a break from me?

She holds up her right hand, wriggling her fingers. "My wrist needed a break."

"What happened? Is it injured?" I ask, just a little too forcefully.

"I'm trying to be smart about not overusing my wrist. It's no big."

"What does that mean?" I ask.

"It just needs a break from use," she says. "Come on, do you have the questions or not?"

I sit on the couch next to her and pull up my email. "It is a woman," I say. "The person on the yacht who we have to fool."

"Eep," she says.

"Her name is Gail Driscoll. We need to convince her two daughters, her sons-in-law, and the cousins, but Gail's the decision maker we care about. She's very shrewd. An excellent businesswoman."

"How old?"

"Seventy-something?"

Tabitha winces. "A woman that age is so done with people's

shit. And she's not trying to impress people, which makes her more observant. She's going to be hard to fool. But—" She puts up calming hands, as though I might break into a rage at any moment. "We got this. Tabitha Evans is on the job."

I nod, feeling this strange sense of...surprise, I suppose. Surprise at her and at her powers of observation. She's right, of course. People who don't give a shit *are* more observant. Gail Driscoll is particularly observant. Is there something more than cotton candy between Tabitha's ears?

She pulls out her phone. The case is new. Black with a brown design.

"Where's the flower and jewel explosion?" I ask.

"I know, right? My pretty case was broken. Your personal shopper and I had to crack it off to get this one on. It goes with the luggage. *Sigh.* Your personal shopper has quite the...uh... classic taste, I guess you would call it."

I lean in. "What did you really want to say? Instead of classic taste?"

She says, "I don't want to insult her. I'm playing a role, right?"

"Tell me," I coax. For some perverse reason, I want Tabitha to give her opinion. I don't know why—I already know it will be utterly Tabitha-ish.

She sinks her teeth into her plump lower lip, as if that might conceal her smile, but her dimples give her away. Tabitha has lots of feelings about her new wardrobe. "I'm playing a role, and this is my costume," she says.

"But how would you describe your costume? Be honest."

"Um, drab and completely boring? Zero sense of style? But hey, I can work with it."

I roll my eyes. Naturally, Tabitha needs a jewel and color explosion on every article of everything that she wears. "We'll get you a brand-new jeweled case when this is all over."

"I think I can buy my own jeweled case with what you're

paying me."

"No, you'll charge it to the account," I say. "Casualty of the job. No reason for you to have to replace it. Now let's go over this thing. I have work to do."

"Okay. Let's go over the questionnaire you guys made first."

I click on the Google Docs link she sent me. She's been busy, color coding the answers—mine in blue and hers in pink. "It's your birthday next month," I say. "You'll be thirty-one."

"And you're forty," she says. "Pushin' forty-one."

I give her a look.

"I'm an Aries," she says. "And I see that you're a Libra. Makes sense."

"I don't do astrology," I say.

"Also makes sense," she says. "Look, neither of us have siblings. Do we bond over being only children?"

"I'm guessing you have an opinion on that."

"We would, right?" she says. "How did you feel about being an only child?"

"It was what was," I say.

"Personally, I would've loved to have a sister or brother. I would've given anything for it."

"I suppose I would've liked a brother," I say.

"Not a sister?"

"Not where I grew up."

She waits, but if she thinks I'm providing more details than that, she's crazy.

"Fine. You grew up in South Boston." She looks up. "Though I have to say, you don't at all sound it."

"I don't," I say simply. She waits for me to elaborate. Also not going to happen.

"Oh-*kay*," she says. "And as you see, I grew up partly in upstate New York, partly in Manhattan. You guys never moved?"

"Next," I say.

"My folks were divorced when I was nine," she says.

"I wish mine would've divorced."

"Why?"

"As my fiancée, you would know that I don't talk about my past."

"Okay, well, divorce sucks, in case you were wondering," she says. "But if there was a kid-of-divorce Olympics? I would kick ass. I got to be a pro at the whole fun daughter gig." She sits back and crosses her legs. "I could make my dad such a sympathetic bachelor, like you can't believe how sort of fun, yet fetchingly needy I could make us seem. And how many dates I was able to help him land. Imagine Hugh Grant with a fun little orphan girl. In coffee shops and at grocery stores? I was the boss of those scenarios."

She gazes out the window at the clouds below. She has that humorous squint she gets, but there's something sad about her now. Of all the words I associate with Tabitha Evans, *sad* is never one of them.

When she turns back to me, she's smiling, though. "I can't tell you how many times I pretended I didn't know how to put on nail polish so that his latest girlfriend could help me. Eventually he couldn't live without me."

"What happened to your mom?" I ask before I think better of elongating this interview.

"Pain pill addiction." She does her one-eye-closed wince. "She came by it honestly. She got burnt in a fire, and it turned out she'd married a jerk who wasn't a fan of the sickness part of *in sickness and in health*. She took up the hobby of watching game shows and soap operas in a dark bedroom twenty-four hours a day. Not the best hobby ever. Personally, I would've preferred she'd gone for knitting."

She tears a corner off her cocktail napkin. She's been favoring her left hand. Exactly how bad is her wrist? I fight the urge to reach out to her, to take a look at her wrist or some-thing. "I'm sorry," I say simply.

"But Dad lived on Central Park in a gorgeous sunny place near everything wonderful." She crosses her arms and fixes me with a happy-go-lucky gleam. "I guess it balanced out."

"Ah," I say, unsure what to make of that.

"You haven't met Mom yet. She's upstate. Assisted living and you know…" She waves her hand. "I go there a lot, but I haven't brought you yet. You've met Dad, but you don't think much of him. You see him as a bit of a jerk, like, not the best dad ever, and sometimes you even get that growly tone when you talk about him. Myself, I take it in stride, and it's some-thing you truly admire about me. Your kitten is such a scrapper."

Before I can respond, she's onto the rest of the back-grounder, laughing at Clark's questions. I suppose she is a scrapper. Most people would be deeply scarred by the tragic little family story she just told, but she really does seem to take it in stride. And she doesn't seem bothered by her wrist, but it has to be affecting her livelihood. Is that why she accepted this role?

Suddenly we're done with Clark's questions and it's time for her questionnaire. She sends me a link to the doc she made. I scan through it. "You've gotta be kidding."

"My answers are already there in red, and we'll put yours in blue."

"Side of bed?" I say. "Nobody is going to ask that. It's ridiculous."

"Why not establish it? And favorite food. We'll be eating with these people. Food always comes up."

"Steak. Medium rare. Sushi."

"I hate wasabi," she says, pointing to the next question, about which foods we hate. "When we go out for sushi, I'm all, get that green stuff off my plate! But as you see, I do love shellfish and all kinds of fish. I think we love going to Japanese restaurants. What do you think?"

I sigh.

"Well, then it's decided. We are sushi fans. Let's make our favorite restaurant be Sushi of Gari."

"Fine. We'll say I'm taking you there for your birthday," I say, eyeing the pocket door, wishing this could be over already.

"I don't do birthdays. Important to know about me."

"Why not?" I ask.

"Just because. Next up, as you may recall, I have a hamster named Seymour. He has a little black dot on his right front paw."

"Yes, I seem to recall you mentioning him once or twice," I say sarcastically, because she talks about him all the time. "And there are those songs."

She bites back a smile. "Do you have any pets?"

"Take a guess."

She types in "NO PETS" after that item. "You were not enthusiastic about Seymour at first, but I believe you will learn to love him as much as you love me, though hopefully not in the same vigorous manner." She looks up, eyes sparkling.

When I don't respond to her ridiculous joke, she presses her lips together, like it's funny that I'm not responding.

"Moving on," I say.

She gazes out the window at the clouds and I study the curve of her cheek. I rarely get a chance to really look at her when she's cutting my hair; either she's behind me or in front of me looking right at me, and it's not as if I can sit there and stare at her.

"The other day you took Seymour out of his little cage and you were holding him so nicely. You always call him little guy. *Hey, little guy*. It's sweet. And when you look at him, you kind of soften…"

She rambles on about me and Seymour, and I can

suddenly see her as that only child, making up stories about invisible friends, wishing she had a sister. It would've been nice for a girl like her.

"I'm kind of glad you don't have pets," she continues. "What if you had a cat? Seymour wouldn't like that."

"There's no way I'd have a cat," I say.

"Okay, but are you comfortable with me riffing about us like that? With that level of detail? That was pretty convincing, right? That thing I said about you and Seymour? A few details go a long way, don't you think?"

"I think this is going to take all week." I scroll down. "Christ, you have over seventy questions! Look, I'm not a sharer. I don't need to know all of this. I won't be at cocktail parties talking about our favorite sushi restaurant. I'm going to have Clark fill this out, okay? Clark can tell you everything about me, and the rest doesn't matter."

"What about my answers?" she asks.

"I know all that I need to know."

"Wait a minute, lemme get this straight. I need to know extra details about you, but you don't need to know extra details about me?"

"Our relationship is unbalanced that way. It's not uncommon in the billionaire set."

"What? Am I just breeding stock for you?"

"I don't have a lot of interest in children," I say. "That part's up to you. If you want children, it's fine, but you have to deal with them."

She raises her eyebrows, dimples in full flare.

I give her a stern look.

"Uhh, okay. Hopefully nobody gets near that topic," she says. "Will I be able to continue my business after we're married? I hope so, because I love running my own business. I have big dreams around it, and it's best to stick close to the truth, especially with somebody like this Gail Driscoll person. You can change my look, but you can't change my personality. After our wedding, I'm not planning on hanging around in the country club. I'm a city girl who loves being near her friends and all of the action. And I love my clients, and I'm really into being a businesswoman. In fact, working with your personal shopper gave me some new ideas for expanding my offerings in a really exciting way."

I'm still stuck on her client comment. *I love my clients.* What exactly does that mean? Are some of these clients male? Not that I care. "You want to work. Fine. I wouldn't like a woman who wants to coast on my money."

"This is good. See how we're creating a picture of us as a couple? I'm not the society-climbing fiancée. I'm the cheerful, playful fiancée who balances you out. I bring fun and joy to your…" She seems to be searching for a word. "…your very *serious* life," she finally says.

What was she really going to say? I study her big brown eyes, though brown's not quite the word, and light brown isn't right either—her eyes have light and depth and richness, and a kind of softness, like a fox-brown gleam.

"We make sense in an opposites-attract way for sure," she continues. "And we're both really focused on our careers, but we fell for each other. How did it happen? That's something people will ask about. We need a couples origin story. How did we start going out?"

"Certain things will not be happening on that yacht," I grumble. "Top of the list: me breathlessly telling people our couples origin story."

"People will ask. I'm warning you—I'm not that good at making things up on the spot."

"Figure it out. I have to work."

"You're leaving our couples story up to me?" she asks. "What if you don't like what I come up with?"

"I don't care either way. I'm the man of few words and you're the sharer."

"There are some important questions here."

"I'm not doing seventy questions. Find three important ones. I doubt there are even three important ones on that whole thing."

She studies the list. "Past significant relationships," she says. "I was engaged when I was twenty-two. Straight out of college, but it didn't last long. We were young. It was stupid."

Stupid? "In what way?" I ask.

She shrugs. "Just stupid." I wait for her to elaborate, but she's back to scanning the list. She went on and on about her hamster, and this is what she decides to hold back on? Maybe it was impulsive. I could see Tabitha getting engaged to somebody inappropriate. Was he the male version of Tabitha? Colorful and happy-go-lucky? Did he wear hats and play the ukulele? I find the idea incredibly annoying.

"And that's it for your significant relationships?" I ask.

"I keep things casual these days," she says. "I'm a friends-with-benefits gal."

I frown, not at all loving that.

"Waiting," she says.

"No significant relationships. Ever. Next."

"Okay, what is your dream? Your ultimate goal in life?"

I fix a steely gaze on her. "I'm a billionaire flying around in my own jet. I'm living the dream."

"Come on," she says. "People never stop dreaming of the next thing. Don't billionaires try to fly to the moon in a rocket ship once they have everything else nailed?"

"A rocket ship is just a rich man's Corvette," I say.

"What do I know? Maybe you're the Corvette type…" Her smile is mischievous. "Some men require a Corvette…you know…"

I lower my voice. "I definitely don't require a Corvette."

She snorts, like it's all so ridiculous, but dusky rose spots seem to heat her cheeks and it's…compelling. We shouldn't have dressed her up in these strange new clothes. It's making me forget that she's Tabitha Evans, the most annoying human being that I know. And I'm still stuck on the engagement detail. Who was he? What happened?

"Come on, you're not cooperating," she says. "Also? I don't believe that you don't have a dream. I don't buy it."

"My dream would be not having to go on this boat trip," I say. "And now that I have to go, my dream would be to minimize any and all social interactions. I'd prefer to spend the trip in my cave. Alone."

Usually people back off when I'm blunt like that, but Tabitha puts on a big frown, rosy lower lip pressed out in a big pout that I can only assume is her way of reflecting my attitude.

It's not a reaction I appreciate.

"Let's finish this. Your turn," I bark. "Your dream."

"Well, like I said, professionally, I have these ideas for building some kind of a style brand. Not fussy high style, but something that helps women express their own personalities. More of a service, I guess. Let's just say I have ideas." She stares into the middle distance. "Also, I wish that the building where I live could stay the same forever. It was sold recently and there's a pretty credible rumor it might get torn down, and I would hate that. I love my neighbors, and my best girlfriends mostly live there. I want us all to stay there forever."

"That's your personal goal? To stay living in the middle of Hell's Kitchen—on 45th Street—forever? And you'd condemn your friends to that, too?"

"What's wrong with where we live?"

I give her a look. "It's an undesirable address. To say the least."

"Well, we desire it. We love it there. The women in that building are like a family."

"This is your dream? That you and your friends would never have nice places to live? Never buy country homes or start families? You all stay living two blocks from Times Square?"

"It's three blocks."

I roll my eyes. "And how about this style brand? What's the idea?"

She studies my face. "It's kind of not worked out."

"So you won't tell me now?"

"No, I don't think I will tell you now," she says.

"You know, entrepreneurs fall all over themselves to tell me their business ideas."

She shrugs. "Also, I want to lose twenty pounds."

"Women," I snort. "You're hardly fat."

She presses her hand to her chest. "Such flattery skills."

"You're not fat," I growl. "Okay?"

She studies my face, assessing…what? Whether I think she's attractive? Does she not look in a mirror? She's not my type, but it would be apparent to anybody with half a brain cell that she's attractive.

"My fiancé should be supporting my dream," she says.

"Sorry, but *my* fiancée would hardly be interested in a pointless weight-loss goal and clinging to a sad little apartment when she'll soon be living in a palace."

"But then what about her friends?" she asks.

"So I buy the building out from under the new owner and give it to you as a gift, and you can keep all your friends there."

"The new owner refuses to sell," she says. "Somebody has tried already."

"Well, maybe I would force him to sell. Maybe I'm the asshole who would ruin him financially until he caves, and then I give my precious fiancée the keys."

"Wow. Thank you," she says with what sounds like gratitude. "I would love that."

Something strange ripples through my chest. "Moving on," I bark.

"Don't worry, your kindness is a secret between us. You're my brutish, gothic Heathcliff, the alpha male who shows his soft side only to me. Ooh, that's good." Here she does one of her upwards finger-pointing gestures. "Right there. That's our couples dynamic."

"What's a couples dynamic?" I regret the question as soon as it's out of my mouth.

"A couples dynamic is a snappy phrase that explains how we fit together emotionally. I'm sassy and fun, and you're the alpha male who's gruff to everyone but me. Only I get to see your soft side. I'm the only one."

"Can we get on with it?" I ask.

"Okay. What is your greatest fear?"

I say, "You already know more about me than every woman I've ever been with."

"Come on. Greatest fear."

"My greatest fear is not landing Gail Driscoll's account."

"It can't be a business fear," she says.

"Who put you in charge of our fear parameters? Landing that account would triple our size. Give me all the fuck-you power I've ever wanted. I can't be where I want to be without this account. I've even hired a fake fiancée."

"All of this for just one account?"

"It's a massive portfolio of funds. Billions more that I'd have under management. The toothpaste that you use, the cars you ride in, your snacks, your cleaning products, your devices —the Driscolls control a stunning number of international brands, and all of those employees earn pensions; Driscoll is one of the few firms that still doles out pensions, and they need me to help them grow that money."

"You think you can grow it?"

"I've *been* growing it. I have a small percentage of their assets under control and I've outperformed everybody else they're working with. This account should be mine, but then Gail seemed to get cold feet, and suddenly she's considering someone else. Something changed. We think it's the article."

Tabitha nods. "Ah."

"The Driscolls are allergic to scandals. Gail's got a stick up her ass the size of Norman Rockwell. You and I are going to show her how wholesome I am."

"You can count on me, okay?" she says. "But if you think that gets you out of telling me your greatest fear…"

"I just told you." I grab my phone for a quick check of the markets.

"Maybe your fear is what happens if you don't get the account," she says. "It's not as if you'll be out on the street. What has you so flipped out that you'd hire a fiancée?"

"I'm not flipped out. I just want it."

"When people are frantically running *toward* something," she says, "it actually means they're running away from something."

I look up. "Says who?"

She tries to look serious, but her dimples give her away.

Something churns in me.

"Says who?" I repeat.

"Um…somebody on *Days of Our Lives*? But it's somebody very wise."

I clench my jaw. I knew it would be something like that. Good god, how are we ever going to pull this off?

"What?" she says.

"We're overpreparing. We'll be spending most of our time in our cabin not talking to people. We're newly engaged, after all."

"Ahh." She smiles mischievously. "Because ours is a very

passionate affair," she says. "Because we've been sneaking around so much that it's a huge deal that we get this unrestricted time together. Now we're secret lovers on vacation together, and all bets are off."

"Though in reality, I'll be working, and you'll be staying quiet as a mouse in your room."

"Yeah, I know," she says, "but please keep insultingly repeating it like I'm gonna be barging in on you every two seconds."

"So are we done?"

She straightens with an expression that says, *definitely not*. It's amazing how I can read all of her thoughts. Has nobody ever taught Tabitha how to do a poker face?

"What now?" I demand.

"Well, we are leaving one thing out. Two things. No! Three things. First, we need a gesture. Like, you tap me on the nose when you're especially proud of me."

"My gesture is silent approval. Next."

"Can I tap you on your nose?"

"Do you value your finger?" I ask.

She beams at me, as though that was an incredibly clever thing to say.

"Maybe I'll tap my own nose when I'm proud of you," she says.

"Don't," I warn.

She grins like a Cheshire cat, and my heart pounds. I'm not used to people grinning when I give commands.

"Which brings me to this finger." She holds up her left hand. Points to a finger. "Rings. We need a pit stop at a jewelers."

"Oh, right. Clark grabbed something...Hold on." I grab my satchel, pull out the velvet bag, and toss it to her.

She catches it. "Oh, my. That is so romantic." She empties the ring onto her palm. And gasps.

"Only the best for my fiancée," I say.

"Clark picked it out," she says. "Right?"

"Probably somebody from reception. They said we can get a sizer if need be," I say.

She slips it on and holds out her hand. "No need." She turns her hand this way and that. The ring sparkles in the low light of the cabin. It's not at all her style; even I can see that. A large rock in a simple setting. Tabitha would want more pizzazz, but her nails make up for it—they're pink and blindingly sparkly, not at all in keeping with her classic wardrobe.

Did my personal shopper overlook the detail of her fingernails? Or more likely this is her small rebellion against the boredom of good taste. She probably went out shopping for the sparkliest nail polish known to humankind to plaster on.

But what am I thinking? This woman would already own the sparkliest nail polish known to humankind. She'd have ten versions of it on a chaotic shelf. I imagine her going through the colors, one by one, wearing the witchy little squint she wears when she's amusing herself. She loves to stir the pot. She can't help herself.

"Wow. Okay, then," she says, tucking her hands in her lap.

"Now can I go to work?"

She does her playful wince. "One last thing. Very important," she adds. "Fake engagement 101. But you're not going to like it."

"I'm sure I won't," I say wearily.

"We need a practice kiss."

My gaze falls to her lips and my mind goes blank. "Did you not read the contract?" I bite out. "This relationship is to be purely platonic."

"Oh, I know. And before you think I'm jonesing to kiss you, please know, I'm just trying to do a professional job at this, and the kiss is important. Because I can tell you right now, when people do the fake engagement ploy and get busted, it's often because they're forced to do a first kiss in front of suspicious people, because everybody can tell a first kiss. Or, if they are pulling it off, a shaky first kiss ruins everything. Raises people's suspicions like nothing else."

"Have you been involved in other fake engagement situations?" I ask.

"No, but, you know, it's a thing. Trust me."

"It's a thing?" I ask, incredulous.

"Well, on soap operas," she adds.

I groan. "Jesus Christ, save me from your ridiculous soap opera wisdom."

"What? There is a lot of life wisdom in soap operas."

I give her a hard look.

"And the fact is, with people who have never kissed, there's a lot of trepidation. They're like, *How do I start off? Where do I put my hands? Which way should I tilt my head?*"

"Those are not questions that would cross my mind during a kiss. Ever."

"Please. Spare me from the knowledge of what crosses *your* mind when you kiss a woman," she says. "I'm just telling you, people aren't stupid. They're capable of recognizing a first kiss. We need at least one practice round. Unfortunately."

I swallow. Somewhere down on Wall Street, trading is in full swing. I have rates to check, reports to analyze, spreads to monitor, strategies to execute on, but the idea of pulling her to me and kissing her crowds all of that out. My hands flex.

A practice kiss. I can't think of a worse idea. "We're not a couple who enjoys public displays of affection."

She does her playful wince. "Okay, buuuuuut…what happens when they toast our engagement? We can't exactly shake hands."

Will people do that? Gather around and expect us to kiss in front of them? I focus on the window beyond her trying not to imagine kissing her. The whole idea here was *not* to be tempted or distracted.

"Ready?" she asks.

"If I decide we need a first kiss," I inform her, "then and only then will we have a first kiss. And I'll do the kissing."

"It has to be more than a peck," she says. "Just in case that's what you're imagining."

"Rest assured, a kiss from me would be the opposite of a peck."

"The *opposite* of a peck," she echoes, as though she finds it funny.

"The polar opposite." My gaze has gone back to her lips. They'd taste like some sort of sugary berry. Her dark hair would be thick and cool in my grip, her ass soft and firm. My mind won't stop spinning on kissing her, now.

"I'm trying to help you pull this off," she says. "Think of the times you've had a first kiss. The wild rush of it. The buzz of it. It'll be so obvious."

I frown. Who the hell has she been sharing these mind-altering first kisses with? Does she do a lot of first-kissing? With these friends-with-benefits types?

"Don't worry, I get this is business," she says. "You're not at all the type of guy I go for, either."

"No? Do tell—what type of guy do you go for?"

"For one, he would scoff at the idea of a private jet. And he would never wear or even possess cufflinks. Or if he did…" She gets up and bends over where I'm sitting on the couch. "There'd be a string attached to the cufflinks because he would've made them into an awesome toy for little Seymour. That would be a guy for me."

"Sounds like a loser."

She smiles. "Now, Rex," she says in a sultry voice. "I'm going to put my lips to yours. There might be a funny feeling in your tummy."

Chapter Five

Tabitha

I'M BENDING OVER HIM, near enough to feel the feather-like brush of his agitated breath on my nose. Definitely near enough to kiss him. Am I going too far?

His gaze is so dark and foreboding. It sends tremors right through me.

But we really do need to kiss. The man's dreaming if he thinks people can't recognize a first kiss. This is the professional thing to do.

Not that I haven't wondered what he'd kiss like…in extreme detail. Not that I don't sometimes breathe in his sharp, spicy scent when I cut his hair, letting it fill and intoxicate me.

"A very funny feeling in your tummy…" I whisper.

"For fuck's sake." He surges up from his seat and grips my shoulders, holding me in place in front of him, like I might suddenly float away if he doesn't keep me firmly in place, two inches from his beautiful, scowly face.

My breath hitches as he stares down at me. His lips hover

over mine, hovering one tiny, electrically charged millimeter away.

And then he brushes his lips over mine.

My body hums in response. I'm a panting rag doll in his hands.

He's peering down at me with those dark eyes. Confident hands pull me closer—close enough now that my breasts are pressed to his chest. I can feel him breathe with my breasts.

It's unbearably intimate. Mind-bendingly hot.

We fit together perfectly. Breathe together perfectly.

"S-so this is how you do a first kiss?" I say. "An almost kiss?"

His expression intensifies. His nostrils flare. It's like he doesn't even hear me over his own ragged breath.

The charge between us ramps up. A certain area between my legs has boarded the crazy train to tickly town. Needless to say, I really want to press into him—hard.

His gaze lowers to our almost-touching lips, enough so that all I see is a sweep of dark lashes.

It's excruciatingly delicious being flush to him, breathing with him, enjoying his sexy man-eyelashes. I slide my greedy palms over his beard the smooth way. My panties might be soaked.

I slide my hands down to his shoulders. I never get to touch him wherever I want. I like touching him like this.

He lets go of my shoulders and cradles my cheeks like two fragile birds, gently cradling them.

"Are you trying to decide how to hold me and which way to tilt your head?" I ask.

"Shut the fuck up." With that, he crushes his lips over mine, kissing me fervently. He presses me to the wall with his body.

The air whooshes from my chest. Did somebody flip his beast mode switch?

I am loving it. And my hands are grabbing his shirt,

greedily holding him flush against me, like I must consume him.

But not in a praying mantis way.

He growls, and the tremor it sends through me is a thousand percent heaven. He feels amazing.

And we really should stop, but his hands are now roaming the small of my back, and then his thumbs skim the sides of my hips, urging me closer.

My sex makes contact with his steely erection, and at this point, I'm more likely to come now than to stop this thing.

His tongue flicks out, and I suck it in—I'm a vampire for his tongue, and it's the hottest thing ever, sucking his tongue while he's pressing his rock-solid rod right into me.

He makes a rumbly sound. He feels out of control. It shouldn't be hot, but it really, really is, because this guy is always in control. I'm hungry for his mouth, barely able to form thoughts.

Suddenly one wicked hand slips under my waistband. The plane seems to dip, to do the loop-de-loop. I hold on more tightly. I give him his tongue back, but I'm all over his lips, starving for them.

One strong hand thrusts into my hair, cups the back of my head; his other grasps my ass, holding me to him.

A bloom of heat rolls through me.

I slide my fingers over his beard, cupping and stroking—and let's be honest, I'm basically mauling his face.

And I make a little *ng* sound.

"Fuck," he groans, kissing me with even more wild abandon.

A moment later, his breath changes. He stills. And with one seemingly effortful movement, he removes his lips and his hands from my body.

I'm a bit wobbly. I blink, pressing my hair behind my ears, trying to collect my wits.

Rex looks dazed. Undone.

"Well," I say, "that'll teach 'em to do a champagne toast in front of the children."

His gaze sharpens. Maybe a joke was inappropriate, but if that's how he first-kisses, I'd hate to know what his second kiss is like. And by hate, I mean, really freaking want to know.

He grabs his phone and taps it a few times. "Can I get to work now?" he asks, as if annoyed. "Or do the sages behind *As the World Turns* have more wise teachings we must follow?"

It seemed like a good kiss—an exciting kiss, even—but the cold, hard way he looks at me makes me think the hotness was maybe all on my side. Nothing is up to Rex's standards, apparently. Not even me.

"By all means, get back to work," I say smoothly, channeling Dorian Lord, my favorite soap opera villainess, waving my arm in the direction of the partition. *By all means* is a total soap opera thing to say.

Without so much as a word, he slides open the pocket door and disappears through, shutting it behind him.

Whatever, dude, I think, but I'm still shaking from the kiss. I wish it had been at least a little bit hot for Rex. But then, I'm the one who has the mad crush on him, not the other way around. And he kisses women all the time, most of them renowned beauties. Statuesque blondes and all of that. Maybe he's used to something more.

I sit on the couch, feeling weird about how turned on I am from the kiss. It was more than I'd ever dreamed.

He's definitely a different species from the men I usually kiss. I haven't gotten together with James, my go-to friends-with-benefits friend, for a few months, but we're always down-right playful when we kiss. And we talk during sex, too—not just technique requests and position ideas, but non-sex things, like we talk about TV shows and takeout food options for later.

No way could I have coherent thoughts about food or TV shows while kissing Rex.

James has an actual girlfriend now. Either he'll stay with her or be available for benefits again, and it's fine either way. I'm not one for drama or angst—there are other friends-with-benefits in the New York sea.

I study my new ring. We shouldn't have kissed—it made things worse for me.

But it was the right thing to do for the job. Rex picked me because he's an amazing leader and somehow he knew deep down that I can pull this kind of thing off. And I feel like we have a connection—I really do. Rex might not feel that connection, but it's there, and it'll help us to convince people we're engaged.

And we can definitely pull off a kiss.

I should be happy with just that. I am happy.

I grab my phone and scroll, scroll, scroll.

A few minutes later, Clark comes through and asks whether I want to watch a movie, and I'm stupidly grateful. Yes, I want to watch a movie.

We choose a documentary on conspiracies, and there's even microwave popcorn. I take a selfie with it when Clark is up front and text it to my friend Lizzie with the words *mile-high microwave popcorn* because she has a major microwave popcorn thing, but my heart's not really in it.

Rex stays in the front for the rest of the flight.

An hour later, we're descending through a layer of fluffy clouds, down, down toward sparkling blue water and coastline dotted with tall buildings. Clark and I return to our seats up front.

"Did you get your work done?" I ask Rex.

"As a matter of fact, I did," Rex says. I don't know why I should be disappointed. What did I expect? For him to confess to being distracted the entire time?

We go down a set of air stairs onto a sunny landing strip lined with palm trees, and pile into a waiting limo. Does Rex just have a network of limos all over the nation waiting to ferry him places? Or do rich guys lend each other their limos? But I don't ask. I'm trying to be cool. That's my new thing.

Rex is all work in the back of the limo, and I catch up on Instagram, making elaborate comments on things I would usually just fly past.

Eventually we pull up to the marina. And the driver opens the door and helps me out. And I look up at the boat—if you can call it that—and my heart is just pounding a million miles a minute.

I knew this yacht would be huge, but it's literally six stories tall, like a layer cake of gleaming white separated by strips of dark windows and brown wooden decks, sleek and ginormous.

Rex comes up next to me. I can feel him looking down at me, but I'm still taking in the yacht. Blue-uniformed crew members come out from the back, which is a sprawling open-air lounge of comfy seating and potted palms. They're setting up some kind of glam gangplank for us.

Rex sets a knuckle under my chin and turns my head to him. It's a romantic gesture until he growls, "Try not to be so slack-jawed for fuck's sake."

I try not to let his growl get me down. I'm dressed as a princess, after all—a boring princess, but a princess neverthe-less—and about to step aboard a giant football-field-sized yacht! A hundred yards longer than a football field, according to Clark. I go onto my tiptoes and whisper into his ear, "I really want to take a selfie of me boarding this boat! You might have to physically restrain me from it!"

He gets one of his disgusted expressions. "Don't," he says.

"But I'm a rube hairdresser you've plucked from obscurity. I feel like I can be a little tiny bit amazed at this thing."

"No selfies. Think about it, Tabitha. We've been having a

secret relationship for two months and I have fully introduced you to all the luxuries of life."

"But do you own a yacht?"

"No." He practically spits it out. Like yachts are the devil.

I suppress a smile because he's so Rex, what with the surliness. "Well, then I think I can be a little impressed."

"You will keep yourself toned down," he warns through gritted teeth.

"What happened to opposites attracting?" I tease.

He gives me a dark look.

"Why do you hate yachts?" I ask.

"Because I do," he growls. "And don't say that out loud again."

"So yachts are out. Now I have to think of another Christmas gift. You are so hard to buy for."

He gives me a warning look. Clark comes around to our side of the limo and takes a selfie with the yacht behind him.

I direct a face of shock at Rex. Because, really? Clark can do it, but not me?

More men in the blue uniforms are grabbing our bags and welcoming us to the boat.

"Thank you," I say as they walk up the plank.

Under his breath, Rex mumbles, "Never thank the help."

I give him a look, because, *hello! I'm the help*! But nothing can deflate my mood right now. "Aye aye," I say.

A row of uniformed women and one man stand at the ready as we step onto the posh lounge area. The first woman has tons of tiny braids, neatly caught in a blue band in back. She introduces herself as Taylor, the head stewardess, and these people are her team. A woman with a close-cropped platinum do is Mary, the first stewardess. Mary holds a clipboard and checks us in. There are other stewardesses, including Renata, a blonde with aviator glasses, who will be showing us to our cabins.

"This is the aft lounge deck," Renata says as she leads the way past live lemon trees and swanky lounge furniture. "You're on the fourth level. I can take you via an elevator at the center or—"

"We'll take the stairs," Rex says.

"Very good." Renata spins on her heel and leads us up a wide wooden staircase.

"Taylor's basically the captain of hospitality," Clark explains as we follow Renata up the second set of stairs and then a third. "Taylor runs the interior, and Mary is her first mate."

We follow Renata along the gleaming wood walkway on the outside of the third floor past an endless row of windows belonging to the guest cabins. Eventually the row of rooms ends, and the walkway opens out to what Renata calls the main foredeck—a vast, sweeping area with pools, bars, bright blue cabanas, potted palms, seating areas, and festive blue flags.

"It's like a little city," I say.

"Almost," Renata says, heading up an open stairway to the fourth level. We pass a small lounge overlooking the massive main deck and head back toward yet another row of guest cabins. "There are sixty guest rooms in all, thirty each on the third and fourth levels, plus the family area and master suites on the fifth. Crew quarters on first."

I nod, acting all casual.

Renata takes us along the outer edge of the fourth level, telling us about the other areas—aft weight room, second-level massage room, entertainment area, dining room.

She finally stops at room 410 and unlocks the door. "Mr. Williamson, you're in here." She leads Clark into his room.

Rex and I look over the rail down at the pier where white limos are pulling up in a row; the smooth sequence reminds me strangely of water ballet. "Those are the Driscolls," he says. "They always travel in white limos."

"You think Gail's in one of those limos?"

"We'll see. There are a lot of Driscolls."

"I gather." On the plane after the movie, Clark showed me pictures of Gail and her three adult daughters. I worked really hard at memorizing their names and faces. I'm not brilliant like Rex, but I know how to work hard.

Gail's youngest is in Asia, so I don't have to worry about her, but I need to worry about Wanda and her husband, Mike. Wanda and Mike run Gail's family ranch in Texas and have three kids. I'm also supposed to care about Gail's other daughter, Casey. Casey is married to a man named Wellington, and they have five kids and are into arts philanthropy in Malibu.

Clark says that the daughters don't care about the business, but they care about Gail.

On the second level of importance are Driscoll cousins and grandchildren, the Driscoll marketing team, and assorted executives. There are also business vendors and partners on the yacht. Clark says I don't have to care about them.

Drivers start opening doors, and people start getting out of the limos. Suitcases appear on dollies.

I turn to Rex. "Clark told me that even when Gail's daughter Wanda got married, Wanda's husband took her last name. They're all really into being Driscolls."

"Common among the family money set," Rex says under his voice. "You keep the money name. If you marry other money, then you go with the hyphen. Jacqueline Kennedy-Onassis."

"They're like another breed."

"Yes, they are." There's an edge to his voice. He came up from nothing, a scrabbly South Boston kid. Does he have opinions on people like this?

"Is Gail a Driscoll by birth?" I ask.

He shakes his head. "No. She came from ranchers. Small-time wealth, but most ranchers, they work. She married into the Driscolls young. Her husband was the one with the real money. He died around fifteen years ago, and she's been running things."

"Wow," I say. "So Wanda and Mike—they took over the ranch from Gail's side of the family?"

"Very good," Rex says.

My chest swells.

"There she is. Black jacket. White hair."

I find her right away. I can't see much of her face from here, but I would've guessed she's the one in charge just from the commanding way she carries herself and the way people cluster around her.

"The Driscoll daughters are lucky she's in charge," Rex says. "She stepped up and ran that business with an iron grip and cool, unemotional decisions. Don't let that white hair fool you. She's straight-shooting, no-nonsense ranching stock. She saved the Driscoll family's ass several times over. She's all about the family. Completely focused on family. You could also say it's her blind spot."

I lower my voice. "If she's so amazing at business, why is she letting some bad press about you get in the way of letting her funds make more money?"

Rex watches another limo pull up, this one black. "An apple pie image has a lot of financial value."

"But you think it's a bad call. Because you would make her *so* freaking much money."

He slides a dark gaze to me. "Yes," he bites out in a forceful way that makes my toes curl.

Four elegant people get out of the limo. Two couples, it seems like. Maybe that one is friends of the family, or business associates like Rex.

"All the people showing up looking fancy," I whisper. "But beneath that veneer of glamour, there are secrets and subterfuge."

"Secrets and subterfuge? What the hell are you talking about?" Rex asks.

"I'm doing a voiceover."

"This is a very boring rich family."

"No such thing. Every rich family has secrets and subterfuge," I say.

Rex gives me one of his warning looks. "I don't want to hear any more of your soap opera theories. Got it?"

"How do you know that's a soap opera thing?"

He raises his stern eyebrows. "Isn't it?"

In fact, it is. The yacht is reminding me very much of a soap opera destination wedding. "Just because it's on soap operas doesn't mean it's not true. Scratch the surface of any wealthy family and you'll find secrets and subterfuge," I say.

"Be done with it," he warns. "I mean it."

I turn back toward the limo party down below wondering what has his boxers in a twist. Or briefs. Who knows. He didn't bother to answer that question.

Renata comes back out of Clark's room. She brings us to our suite, 412. It has a luxurious center living room and bedrooms on either side, and our bags are already there.

"Ms. Driscoll said you'd want to repurpose one of these bedrooms into an office," Renata says. "If the corner desk isn't large enough, crew can pull in something more suitable." She shows us to a bathroom with a spa-like tub, and then she shows us a little control panel with switches to control the lights and the opaqueness of the windows that line the exterior wall.

Rex keeps looking over at me. I'm acting bored, but it's not easy, because, what witchcraft is this? The literal tint of the windows lightens and darkens with the turn of a dimmer switch.

"Do you have housekeeping preferences?" Renata asks.

"Our preferences are for nobody to disturb us or come in a room at any point," Rex says. "We will request housekeeping when we feel that we need it; otherwise we would prefer to be left alone."

"Very good," Renata says. "Your itinerary should be up on your phone. Launch toast at three."

"Thanks," Rex says.

"Yeah, thanks!" I echo.

Renata smiles and leaves.

"So it's okay to thank her," I say.

"It was a conversation."

"Do we not tip her?"

"They get a tip all at once at the end. In one big chunk," he says, like he's exasperated just from me asking questions. *Sorrr-reee!* I want to say. Instead I walk around touching things. Now that we're alone, I feel that I can do that. Every surface is special in some way—polished wood, sleek metal, fancy inlays. I feel Rex's eyes on me.

"It's one of your more high-end megayachts," he says. "I think they bought it from a sultan or a prince or something."

I spin around. "Are you shitting me?"

"No."

"Wow."

"That will be your room; the middle is my office, and this bedroom's mine. You can do whatever you want in your room; just don't disturb me when I'm in my office, and my room is completely off limits to you. I'll let you know when there's a function we should attend together, otherwise I prefer you remain largely inside your room."

"Wouldn't it be more natural for me to socialize with people, or at least be up on deck with a book while you're working?"

"I think that limiting your contact with people is really the best policy, don't you? Less room for error?" he says briskly. He definitely seems surlier since the kiss.

"I hear what you're saying, but too much of that could

seem antisocial, don't you think?" I say. "But I get it. You need to see how awesome of a partner in the realm of fiancée fakery I can be before you're comfortable with me hanging out on the loungey decks. So I'll hold off for now."

"You're not hanging out on any of the decks, ever," he says. "I'm keeping you busy."

"You're keeping me busy while you work in your office? That is some multitasking mojo right there!"

He frowns, unamused.

"Maybe I'm exhausted by your enthusiastic lovemaking," I suggest. "So I sleep it off while you work. Is that what you want them to think?"

"I don't give a shit what they think. You exist in that room until I decide to trot you out. End of story. Questions?"

"What's a launch toast?"

He pushes off the doorframe and grabs his suitcase. "It's a ridiculous and boring tradition where we all go up on the main deck and stand together and drink champagne and watch as the boat pulls away from the pier at an excruciatingly slow pace. It's a tradition in yachting that you always toast the launch."

"Is this a dress-up thing?"

"No, you're good."

"Okay," I say.

"You're going to change anyway, aren't you?" he grumbles.

"I feel like my character would change. She wants to make a good impression."

He turns and goes into his bedroom. I wander into mine and heave my giant suitcase onto the bed and start unpacking and hanging up my clothes. I suppose it's best that Rex was all growly about no housekeeping coming in here except when we specifically request it, being that we're in separate rooms. That is not fiancée-ish at all.

I change into one of my favorite outfits that the shopper

got for me: a black halter-top jumpsuit with gaucho-length flared pants. It's not my style, but it's elegant yet casual and vaguely sailor-ish.

I emerge from my posh prison to find Rex in a linen jacket, noodling on his phone. He looks up when I come out and seems to stiffen with this whole stormy expression.

"Behold the gaucho," I say. "It looks like a skirt, but it's pants!" I twirl around.

"It'll do," he grumbles. "Let's go."

We head down to the main lounge deck, which is draped with white and blue banners, and there are bouquets of white flowers spilling out from everywhere. Several dozen people stand around in small clusters up and down the dockside of the yacht, some standing at the railing, watching the dockworkers do whatever they do. Waiters circulate among them bearing trays of champagne glasses.

Other people are bunched around the bar or cluster at the far side watching clumps of kids racing around on some sort of games court.

I spot Gail near the bow of the ship. She has white hair and fun blue glasses and a button nose, and she's built like a tank—not overweight so much as strong and vital.

Rex turns to me. "I think it goes without saying that you cannot get drunk."

I take his arm and smile. "Dude, a little faith."

We linger around while she receives people like the queen of the yacht. Eventually we head over. Gail smiles when she sees us coming.

"Rex!" She clasps his hand warmly in both of hers—she's definitely not the air kisses kind. Then she pulls back and inspects me. "And you must be Tabitha!"

I smile. "It's so nice to meet you, Ms. Driscoll."

"Gail, please." She takes my right hand in both of hers and squeezes. Even in her seventies, she has an outdoorsy look—

sun-weathered skin, rosy cheeks, a smattering of freckles. And she really does seem to be happy that Rex has come on the yacht, or maybe she likes that he has a fiancée.

"Your yacht is lovely," I say. "We really are so grateful that you've invited us. We've been so looking forward to it—you have no idea." I gaze up at Rex. "It's hard to get this guy out of the office."

"Somehow that doesn't surprise me," Gail says.

"Right?" I say. "There's definitely no talking to him before the closing bell. The way he sometimes looks at those monitors, you'd think he's trying to melt them with his mind."

Gail laughs. "Oh, I know the look. I know it well."

Rex is staring at me strangely. Was that too quirky to say? I thought it was nice, and also, it's true.

Gail beams at us.

Encouraged, I reach up and brush the side of his beard with the back of my hand. "He's the most focused person I've ever met. He's just amazing."

He looks bewildered for a moment, a deer caught in head-lights, then he takes my hand and kisses my knuckle; the hot shock of contact knocks the breath out of me. He turns to Gail. "We really are grateful, Gail."

"Glad to have you aboard," she drawls, and starts intro-ducing us around. There's Gail's daughter Wanda and Wanda's husband, Mike, and a few of the cousins—I recognize most of them before Gail even says their names. I was never good in school; I always hated memorizing things, but I know how to work hard. Rex is paying me well and I plan to be an amazing partner.

Wanda Driscoll and the Driscoll cousins all have wide moon faces—all the people in the Driscoll bloodline seem to have them, which is something that didn't come through in the photos on Clark's cheat sheet. I can't tell if their heads are really large, or if their faces take up more area on their heads. Or is it that their hair takes up less area?

I really want to talk to Rex about it and see what he thinks.

The members of the Driscoll bloodline also seem to have brows that slant down at the outer edges, like the opposite of villain eyebrows. On some of them, like Wanda, it's a cute look —there's even a certain sweetness. But on the guys, it's more of a hangdog look.

Gail, being a Driscoll by marriage, doesn't have that Driscoll moon face or the Driscoll brows.

Eventually we're introduced to a blond man named Marvin, who wasn't on the cheat sheet of people that Clark gave me, but Gail seems to regard him as important. Who is he?

Marvin looks to be in his thirties. He's not a Driscoll by blood, judging from his normal-sized face. In fact, he has Gail's stocky build and button nose. He also has a fake tan and wears his sunglasses perched on top of his head. My hairdresser's sixth sense tells me that the sunglasses on his head are a central part of his hairstyle strategy.

Gail beams at him. "Marvin's my nephew. My sister's son."

We say hi, and introductions continue around from there, but I can't get past Marvin. Something feels off about him. He shakes Rex's hand and then mine, meeting my gaze with a smile as fake as his tan and an expression that I would describe as assessing. Like he's on guard, somehow.

"We didn't even know Marvin existed until this past August," Gail says. She goes on to tell this tale about her wild-child sister, Dana. Dana took off after high school to lead a carefree life of boozing it up on beaches while Gail stayed at the ranch. Dana cut off all contact with the family and died in her thirties. It was only when Marvin made contact last year that they learned she'd given birth.

I try to make my expression blank and not at all suspicious, but seriously? The ol' secret-baby-coming-out-of-the-wood-work story? Related to billionaire Gail Driscoll? Nobody finds it surprising?

It's like if your friend got a bunch of money from a Nigerian prince, like, literally got the money, wouldn't you laugh and be surprised, and maybe say something like, *who would ever think such a thing could actually happen in real life? Crazy, right?* People would acknowledge the weirdness of it. It's so clichéd!

I look around, checking if anybody else seems to find the secret-baby thing unusual. Do these people not watch soap operas?

Then I look over at Marvin, and he's totally frowning at me.

Shivers go over me—not the good kind of shivers, either. I turn my attention back to Gail, who's going on about wild Dana giving little Marvin up for adoption and not telling the family.

People are saying nice things now.

"That is…really *amazing*," I say, struggling to sound like it's so believable. I furrow my brow, like I'm so convinced. "So amazing that you found each other."

"So amazing," Gail says, smiling at Marvin. "He's the spitting image of Dana. To think we never knew. All alone in the world."

"I wasn't exactly alone. My adoptive parents were very kind," Marvin says, no traces of his weird frown that he apparently had just for me.

"Still," Gail says. "All the time we missed. The birthdays. The small steps."

"I'm just grateful I got it in my head to do the search," Marvin says. "I wasn't sure if it was a wise thing to do, but I had to know, so I gathered up my courage."

People smile, like that is so sweet.

"You hear of those searches going poorly so often," Marvin continues. "Turning out devastating in some way. I was heartbroken to hear my mother was deceased, but then I found my aunt, and it meant the world."

I tend to observe people closely in my job, and I can usually tell when they're lying—it's one of those skills a hairdresser develops. His words just don't ring true—deep down I feel it!

Rex asks when they first got in contact with each other. Gail describes their first meeting and the way she recognized Marvin from across the coffee shop. Saw her beloved sister in him.

But a lot of people look like other people. And it drives me crazy that nobody seems to think there's anything strange about a secret baby who's closely related to a billionaire turning up.

Hello! It's the exact thing that happens on every soap opera, and the person is always a fraud. I'm sure they checked Marvin out. Still. A long-lost relative coming out of nowhere?

And he's acting so shifty!

I force my gaze to the horizon, which is filled with crane things looming above the ships. I tell myself that it's not my problem if Marvin acts suspicious and sounds like a liar. I'm here for Rex. I'm doing an important job for Rex.

At one point, Gail is talking about their meeting, and everybody is watching her, listening to her, and I happen to glance over at Marvin and he's giving me the frown again.

A chill rockets down my spine because his eyes are weirdly flat—I'm talking dead-fish-eyes-in-a-butcher-case flat.

What?!

I look around. Nobody sees him staring at me like a freak; everybody else is listening to Gail. I look back at Marvin and he's still fixing me with that frowny stare. The chill seeps into my veins.

His frown feels like a threat. Does he know I'm suspicious of him? Is that it?

Suddenly his expression goes back to normal. The attention is back on him, and he's smiling and adding details to Gail's story. Apparently they both ordered a blueberry muffin.

I smile brightly and link my arm into Rex's. "So *amazing*," I say, heart pounding like mad.

The talk turns to books. As luck would have it, I've read one of the books that Gail has read—a fictionalized account of anthropologist Margaret Mead—and we bond over it, and I fall back to being my normal self, and completely avoid looking at creepy Marvin.

I'm relieved when Rex and I are finally alone, leaning over the railing. Down on the dock, men are doing things with chains and winches.

"Will they never shove off?" Rex mumbles. "I have business to attend to, and there's a limit to how much I can look at my phone with our hostess right there."

"So what's up with Marvin?" I say.

"What do you mean?" he asks.

"The suspicious surprise nephew?"

"What about him?" he asks.

"Do you not find his story a bit odd?"

He turns to me fully now. "What do you mean?"

"A surprise nephew comes out of the woodwork, and nobody bats an eye? The surprise secret baby, relative of a billionaire? You do know that the secret nephews always turn out to be fake, right?"

"Marvin's not a Driscoll by birth; he's a Turlington. Like Gail. He wouldn't be in line to inherit the Driscoll money."

"Well, he's drinking champagne on a yacht with the billion-dollar club, isn't he? And didn't you get a sense that he's kind of...not right?"

"Mentally, you mean?" he asks.

"No, he's just wrong," I say. "A freak, if you will?"

"He's a bit ingratiating," he says. "But he's with his new family. Maybe he's feeling awkward."

"But seriously, you don't find it suspicious? Somebody coming out of the woodwork to be part of the jet set?"

"Well, of course Gail would've had his DNA tested. She's not a fool. She wouldn't take a person at his word."

"Yeah, but you can't really trust a DNA test," I tell him.

"Yes, you can," he says in his stern tone. "DNA tests are established science with a very small margin of error. Marvin wouldn't be here if he wasn't who he says he is. Gail would've had him fully investigated. She probably ran two tests."

I shrug.

"What are you saying? You don't believe in genetic science now?"

"Oh, I believe in genetic science for sure. But a DNA test is only as strong as the weakest link in the chain from the DNA sample to the lab. A lot of people are handling that genetic material. A DNA test or two…please. A few well-placed bribes and you have yourself an instant relative."

Rex gives me one of his trademark scowls, sooty brows drawn together over gray eyes. That scowl reaches clear through me, deep into my belly where it plucks a forbidden low note. "That's not a thing people do," he says in a stern and rumbly voice.

"I think some people do it."

"You know of people faking their way into prominent families by fixing DNA tests?"

I shrug.

His eyes sharpen. "Who exactly are we talking about here? If anybody was faking their way into families like the Driscolls by fixing tests, I would've heard of it. I've worked with half the billionaires on the East Coast. Who *specifically* has this happened to?"

"Uh…the Quartermaines…the Chandlers…" I mumble.

He looks confused, searching his memory for a moment, then, "Oh, Jesus Christ. Are you talking about your soap opera?"

"Well…" Soap operas, plural, but I don't say that.

"Seriously!?" he whisper-barks.

"What? You asked. You can't kill the messenger."

"Actually, you *can* kill the messenger," he says. "There's a long tradition of messengers' severed heads being sent right back to the sender of the message as a way of strongly rejecting that message."

I sit there wishing I hadn't mentioned the Quartermaines and the Chandlers, because in spite of everything, I want him to take me seriously. And I know for a fact there was a moment of weirdness between Marvin and me—I felt it right to my bones, and I want Rex to believe me. The facade came down between Marvin and me—just for a split second, but I really felt it.

"A soap opera," he says with maximum derision.

"Just because something is on a soap opera it doesn't mean it doesn't also happen in the real world," I say. Except maybe *Dark Shadows*, but I'm hardly going to bring a vampire soap opera into the discussion at this point.

Rex switches gears to muttering and glaring darkly at the dockworkers, as if that might speed them along. You know he wishes so bad that he could yell at them.

"I'm just stating facts, Rex," I say in my voice of calm reason. "Fact: tests can be fixed. Fact: bribes can get you anywhere. Fact: there was this moment of weirdness between Marvin and me where he was looking at me like, *I see you seeing me*. Like all his pretense fell away for a moment and I got this glimpse of his weird, creepy wrongness."

I have Rex's full attention now. "Are you telling me that Marvin was *hitting* on you?"

"More like, giving me the fish eye."

"Sounds like he was hitting on you," Rex grates out. "That is *not* acceptable." He turns his dark gaze toward Marvin, who's deep in conversation with a Driscoll.

My heart pounds, because Rex's sudden anger is magnificent. Rex is a bird of prey unsheathing his claws, and those claws want to rip Marvin's face off.

"It wasn't sexual," I say.

Rex looks unconvinced.

"Not everything is sexual," I add. "It was Marvin momentarily dropping his mask, and showing me that he's just...not on the up-and-up."

Rex folds his arms. "He unwittingly revealed to you his criminal identity? Is that what you're trying to tell me here?"

"Not revealing, but..." I feel so frustrated, because I know what I felt. "Marvin gave me a super-weird feeling."

Darkly, Rex says, "If he's hitting on you, he's going to have to deal with me. And he won't like it, I assure you."

This pleasant little trill ripples through me. So wrong.

"I don't care who he's related to," Rex continues. "This wouldn't be much of a fake fiancée charade if I let some weasel hit on you."

"After many years of life experience, Rex, I think I'd know when a man is hitting on me," I say. "I'm telling you, he's up to something. And that makes him paranoid. He's paranoid of people who might be suspicious of him."

"Meaning you."

"Yes," I say.

Rex discreetly checks his phone, then pockets it. "I hate to destroy your fake nephew theory, but pulling off a significant identity scam like this with all of the bribery and fraud that's involved, it wouldn't be worth it in Marvin's case. Gail's the one who married money—her sister's kid is in no way a direct heir to the Driscoll fortune. So, posing as Gail's nephew wouldn't be worth risking doing time for. The best he can do is get a job in the family company, nice Christmas gifts, and the occasional ride on a yacht. Maybe a loan or two from Aunt Gail. Not that that's nothing. I mean, he's not exactly working as a swamper at the burger shack at this point. But for that kind of financial outlay and legal risk? The return on investment simply isn't there. Now if he was posing as a fake Driscoll heir, that's different. But the Driscoll money does not flow sideways to Gail's family of origin. And again, she would've checked him out. A family like that has investigators and lawyers on retainer."

"All I'm saying is that there's something fishy about him."

"Well, guess what?" Rex says. "You're not being paid to think about what Marvin's up to, are you?" He pauses here. "Are you?"

A bolt of annoyance goes through me at his utter jerkiness. "Well…"

"The answer is no. You're not being paid to talk about Marvin or report to me about Marvin or worry about Marvin in the least. Got it?"

"I got it," I mumble, grateful one of the cousins has chosen this moment to come up and chitchat with Rex about the market so that I can stew in silence.

Rex is right, though. I need to forget Marvin. I resolve to leave it. Another cousin joins us, a younger woman, and we smile and laugh while Rex grumbles about the market with the first cousin.

The other cousin and I go on to gush over the yacht for a while. We totally hit it off, and then she flits off to grab another drink.

I go up on my tiptoes. Into his ear, I whisper, "Killing it." I don't really have to whisper into his ear being that there's nobody around, but it looks couple-sy.

"So far."

"I'll take that as a very sad compliment," I say. "Though do you get the feeling that Gail really wanted to ask how we got together? I think she wanted to ask earlier. We need to work out our couples origin story."

"Just make something up," he says. "You think you can do that?"

I swallow. "Yes, I think I can do that."

He sighs, like my very presence annoys him, and checks his phone again.

I grit my teeth, feeling this awful sense of déjà vu; it doesn't take me long to put my finger on it—he's acting like my dad after the fire and the divorce. Annoyed with my presence. I suck in a breath, hating that feeling, that old sense that somebody will hit the eject button the moment I stop being useful.

Clark comes up. "How goes it?"

"Glad you could make it," Rex grumbles.

"A few glitches hooking up our network." He turns to me. "You look amazing."

I give him a sunny smile. "Thank you."

"Everything going good?" Clark asks.

Rex lowers his voice. "Aside from the scandal with Marvin that Tabitha has turned up?"

"Marvin?" Clark asks.

"The nephew," Rex says darkly.

"Oh, right," Clark says. "Yeah, I met him just now. He wasn't on the guest list."

Rex gives me a level look. "According to Tabitha, he's a fake. He falsified DNA tests and everything."

"What makes you think he's a fake?" Clark asks.

"He looked at her weird," Rex says.

"He's acting suspiciously," I say. "Like he's up to something and just a little paranoid."

"Well, if that's true, he picked the wrong side of the family to fake out," Clark says.

"That's what I told her," Rex says.

I shrug. "So it's not a fake heir thing. But it's something."

"Starts with an *H* and rhymes with corndog," Rex says.

"Horndog?" Clark frowns. "Let's hope not."

"No. Won't look right if I tolerate some random nephew giving her energy," Rex says. "Hitting on my fucking fiancée."

"It's not a horndog thing," I say. "I would know. A woman knows."

But they just talk over me, like I wouldn't know. "You'd have to push back at some point," Clark says. "And Gail won't like that."

Rex grumble-swears.

People cheer and raise their glasses. The yacht has broken away from the shore, towed by one of the two tender boats that go everywhere with it, because even a yacht has underlings. Another Driscoll wanders up, and the talk turns to some merger. It seems that everybody wants Rex's thoughts on financial events.

I'm left to my own devices, namely staring at the shore and the receding rows of pleasure boats and lesser yachts, lined up along the pier like shiny little soldiers at the edge of the sparkling water.

A gorgeous blonde woman comes up next to me, leaning over the railing. I recognize her from Clark's cheat sheet as Serena Driscoll. The giant Driscoll face and the puppy-dog Driscoll eyes definitely work for Serena. She's a South Carolina cousin, not one of the main Driscoll kids, and not one of the Driscoll decision makers, but a Driscoll all the same.

"So you're engaged to Rex?" she asks with a pretty southern twang.

"Yes," I say. "I'm Tabitha Evans." I hold out my hand.

She hesitates, then takes it. "Serena Driscoll."

"So nice to meet you," I say. "You know Rex?"

"Oh, yes," she says, not elaborating, which I definitely take as, they slept together. My heart pounds. "And how…did you two meet?" she asks.

"I was his hairdresser," I say, wishing I'd worked out our story.

"*Hairdresser.*"

"Yeah."

"Oh." She tilts her head and narrows her eyes. "Wait, you're not kidding?"

"No." I shrug off the jab. "I've been doing his hair for years so—"

"Y'all are telling me Rex O'Rourke is marrying his *hairdresser*?"

"Yes," I say. "Why?"

She smirks and looks out at the shore. "Just…unusual."

"Not to us," I say. "We spent a lot of time together, and we fell in love, and now we're engaged, so…"

"Yeah, I don't know. Men like Rex…" She pauses.

I wait, though her meaning is clear—men like Rex don't marry women like me.

She turns to me, lips pressed smugly together. Slowly she shakes her head *no*. As if *that* weren't clear enough, she adds, "You're not his type, is all."

"Yet we fell in love," I say, "so we must be each other's type."

"You think?" she asks me. "Rex is all about work. It's all he cares about. Men like Rex would go for somebody who adds value on a connections level. Not that it's not sweet to marry for…*love*," she adds, quote fingers fully implied. "It's just not Rex's style."

"Turns out it is Rex's style," I say, feeling nervous. Is she right about Rex? Is she seeing through our charade? Marvin's not the only person with something to hide on this boat.

"Well, it *would* be his style to bring a little something for the cabin."

My blood turns cold as I get what she's implying, but I smile in a sunny way, like I don't care. It's a million-watt smile, because if there's one thing I've learned in life, you never let them see you sweat. And you never *ever* let them smell blood in the water.

"The thing is," I say, "when you meet the right person, it's just an amazing feeling." I gaze over at him. He's talking sternly to the little group of men, who are all hanging on his words. "People say to me, why Rex? He only cares about business, and there's his track record with women. But I'm the one he shows his sweet side to. His soft and sensitive side." I turn my gaze back to her. "People don't believe he has that side, but he shows it to me."

She gives me a smile. She's as good at fake smiles as I am. It's the duel of the fake smiles. My blood races.

"It means everything that I'm the only one who gets to see that side, you know?" I say sweetly.

Her smile falters. She is not loving this. "Very special," she says.

"Very," I whisper.

I feel Rex before I turn and see him strolling over like he owns the place, dark chocolate sports coat picking up the rich tones of his hair and beard, dark eyes fixed on mine.

"Rex! What a lovely surprise!" Serena inserts herself between us and hugs him and kisses one cheek and then another, pressing a bit too hard if not downright smooshing her face to the side of his.

He directs a vaguely pained glance at me, and for a second, it feels like we're allies. It's nice.

"I've been chatting with your...*fiancée*," Serena says to him, managing to insert more air quotes with just her silky tone. "Hairdresser. How unexpected," she says. "You took up with your hairdresser."

"It wasn't unexpected to me." Rex looks down at me. "I always knew there was something about her. Always."

This strange bright feeling flits through me, and I beam up at him. He said it so convincingly, like he felt something about me, too, his gaze softening even through the scowl.

I know he's acting, but it feels real.

"Huh," Serena says.

Gail stands on a raised platform up at the bow of the ship, glass in hand. She's calling for silence. Marvin and her two kids are next to her, shushing people. The yacht is finally heading out to sea.

Chapter Six

Rex

TABITHA IS INFURIATING AND IMPOSSIBLE. But when that infuriating, impossible power is turned on Serena Driscoll?

Priceless.

I'd slept with Serena years ago. She's beautiful and competitive with a cruel streak a mile wide. That cruel streak felt like worldliness when I was in my twenties.

I could see what was happening even if I couldn't hear what they were saying, and I had to come over. Not that Tabitha needed a save. Tabitha is the last person who needs a save. If anybody needed a save, it was Serena.

I slide an arm around Tabitha's sun-warmed shoulders, sucking in her berry scent, watching her chest rise and fall, imagining finishing what we started in the plane.

The kiss was a mistake—a very hot mistake, but a mistake all the same, because it got me thinking about her in a sexual way, which is so outrageous, because this is Tabitha, the most annoying woman in all of Manhattan.

It doesn't matter. The feelings will pass. When I focus hard enough on work, everything goes away. Work is my fortress, my refuge, my escape hatch.

Gail's talk is long. *Thank you for being here, importance of family, good things in life,* yada yada.

Marvin stands up with Gail like a little lord of the manor. I grit my teeth. Hitting on Tabitha like that? No way. Not on my watch.

I slide my hand up and down her smooth, muscular arm, palm like a hungry ghost, touching, consuming, but never covering enough of her skin to be satisfied. I tell myself that one inch of her skin is the same as another, but I can't seem to stop. Our small contact burns in a way that feeds me. A strange sort of nourishment.

I need to focus. With my free hand, I pull out my phone and do a discreet check of the market, disengaging my attention, but I can't quite bring myself to disengage physically.

I shouldn't have kissed her like that.

It was just that, back there in the plane, when she was talking about us kissing, I got this perverse idea that I needed to take back control. And suddenly I was yanking her up to me, holding her still, our lips a hair's breadth apart.

If anything, holding her like that made my control disintegrate.

With every moment I held her still, I'd needed to kiss her more. I was trembling with it. And she was being full-on Tabitha, a panting confection. So that didn't help.

I'd forced myself to hold her there longer. To make her wait until I didn't need to kiss her anymore. But when I held her like that, the urge to kiss her just built and built until I couldn't stand it. So I just kissed her, thinking to get it over with.

But once it started, it was difficult to end—I don't know why. Maybe it was because we'd been sharing those stupid confidences, creating this faker's intimacy. I was falling for our own PR.

Eventually I tore myself away. I'm an Olympic-level athlete when it comes to the sport of self-denial, and I tore myself away from the kiss and grabbed my phone and forced myself to type out a message. The message was nonsense, but sometimes you have to settle for the appearance of control on the way to getting it.

Gail prattles on, bringing me back to the present. Tabitha listens, rapt, arm warm and soft under my palm. I scroll through a report, not really seeing it.

It's so Tabitha to think that Marvin is running an elaborate and entirely pointless identity fraud scam rather than the far more obvious and likely scenario that he's a jackass who wants to get into her pants.

Heat rises up my neck. I glance over at him and grit my teeth.

Marvin's interest in Tabitha is a complication I don't need. What if he openly hits on her? I'll come down on him like a ton of bricks. It's what a fiancé does, or at least, it's what I would damn well do. But then I risk alienating Gail.

Gail finally wraps up her speech with instructions to show up for dinner in the stateroom in two hours. Already this trip is proving to be more time consuming than I'd imagined; my usual twelve-hour workday has been reduced to a small handful of hours and whatever I can secretly do on my phone.

Unfortunately, I can't blow off the first dinner.

We leave Clark at his door and head to our room.

"Serena," she says as soon as I shut the door. "Old flame?"

"I don't have flames, old or otherwise." I inspect the command center that Clark set up in the center room—three monitors, two laptops, and office supplies arranged the way I like them, right down to the small flip pads I like to jot notes in.

"I thought it went well," she says.

What? She wants to discuss our performance now? I pull off my jacket and toss it on the couch with maximum annoyance, and then I sit down and tap the laptop to life.

She's still there. Waiting.

"What?" I bark, keeping my eyes on the set of charts on the central monitor, but not really seeing them. "You need something?" This is usually enough to send people running.

"No," Tabitha says, standing there with that amused sparkle—I can't see it, but I hear it in her voice.

"We pulled it off. Keep it up," I say.

When she doesn't stir, I turn, annoyed, because instead of attending to the Yorkbridge IPO, which we've shorted the shit out of, I'm letting Tabitha distract me.

"This is my work area," I say. "This whole room is my work space. And where do you live during this trip? Can you remember what you promised?"

She frowns. A frown is definitely the proper reaction, but Tabitha's frown is more of a pout, as if she's playfully mirroring my mood. "You don't have to say it like that."

"Don't I?"

"Try a little niceness, maybe?" She heads into her room.

"Wait."

"Yeah?"

"First dinner's a black tie."

"I got it. It's on the schedule." She shuts the door behind her.

I turn to focus on the day. I get on to Slack on one monitor while I pull up shared screens with my top traders on another. The data streams in, and I start reacting, falling into the comfortable pattern of work. But I'm thinking about her. What? She's pouting now?

A knock at the door. Clark.

"Come on in," I say.

Clark comes in with his tablet. "Where's Tabitha?"

"Doing her job of staying in her room and not bothering me while I try to squeeze twelve hours of work into two."

"Ah," Clark says. Clearly he has more to say about Tabitha, but my look tells him that I'm not in the mood to hear it. We fall to reacting to the data that's streaming across the bottom of the screen. Nothing's blown up. People are on track for their quarterly numbers. There's currency stuff popping, but my people have it.

"Things seemed to go well," Clark says during a lull in the action.

"I'll say. Can Wydover be more screwed?" Wydover, my main competitor for Gail's accounts and the general bane of my existence, made a dubious play today. It's always nice to see Wydover get stung. People who break the rules don't get stung nearly enough.

"I mean, things went well at the launch party," Clark says. "You and the future Mrs. O'Rourke."

As if Tabitha would change her name. "If things hadn't gone well, I'd definitely have something to say," I grumble, turning my attention to the Tokyo futures.

A few minutes later, the shower in Tabitha's room goes on.

I try to focus on the flashing numbers, but then I hear the shower door open and close, which tells me she's in there, showering, turning under the water in a way that maximizes the volume with which the spray hits the door, all the better to let everybody in the world know that she's naked now, taking a shower.

"Rex?" Clark says. He's been saying something about Hong Kong. I make him repeat it.

Eventually, the shower is finished.

Some time later, Tabitha comes out of her room in a long brown gown that's…too something. She twirls around, and my mind starts buzzing.

Maybe it's the way the dress hugs her curves, or the way

her neck looks so long and graceful, or the excruciatingly bare expanse of her back, or the way her breasts are pressed together.

I need to fire that personal shopper. Do people not understand the meaning of *no distraction*?

Admittedly, it's more chaste than most gowns people wear at these sorts of things, but there's something about the way she wears it that makes it way too dramatic, impossible to ignore. And I can't stop looking at her breasts, specifically at the place where they crowd together. Two smooth globes, pressed distractingly together.

"Tabitha, you look stunning," Clark says.

"Thank you," she says.

They both turn to me, the asshole in the room with the buzzing brain. It's just that, does she have some special bra on? Some new innovation in female witchery?

The dress is all wrong. I barely ever notice women's clothes unless they're difficult to remove. But this dress? Absolutely too overwhelming.

And what about Marvin, horndogging all over her? If we thought he was bad before, what about now? Was any thought given to that? Because the idea of his eyes roaming all over her —I really will come down on him like a ton of bricks.

"My personal shopper came up with this?" I bark. "*This* is what you guys decided would be good to wear?"

"D-don't you like it?" she says.

Clark fixes me with a dark look. "What's the problem?"

"It's a bit...*much*." I make a hand gesture in the vague region of my torso. My neck. My head. She's piled her dark hair up onto her head, which just accentuates the effect of her neck and her large eyes, her regal bone structure. It's all of her, like a shiny lure, tailor-made for creating more Marvin problems.

"A bit much in what way?" Clark asks.

"Every way," I say.

Tabitha looks down at herself. "I thought it was pretty."

"It is," Clark says. "It's elegant and tasteful."

They're both looking at me like I'm the bad guy now.

The fog clears from my head long enough to realize that, objectively, it's not too much. Can she at least wear a shawl over it? Or better yet, an XXL Irish fisherman's sweater?

I force my gaze away from her dress and her graceful neck and her fucking breast globe meet-up and back to the Tokyo charts. "Very elegant and tasteful," I say.

"Well, dinner's in like ten minutes," she says.

"I can get dressed in two," I grumble.

Clark says, "You really do look nice."

"Thanks!" I can hear the grin in her voice. I can just hear it.

In a dark mood, I head to my room to change into my tux.

A few minutes later, I have Tabitha's arm, and I'm trying not to look at her. She's a prop, nothing more.

I have to admit, though, she's been doing a good job. She did handle the launch party well.

We follow Clark along the fourth-level walkway. On one side of the walkway are the guest suites; on the other is a railing separating us from the tedious expanse of ocean. The moon reflects in a splotch of light that everybody will be taking pictures of soon. Pictures they will never look at again.

"I'm glad every dinner isn't black tie," Tabitha says. "The shopper definitely didn't have me bring enough fancy dresses."

"The first dinner is often black tie," I explain. "It's about setting a tone for the trip. The last one'll be black tie, too. It's how Gail's set rolls."

"Gail's set?" Clark turns to walk backwards in front of us. "I hate to break it to you, but Gail's set is your set." He turns back around and continues on.

"Hardly," I say. "Once I have her portfolio locked up, maybe then."

"No, it's your set right now," Clark says over his shoulder.

"Not when I'm not here by choice."

Again Clark walks backwards, and this time he addresses Tabitha. "Rex is all about the hunt. He's obsessed with bringing down prey, and once he does, it's on to the next thing. He never relaxes. Never stops."

Tabitha looks up at me, gauging my reaction.

"Always moving the goalposts on himself," Clark adds.

"It's not true," I grumble.

We start down the stairway. Instead of heading to the third-floor deck, we keep going, following a red carpet that coils around into the interior of the ship and then opens out into a grand marble staircase that leads down to a large, candlelit dining area.

Tabitha stops at the top of the staircase. "Oh, my!"

I follow her gaze down to the dining area, trying to see it from her eyes. Gleaming marble tile, triple crown moldings, potted palms, ornate woodwork, soft lights glowing from wall sconces. In short, the place is bathed in candlelight and ostentatiousness, pretty much everything you'd expect from a yacht built for minor royalty.

A harpist and a cellist do a soft duet from a discreet corner; fine china and silver settings gleam on white-cloth-covered tables that are arranged across the vast floor.

"It's magical," she says.

"Right," I grumble, scanning the room. "All we need is a liveried guard in a powdered wig to announce us, and the disaster would be complete."

Clark nods at Tabitha. "What's in the box?"

It's only here I notice that she's holding a cardboard box the size of a small suitcase, complete with a cardboard handle. I was trying so hard not to stare at her I didn't see it.

"My friend made special yacht cookies. As a gift!" she says brightly, still blinking at the dining room below us. "Nine dozen, thank goodness. I thought there would be too many, but I guess not."

"No, no, no, no," I say. "You can't show up with cookies like that."

"Why not?" she asks.

"It's not done," I say.

"There's no rule against cookies," Clark says. "It's thoughtful."

I shoot him a look. "These yacht chefs are notoriously touchy. We can't add a food item to replace a dessert they've slaved over."

For once Tabitha looks chastened. "Should I put them back in the room?"

"No, there's no time—we're late already," I say. "Just don't break them out, for crissake. It's decorum. We'll find our seats, and you'll hide them under the table or something."

Clark has feelings about the cookies, I can tell.

"What?" I say.

"It's just cookies," he says.

"You just got done insisting it's my set," I say to Clark. "It would follow that I'd know the rules of decorum, then, wouldn't it?"

"A small food gift is hardly bucking decorum," Clark says.

Clark thinks I'm being unfair. Maybe I am. There's something about the dress that's affecting my mind. I tell myself to focus on dealing with Gail and on getting this account.

We descend the broad, gently curving staircase.

"And we're not drinking," I say to her. "We're going to act sedate and normal and leave at the first opportunity."

"Oh, Rex," Tabitha whispers, taking my arm.

"What?" I say.

She grins, gazing up at me from under her lashes. I want to

tell her to stop it, but what does that mean? To stop what? Being so Tabitha-ish all the time? Wearing yacht-appropriate clothes? And there's that buzzing in my head again.

We head toward a bank of chichi cocktail seating, square and deep, dotted with red pillows.

At the far end is a bar complete with a polished wood back-drop—the whole "mirror and bottles and carved cherry cabi-netry thing," rumored to have been the interior of a fabled Irish pub fallen on hard times, dismantled and brought onto the yacht, lock, stock, and barrel.

We weave around the tables. I'm surprised when Gail waves at us from the bar. We go over to say hello, and I order sparkling waters for Clark and myself while Tabitha asks for a Shirley Temple. "Two cherries," she says to the bartender, and then she turns to Gail. "Maraschino cherries are my favorite fruit."

Gail laughs. I'm sure she imagines it's a joke. I'm guessing it's not. It's perfect that maraschino cherries would be Tabitha's favorite fruit. There is no other possible fruit that could be her favorite. Tabitha and Gail go on to make much ado over each other's gowns. Gail clearly approves of our drink order, and she really does buy us as a couple. She seems even to approve of us as a couple.

I'm slowly calming down as the night seems to be starting out as a win until Gail spots Tabitha's box. "What's in there?"

"Oh!" Tabitha looks at the box. "It's something for later. I shouldn't have brought it to dinner."

"What is it?" Gail asks.

"It's nothing."

I think Gail's going to drop the subject, but then Marvin chooses this time to show up at Gail's side. "What's nothing?" he asks. Has he been listening in?

I grit my teeth, monitoring his eyes to make sure he doesn't leer at Tabitha; I'm more than ready to back him off if he so much as looks at her wrong.

"My box," Tabitha says. "I had things a little mixed up, though, so never mind."

"It's nothing, really," I say. "But this duet! Gail!"

"I'd been meaning to ask where you found them," Clark says, perfectly in sync with me, as usual. "They really are talented."

"Boston," Gail says, and what she really means is *Boston Philharmonic.* "I get them when I can."

I say something about having met a one-man-band guy at the launch toast, and she explains that's for the kids. "He's playing on the kids' deck tonight. There'll be pizza followed by a make-your-own-sundaes dessert buffet."

"And then they'll hopefully burn off all that sugar in the bouncy castles," Marvin adds. "Or their parents will have our heads."

Gail gives him a warm smile. "Yes, they will."

How close have these two become? Did Marvin actually help create the activities? Has he moved into her home? But then, I suppose they have a lot of time to make up.

Gail suddenly turns to Tabitha. "Rex tells me you own a hairstylist business. My stylist and I tried this new cut...I'm not sure..."

Tabitha's eyes go wide. "It's nice."

"Come on, now," Gail says. "This guy's new for me, and I'm not sold on what he did."

Tabitha tilts her head. "It's a quality cut," she says. "But if you don't like it, that's what matters."

Gail laughs. "You don't want to dog one of your peers. I get that, but come on now, what do you think? Because I'm not so sure I like it, but I don't have the words for why."

Tabitha has the words—I can tell by her eyes—there's a certain bright energy in them. "I think if someone were to thin it out by your ears, it would make your cheekbones stand out more."

"You think it's too fluffy on the sides? Is that what you're telling me? Because I kind of think that might be it," Gail says. "And don't you bullshit me, now."

Tabitha bites the side of her lip. "I'm just saying what I'd try. Every hairdresser has a different vision."

Gail's nodding. "I think I want your vision. How hard would it be?"

"Well, not hard…but only if I had my shears."

I frown. And what about her wrist injury? Isn't she supposed to be resting her wrist?

"Well, we have a fully stocked hair salon here," Gail says. "You think you would have some time on this trip to do your magic? Not to put you to work when you're a guest here—"

"I love cutting hair! And this change on you would be…" She pauses, eyes sparkling. "*Chef's kiss*," she says—instead of simply doing a chef's kiss with her fingers. "But…" Tabitha looks over at me. As though I might forbid it.

"Oh, you can let your girl out of the room for a bit now, can't you?" Gail says to me.

"Why not?" I say, having exactly zero choice.

"Great!" Tabitha grins at Gail. They're talking schedules.

I stiffen when I catch Marvin's eyes on Tabitha. I shift a little to let him know I see him. Gail's nephew or no, a man doesn't stare at another man's fiancée. Or at least not *my* goddamn fiancée.

"So you're not going to tell us what's in the box?" Marvin asks.

"No," Tabitha says. "It's for maybe tomorrow."

I sling an arm around her, eyes on Marvin, who has wisely removed his gaze.

"I'm *intrigued*," Marvin says. "What could be in the box that's so incredibly secret?"

I grit my teeth.

Serena comes up now. "What's going on?"

"Something hush-hush in Tabitha's box," Marvin tells her conspiratorially. What the hell? Does Marvin sense Tabitha's hesitation? Why push it? Does he want to make her look bad?

"It's nothing," Tabitha says.

"Do tell," Serena says.

"Now y'all got me curious," Gail says. "We can't get a sneak peek?"

Marvin's smiling at Tabitha. "You know you can't keep us in suspense."

Tabitha glances apologetically at me. There's no getting around it now, that's for sure. I pull her close and kiss the top of her head. "Show them." I look up. "It's just a little something we thought would be fun." *We*, because Marvin needs to see that if he messes with Tabitha, he's messing with me.

Tabitha sets the box down on a side table. It has a little Cookie Madness sticker that glints in the light. She undoes the bright ribbon, opens the top, takes out a cookie, and shows it to Gail.

Gail gasps. "Will you look at that!"

I blink. The cookie is in the shape of a Flying Fox megayacht, frosted in white with the decks indicated with slashes of chocolate.

"This is incredible," Gail says. "Well, this is my boat to a T. My god..." She looks up, glancing between us. "This is the most thoughtful thing anybody..." She looks down at the cookie in her hand. "It's so intricate...I can't even imagine."

"My friend has a cookie shop," Tabitha says.

"Very nice," Marvin says, but what he really seems to be saying is that it's not nice at all. Now I'm glad the cookies got opened.

"Nice?! These are wonderful!" Gail corrects him. "Thank

you! What on earth made you think these weren't something we'd want to be seeing tonight?"

"We didn't want to upstage your chef," I tell her. "We realized a bit late that they probably had a specific vision and wouldn't like an addition."

"Honey, if I got a chef who'll pitch a fit over something like these cookies, that's what I call a diva, and divas don't tend to last long in my employ. I mean, it's not like you brought in a pig on a spit."

Tabitha does her smile-wince. Without missing a beat, she says, "There goes our breakfast surprise!"

"Don't you dare!" Gail says, laughing. She grabs Tabitha's arm and leans in with a twinkle. "Don't you dare, little missy."

"That's a no?" Tabitha says. They go back and forth, keeping the joke rolling, laughing it up.

Marvin's frowning, which pleases me greatly.

Gail sends the cookies back to the prep area. She wants them out with the coffee and cake round. "Wrong night for them indeed. Tonight's the perfect night. This is the launch dinner, honey!"

Tabitha gives me a wide-eyed smile. Anybody else looking at her might see an adoring fiancée gazing at her beloved— even Clark might mistake it as that. But I see her. I know what that look is all about. It's the look of *oh, snap!*

That little vixen is gloating. I grit my teeth against the strange feeling bubbling up in my chest.

I raise one eyebrow. *Don't get too cocky*—that's what my look says to her.

She turns to sparkle and laugh at something her new friend Gail says.

Soon enough it's time to sit. We find our place cards at a center table, right next to each other, thankfully.

"Well, I guess frosted cookies are the way to Gail's heart

after all," I say. I really want to tell her that she's doing a good job. I should say it.

"Right? I was kind of worried." She leans in close. "Gail is totally hilarious."

"Hilarious as a mama bear."

She seems to think this is amusing. "She is very no-nonsense."

"That's an understatement," I say. "She married into the Driscoll money, but she's the one responsible for getting this family into the megayacht set. She'd shiv you if she thought you were crossing one of hers."

"That kind of makes me like her more," Tabitha says.

"It makes me like her more, too," I say. "But not when she's jerking me around with this review. This vacation."

"A vacay on a yacht—positively medieval," Tabitha says. "Thumbscrews would be better!"

"Actually, thumbscrews would be better," I say. "I'd vastly prefer thumbscrews to a two-week yacht trip."

"What do you hate about yachts so much? A yacht is exciting."

"A yacht is objectively not exciting," I say. "The view is nothing but the endless monotony of sky and sea, and there's nowhere to go. A yacht is just a hotel on water, except you're trapped together with everybody else who's in the hotel. And everybody is a stranger in a regular hotel and you're not expected to talk to them. Here? You're supposed to talk to people. And this isn't even a five-star hotel. It's more of a four. A boat simply isn't large enough to have the amenities of a five-star hotel. Why? Because it's a mode of transportation. Humankind should've left it as that."

Tabitha's suppressing a smile—I can tell by the way she's moving her cheeks, her lips. The deepening of her dimples.

"Do I amuse you?" I snap.

She tries to disguise her smile by biting her bottom lip. Pretty white teeth crushing her bottom lip. It doesn't work.

"Yachts." I grab my straw and shove it into my seltzer, focusing on the bubbles. "Can you argue with any part of what I just said?"

"No!"

When I look back up, her bottom lip is rosy and plump from the force of her teeth, and I have this nearly uncontrollable urge to press my thumb onto the pillowy center of it, just press my thumb onto her lip and stop her from being so... Tabitha-ish.

But more than that. I want to slide my thumb in past her plump bottom lip and right into her mouth. Something in me ripples at the knowledge that she'd suck on it, because that's a move of hers—that's what she showed me on the plane.

It would be so wrong.

She'd suck on my thumb the way she sucked on my tongue, gaze just a little bit sassy, with this insinuation that she might not let it go. A messed-up little move that is so her, because she pushes everything. It comes to me then that that's exactly the way she'd suck my cock, too—pushing things, not letting me go. Because she always needs to make you crazy. Tabitha and her sugar-berry lips and those breasts pushed together just so.

I shake myself back to reality. "What's more, this constant demand for socialization makes it nearly impossible for me to work. I have a massive global empire to run, and instead I'm stuck in this windowless hellscape of socializing."

Tabitha's working yet again to hide her smile, but her dimples have reappeared, giving her away.

"What now?" I demand.

"*What* kind of empire?" she asks. "What kind of empire are you running?"

I give her a dark look.

Two of the Texas cousins, two teenaged granddaughters,

and the family's interior designer choose this moment to join us.

I look around and spot Clark up at a front table. Serena is thankfully at a table with some of the vendors. Gail's at a table with her daughters and their husbands.

Now the family's PR woman sits and introduces herself as Nala.

It's Nala's birthday. One of the women proposes a toast and everybody is laughing and clinking glasses. The talk turns to birthdays, everybody telling birthday stories. Tabitha gets deeply involved, which works for me—I do some discreet work on my phone.

One of the Driscoll cousins tells a funny story about a birthday gone wrong while I text with my quant team leader.

I'm vaguely aware of Tabitha telling a funny birthday story a few minutes later, something about her as a kid at the TipTop, which is one of those restaurants at the top of a skyscraper where the floor revolves around to provide views of the city. She has the women on the other side of the table roaring with laughter at her description of herself as a twelve-year-old girl all alone, waiting for her dad, crying in a party dress, and how she'd adjust her party hat to milk the sympathy.

"You can't believe how many free desserts I got," Tabitha says. "The pretty waitresses would come over on their breaks. It turned out to be a great birthday!"

There's more laughter as she demonstrates the faces she'd make. She has the table in the palm of her fun-loving hand.

Somebody else starts telling a Valentine's breakup story. It's amusing enough, but nobody has the mastery of Tabitha, and nobody gets the laughs Tabitha got. I feel perversely proud of that.

There are more stories. This is apparently the humorous story table.

Tabitha has yet another tragicomic tale, this one about her

college sweetheart breaking off their engagement while she was in a hospital after a bicycle accident. She makes one of her funny wince faces and delivers a wry aside that gets more laughs.

She then recreates a conversation that ends with her calling him a douche and a funny line about her ruptured spleen. The girls are nearly falling out of their chairs with laughter.

I pause in my texting, frowning. Tabitha knows how to tell a story to get a laugh—it's a talent of hers, one that's coming in handy on this trip, but when I actually think about the stories she's telling, they're not funny at all. What kind of father lets a twelve-year-old girl sit alone in a Midtown restaurant on her birthday? And what type of motherfucker breaks off an engagement while his fiancée is in the hospital? The more I ruminate over these tales of hers, the angrier I feel. These are two men from her past who definitely need to be hit, and I would be more than happy to oblige.

More than happy.

Eventually the stories end, and so does my secret phone checking, because Nala is taking shots for lord knows what social media outlet. There's nothing worse than being caught looking at your phone in party pictures.

Naturally, Tabitha's posing with maximum enthusiasm, and Nala is clicking away.

Whereas most women care about looking good in pictures, Tabitha goes for a comedic effect. Her new PR soulmate is eating it up, and they're feeding off each other.

Inspired by Tabitha's antics, the cousins and Gail's teenaged granddaughters start silently gesturing across the table at Tabitha, who gestures back at them. Soon, they're all making faces and striking poses to suggest they're in an animated and highly dramatic conversation.

The whole table has become an over-actors anonymous meeting, making my pulse race with the sheer fuckery of it.

I refuse to join in, much as my tablemates are trying to get me to. I stir my drink, feeling awkward. I never did know what to do with people being playful. I grab the program, unhappy to see there will be singing children. Of course I can barely think at this point.

When everybody's finally finished laughing at their own ridiculous antics and the spotlight is off of us, I give her a look.

"What?" she says.

"Maybe turn things down from eleven?"

Hurt flashes across her eyes. "I'm not on eleven."

"Good god," I grumble. I check my phone under the table, monitoring Tokyo. Am I being an asshole? Yes. And I don't want her to turn down from eleven. I don't know what I want. I just feel…uncomfortably stirred up.

Right then, I feel her stiffen. I look up and see that Marvin has settled down on the other side of her.

I grit my teeth.

"Uh-oh," she says to Marvin, and she points to the place card, which says *Charles McKenzie*, one of the distant cousins. Thank goodness for that. Marvin is the last person I want next to Tabitha.

"I think that's for this place." Marvin moves Charles's place card to the other side of him.

It's not right. Marvin is definitely in Charles's place.

My pulse ratchets up murderously. What is this guy up to?

The cousins and granddaughters have fallen to chatting with PR Nala and the designer on the other end of the table, oblivious to the utter weirdness and the fact that one of them has two place cards, thanks to Marvin.

"But…where's your place card?" Tabitha asks innocently.

Ignoring her, Marvin pulls out his phone.

I lean forward. Trying to keep the edge out of my voice, I ask, "What are you doing, Marvin?"

He keeps his weasel eyes on the phone. "Hold on." He's texting.

Tabitha turns to me, eyes wide.

An older man bumbles up and stands over Marvin, who proceeds to ignore him. The man gestures at the place setting. "I think this is me?"

Charles McKenzie to the rescue, I think.

Marvin's got his phone up to his ear now. "Sorry, this is my seat," Marvin says before he returns his attention to the phone. "Can you just...no, sorry, not you," Marvin says into the phone. "I'm sorry, what were you saying?"

Charles looks bewildered. He's a minor cousin and won't be any match for Marvin, who is clearly determined to sit next to my fiancée.

"It's your place," I say to Charles. "Marvin," I say. "This is Charles's seat."

Marvin shakes his head and puts a finger in his nonphone ear, as though to signal that he's on an important call.

Charles is not helping. He's doing a polite little pantomime now, acting out his thought process. "Well...this is Kitty Driscoll, and there's Kitty Driscoll...this says Charles McKenzie, and I'm Charles McKenzie, so..."

Marvin points to his phone. "Sorry, I need to deal with this, Charles. It's really not important, right? They change the seating every day. Just find a place to sit. Wait, hold on, what?" His attention is back on the phone.

Charles turns and wanders off. I guess I can't blame him; Marvin has far more pull inside the Driscoll machinery. The people here are ranked by their proximity to the main family.

I feel a hand grip my thigh. Tabitha's wearing an outraged gleam. I return her look with an annoyed one of my own. For a second, we're together.

It feels...good.

I reach up and slide a lock of her hair through two fingers.

If Marvin thinks I'll let him sit next to Tabitha, he's dead wrong.

I twist her hair around my forefinger. "Baby, will you go get us another round?"

She looks at me gratefully, reading my intention, I suppose. "Kitten would be happy to," she says. "Excuse me." Off she goes.

Marvin's off his call soon enough. Because there was no call.

I set my arm over the back of Tabitha's empty chair. "You're from Ohio," I say to him.

"Yes," he says. "Dayton."

"Tell me," I slide into Tabitha's seat. Does he think he's a match for me? Does he really think he gets the seat next to Tabitha so that he can hit on her all night? Accidentally brush against her and all that? "Are you a Buckeyes fan?" I grill him on the Buckeyes. If he's unhappy, he doesn't show it.

Tabitha comes back and takes my place.

I turn to Tabitha when Marvin's engaged in conversation with the cousins. "So much for the soap opera theory," I say in a low tone that only she can hear.

"I don't see it being wrong," she says sweetly.

Horndog, I mouth.

Softly she says, "Just because *you're* obsessed with my beauty doesn't mean every man is."

She glances over my shoulder. Is he looking at her?

I lean in. "Ten months ago he's a nobody, and now he's a little nobody prince who sees something he wants and he's pushing his boundaries.

She leans nearer to me now, sets her chin on my shoulder. "You shouldn't automatically discount my theory," she says in a low tone. "I know it seems implausible, but you should trust your teammate."

Did she feel it too? That sense of us as a team?

"But what if my teammate's perception is based on an idiotic soap opera plot?"

She grumbles in my ear.

Suddenly they're serving the appetizers—each plate has a hunk of sushi-grade tuna on it, festooned with a vertical sesame rod like a curly flag, set atop colorful drips of sauce.

"Sushi," I say, because that's our fake favorite food.

"Like they knew we were coming!" she says.

After what seems like an endless appetizer course and a song sang by children that is long and boring and makes me glad they are sequestered on a deck of their own, the main course is served. Tabitha and I both choose the fish with a hazelnut crust.

"So where did you two meet?" Marvin asks, looking from her to me and back to her.

"Work," I say curtly.

There's an awkward silence, and I know I should add something, but I would so much rather drive my fist into his face. If Marvin so much as breathes in her direction again, he is going to find himself laid out on the floor eating his own broken teeth.

Unfortunately, other people are listening. "Work?" one of the cousins says.

Tabitha puts her hand on my arm and leans forward. "I was his hairdresser. I have mobile styling business, and Rex was one of my clients." She grins at me.

I tilt my head. "Two years you were cutting my hair."

"And then what?" Marvin asks.

"Yeah, what's the story?" PR woman Nala asks.

"We always had this fun jokey thing going when I'd give him his weekly trim." Tabitha gazes at me. "We were kind of simpatico, right from the start."

"Simpatico," I agree, looking at her, waiting for her origin story. She was the one who thought we needed one.

She beams. "It was all very professional, at first, but in a fun way. Us talking about our days…" She trails off.

Is that all she has? Shit. I grab my drink, and take a swig.

She blinks, looking like she's racking her brain. "Buuuuut then I was out for tapas on a Tinder date one night. And out of the blue, I spotted Rex across the place. He was with some guys. Important clients from Tagastan, I found out later."

I nearly choke on my drink. That's not even a country. "You mean the Greeks," I say.

"Right," she says. "And remember how you kept looking over at me?"

"Well, it was strange to see you out of context."

"Oh, yeah, that's all it was," she says sarcastically.

Her fox-brown eyes look soft and translucent in the candle-light. She reaches up and smooths a bit of my hair sideways.

"He was burning up with jealousy," she continues. "And he didn't realize what a high point of his week my haircuts were until he saw me with another man."

I hold my breath. Where is she going with this?

"He didn't like it at all," she continues, beaming at me, "but of course, he would never come over. Rex would never hit on another man's woman."

It's true, actually. It shouldn't mean anything that she'd guess such a thing, but I like that she did. "A man doesn't hit on another man's partner," I growl.

This seems to delight her. "You have a code. It's one of the things I've always admired about you."

I swallow. I do have a code. Does she really admire it?

She grins. "The Tinder date was going poorly. The guy was drunk. And suddenly he gets kinda handsy. I was like, 'no, thank you, dude.' But some of these Tinder bros…"

"Oh my god, right?" Kitty Driscoll shrieks.

Tabitha flings up a hand. "Save us from the Tinder bros, right?" The Driscoll girls are laughing. "And suddenly Rex is there," she continues, gaining steam. "And he clamps his hand on the guy's shoulder, like really hard, and he growls."

Nala claps. "Love it!"

The other women are smiling at me.

"And my douchey date is like, wuuuut?" Tabitha continues, looking into my eyes. "And so cool and calm, Rex goes, 'If you touch her again, I will rearrange your face like a marble cake.'"

I narrow my eyes. A *marble cake?* What man says that? "Are you sure I said marble cake?"

"Oh yes. It's what you said." She beams at me. "It was amazing."

My blood races. Something that's not exactly annoyance rises up in me. I want everybody gone. Except Tabitha. Marble cake? This is what she came up with? But it's not just about the marble cake.

I slide a knuckle across her jawbone, wanting to, I don't know what—take back control of the situation. Engage with her. Prod her.

"And the douche backs off," she says, gazing into my eyes. "He's mumbling something jerky, like, 'she's not all that.' And Rex growls, like, a dangerous growl, and the guy is out of there so fast, it was kind of hilarious. One growl from Rex and the douche is out of there like a bullet."

"I love that!" Nala exclaims.

"Rearrange his face like a *marble cake*," Kitty says.

"Right?" Tabitha says brightly. She goes on to weave a tale of how we had drinks followed by a midnight walk in the park, and then I'd brought her home and kissed her on her doorstep, the perfect gentleman. The next day the flowers started coming.

You couldn't invent a more girly story.

"How long were you going out before you got engaged?" Marvin asks.

I turn to him. "Long enough." Does Tabitha have that

timeline worked out? Maybe it was in her ridiculous question-naire. Which I clearly should've taken more seriously.

"We'd known each other two years, after all," Tabitha says. "When Rex decides he wants something, there's no stopping him."

"Yet you decided to keep it a secret…" Marvin says.

I give him a cool look.

"My request," Tabitha says.

"What made you change your mind?" Marvin asks. "I mean, here you are going pretty public and all…" He gestures at Nala with her camera.

I focus more directly on Marvin now. These questions are starting to feel like a power play. "It was time," I say simply. I keep my gaze on him, square on the bull's-eye of his face until he looks away.

Eventually dessert is served, buffet-style, and we're released from the hell of the table only to go to the hell of the dessert buffet line.

The cookies are a huge hit. Everybody's photographing them and photographing each other eating them. I grab a cup of coffee while Tabitha loads up a plate with every type of dessert.

We stake out near a ledge next to the piano player. A nice, visible spot where everybody can see us being out and about, hopefully buying myself a lot of cave time in the room. *Here we are after dinner, folks.*

Tabitha sets her loaded-down plate on the ledge next to my coffee.

"Maybe you should've just pulled up a chair to the buffet," I say.

Tabitha snorts in her classic *Oh, Rex!* way and takes a bite of cookie.

I glance over at Marvin, across the room. "Sitting next to

you? Does he have a fucking death wish? Did he actually think I'd let that happen?"

"I know. The way he was grilling us? He is completely suspicious of our engagement."

"The man is fixated on you," I bite out with maybe more force than necessary, but I'm imagining him doing some kind of pass-the-butter tit feel, and it's overriding my rational brain. "Account or no, one move and I *will* rearrange his smarmy little face." I look down at her sparkling eyes. "And for the record, we're talking ground chuck, not marble cake."

She grins at me. She might be the only person in the world to have such an idiotic reaction when I'm annoyed. "Ground chuck would've been better."

"I don't even know what a marble cake is. I mean, what the hell?"

"Kind of swirly?" She leans in. "That's not important. I'm telling you, he didn't sit next to us out of sexual interest. He was trying to trip us up."

"You don't know men very well, if that's what you think."

"Oh, I know men well enough," she says.

Something twists uncomfortably in my chest. What the hell is that supposed to mean? What men?

I force myself to form words. "I know men better," I say. "That was a power play. Marvin was trying to control the field with questions. Sitting next to you didn't work, so he tried to do an alpha thing."

"Gawd," she says. "Poor Charles, right?"

What am I doing? I need to get back to work. I grab my bone china coffee cup and empty it in one gulp, setting it down beside her dessert tower. "We need to start our exit."

Tabitha's not finished. "Marvin's suspicious of us," she says. "It's important for you to understand that. And when people are weirdly suspicious of other people? It means they're up to something."

I turn to her. "You'd better not be getting that from your soap opera."

"Wellllll." Here she does her one-eye-closed wince.

"Oh, Jesus Christ," I growl. "You have to stop talking about soaps. People will think you're addled in the head."

She takes a bite of a mini-powdered donut. "Addled in the head," she says, amused, because everything on the planet amuses Tabitha.

She looks up at me from under thick, dark lashes, and the boat seems to lurch.

I have this urge to remind her to tone it down, but the truth is, I don't want her to tone it down. I don't want her to turn down from eleven. I wouldn't mind twelve, or maybe thirteen.

Suddenly she's licking the powdered sugar off her lips, little tongue darting out here and there. And then she's sucking it off her fingers, one after another. Sucking.

A gentleman might grab her a napkin, but I wouldn't end this little display of hers for all the gold in Fort Knox. She starts on her other hand. My pulse races as she presses one finger into her lips, in and out, then another.

Heat spreads down my spine.

"Addled in the head," she says.

I look at her, pulse racing, barely registering her words. I tear my gaze from hers and fix it on Marvin. He's with Gail and some people, back turned.

"Anyway, I didn't get it from my soap operas," she continues. "I mean yes, it's a feature of soap operas. But only because that is how people act in real life. At any given time, half the Quartermaines think other people are up to something, but it's always the Quartermaines who are. Or Dorian Lord. She always thinks people are up to something, and she literally kept her rival in a cage in her basement. And don't get me started on Stefano DiMera." Here she swipes an already-cleaned finger through some frosting and licks it off.

My mouth goes dry.

"Did I hear a plural there?" I say. "Does this mean you watch more than one soap opera?"

"I switch around based on excitingness of storyline, but usually I'll at least double up."

I frown. Is this how regular people live? They sit down and watch several hours of TV without a second thought?

"The point is, when somebody's up to something, it gives them a kind of radar for other people who are up to something. You know it's true. Marvin is up to something, and it's big."

"Good god, are we back at the DNA-test thing again?" I pull out my phone, needing to tamp down the feelings swirling through me. Being separated from work this long is causing me to give way too much attention to Tabitha's lips and fingers. Why am I even reacting? Who cares?

"Here are several facts about Marvin," she continues as I scroll. "One, the man is watching us. Two, it's not horndoggery. Impossible as that is to believe, of course. I mean..."

She stops speaking for an oddly long time. I make the mistake of looking up, and I find her striking one of her little poses—one hand on her hip, one holding a half-eaten brownie at shoulder-level. Her head is tilted, lips slyly pursed.

An uncomfortable feeling of lightness fills me. I roll my eyes to cover it.

"Right?" she says. "So impossible to believe, yet true."

"You said several facts," I snap. "Several facts suggests more than two facts."

"That was three facts." She counts them off: "One, he's watching us. Two, his interest is not sexual, or I would know. Three, people who are up to something always think others are up to something. As established."

"I have to get out of here." I hazard another glance at Marvin. Clark is chatting up the captain. "I need to be back at work, and you need to be in your room. I sense a long day of us not being up on deck ahead."

She frowns. "Gail says there's whale watching tomorrow. We might be going near some pods or something. It might be a fun activity…"

"Nope," I say.

"But everyone's so excited. Everybody's gonna go…"

"Not everybody. Not a certain man who is running his company and not his hairdresser who is being paid way too much money to sit at her workstation. And do you remember where that workstation is?"

"I remember where that workstation is," she says hotly.

"Where?"

She twists her lips by way of answer. "I'm just saying, people saw that I was excited about the whales. You hired me to do a job. You should trust me to do it. Trust my recommendations. I recommend we go because it might be weird for us to blow it off."

"Why would it be weird? They'll just figure that I'm not into it. And when it comes to a choice between being with your loving fiancé and seeing whales, you'll always pick your fiancé."

"However, as my loving fiancé, you'd want me to see the whales. You'd want to be there when I see them just to enjoy the delight in my eyes. You feel curious and enthusiastic about things that I enjoy. That's how a relationship works."

"That's not how my relationships work."

"Ugh," she says. "Spare me."

Our strange friction has me stepping closer, itching to touch her. I lower my voice to a deep register. "You're already going to play beauty parlor; is that not enough?"

"It's not playing," she snaps. And then she swipes a finger through cupcake frosting yet again, and slides it into her mouth. Then pops it out. Impudently.

Her eyes sparkle. We're flirting. It's what we should be

doing—we're making it real, aren't we? But I need to touch her, and it has nothing to do with our roles.

I draw a knuckle along her jawline. Her skin feels soft and warm.

Her chest rises and falls. I get to the end, to her chin, and force myself to drop my arm to my side, when really what I need is to kiss her.

I tell my people to never lead with need. Need clouds your mind and destroys your bargaining skills. But everything in me is surging for her. Every molecule transformed into a little compass straining toward her north.

I remind myself how wrong this is. I can't be attracted to her; that was the whole point of bringing her. This heat has to stop.

"If you want to watch whales," I say coldly, "you can take the massive sum of money I'm paying you and book your own cruise."

"Maybe I will," she says.

"The next few days will probably be buffet-style meals," I say. "We'll grab food, chat up Gail, and get in pictures whenever possible. Other than that, we're AWOL in our room."

"What about when we dock on St. Herve? You'd want to walk around St. Herve, right? It sounds really beautiful."

"We will not be exploring tropical islands. You will be sequestered in your room while Clark and I focus on our projects. And we won't even know you're there until we need you for on-deck appearances."

"I'm just saying it'll look a little unnatural. I mean, are people supposed to think we're banging the whole time?"

My mind races with images of pressing her up against the wall, of plunging my fingers and possibly even my face into the place where her breasts meet. I try to stop my thoughts, but I can't. "Yes."

"You have a high opinion of your stamina," she says.

"My stamina is extremely impressive," I say.

"Oh, I've had better," Tabitha says coolly, but those rosy spots have appeared, heating her cheeks. I imagine cupping them, touching the curves of her cheekbones. I imagine tasting the soft warmth of her lips. The breathy sounds she'd make as I fit her up against me.

Chapter Seven

Tabitha

I SWALLOW, remembering our breathless kiss on the plane. The way Rex held me, so fierce and intense. The air is electric between us. "I've definitely had better," I say.

"Doubtful." Rex leans against the marble pillar, the picture of evil cool in his tux.

I can't pull my thoughts together enough to form a sentence, so I shrug. I don't know what's for show anymore.

I'm used to jokey, friendly sex, not friction or strong feelings. Friction and strong feelings seem dangerous.

"Baby," he says, voice gruff, "I'm doing things you never imagined."

I need to make a joke to cut the heat, but I can't think of a joke when his sexy scowl is bolting down into my belly.

"Things I've never imagined," I whisper stupidly, as though I don't believe it. But I so do.

"That's right," he says.

By some miracle, I gather my wits. "Well," I say. "I never

imagined a man gently slathering jam onto my chest while patriotic marching band music plays. I never imagined that."

"Baby," he rumbles, "the things I'm doing are good things."

Shivers fly over me. "You'll address me as kitten," I whisper, heart thundering like a jackhammer.

His lip quirks into a lewd, lazy half smile that warms my core. He'll do what he wants—that's what his half smile says.

"Gulp," I whisper.

He says, "You're doing good things, too. Your mouth is fucking amazing."

I shouldn't have taunted him—he's a powerbroker with control issues. But something keeps driving me on. "My mouth *is* amazing, but not as amazing as the rest of me."

His gaze intensifies. His dangerously sexy villain vibe has me immobilized. "True enough," he says.

"You worship every inch of me," I say.

"Every hour of every day," he says. "That's why they never see us."

I sigh, but I'm not at all weary. I'm excited, and it's terrifying. I work overtime to keep things light and fun and manageable. Rex is scary and unmanageable. I love it and I hate it.

"Sometimes you wake me up begging for it," he says hoarsely. "You're lying there in the middle of the night, and I wake up to you straddling me, and then I flip you over and I take you how I want. I'm not the only one who's insatiable."

My breathing speeds.

"I like to keep you really close to the edge," he continues. "When I have you where I want you, trembling with need, begging for that final stroke that makes you shatter into a million pieces…"

I roll my eyes, desperate to get back to some humor and control. Desperate for something clever to say, but my entire psyche is busy digesting his little scenario. My entire psyche likes his little scenario.

Then he reaches out. He sets one feather-light fingertip on the base of my throat, right in the center, that vulnerable center divot.

My belly quivers.

His touch is so light, it's barely a touch, but my mind turns to gossamer, flowing brightly in the wind.

Rex's eyes darken.

My pulse speeds.

This isn't for show anymore. The show is running away with us.

Slowly—ever so slowly—he slides his finger down, down the hard plate of my breastbone, down to the point where my breasts are pressed together, courtesy of a Victoria's Secret push-up bra. His finger presses down between my breasts, plunging down between them, tracing a bold line, cool and alive, through the place where they squish together.

And I'm panting. And my eyes fall to his warm, kissable lips, framed in a field of whiskery goodness.

His finger has made it down beyond my breasts only to be halted by the V-shaped base of my bodice. He hooks his finger around it, and slowly he pulls me to him, pulls me close until our lips are near, like he might kiss me again.

We're gazing into each other's eyes and there are no more games; there's just this unspoken need between us, as if we're sharing one reckless, lust-soaked brain.

His eyes are warm, and I know he knows. And he knows I know.

And we're breathing together, and right then, I've never felt closer to a person. It's scary, but I also love it. I want to lose myself in him.

We're about to fall together—to grasp hands and fall.

"Get a room!" Clark's face bursts into our reality like ice

water, shattering the spell. He claps his hands onto each of our shoulders. "You two! My god!" he says, playing his part.

Rex releases me, all of the warmth draining out of his gaze, until he's cold, surly Rex again.

I stiffen, come to my senses. What was I thinking?

We'd forgotten ourselves. But not anymore.

"And the Academy Award goes to," Clark mumbles under his breath.

"Oh, I think we should share it," Rex says coolly, watching my eyes. "Don't you?"

I swallow, straightening up with this horrible sense of loss. "A pair of sterling performances," I say.

"Absolutely," he says.

And in this way, we redefine what just happened as a performance. Nothing but a show. Nothing to see here. Please move along.

Chapter Eight

Tabitha

OUR WILDLY OVERHEATED interlude seems to have chastened Rex—he plays the perfect gentleman as we head back to our cabin with Clark. We disappear into our respective bedrooms.

It really is for the best. Strong feelings like the ones that I have for Rex are the kind you should never give into.

Over the following days, we make appearances for meals and other mandatory events, we turn up for every show we think Gail will attend, and we try to get in pictures together.

If the event is long or the lights are out, like for a movie, for example, Rex leaves me with Clark so that he can do his Very Important Work, and I text Rex to come back when I sense that the lights are about to come back up.

There are no more almost kisses. No more sexy touches.

If there's the occasional sizzle between Rex and me, he doesn't seem to notice, and I act like I don't. And when the random touch melts me inside, or when one of his scowly faces gives me a pesky little zing of excitement, I stuff it back down into the place from whence it came, and he does, too.

Or maybe it all was an act. I don't entirely trust myself to know.

Most of the time, Rex and Clark are in their war room in front of three monitors with numbers that flash across constantly, and I keep to my room, streaming shows, playing Tomb Raider, and reading on the little deck off our cabin.

I also text Jada a lot, possibly too much. Now and then, she warns me to be careful with Rex—she knows about my crush on him, though I don't confess to her how it's spiraling out of control. Jada would worry if she knew—not just about how one-sided anything with Rex and me would be; she also knows about Jacob.

She knows what it did to me when Jacob broke off our engagement while I was in that hospital bed, frightened to go into my fifth surgery after the bike accident. She knows how young I was, how alone I was. How devastated.

She doesn't want me to be in another one-sided romance. I love her for reminding me of it, for caring like that.

I joke about Rex as a way to reassure her that things are strictly fun and transactional. I say things like, *Captain Sternpants and I are going at it in our room for the twelfth time today,* always with some clever emoji, and then she emoji laughs back, because of course I told her about Rex's stamina claims.

But that thing I said to Serena about Rex showing me his soft side? I really do feel like I can see it sometimes. I think I see it in countless little chivalrous actions. The way he gives me his jacket when he notices I'm cold, even before I can ask. The way he unwrapped a little hand wipe for me after a breakfast of caramel rolls one morning, even before I realized my fingers were impossibly sticky.

I imagine I see his soft side even in the way he listens to me, like he really hears what I have to say. Even when I'm telling silly stories to people at various functions, he seems not only to listen but to silently reflect on what I have to say.

I think I see it in his hawkish monitoring of Marvin. I get that we're supposed to be fake engaged, but some little part of me thinks it's more. Wants it to be more, anyway.

Maybe I am a masochist, like my employee Amanda suggested.

Now and then, when I'm stuck in my room, I put my ear to the door to listen to them talk, or I crack it open and peek at their backs. I enjoy seeing Rex in action.

Also, I'm not used to these long stretches of solitude. The sky and water view really *is* monotonous after a while.

I try to get in a lot of socialization at mealtime, but it's not enough compared to what I'm used to.

I miss two whale sightings.

Sigh.

Supposedly there will be more of them, but I really wanted to see a whale, and even more than that, I wanted to be with the group, to share the excitement of it.

But like Rex says, I'm getting paid well for doing nothing.

Sometimes I hear laughter as people pass by the window, and I try to put the voices to faces. I really like the people that I've met—except for Marvin and Serena.

I'm definitely looking forward to doing Gail's hair. I run into her at breakfast one day, and we set an official appointment to meet in the salon room for the following Sunday. Rex acts grumbly about it after she leaves our table, but he mostly seems concerned about my wrist.

I try not to let his concern for my wrist touch me too deeply. I try not to let it make me hopeful, because that is where the danger is.

Rex works like a demon—he really does. Part of his work seems to revolve around testing *the algo* with his *quant team* back in New York. Which is all about using computers to do really fast stock trades.

As if that's not enough, it turns out that there is some kind of stock market open no matter what time of day it is, though Rex seems particularly obsessive about the London and Tokyo markets, which he merely calls *London* and *Tokyo*, because to Rex, the entire significance of each city is the numbers that spill out of its markets and how that relates to his world domination plan.

Rex and Clark are always secretly checking the overseas markets on their phones.

And if they have to be involved in some social activity during the hallowed trading hours of the New York Stock Exchange? And people are watching them so that they can't check their phones? Let's just say that the futures are soaring in Crabbins City.

Not to toot my own horn, but over the next few days, I get really good at sensing when they're freaking out on their phones, and I work extra hard to monopolize the attention of whoever's around, turning myself up to eleven, as Rex would say, to give them space to work.

Rex's other main business activity seems to be creating some kind of proposal or vision for Gail's review—a kind of vision of what he'd do if he could get Gail's funds fully under management. Plans and charts and whatnot.

"Do you guys think you can get the account?" I ask Clark while Rex is on a conference call in the other room one day. "How likely is it that you win this review?"

"I don't know," Clark says. "The whole thing's a mystery. She's definitely buying you guys together, and she really does like you. But she's still forcing this review. Why? Why is she pitting him against a less worthy competitor? Is it still about Rex's bad publicity, or is it something else? And if so, what? It's a mystery to me."

"I get the feeling she likes Rex," I say.

"I think she does. So what's going on, then?" He lowers his voice. "Rex came up poor as hell, you know that, right?"

"Yeah," I say. "I mean, I read about it on the internet."

"Early on, less qualified competitors beat him out for accounts because those people had money and connections that Rex didn't have," Clark says. "When you lose to somebody like that, it's never spelled out, it's always a decision that didn't make sense otherwise. I was there, I remember."

"You've been with Rex from the beginning?"

"Since he was working out of the studio he slept in. And the weirdness of this feels like that to me. It feels as though somebody's got their thumb on the scale. Nothing about this review makes sense."

"Is a review like a stock market guy competition or something?"

"Sort of. Rex and his competitor, Wydover, each have a small bit of Driscoll funds under management," Clark says. "Kind of like a test."

"Wydover's the asshole."

"Right—total asshole," Clark says. "But connected. Anyway, Gail and her board will be comparing Rex and Wydover's performance over a specific frame of time—we don't know what, but Rex usually does better than Wydover. Though Wydover can be erratic. He does risky, quasilegal things. Anyway, we think Rex will also have to present something to her and her board, which is ridiculous. The whole thing is driving Rex up the wall. I don't love seeing it. He's stressed out enough."

I nod. Over the two years I've been working with Rex, this is the most stressed I've ever seen him. "It's not good for him," I say. "He needs to go in the hot tub."

"Good luck getting him to do that," Clark says. "There are exactly zero business reasons to go into the hot tub."

"It would relax him, and he'd be better at thinking. Relaxed people are better at thinking."

"Hey, I'm not arguing. It would be the best thing in the world for him to sit in the hot tub or lounge in one of those cabanas," Clark says. "And there is exactly zero chance that it will happen."

"I'm going to make it happen," I say. "I'll find a way to make him relax."

I make him have head massages, right? Sure, he doesn't know they're massages. But still.

Clark laughs. "Rex doesn't give in to the best negotiators in the world when he doesn't want something. A hot tub? A cabana? Not in this life."

Chapter Nine

Tabitha

I'M EXCITED for my midmorning salon date with Gail the next day. I follow the yacht map to the spa area, just one door down from where their massage person will never ever set their hands on Rex.

Gail is already there when I arrive. The place is beautiful, with chairs and mirrors arranged around massive tropical plants, soaking up the softly muted sunshine that's coming through skylights.

One of the stewardesses is setting out tea and fruit and candles that smell like jasmine.

We chitchat a bit, and I look through drawer after drawer of stuff. The place is amazing. It has every hairstyling implement known to humankind. "It's like Oscar Blandi himself stocked it," I say. I pull out a beautiful pair of shears and give them a couple of snaps. My wrist feels okay. One haircut won't set me back, and I'm happy to do this thing for Gail. I like her.

"We never really use this area," Gail says.

"I suppose it would be handy if there was an onboard wedding or something." I drape a cape over her pretty yachting shirt. The rich have actual shipboard clothes the way that baseball players have specific types of uniforms. A lot of linen fabrics in solid, bold colors. Flowy construction. Stripes and boat shoes.

I comb Gail's hair out. Diamond white.

"This really is a beautiful color," I say. "A lot of women pay good money and spend hours a month maintaining this kind of color."

"How do you know it's real?" Gail asks.

I smile at her in the mirror. "I have my ways."

"It grows really fast, though," she says. "Which was good when I was a girl getting crazy hairstyles, but not so much when I used to color it, so I let it go natural."

Carefully I begin to snip away. This is definitely a high-stakes haircut; Rex would kill me if I screwed up Gail's hair. But really, every cut is high stakes.

"How are you enjoying the trip so far?" she asks.

"Loving it," I say. I hate the idea of lying to Gail, but this, at least, is true. Except when I'm stuck in my room too long. "Rex is not a man who relaxes much, so this is really amazing for him."

"A man like Rex doesn't get to where he got by taking it easy," Gail says. "My late husband never stopped working—not until the day he keeled over of a heart attack."

"Oh. I'm so sorry, Gail," I say.

"It was a long time ago," she says. "But thank you. Dieter never stopped working on the business. Day and night. He wasn't much older than Rex when he went."

Dread flows through me yet again as I consider Rex's nonstop work habit. He eats well and works out, but even that feels more like punishment than self-care. My gut twists at the idea of him having a heart attack.

"I do worry about his pace," I confess.

She nods. "It's good seeing Rex get at least some relaxation in. See you two getting your lounge time."

She asks me about my business, and I give her my stock answer—it's good and I love my clients, love working for myself —because I can't get my mind off Rex. He really is wound up all the time.

Unsurprisingly, my stock answer doesn't satisfy Gail. She's interested in how I got the idea for the mobile side of it, and soon I find I'm telling her how I love the idea of doing every-thing really high-end—simple and high quality for those who are too busy and successful to go anywhere. I tell her how exciting it was to hire my first employee, how it made me feel like a real entrepreneur, and how I even like filling out the paperwork.

She wants to know my rationale for various choices and we get to talking nuts and bolts, which I never do with anybody. Being a mobile stylist with two people under me is a lonely thing, in the sense that I don't have co-workers—it's me alone bossing two women.

I end up telling her my crazy new idea I got from working with the personal stylist/shopper Rex sent for me, how I think it would be amazing to combine styling someone's hair with a kind of personal-stylist-lite experience—something that's more personal than a box in the mail, but less high-investment than a private stylist. It could be something mobile, like training mobile stylists in fashion, or else go all out with makeover store-fronts that employ personal stylists like movie stars have.

Gail is really interested in the storefront aspect. I explain my idea to have runners who would shop for clients while the clients are in the store getting their hair done, and they'd do a fitting session after the blow-dry session, and the runners would return the stuff that doesn't work. It would combine the best of online and brick-and-mortar shopping—you can try the stuff on without having to go anywhere, and there's a stylist to guide you, and there isn't the hassle of returns. She asks me whether I got the idea from restaurant-runner or grocery-delivery services, and I tell that I did. I was thinking, too, that there could be group experiences. Special-occasion parties. Champagne makeover nights.

"I like it," Gail says.

"You do?"

"A lot," she says. "It's niche, it saves time. It's good. Have you written up a business plan?"

"It's a new idea," I say. "I don't know *if* or *how…*"

"Well, how about we figure it out."

"You and me?"

"Yes, you and me," she says, like it was a ridiculous question.

Before I know it, we're brainstorming different approaches and different angles. Not only does she see a cool business operation, but she also sees an entire nationwide franchise operation with really specific branding. I can't believe how big she thinks.

"If you ever work up a business plan and pull these details together, you need to show it to me. I could be up for investing, partnering, if that was a way you'd want to go. I'm not promising anything, but it's the kind of thing I like getting my teeth into."

"Oh my god, Gail, I completely was not soliciting your investment!" I say. Because Rex would kill me if he thought I was hitting up Gail.

"I know you weren't soliciting my investment," Gail says, "but now I'm telling you I like it, and I'm telling you that I want to take a look. I know Rex could fund it, but it's not his wheelhouse, and you want to be thinking about somebody who has the vision and the funding and the willingness to get in there and go shoulder to shoulder with you. I don't invest in much, but I'm hands-on when I do." She punctuates the sentence with a curt nod.

My heart pounds like crazy…Gail Driscoll wants to work with me?

But then I realize I can never work with Gail. What am I thinking? I'm here under completely false pretenses. I could never build a partnership on a lie, especially not one where we work closely together.

"I'm flattered, but I don't know if I can," I say.

"Why? You know how to run a business. You're excited about the idea. It's just a matter of implementing it and then scaling up." She gives me the eagle eye in the salon mirror. "You planning on staying home and baking meatloaf for little Rexes? Is that it?"

"No, not at all. I plan to keep working. It's just, uh, thank you…" I stammer. I go around to the other side of her, carefully snipping away. "It means a ton that you're into it."

"It should mean a ton," she says. "I hear a lot of ideas. What you got here is a nice little niche-plus service. I like you partnering with these brick-and-mortar stores."

"Right!" I say. "It would be really cool to partner with mall stores. They put the stuff up front for pickup, or I send the pickers."

By the time I've finished the cut, she's talking about launching with a lab or popup somewhere like Tribeca. "The worst thing to do is to kill yourself planning. I always say, bring things to the market half baked and let reality be the feedback that perfects it, then you brand and iterate the ever-lovin' shit out of it."

She's hilarious, and I love talking about it even though it can never happen—not with us as partners.

Just then the door to the salon opens, and Marvin walks in, his ever-present sunglasses perched on top of his head. "How's it going?" he asks.

He's got two beverages and he sets them down. "Fresh-squeezed lemonade with basil. The stewardess just served it. So good."

"Thank you, Marvin," Gail says brightly.

Marvin gives Gail a very normal-looking smile. Does he reserve the weird faces for me? Is that it?

It seems strange that he's even here, but Gail seems happy. Rex did say she was obsessed with family, and Marvin is her new family—her only remaining connection to her dead sister.

I'm not at all happy, and not just because he's a freak. I was having fun talking with Gail, dreaming big with her. I've never done that with somebody so knowledgeable.

Marvin turns to me. His back is to Gail, and there it is, his unfriendly flat-eyed look that's definitely not horndoggery—a woman knows.

"I wonder if you could fix this one area of my hair for me…" Pulling his sunglasses off his head, Marvin turns and points to a divot in the back of his really perfect feathered hairdo.

I take a look. "What happened?"

"Is it that noticeable?" he asks.

"No," I say, and it's mostly the truth; it's not noticeable… unless you're a stylist; then it's just completely bizarre.

Sheepishly, he says, "I think my barber might've made a slip."

I smile and nod. "Maybe come back in ten, fifteen minutes? I'll do that while Gail's oil treatment sets?"

"I'll wait."

"Please do!" Gail says brightly.

Ugh. I'd wanted to finish my conversation with Gail.

I finish up Gail's cut, then use the fancy Parisian oil I found in one of the drawers to moisturize her hair while she talks to Marvin.

The divot really *is* weird—just this blunt sideways chunk.

It's a tiny cut to a layperson but a glaring error to somebody like me.

Other than the divot, his haircut looks very expensive. And even a cheap, incompetent barber would've at least tried to smooth it over.

Also, I would've noticed it earlier.

Did he just now cut that divot as a pretext to come up here? If so, why? No way is this about hitting on me—not in front of Gail, and not with stupid hair as a pretext.

I put the wrap on Gail's hair and put her under the dryer and gesture for Marvin to take the other seat so that I can fix his freak divot.

Of course I take the opportunity to inspect it. The divot was cut within the past day or two; I can tell by the bluntness of the ends themselves—a newly cut strand of hair has a cleaner tip than a strand that was cut a week or two prior. But even more than that, I can tell by the blunt line of the cut. Hair strands grow at different rates. In other words, a blunt cut doesn't grow out perfectly blunt.

The only scenario I can think of is Marvin cutting it himself as a pretext to join us. Why?

"We'll get this perfectly integrated," I say, snipping away, because as any watcher of soaps knows, you never tip off the bad guy that you're onto him.

He wants to know what we've been talking about.

I stiffen. I don't want Marvin knowing my idea. I just don't trust him.

"Salon business stuff," Gail tells him, nice and vague. "Style and so forth."

Soon after, he engages Gail in a conversation about people they'd been with in Scottsdale. He's heard news, some continuation of a conversation. He launches into a story that Gail is, admittedly, interested in. Which I have nothing to do with.

It's almost as if he's monopolizing her on purpose.

I'm thinking back to his seeming unhappiness about her delight in the cookies. Does he feel threatened and possessive of Gail? Like he doesn't want us to be friendly or something? Does he not want Gail to like me?

"There we go!" I say. I give him the hand mirror and spin him around so he can see the back. "Divot no more."

He thanks me, but makes no move to leave. He stays chatting away with Gail while I wash her hair and blow it out.

Marvin keeps Gail talking about things in their lives, and I keep working on Gail's hair.

I guess I'm the help now, at least in Marvin's eyes. But then at one point, as casual as can be, Marvin turns to me and says, "Is Rex busy preparing for the review?"

I detect a micro scowl on Gail.

"Umm…" I shrug. "I don't get into that side of things."

Marvin turns to her and says, "We really should establish a timeline for the whole thing."

"I'll decide on the timeline when I decide on the timeline," Gail says casually.

"I'm just saying it would be helpful to our guest to know the time frame he's working with," Marvin says.

"I've got it under control," Gail says with a smile.

He seems to want to say more, but Gail's sweet steely thing seems to stop him. I wait to fire up the blow dryer, hoping Marvin says whatever he wants to say.

Something *was* weird—Marvin said "*we* should establish a timeline," and then Gail came back with "*I* will decide."

Does Marvin think he's helping to drive this review? *Is* he helping to drive it? Is he involved? It sure sounds like that! Which is something that will be very interesting to Rex.

Is Marvin the one putting his thumb on the scale?

Marvin says no more, so I blow out Gail's hair. I'm feeling extremely pleased with her cut. The result is more brilliant than I could've imagined.

"Gail," I say, grinning. I spin her around to the mirror.

She brightens up and touches the side of her head. "Oh. Wow. Thank you! I love this. I love how…"

She doesn't have words, but I do. I explain how I've thinned out the bulk on the sides and added layers to free up the natural curl. The shape gives her face a kind of lift.

Gail's beaming. "It's perfect!"

"*Very* pretty," Marvin says, but in an uncertain way. Like he doesn't think it's very pretty at all. What an asshole!

I don't even care. Gail knows it's good, and I do, too. And everybody will tell her so. And most enjoyable of all, I have an interesting puzzle piece for the mystery of Gail's assets not being already in Rex's lap.

Chapter Ten

Rex

SHE BANGS into the suite while I'm busy at my desk, and instead of proceeding to her room as she's supposed to, she stands behind me. I can feel her eyes on me, wanting me to turn around, give her attention. Tabitha is constitutionally incapable of not interrupting me.

"Do pass go," I growl, eyes fixed on the screen. "Do collect two hundred. Do proceed directly to your room."

"You wouldn't be talking like that if you knew my news," she says.

"Don't tell me you messed up the haircut." Not that I think she would. Tabitha's a pro.

She sighs. I hate how badly I want to turn around and see what kind of annoying expression she has on her face. I hate how badly I want to go to her and breathe in her floral scent, or say something rude just to enjoy her reaction.

Her silence finally drives me crazy enough that I spin around. "What?"

She's wearing white shorts and a snug little brown striped top that perfectly highlights the contours of her breasts and the pleasing line of her collarbone, but it's her proud expression that gets me.

"The cut turned out more brilliant than brilliant," she says. "I knew I was going to improve Gail's hair, but that was some major haircut magic. Chef's kiss!"

"A chef's kiss is a gesture, not a phrase," I inform her. "It's a gesture where you kiss the tips of your fingers. Why not just do the gesture?"

"Because," she says happily.

"So what's the news? Ridiculous things I'm supposed to have said or done?"

"Believe it or not, there are other shipboard subjects besides you and your fantastical stamina. Though Gail does think you work too hard. Her husband died of a heart attack from working too hard. Did you know that?"

"Old news," I say.

She flops down in Clark's chair, careless of the fact that she's interrupted a very complex task. "You work way too much. It's not healthy." She crosses her long, shapely legs.

I force my eyes back onto the monitor.

"You need to think about your health. But that's not what I need to tell you."

I should order her out. She's my employee, after all, but for some perverse reason, I want to hear what she has to tell me. It'll be useless and infuriating, but I need to hear it. And her just blurting it out would be too easy. She's waiting for me to ask her. Tabitha never fails to disappoint.

I frown. Is it her hand? Did the haircut set back her injury? I spin back around. "Tell me."

"Some very important information on Marvin."

This gets my attention. "What about Marvin? Did he try to talk to you again? Do I need to get thick with him?"

She bites her bottom lip, as though she's trying not to laugh. I want to go over there and…I don't know what.

"I *hope* you don't get thick with him," she says. "I think it would be inappropriate for you to get thick with Marvin, don't you? Considering you have a gorgeous fiancée right here on board? I mean, what would Gail say?"

"That's not what *getting thick* means," I say through gritted teeth.

"I assure you," she continues, "he is not hitting on me."

"Why don't you tell me what happened and I'll decide."

"He might have said something that has to do with this review you and Clark are so curious about. Something that could provide insight." She uncrosses her legs and crosses them the other way, slow and sultry, and then settles her hands in her lap.

"What? What did he say?"

"Oh, wait…" She touches her cheek with the tip of her finger. "I'm sorry, I just remembered that I'm not being paid to talk about Marvin or report to you about Marvin or worry about Marvin in the least." She tilts her head. "My bad."

I stand. "If you have some information that's important to me, you need to tell it to me."

"I will. But you'll have to do something for me, then. The telling of the information will occur in the hot tub up on the high deck."

"No, it'll occur here," I say.

She winces. "Sorry. I'm going to the top deck and getting into the hot tub and that is the place I will tell it. And I assure you—it *is* eyebrow-raising."

"I don't do hot tubs," I bite out.

"Well, that's the only place that I'm gonna tell you this very important information. And you need a break anyway. Have you not heard the studies of how you need at least a fifteen-minute break for every twenty-hour work sprint?"

"What does Marvin have to do with the review?" I ask.

She sits there like the cat who swallowed the canary. "Tune in at the hot tub to find out!"

I go right up to her, grabbing the armrests on either side of her, caging her with my arms.

Her pupils darken.

"Do you have actual information on the review, or are you just jerking me around?"

She bites her lip, looking witchy. I'm getting addicted to provoking her. I'm getting addicted to her reactions.

I lean in close enough that I can feel her body heat; it's as if I feel her on my skin, through my clothes.

She releases her lip, and it glistens plump and rosy. I can't tear my eyes from it. I want to taste it. I want to press my palms to her cheeks and take that little mouth for my own.

How is she so infuriating? Why do I let her drive me crazy like this?

"You so want to know," she says.

"Then tell me."

"I will." She slides downward out of the chair, limbo-style, and gracefully twirls out of the cage of my arms, ending up behind me. "Put on your bathing suit and meet me in the hot tub." She beelines to her room and closes the door.

She's bartering with me now? That's not how it works. I call the shots with women, not the other way around. Calling the shots is one of the privileges of having climbed as far up the food chain as I have.

But here I am—with a woman I specifically chose for her repellent qualities trying to call the shots.

The worst part of it is that I *want* to go up there and hear whatever thing she has to say.

The zip of a suitcase sounds out from her room.

I should blow it off—that would teach her. If they

mentioned the review in front of her, there's no way it was anything important.

Except that every bit of information is important. I made my fortune by taking scraps of information that other people passed over and putting them together in a way that lets me see around corners.

I make cool, emotionless decisions, and then I execute on them.

I need to know what she thinks she knows.

And I can't have her parading around deck in a sexy suit without me.

I throw down my pen and storm into my room and try to find my suit. My assistant said he packed me one just in case. I riffle through, unsure where to look or even what color the suit would be. I stiffen at the sound of the outer door closing. She left without me?

I finally find the thing and change. I put on a short-sleeved shirt and head to the end of our level. On the deck below, people are lounging in cabanas and sitting at the bar. Somebody waves, and I wave back, walking with purposeful strides toward the steps that lead to the uppermost deck where the hot tub is.

I grab the rail and start banging up, up one level and then the next, arriving on the top deck.

The top deck is smaller than the other decks, like a platform suspended some six stories above the ocean, all potted palms and posh loungers and the feeling of being on top of the world.

Stretching out from the shadow of the towering structure that holds the ship's communication and navigation array high in the sky is a giant hot tub. Tabitha is on one side of it, grinning. I'm irritated to note that she's not alone; two guys are sitting across from her—drooling over her, no doubt. Neither are Marvin. Luckily.

Still, how are we supposed to talk with two guys sitting there?

I reach the edge. Tabitha smiles up at me, droplets of water glistening like diamonds on her smooth shoulders.

There's no way they aren't drooling over her. I give the guys a hard look. An *I-see-you* look.

"You made it," she says.

"How could I not?" I grit out, with a look that says, *you'll pay for this.*

Her grin is wide and devilish, and it goes straight to my cock.

I sit down on the edge, sink my calves into the hot, bubbling water, and take a deep breath. It does feel nice.

"Pretty relaxing, huh?" she says. "You should get all the way in."

"This is good," I say.

"But the telling of the information," she says.

"Will occur while you're in the hot tub," I say. "Looks like you're in the hot tub to me."

Her pout sends a little glow through me, and suddenly the memory of our kiss on the plane is flowing through my mind, through my body. Without even thinking, I brush a droplet off of her shoulder.

Her chest rises minutely, as though to suck in a silent breath. As though my touch affects her that deeply.

The idea of that pleases me way too much.

I touch her chin and nudge her face up to mine. The tiny flecks of gold around her irises have become more intense in the sunlight.

"What?" she asks in a lightly mocking tone.

Before I can think better of it, I lean down and brush a quiet kiss over her lips.

Her gaze falters for just a moment—just a moment—and then her eyes dance, and her brows lift. *Aren't you glad we prac-*

ticed kissing? That's what her expression is saying. *Didn't I tell you so?*

My eyes fall once again to her lips. I need to kiss her again. What is happening to me? I force myself to release her. I tip my head back and gaze up at the clouds, ignoring the young guns, willing them to leave so that she can tell me what she has to tell me.

The water is a perfect temperature on my shins. I let them float.

"Well, *I* think it's nice," she says.

"For a bath."

The side of my foot accidentally brushes against the silky warmth of her thigh. Energy surges through me at the contact.

I picture sinking into the water. I could sit right next to her and slide my hand up along her smooth thigh, lazily enjoying the feel of her, slippery as silk under the foam. I imagine sliding my hand between her legs—slow enough that she could stop me if she wanted. *Would* she?

Or would she watch me, still with that mischief in her eyes, playing a game of chicken, wondering if I'd really go there?

Hell yeah, I'd go there. I'd go right there, watching her eyes, her breath, modulating my pressure, my stroke, learning every last one of her preferences and her secrets. It wouldn't take long—I'm a good observer, and more than that, Tabitha's expressions are just that obvious.

I'd get her off and replace that mischief in her eyes with pure fucking stars. It would be so wrong. So damn good.

"Excuse me, Mr. O'Rourke," a male voice says.

I jolt out of my mad reverie and turn my attention to the two young bucks.

"Hi, I'm Michael Washington," the one says. "I just wanted to tell you, I did my master's thesis on the quick-turn credit derivatives system you pioneered the year before last. I thought it was genius."

"It's not really that unique," I say.

"But you were the first." He motions at his friend. "This is Sam Singh. We both graduated Wharton together last year."

Sam says hi.

"I hope I'm not disturbing you," Michael continues, "but I wanted to ask you what you make of that last rate change vis-a-vis the OTC market." He goes on to explain his question in detail. I watch him, pondering. I'm not pondering the question, which is a relatively simple one, but rather, whether a curt answer or a complex answer will get them out of the tub faster. Of course, being an asshole would get them out of the tub fastest, but this isn't the place. So I go with a complex answer. I take more time than I'd like. Their follow-up questions feel endless.

The sounds from the side of the deck announce a new arrival.

It's Gail. She pops up the last of the steps and comes to stand over us. "You finally got to pin him down," she says to Michael, making me extra glad I followed my no-asshole instincts. "Croquet at three, people! I'm recruiting for my team. Who's in?" She's inviting all of us, but she's looking at Tabitha. She wants Tabitha on her team.

Exactly how much did they bond?

Tabitha looks over at me, because I don't like her being social on deck without me.

"Are you in, Rex?" Gail asks. "You and Tabitha? On my team?"

And with that, I'm trapped. "Sounds fun," I say. "Sign us up." The guys volunteer to play on her team, too. All of us on a fucking team.

I stare at faint wisps of clouds at the edge of the blazing blue sky.

Gail leaves, and finally the two guys heave themselves out, dripping like wet dogs.

"A hot tub and now croquet?" I mutter once we have the entire deck to ourselves. "Whatever you tell me had better be good, because I'm doing time in a hot tub, and now I'm roped into croquet? You know what I hate more than getting turned into a stewed turnip in a tub? Do you want to guess?"

Her mouth twists into a merry little bud. Only Tabitha would think this is amusing.

I stare at that half-smirking twist of pink lips, fighting the urge to grab her hair and pull her face to mine, and it wouldn't be a brush of a kiss that I give her this time. I'd do every kind of lewd thing to those pretty little lips.

"Umm…" she finally says. "You hate games? I'm guessing all games?"

"That's right. I hate all games." I twirl my finger in a strand of dark hair. I let it tighten, lowering my voice, tugging softly. "I hate them very, very much. So let's hear it."

"Uh," she says, eyes flared, lips parted, her tell that she's turned on, I've noticed. I love that look on her.

My blood races. I shouldn't be touching her, but I can't seem to stop. "Spill it," I grate out.

She sits up and pushes away my hand, forcing me to relinquish the curl. "It's two things, actually. Wait—three."

I put my hands on the tiles behind me and lean back, forcing myself back under control. "I don't need you to tell me how many individual things you have for me. We both know the number will be wrong anyway. Just tell me what you need to tell me and be done with it."

"My goodness," she says, turning to face me with a shift of water I can feel on my feet. She's facing me now, elbows up on the side of the tub. Her wet arms glisten in the sunshine. She looks sexy, and mind-bendingly fuckable. It's not even about fucking, really; I want to make her feel good. I want to see that turned-on face even more turned on. I want to see her coming face.

What is happening to me?

"Get on with it," I say.

"*Somebody* needs a jasmine-scented towel over his eyes."

I raise my eyebrows.

"Fine, fine!" she says. "Fact one, Marvin doesn't want me bonding too closely with Gail. He can see that we have a fun connection, and it threatens him. You wanna know how I know?"

"I'm sure you'll tell me."

"He got some scissors and cut a *divot* into his own hair, just so that he'd have a reason to play beauty parlor with us. He literally ruined his own very nice haircut as a pretext. He said it was a barber flub, but it wasn't."

"How do you know?"

"Beyond the fact that no barber would let a client walk around like that? Because we've been on this boat for a few days and that snip was fresh."

"You can tell a fresh snip?"

"It's my business to know these things, Rex. And even if I hadn't examined the follicles up close, I think I would've noticed a freak chunk out of his hair the day we boarded. He thinks it's small, but to my eye? Please. He cut it and ran up there to join us."

I frown. "Maybe he hoped that Gail would leave so that you two would be alone."

"He makes his hair look stupid as part of his seduction technique? No. Anyway, he specifically wanted to interact with Gail, not me. He was all about Gail and taking Gail's attention off of me. I mean, he sat down and he just started talking about stuff that I wouldn't know about. Conversations that specifically excluded me. I think Gail was a little miffed, but she is really sweet, and she's trying hard to include him in the family."

"Family is her blind spot," I say. "But this only suggests that he's ragingly insecure. And it has nothing to do with the review."

She says, "It comes out, in the conversation, that Marvin is driving the review. Not Gail."

I straighten. "Marvin's driving it? They said that specifically?"

"No, it was subtle. Marvin at one point asks me if you were preparing for it. I, of course, acted clueless. Then Marvin turns to Gail and he's all, 'we should establish a timeline for that review, let him know the timeline he's working with,' something like that. And Gail turns to him and she's all, 'I'll decide on the timeline when I decide on the timeline.'"

"Really."

"Yeah. He acted like they were a team on it, using the pronoun *we*, and her communication to him seemed to be, you've reached the limit of how much you can push this thing. And she stressed that *she* will decide—not them together, but her. Do you see how the two pieces of information work together? If he is driving the review and has some reason to want you to lose out on her business, the last thing he'd want is for her to be having a magical time with your fiancée, which for the record, we were having a magical time. I think she's really interested in making him welcome in their family and she's tolerating the review that he's avidly pushing for, but I think he's really pushing it."

"You're sure…"

"Yeah. And it's not only what they said; a lot of it was nonverbal. I know how to read people. I'm in the people business. I'm telling you—Marvin was pushing, and she was drawing a line."

I brush another droplet off her shoulder. "And you think he's driving the review. And she's humoring him."

"Why else discuss the timeline? My theory is that she's really going to pick you in the end, but she's doing the review to humor her new nephew. What kind of position does he have in her company?"

"Something vaguely vice presidential. A firm like hers has lots of vice presidents, though."

"You don't find this all in the least bit suspicious?"

"It doesn't make sense. Even if Marvin is behind the review, what possible reason could he have for steering the Driscoll portfolio away from the person who'd get them the best return? He's not entitled to any of that money, so it would just be him making a shitty recommendation."

"Mmm," she says.

"So then, what's in it for him?" I ask. "Nothing at all, unless he's financially associated with my competitor. And I guarantee you, the first thing Gail would do would be to look at that."

She pulls herself up out of the tub and onto the edge, water dripping off her, except for the few droplets that remain behind, quivering on her sexy skin like diamonds. Her black one-piece hugs her breasts deliciously. "I'm telling you what I heard."

Is she annoyed that I don't seem to believe her? Some kind of retort forms in my mind, and just as quickly it floats away—up, up and away like a balloon.

"Don't believe me at your own detriment." She stands up.

My vision fuzzes at the edges as she grabs a towel and begins to rub it over her long legs, her stomach, her arms. And then she turns to grab her robe, and I see how the suit clings to her ass, and all thought drains from my brain.

"I'm thinking croquet requires sunscreen and a costume change," she says, putting it on. "We should go get ready."

Going back to get ready requires crossing the main deck, and everybody seems to want to talk to her, to the extent that she has to tell everybody that we're rushing back to change for croquet. And suddenly there are more people wanting to play. What is happening here?

It's not like I haven't noticed her laughing with people during mealtimes, but I wasn't thinking about it too hard; usually I'm hiding with Clark or talking to Gail or the adult children during meals. They're the ones who matter.

Finally we're heading down along the walkway to our door. "Somebody's the social butterfly," I say.

"Your kitten is a super-fun person who can get along with everybody. It's why you worship the ground I walk on."

"Is that how our engagement goes? I worship the ground you walk on?"

"Oh, yes," she says.

I open the door to our suite, still stuck on the way her suit clung to her ass when she emerged from the hot tub. The image is burned into my brain.

"What?" she says. "You don't agree?"

I close the door behind us, back up against it. The idea of wet black nylon cupping her ass somewhere under that terrycloth robe she's currently swaddled in has pushed all other conscious thought from my mind.

In a matter of moments she'll head into her bathroom, take off the robe, and then peel the damp suit off of her perfect ass, and then she'll get under rushing water, let it pour all over her perfect little body.

She throws a towel over a chair. "And FYI, when I tell you a thing, you completely believe me, because you know how good I am with people. How tuned in I am to people. And if you were a proper fiancé, you'd be suspicious, too. Because isn't that so weird that Marvin said that? What is he up to with that review? Because you know he's up to shenanigans. I'm not saying he's for sure a fake nephew..."

"Good god, you're still on that thing?" I move near her. I can feel her heat all over my skin—it's as if she radiates heat.

Her neck pinkens. Her words, when they come out, are breathy. "Something very fishy is going on."

I say, "You're seeing things that aren't there."

"Is that so, Captain Sternpants?" Her eyes flare, like she can't believe she just said that. "I mean…umm…"

Captain Sternpants? I narrow my eyes. "What did you just call me?"

"Nothing."

But her cheeks are all rosy suddenly. "Didn't sound like nothing to me."

"Uh…"

I take a step closer. "I'm in the business of knowing when something is nothing or not."

Her gaze is hot and hectic. She doesn't want to repeat it for whatever reason, which makes me want to make her repeat it—several times over, just to see it coming out of her lips, up close and personal.

She steps back and hits the wall. I cage her against it, palms flat against the textured plaster, forearms brushing against the terrycloth tips of her robe. I have to make her say it again; I don't know why, I just do. I'm out of control. Obsessed, even. It's wrong, wrong, wrong.

And I want her. I can't see anything else but her.

I lower my voice to the deep register that she seems to respond to. "Now, what did you just call me?"

She fixes her gaze on mine, lips parted. "Captain," she says with dramatic enunciation. "Stern. *Pants*."

"What's that supposed to mean?" I rumble.

"Just a name."

"Is it your name for me?"

She clearly doesn't want to tell. I don't give a shit about the name, but I like making her confess things.

"Is it?" I ask.

She twists her lips as if that will ward off the smile that's pressing at the gates. "Fine. It's me and my roommate's name…for you."

"You talk about me with your roommate? And that's what you call me?"

She swallows, searching my face. I'm overwhelmed by her girly scent. Her heat. This is everything I was trying to avoid, and there's nothing else that I want. "Sternpants? Why?"

Her lips part—it's her turned-on tell. "I don't know," she whispers huskily.

"I think you do."

Her eyes twinkle, the little vixen. She says nothing.

"Is it how you imagine me?" I lean in closer, lips grazing the shell of her ear. "Like some stern control freak?"

She sucks in a ragged breath. In a hoarse whisper, she says one word: "Yeah."

Heat licks over my skin. "Do you think that's how I fuck? Is that what you think?"

"Yes," she rasps, cheeks glowing dusky rose.

Images of taking her right against the wall crowd my mind. They morph into images of bending her over my bed, ass bare. "That's what you think?" I repeat senselessly.

"Uh-huh," she says.

"Then you'd be correct," I whisper, right before I press my lips to hers.

Chapter Eleven

Tabitha

I'M DYING.

He has me trapped against the wall, and he's kissing my lips, then my neck, and I'm dying. I'm melting. I'm happy, panting putty in his wickedly roaming hands.

He traps me harder, and I'm pulling at his shirt and meeting him halfway in a manner that might best be described as *grinding back atcha*.

He pulls back to look at my face. I should be scared of the stormy look in his eyes, the way he seems to be losing control again, but I love him like this, unspooling just for me.

I lick my lips. His eyes follow the motion of my tongue, which just makes everything hotter. I love that I can do this to him.

He grumbles and slides a hand over my hip and around to my ass, which he clutches through terrycloth.

"Captain Sternpants," I whisper, "are you getting *thick* with me?"

"Very," he snarls against my skin.

Butterflies go wild in my belly.

I should know better than to give in to the crazy chemistry that we have, but right now, I'm telling myself it's okay to do casual sex with him. I do friends with benefits all the time, right?

Except I'm not head over heels for my friends-with-benefits friends. Still, I tell myself that this'll be okay.

Anyway, I can't stop kissing him. I can't stop stroking his beard and mauling his shoulders. I can't stop meeting him halfway with my pelvis. Feverishly, I start to unbutton his shirt.

"No, no, no," he breathes, and suddenly he has my wrists. He lifts my hands above my head and presses them against the wall with just one hand.

"I don't get to unbutton your shirt, but you get to disrobe me?"

"That's how I like it."

"You keep your clothes on? Oh my god, control freak much?" But I like it, too.

Umm…a lot.

With his free hand, he yanks open the ties of my robe, just yanks them apart with way more brutish force than necessary, but it's just the right amount of brutish force to overload me with lust. The boat seems to be tilting. Are the seas swelling? Have extra seamen come aboard?

He still has that stern scowl, acting all in control, but the rough in-and-out saw of his breath says otherwise.

The cool air of the room caresses my bare flesh, my damp suit, even as heat blooms up my core.

He slides his hand down over my breasts, my belly, my crotch, all the way down my thighs and then around to my ass. "This fucking ass," he growls, taking a handful and giving it a squeeze.

The squeeze does something amazing to my clit. Then he

pushes his hand up the inside of my suit and makes contact with my bare ass skin.

I press into him, nipping his earlobe. Suddenly his wicked fingers are on the move again, heading back up to my breasts.

I swallow. "Wait."

He stills. "What?"

"Go back down again," I say. "With your hand."

"Are you telling Captain Sternpants what to do?"

"Um…trying to?"

His eyes darken. "That's not how this works."

I say, "You are so bossy…"

"I think you like it," he rumbles.

He's right. His scowly, bossy face makes me want to lie down and bare my belly, not to mention my pussy and everything else that the law likes covered.

"Now get those fucking legs spread apart," he says.

His words hit me like a drug, and I do as he says. He's such an unbelievably gruff jerk, and now, after months of pining after him, months of fantasies, I'm going with the full barrel roll. It's everything I promised myself I'd never do.

Which maybe makes it more delicious.

"Captain Sternpants?" he growls, sliding my suit top sideways off my breast, kissing the side of it, marking it with his whiskers, a white-hot swipe of yummy Rex harshness, before tonguing my nipple with wicked abandon.

And suddenly his hand is between my legs. "You are such a little tease," he rasps, helping himself to my pussy, the most willing and eager dance partner he will ever encounter. He finds my aching clit. He begins some kind of sexy finger sorcery there.

I sag in his arms, managing by some miracle to keep my groan of pleasure at a conversational level.

I can't think. My clit apparently contains my entire mind, and he's doing things that make it hum.

A knock at the door jolts me out of my lust haze, makes Rex's hand still. A female voice I don't recognize. "Gail sent me down to let you know it's starting."

"We're getting ready," Rex grunts.

The footsteps clunk away.

"It *was* starting," I say.

He grips my wrists harder in his hand. "Come back," he whispers, watching my eyes, touching me. "Come back to me."

"But…Gail. C-croquet," I whisper.

"Yes, and whose fault is that?" he rumbles. "Whose fault is it that we're going to play that ridiculous game?"

I wheeze out a breath that maybe sounds like *huhhhh.*

"Say it," he growls, doing my sex in a new and awesome way. "Whose fault?"

I'm panting. "More, please."

"Whose?"

"Mine," I gust out. "My fault."

Finally, he gives me what I want, and it's like my pussy spent the past five centuries in a cage under the Italian Alps, deprived of touch. And now his finger is there, a full, brilliant 3-D experience. It's so much—too much. An orgasm explodes over me.

"Ride it," he says as he slows his finger, letting me move on him. "All the way," he rasps into my ear as I come.

And come.

And come.

When I flutter my eyes open and meet his gaze, I know he's been watching me. And it feels amazing in a way I can't describe, just that he was watching.

"God, you're the most maddening fucking…" he grates, and suddenly he's kissing me. And I have my hands back and I'm grabbing the shit out of his shirt, pulling him to me.

Right then the footsteps show back up.

"That better not be somebody else coming to get us," he whispers.

The footsteps slow in front of our door. Somebody feeling uncertain.

A menacing rumble in my ear, "You see what you've done?"

A soft knock.

"Two minutes," a voice calls out.

Rex detaches us and points at my room. "Go. Change."

"What about…" I look down at his cock. But then he glowers, and I do as he said, because professionalism.

I go in and do a speed shower and record-breaking costume change. I put on a short brown jumper with white piping around the collar and awesome brown and white Fly London sandals. I put my Smuckers pendant around my neck, just because.

When I emerge from my room, he's at his usual station, glowering at his laptop. He grabs his phone in the bold, angry way he has, and I'm flooded again with the memory of how he touched me and the things he said.

And the way he seems to care, even though he acts like he doesn't.

He's barking something into the phone—talking with Clark, obviously. "Bring your go-folder and cover for me, just fucking get over here. Bailey Tech's popping." He slams down the phone and turns to me, and my belly twists. He's in a loose white linen shirt and tan pants and he looks amazing.

I feel nervous for a moment, because I like him so much, but the fact that it ends contractually after the yacht vacation is over makes it safe to have a fling. That's what I tell myself.

"You're ready," he says.

"I'm a professional freaking fiancée," I say. "You're ready, too."

"I'm a guy."

His gaze drops to my chest. "Something tells me my shopper didn't pick that out."

I look down and see that the Smuckers pendant is showing. "Oops," I say, tucking it in. "That's just for me."

When I look back up, he has an expression I can't read. Is he unhappy to have seen it?

Clark's distinctive rap breaks the strange silence. I pull open the door, and he comes in with a bundle of stuff in his arms. "What's going on?" he asks.

"This one got me roped into a game of croquet," Rex says. "I need you to be at the helm here."

Clark looks astonished. "Croquet?"

"Don't ask," Rex says. "We were up in the hot tub and just…don't ask."

Clark looks stunned. "You were in the hot tub?"

I give him a smug little smile.

"What's up?" Rex barks.

"Bailey Tech hit forty-five." Clark arranges his papers on the desk, and they start carrying on a conversation in half numbers that I completely don't understand. It sounds urgent, like something's happening.

I wander over to where Rex is assembling his stuff. "Is everything okay? I can probably make excuses for you if it's something urgent."

"Everything that I do is urgent," Rex says, turning around just as Clark's reaching sideways.

A coffee mug goes over. Rex swears and grabs a keyboard and a laptop, and Clark dives for another laptop, and that upsets a box that's balanced on something and suddenly papers and folders are all over the floor.

"Fuck!" Rex says, sliding his fingers across the laptop keyboard, checking for water. "Dry."

"Wet." Clark's got his laptop tipped upside down. He peels off a keyboard cover. Rex goes for some towels.

I start gathering up the papers, trying to keep the general order of them, when my eyes are drawn to a little sheet of paper that's paper-clipped to the inside of a leather folder that had fallen down in a spread-open position.

Before I think that it isn't something I should be reading, my mind registers three things simultaneously: One, a gold insignia with the name Rex O'Rourke at the top.

Two, an underlined heading written in Rex's characteristic scrawl: REX HATES.

And then a series of items: *Bubbly personality. Into soap operas —thinks they're profound. Pathetically impoverished. Laughs at anything.* I grab the folder, heart pounding, clutching it, reading down every one of the items listed.

Clark's voice. "What are you doing?"

Stupidly positive attitude. Fashion choices: colorful hair streaks, sparkles, Hello Kitty shit. Narrates her expressions and reactions to things. Turns popular songs into songs about her pet and thinks other people might actually find that amusing.

I blink, mind spinning. Is it some kind of joke? Why would Rex make a list like this?

I look up, feeling a weak smile playing upon my lips, because I need it to be a joke so badly. I need, need, need it.

Then I meet Clark's horrified gaze. And I know it's not a joke.

My heart pounds like mad. "W-what is this?"

Clark and Rex are both staring at me now.

"I made it," Clark blurts.

"Oh really? *You* made it?" I yank the list from the paperclip that holds it to the folder and stand. "In Rex's handwriting on Rex's personal stationery? You're saying you made it?"

"I made it," Rex says. "Seriously, it's nothing." He moves to take it away, but I pull it out of range.

Trying to keep my voice from shaking, I say, "Why don't you tell me about it and I'll decide if it's nothing."

"It's not what it seems," Rex says.

"It's nothing," Clark says, "it's nothing."

"Nothing," I bite out, staring at Clark. Because right then, I'm remembering his weird expression every time I wondered aloud why Rex would've picked me. His weird look when I confessed to him that I didn't even think Rex liked me.

God, I felt so lucky, so special. I turn to Rex. "Did you pick me for this job because I'm hateful to you?"

"You're not hateful to me," Rex says.

My blood whooshes in my ears. "That's not the question," I say.

"It's the important question," Rex says.

"Oh my god, that's a yes!" I say. "I always wondered why you picked me." I hold up the small paper in my trembling hand. "I thought it was such an honor to be picked by you. You have no idea what an honor. But you picked me because of this. Because I satisfy your hate list."

"I don't hate you," Rex says.

"Well, it says here you do. Or at least you hate everything about me, which is basically the same thing. I mean, how much more clear could it be? It says 'Rex Hates' followed by a colon. In your handwriting, on your stationery. I don't feel the need for a witness affidavit that you created it."

"Tabitha," Rex says.

"I don't want to hear it." My voice sounds strange to my own ears—raw, somehow. "What I don't understand is why you would want somebody who is so hateful, so repellent to you, to spend this time with you. Narrating my expressions and reactions and all that." I think of all the times I said *ragey* or *sadface*. I actually thought it was fun and humorous, like we were in something together. But I was only being hateful to him. "Joke's-on-me face," I whisper hotly.

"Don't," he says. "Let me explain—"

"But apparently," I continue, "you don't hate me enough not to make the moves on me when you're in the mood. Did you have to close your eyes and think of your precious Tokyo?"

Clark gives him a dark look.

Rex finally succeeds in snatching the paper from my fingers. "It's not like that."

"What is it like, then? You don't hate me all that much? You find me tolerable enough now to promote me from hate-able fake fiancée to fuck buddy-slash-fake fiancée? Check it out, folks, a two-for-one! Is that maybe what it's like? Uhhh!" I storm off into my room and slam the door.

I sink onto my bed, arms wrapped around myself, mind whirling.

I'd thought I was special. I'd thought that he'd seen some little spark of something in me. And god, the way he'd kissed me, the way he touched me.

But he can barely stand me.

Six more days on this yacht.

With *him*.

I can't hug myself hard enough to erase the hole in me, but I seem to be trying.

"Tabitha," he says from the other side of the door. "Can I come in?"

I get this little pang of something sweet and sickly, like some part of him has taken root in me and wants to let him in. How pathetic is that? The hate list has killed every nice feeling in me, but somehow my stupid crush on him has survived. "Go away."

"I'm coming in."

I glare at the door. Slowly he creaks it open and then he's standing there, inky brows drawn together, so intense and serious. "I don't hate you. Far from it."

"Your list would beg to differ."

Clark's at the door behind him. "I'm gonna go make apologies for you guys for croquet."

I stand. "I said I'd be there. I'll be there."

Rex looks concerned. "You don't have to—"

"Nothing's different," I snap. "I don't need you to like me. I just need you to pay me for the job I signed on for. The job I'm doing amazingly at in spite of these bullshit work conditions." I storm to my bathroom and swipe on some lipstick, proud that I'm not crying. Not one tear did I shed, and not one tear will I shed.

They're all trapped in my chest, my throat—sad little prisoners he'll never get to see.

I swing past him, past Clark, who's mumbling how he'll handle whatever business thing is up, heading for the door. I head out the walkway and stomp toward the front of the yacht, fingering my little Smuckers pendant.

Rex catches up to me. "Tabitha."

"We don't have to like each other to pull this off. End of story," I say in a low voice as we pass by other people's dark cabin windows. "The fact that I'm a horrifying individual to you makes it cleaner somehow—"

"You're not horrifying—"

"Just stop," I bite out.

I always make things fun, even when people are assholes. I'm the fun girl everybody wants around—it's been who I am ever since I was a little girl. Ever since the fire.

So it's weird to be all-out angry at a guy, but with Rex, it feels pure and real. Good, even.

"Tabitha—"

"*Not horrifying*," I say, crossing the mini-lounge area. I spin around at the top of the stairway that takes us down to the third-floor party deck. "Would it be cool with you if I put that on my website as a customer testimonial?" I raise my hands in the air in front of us, as if to frame the thought. "Not horrifying! So says billionaire client *Rex O'Rourke*." I smile, game face fully intact. "Not horrifying is one of the most important features of a hairdresser, did you know that? Most people don't realize that."

"I'm sorry," he says. "And you're wrong about the list."

"'You're wrong.' That *would* be your apology." I turn and head down the steps.

It's a lovely afternoon, and the guests are all out, massed around the pool and the bar area, with a good dozen of them at the croquet area beyond, waiting for us on the bright green AstroTurf in their yacht clothes and hats, croquet mallets in their hands.

He catches up. "Hate isn't at all an accurate description of my feelings—"

"We don't have to actually talk until we're with people," I say, speeding up.

He catches up to me. "I'll double your bonus."

"Oh, great. More money. That'll fix *everything*."

"Consider it hazard pay," he says.

"Don't flatter yourself. You're hardly a hazard. And this is just a business relationship."

"Tabitha—"

I give him a hot glare and round a potted palm, heart secretly breaking.

How could I have been so stupid? Guys always put themselves first—you never want to depend on them, and you never *ever* put your heart in their hands.

Putting your heart in the hands of any guy is the recipe for ruin, and what did I do? Exactly that.

I paste on a smile and wave energetically.

And then I think, *have I lost my mind?* I link my arm in his. "I changed my mind. Double the bonus. Yes, please."

He says nothing, and then we're in the thick of it. "We're ready to rumble!" I say, grabbing a mallet.

Nala high-fives me. Serena watches me coldly, but I'm already chilled to the bone.

I make the game count, laughing and trying to get into it, doing a good job. I don't need him to see he picked right, I just need to last.

And somehow, forget how hard I was falling for him.

Chapter Twelve

Tabitha

ONE THING REX is right about when it comes to yachts—it sucks to have nowhere to go.

Especially when you want to be away from everybody.

After a game of croquet that felt like five hours, but was probably just one, Rex and Clark go back to work. I retreat wordlessly to my room, but I really, really want to not be there. I want to be away from Rex and Clark, and away from all of these nice people we have to fool and the not-nice people like Marvin and Serena.

I change into dark clothes and head through the main area. "I'm going for a walk," I say. "Don't worry, I won't talk to anyone. I don't plan on seeing anybody."

Rex doesn't try to stop me.

I get out of there and I walk around the edge of the ship and toward the back, pretending I'm on my phone, waving when I have to. I climb down some random steps and cross through the dining room, empty aside from a pair of stewardesses setting up the tables.

I finally work my way to the back of the ship where fewer people seem to hang out. I discover a small spiderweb of staircases apparently leading along the outside of the decks like scaffolding, probably used to serve when things are going on.

They're empty now.

I climb up, discovering a small sunny landing, and then I climb up and there's another landing. I reach a small landing just above the fifth deck, the very top of the staircase, and that's where I stop. I'm away from them all as much as I can be. It's just me and the sky and my phone.

I place a call to Jada, willing her to pick up, but she doesn't. It's yoga time, dammit.

"You got this," I whisper to myself, but it seems just trite. I tell myself that I'll do this job well over the next six days and then get away forever. And no way am I cutting his hair ever again. And Amanda won't have to, either. He can hire a new service. After this caper, I'll be through with him for good.

I hate how sad the thought makes me.

I huddle down on the corrugated metal surface, back pressed to the warm hull of the ship, feeling so lonely and really just unlovable. Or more accurately, hateable.

So much for the stupidly positive attitude.

And I can't believe I let him touch me the way I did. And all the while, he thinks I'm this bubble-headed idiot?

There's that saying—*when somebody tells you what they are, you should listen.* I definitely didn't listen to Rex when he told me that he was a jackass over the two years I knew him. And all the papers and magazines told me that, but did I manage to listen?

No.

I saw him as thoughtful and passionate and achingly human

behind that gruff façade. I'd imagined we had a connection. There was playful banter, or at least, that's what I thought it was. And those lingering looks—maybe it was annoyance the whole time.

After more self-berating, I turn my mind to food. I'm thinking of having a lot of desserts, because food therapy definitely works on me. I sit there imagining the desserts I'm going to have and the ways I'll spend the new double bonus when I hear a male voice on the landing below me.

It's Marvin. Even if I didn't recognize his voice, I'd know the top of his head with those sunglasses anywhere.

Grrrrreat.

If he turned and bent backwards, he could see me, I suppose. Or if he decided to come all the way up. I could rush away to the fifth-floor deck from here, but I don't want to draw his attention.

Anyway, he seems to have stopped moving, so I hunch down into the shadows, hugging my knees. Of all the people I don't want to see.

He's involved in some heated conversation, something about funds.

I will him to move on—because the longer it goes on, the more awkward I feel, because it really will seem like I am eavesdropping, and I'm so not. I don't give a shit what happens to all these people and their stupid intrigues. I'm just doing a job.

"She's not giving us a timetable," Marvin says. "I can't ask her again. I don't even know if she's serious about conducting this review or she's just leading me on. We need a little stimulus to get her off her bony ass."

I stiffen because I'm pretty sure he's talking about Gail. I mean, who else?

I listen in earnest now, though it's hard to know what he's talking about. Hard to follow his conversation because it's fast and there are a lot of terms that I don't understand, but one thing he keeps repeating is something about the review numbers and also Bellcore or Bellcorps maybe. "It's time to pull the trigger on Bellcore," he says. "It needs to go down while he's bullish on Bellcore."

Is he talking about Rex?

There's a breeze going, and I don't hear some things, but he's really being intense. And I may be a babbling, soap-opera-obsessed, blue-streaked-hair girl, but even I know when somebody's up to something.

I huddle down even lower, because now I really, really don't want him to know I'm listening.

Anger and triumph heat my body like a righteous fuck-you furnace. Marvin is scheming—full-on scheming!

He's scheming on Gail, and he's quite possibly scheming on Rex. I'm not sure until I hear the phrase "kissing up to her with his fiancée."

My heart pounds a million miles a minute. I *knew* it wasn't a horndog thing! It would serve Rex right for me to not tell him. Better yet, I would tell him, and of course he wouldn't believe me, and then later he would realize his mistake in not believing me.

That would definitely be satisfying, even if I couldn't see his face for the reveal.

But then I think of Gail. Gail has been kind to me. So kind and so supportive, and it has meant a lot. Gail doesn't deserve to be screwed. I sit there considering telling Gail, but would she believe me? She really seems to adore Marvin. Marvin is family.

Or is he?

With a jolt, I remember that my phone is on loud. What if Jada calls back? I reach for it, accidentally scraping my foot along the corrugated metal surface.

I freeze.

Marvin stops talking.

Did he hear me?

I wait, blood racing. The breeze whooshes.

Marvin mumbles something I can't hear. The talking starts up again, tone casual...I think. He's moving though. Is he coming up here? Trying to move to get a better view?

I ease off my sandals and stick the straps in my mouth, then stretch myself low along the warm metal, and then I begin to scuttle away on knees and forearms, trench warfare-style. It's a little crazy, but this whole thing is crazy! I move on, carrying my sandals like a dog, thankful for the many plank poses I sweated through in yoga this year.

When I get to the interior space, I crawl over the rail onto the lower deck and rush down some steps, heart pounding in my throat. I go into the dining room and cut through and head back to our quarters.

Clark and Rex spin around when I yank open the door.

Rex takes one look at my face and stiffens. "What's going on? Is everything okay?"

I close the door and lean back against it, clutching my sandals, taking a moment to compose myself.

"Are you okay?" Clark asks.

I push off the door and strut across the room like I'm the queen of the world. I pour myself a drink and slam it back, just to put them off balance, and also, I'm a little shaky and I just want a drink.

Then I turn, hand planted on my hip, and I smile my most dazzling, most brilliant smile. "'A bubbly stupid girl into soap operas,' they said. 'Stupidly thinks they're profound,' they said."

Rex says, "What's going on, Tabitha?"

"What's going on is that it's *so* like a jerky, rich asshole to mock my female intuition, to mock the most awesome type of show ever, namely, the daytime drama."

"What are you talking about?" Rex asks.

"Tabitha," Clark says.

I'm feeling so strange, standing there. Like I'm on this high mountaintop where I've never been, being totally unlike myself, and I no longer care about being fun. I have very little to lose where Rex is concerned. He hates me. He hates everything about me. You can't turn that around by being fun.

It's…freeing.

"If it wasn't for Gail," I continue, "I wouldn't bother telling you jackasses what I just learned about Bellcore." I fix an eagle eye on Rex. "You *are* bullish on Bellcore, are you not?"

Rex blinks. I suppose market talk like that sounds as weird coming from me as it would coming from a passing whale pod.

"Are you?" I ask. "Strong on it?"

He tilts his head. I hate how I still feel our connection. I hate how his beauty affects me. "Sure," he says.

"Well, there's a plan afoot. It's going down while your position is strong."

Bewilderment transforms Rex's hotness into, well, a bewildered version of his hotness. He and Clark exchange significant glances.

"Where's this coming from?" Rex asks.

"Soap opera 101. When you're sitting around somewhere and somebody who is a totally suspicious character is talking on the phone saying super-suspicious things, announcing yourself is a definite soap opera DON'T. But staying hidden and listening? Total DO. It's a Dorian Lord DO. A Stefano DiMera DO."

"No, I mean, where did you hear it?" Rex asks.

His gravelly voice pulls at something in my groin. I try to wipe away the memory of his lips brushing my ear, his hands inside my bathing suit bottom.

I inspect my drink. It's scotch I'm apparently drinking. I don't usually drink scotch, and now I see why. It's bitter and unpleasant, but I like the idea of it. Maybe it can be my new drink now that I've unleashed my inner bitch. It would be even better if the scotch had been contained in a crystal decanter on a liquor cart in the corner of the room, and I'd poured the scotch from the decanter into a cut crystal lowball glass—then my soap opera bingo card would be complete.

This glassware is smooth, however. Nothing to be done. I swirl the liquid.

The guys are waiting. I should put them out of their misery, but why? Rex hates me. Clark doesn't give a shit. I have nothing to lose.

It's just so freeing.

"This is important," Clark says.

"She knows it's important," Rex says.

I turn my hard gaze back to him. *Too little too late, Sternpants* —that's what my gaze hopefully says at this point and not, *I've only replayed that* Am-I-stern in bed? You-would-be-right *moment twenty-eight times.*

Erp—twenty-nine.

And the knowledge that he's a control freak who keeps his clothes on during sex. I hate that I know that, and also, I hate that it's hot.

"It's Marvin," I say. "Marvin was completely conspiring on the phone with somebody. Which, if you'd paid attention to my soap opera wisdom, wouldn't surprise you all that much."

"What did he say?" Rex asks.

I take a leisurely sip of scotch. The truth is, I'm pretty surprised the soap opera thing came true. I do think most wealthy families have shady things going on, but I didn't expect anything like this. And it's not all that likely that Marvin faked the DNA, but what if? The thought is kind of exciting!

After I feel they have waited long enough, I re-create the conversation best I can. Followed by my dramatic escape, which I recap to sound more stealthy than crab-like, because I still have some pride.

Chapter Thirteen

Rex

I RARELY WORRY about people's feelings. Why should I? People will have their feelings whether I worry about them or not. If I sat around worrying about it, I'd never get anything done.

But Tabitha pissed off? A thing of beauty.

But underneath that, I know there is so much hurt. I really screwed up with that list. So instead of focusing on this potentially serious evidence of a corporate enemy, my mind is spinning on how to fix things with her. How to soothe her feelings, how to apologize.

I'm not sure what to make of my feelings about Tabitha, but they're not hate.

I didn't realize it until she had the list in her hand. Why the hell won't she believe me when I tell her that it's not hate? My mind spins on ways to apologize, how to get her to laugh again. How to get back to us as a team. I loved us as a team. I loved that strange, delicious friction we had.

I tell myself to focus on the important issue at hand. I tell myself that I should feel relieved—our relationship is more clearly defined than ever as the economic transaction that it is: Tabitha fits a job description, she's accepted the job, and she's getting great pay.

"You're sure that's what you heard," Clark says.

She glares at him.

"She wouldn't be saying it if she didn't hear it," I say to him. The fact that Clark asked that shows he doesn't really see how sensitive and perceptive she is. Maybe nobody does. She doesn't make it easy with her bubbles and sparkles. Why? What is she hiding? Or more like, what is she hiding from?

Tabitha glowers at me now. Her gaze cuts to my core, and I can't look away. I don't want to look away. Fun Tabitha is mysteriously compelling, but furious Tabitha is a force of nature, burning with sexy glory, and I want to pull her against me and feel her delicious skin against mine.

"But maybe she misheard," Clark says, skeptical.

"*Pull the trigger on Bellcore* is not a thing you mishear," I say.

"But why would Marvin want to see Bellcore tank?" Clark asks. "Even if he wants us to look bad in the review, we've got Gail heavy into Bellcore, and Gail's his family."

I steeple my fingers. That's the million-dollar question. The portion of Driscoll funds we control is a drop in the bucket for Gail, but it's not nothing. If Bellcore tanks, Gail would lose a lot of money. And we'd look bad for the review.

Tabitha tilts her head and I know what she's thinking—*is* Marvin truly family?

"The fake nephew," I say. "Just say no."

She sniffs angrily. "You're that sure? As I told you before—scratch the surface of any wealthy family and you'll find secrets and subterfuge. That is something that the soap operas teach us and it turns out to be true. A fake DNA test isn't such a stretch anymore, is it?"

"Actually, it's still a stretch," I say. "But Marvin could be in league with a competitor. Any chance you heard any names? Pete Wydover? Randal Ackerman? They'd be the other ones Gail's looking at. They could handle this kind of account."

"No."

"Of course, Marvin may have been talking to Wydover himself," I muse. "It's not as if he'd address him by name."

If anybody would do something shady, it's Wydover.

"Except Gail would've looked at Marvin's connections to people like Wydover once he started agitating for a review," Clark says.

"Exactly, but what if the connection is new?" I say. "Try this on for size—Marvin's related to Gail, but it doesn't get him a payout. It's just not worth much."

"Right," Clark says.

"Marvin's bitter. Because hey, he finds out he's related to a billionaire and it gets him peanuts? Wydover hears about it and approaches Marvin. Wydover tells Marvin that if he, Marvin, can help shake our business loose from Gail, swing it to Wydover, Wydover would give him money."

"It's a lot of legal exposure for Wydover," Clark says, "but then, the account *is* worth millions."

"Wait, what? Millions?" Tabitha says. "People pull way bigger scams for a fraction of that."

"I'm not sold," I say.

"Either way we have to tell Gail," she says. "Marvin's clearly up to something shady."

"No, wait," I say. "Not yet."

"She deserves to know," Tabitha says.

"Of course she does," I say. "But right now it's your word against Marvin's. She likes you, Tabitha, but not enough to take your word over Marvin's."

She frowns. She knows it's true.

"Here's what I'm thinking. We're going to put our investigator on Marvin, look at his financials and associations, see if we can find something Gail's people didn't," I tell her. "We're going to see which of our competitors has been dumping Bellcore, and look at Bellcore itself."

Clark reminds me that he was at a charity golf outing with the Bellcore CEO. We decide Clark should be the one to reach out.

We work up a battle plan.

"Marvin said 'pull the trigger,'" I say. "That suggests a specific negative event to me, considering that Bellcore's flying high right now. Maybe something like bad publicity or sabotage of their upcoming medical device launch. Irregularities in testing. They know where their vulnerabilities are. They need to plug those holes. And keep us in the loop. And get our investigator back on them to make sure they're not hiding something."

Clark's already got his phone. "I'll get the ball rolling on all of these things," he says. "You guys have that charity cocktail hour in twenty. I can blow it off, but you shouldn't."

I swear under my breath. Bad form to miss Gail's charity things.

"Shouldn't you dump the stock before it crashes?" Tabitha asks. "Right? To keep Gail from losing money?"

"I'd rather turn the tables," I say. "I'd rather screw up my competitor's plans to tank the stock and make them look bad. The best defense is an offense."

"Of course you'd say that," Tabitha says.

"Dumping that stock also tips our hand to whoever's targeting us," Clark says. "Not to mention the appearance of insider trading. Rex's idea is best. If somebody's doing something shady, this is our chance to ruin their plans and maybe even expose them."

"If nothing else, we make them look like a fool for offloading a great stock," I say.

Clark goes into my room and shuts the door, giving our guy instructions.

It's just Tabitha and me. And her anger. And her hurt. It's been all I could think about since she saw the list. Sitting there on one conference call after another, wondering where she'd gone, replaying the look of hurt on her face.

"Gail needs to know that Marvin's not an honest person," she says.

"He'll still be dishonest tomorrow."

"I won't wait long," she says.

"You and Gail have a bond," I say. It's something I've come to respect, how easily Tabitha won her over. Would it have killed me to say something?

"So…that cocktail hour now." Her tone is glum. She usually looks forward to being around people.

"Thank you for bringing this to my attention," I say.

"I did it for Gail. And I *am* going to tell her about what I heard at some point." She heads into her room and shuts the door behind her.

I stare after her, unsure what to do for once in my life.

Suddenly the door opens again. She pops her head out. "And newsflash: from now on, I'll be answering to kitten. Because I'm unbelievably cute, but oh my god do I have claws." She shuts the door again. The sound seems to reverberate in my chest.

I need to handle this crisis, but all I want to do is go in after her—and do what? Talk to her? Kiss her? Call her kitten like she asked?

Good luck with that, I think, shoving a hand through my hair. Instead, I go into the room I've been using as a bedroom and check on Clark. He's on top of things, as usual. He's perfectly capable of handling this investigation, possibly more capable than I am at this point.

He gives me an update and leaves me to get ready.

~

TABITHA COMES out in a green cocktail-length gown with gleaming jet buttons down the bodice that match the black shoulder straps. Her thick, dark hair is in a straight style, pulled back into a polished ponytail. She looks strong and statuesque, so goddamn gorgeous I can barely think straight. She really can pull off elegant clothes—far better than any of the haute-couture clothes horses on this yacht.

"You are...stunning," I say.

"Save it for the deck."

"I mean it," I growl. "I'm an asshole, not a liar."

She gives me a dismissive snort.

I straighten. I've never seen this edge of her and I find that I like it. She feels more real, somehow. Usually I cringe inwardly when people reveal hidden facets of themselves—it's all I can do not to beg them to stop for fuck's sake! But with Tabitha, I just want more.

What have I done?

We head out in silence. Just as we emerge onto the cocktail deck, I hover my hand over the small of her back, playing the attentive fiancé without touching her.

This is how it is, now.

We get waylaid by the Wharton grads, and Tabitha leaves and drifts over to a knot of women.

I watch her smile as people talk at me. What would she have worn to this charity cocktail party if she'd been able to pick something from her own closet? What kind of infuriatingly sparkly devil-may-care whirl of color would she have showed up in? Or maybe it would've been something with cats or Hello Kitty. Tabitha will take big-personality outfits over high-fashion elegance any day of the week. Instead she's wearing a dress that a stranger picked out for her, a dress designed to hide who she is.

I watch her discreetly, looking for one of her small rebellions—sparkly nail polish, a quirky dog pendant, the sparkly pink barrette she sometimes wears, but she seems to be a hundred percent in disguise now.

Not that it works—Tabitha's spirit twirls and shines like a disco ball. It used to bug the shit out of me. Fill me with this weird urge to get in her face, to tamp her down.

But now, looking at her, all I can think about is the way she felt in my arms. The little sounds she made. The softness of her skin. The perfect handful of her ass. The way her face softened when she came, lips parted.

She's laughing, now. If I hadn't seen the rage and the devastation in her eyes, I might believe the laughter. She's such a little actress.

Gail chooses this time to come up and stand next to me. Maybe she sees me staring at Tabitha like the madman that I've apparently become. "Watch out for that one. She may just outstrip you," Gail says.

I turn to her. "What do you mean—outstrip?"

"Her ideas for her style storefronts? They're exciting. She could really do this thing."

I blink. She told Gail her business idea instead of me. But then, I didn't exactly ask her.

"She has amazing vision," Gail continues. "I can see how people might underestimate her. But you didn't, did you?"

"There's nobody like her," I say.

I can feel Gail's eyes on me. "I'll admit, I found it unbelievable that you were suddenly engaged like that," she says. "To your hairstylist, of all people. But now I get it."

I want her to say more. I want her to tell me the story of Tabitha and me the way she sees it.

"She likes the term *hairdresser*," I explain. "She told me that when we first met. It's just like her to prefer the quirky, old-fashioned term. It's sometimes used in a belittling way, but Tabitha makes it hers."

Gail seems to like that, but just then, she's pulled away, and I'm back in the hell of my own company.

Of course Tabitha would be amazing at business. But she didn't trust me enough to tell me her idea.

The noise around Tabitha heightens. The girls are making jokes. Tabitha does one of her poses, comically off balance. "Sadface!" she declares.

One of the younger Driscolls does a little pose that's very Tabitha-ish and says, "Shockface!"

Washington and his friend have gravitated back over to talk currency plays. It's good to pay attention to the younger guys—especially this Washington kid; he could be somebody someday, but I'm only half there. I'm inexplicably desperate to…I don't know what. Run ten miles. Flip a few tables. Turn the world inside out.

Or maybe just get back to that place where Tabitha's staring up at me, drugged with pleasure. And our hands are on each other, and it's almost as if we're breathing together.

I need to win her back, but it's too late.

Or is it? I've done the impossible before. I crawled out of that shithole bar I grew up in. I avoided making every mistake my parents made. I earned a billion dollars without having set foot in college and beat out rivals who had every advantage over me.

I can win back Tabitha's affection. I have to. For once I'm on fire with a goal that has nothing to do with my carefully mapped-out business objectives. But right now it's the only goal I care about.

I'm thinking about something she said before—how people in relationships bond by being enthusiastic about things the other person enjoys. I can do that.

I watch her, thinking about what she enjoys. Hello Kitty

stuff. Soap opera intrigues. Hair and fashion. Animals. The color pink. Sparkles and sweets.

I decide to go for the low-hanging fruit first—sweets. A small peace offering in the form of one of those foofy pink drinks she likes. I take my leave of my acolytes and head to the bar. Unfortunately, it's a new bartender who doesn't remember the concoction Tabitha's been drinking on the trip.

"Just make something really special, with cherries and whatever else. Pink and sweet. No straw," I add, because she always remembers to say that.

He whips it up, and I head over to her with it. A few more people are around her including Gail herself. Good.

I walk up, taking care not to touch her or startle her in any way, because she is mad, after all. "Kitten," I say. "I took the liberty of ordering you your favorite."

She blinks at the drink. "Thank you," she says, taking it, sounding pleasantly surprised.

One of the guys groans. "What is that?"

Tabitha smiles, because sweet pink shit is her jam. "Something delicious," she says.

Warmth ripples through my chest. Success is about knowing what people want and delivering. So few people get that.

She takes a sip and swallows. I watch the progress of it down her smooth throat, imagining her feeling grateful, thinking again about how she felt against that door.

She looks up at me with a slight pink moustache above her upper lip. She plasters on a smile and says, "Mmm."

My belly twists. She's fooling these people, but she isn't fooling me—she hates it, and she's trying her best to hide it.

I messed this up. Royally.

She schools her features and beams at me, ever the pro.

"You're actually gonna drink that?" one of the men asks. Even Gail's attention is on us now.

"Of course!" she exclaims. She has no choice—it'll look weird if her fiancé didn't even get her drink right. I said it was her favorite, after all. Wouldn't I know?

They groan and watch her, waiting for her to drink it. Somebody calls it disgusting.

I take it from her hands. "Don't knock it 'til you try it, guys. These things are great."

Her eyes widen as I take a swig. God, it's terrible. Sickly sweet. "Hey!" she says.

"What?" I say, drinking more of it, feeling her amazed gaze. Amazed I'm taking this bullet.

God, what kind of man does she think I am? The kind of man to let a woman pay for my mistake? That's not me.

I'm all-out chugging it now, faster and faster, sucking it down, trying to let it bypass my taste buds, though that is definitely not working. If I survive the sugar coma I get from this, I might go over and strangle that bartender. Finally the glass is empty. People are laughing, groaning.

I'm just trying not to vomit all over the beautifully polished cedar planking. "Let's get you another," I say, heading off toward the bar.

She catches up. "I could've drunk it."

"The only one who falls on my sword is me," I say.

She gives me a suspicious look.

The bartender is nowhere to be seen, but Gail's up front, starting her talk.

We move back a bit, as other people crowd forward. It's some kind of childhood disease prevention charity. I already had my guy in New York wire over a donation, but I like to look like I actually care.

Gail drones on.

The pink-drink thing was a disaster, but it was the right idea. There are other things Tabitha is into that I can show an interest in. I run back through the list again. Hair. Sparkle shit. Hello Kitty. Then I hit it.

I lean in. "Question," I whisper.

"What now?" she sighs.

What now? I don't know why the re-appearance of her sassy attitude should please me. I tamp down my reaction and lean in. "What would Stefano DiMera do?" I whisper under my breath. "About Marvin?"

"Oh, please."

"What? I'm really asking. Given this circumstance, him scheming like you think, would he say *'screw it all'* and tell Gail? Or would he investigate the enemy? Figure out the play and hit back?"

"I won't be patronized by you," she says. "I hate when people patronize me."

I grab a glass of champagne for each of us from a passing tray. The speakers are changing. Now it's one of the daughters. I'm grateful we're in the back.

"I'm allowed alcoholic drinks, now?" she asks. "Or are you going two-fisted?"

"For you. It's probably excellent," I say.

"I do like a nice glass of bubbly."

"Take it."

Our fingers brush as she takes it, a small sizzle that burns. She averts her gaze from mine, watches the daughter talk as she sips. Did she feel it, too? The forbidden heat of our connection?

It drives me crazy that I can't read her right now. It drives me crazy that she isn't wearing any of her secret little Tabitha things. She's everything that drives me crazy, and everything that I ragingly, infuriatingly, frustratingly want.

"You think you can get me drunk and find out what Stefano DiMera would do?"

"Can I?" I ask, settling two fingers on the small of her back. "Would it work? Would you tell?"

She rolls her eyes. "Screw off."

Now I need to know what kind of drunk she is. Is she a happy drunk? A reveal-all drunk? A reckless drunk? Who is she when she's rid of her inhibitions?

"It won't work because you don't deserve to know," she says.

"Maybe it's not either of those things. Maybe he wouldn't investigate the company *or* tell Gail."

She's shaking her head. Refusing to tell me, but I know she wants to.

Eventually, the presentation is over. Or I'm hoping it is. This could just be a break. I'm keenly aware of Marvin's gaze drifting over to us from his place at Gail's side. "You see that? Him watching us?" I ask her.

She levels her gaze at me. Meaning *yes*.

A few of our fellow cruise prisoners drift by, telling her about the whale pod sighting. Everybody is very excited about it.

Tabitha folds her arms over her chest when they leave. "Alas, I was in our suite banging you all day."

"And you're so grateful," I rumble. "It was so much better than a whale pod."

She shakes her head. "I'm afraid the whale pod would've been better," she sighs. "Frankly, a lone little mackerel would've exceeded it."

"Trust me, it's far more impressive than a mackerel," I say. "Even a very large mackerel."

She rolls her eyes.

"Though the most apt comparison would be python," I continue, enjoying her smile. "A large adult male python."

"*Pul*-ease," she whispers. "You are so full of yourself.

Anyway, I thought you kept your clothes on during our sexy times. For your power play."

I glance toward the front. "He's watching us again," I mumble.

She stares into my eyes—it's her fake lover's gaze, but even so, it connects to my groin. "Of course he is. Scammers have a special radar for each other. They have scam-dar."

"We're not scamming."

"We *are* a scam," she says.

Ouch.

Commotion up front. Children are lining up along the rail against the backdrop of the sea and sky. They begin to sing a sad song. Even that doesn't cut my raging libido.

I lean in, lips hovering over the shell of her ear. "God save us from songs sung by other people's children."

She sucks in a breath, trying not to smile.

"Where is a giant, annoyingly loud gong when you need one?" I add.

"Don't you dare make me laugh," she breathes. "They'll think I'm laughing at the song!"

They sing an even sadder verse. A sweet and tender verse that pulls at the heartstrings.

"*Gonggggg,*" I whisper.

"Oh my god," she breathes.

The song goes on. I press my hand to the small of her back, guide us to the side and back even further, back behind some people and a large winch-type thing.

She leans back against the rail.

I twist up a lock of hair with my finger. "You never answered my question about Stefano DiMera."

"And I won't."

I tug a bit on the hair. "Tell me what Stefano DiMera would do."

She slides her glare to me. Heat kicks up between us. She likes the tug.

I go a little harder. "Tell me, kitten."

A vague smile plays upon her lips. "*Now* you call me kitten."

"Would he try to prove Marvin's an imposter?" I ask playfully. "Is that it? Would he sneak up and cut some of Marvin's hair?"

"I thought the great Rex O'Rourke decided the fake nephew angle is ridiculous," she says.

I shrug. Tabitha enjoys soap-opera-style intrigue, so I'm officially enthusiastic about it now. Me and my caveman lizard brain are both very enthusiastic. My lips hover over her ear. "Tell me."

"Shut it. The children are singing." There's that edge again, and something in me heats. She cares about the job; she'll do the job, but she doesn't care about being agreeable to me. It's intoxicating. This is the real Tabitha, giving as good as she gets.

The children have broken into some sort of dance and they're making people join. We back up, as if guided by a single survival impulse. We end up in a shady nook near a service stairway. Hopefully out of the view of the children.

"Come on, tell me," I say. "That's what he'd do, right? He'd sneak up and cut off a bit of Marvin's hair for testing?"

Tabitha shakes her head, disgusted. But I know she wants to tell—I can see it all over her face, and it makes me want her even more.

"He wouldn't get his hair tested?" I continue. "Secretly snip some off and send it to a lab?"

"Uh! Stop, please!"

"What?"

She lets out an exasperated huff. "*Snip his hair.*" This like it's the stupidest thing ever.

"Why not?"

"Fine! Yes! He'd be all over the testing," she says. "But unlike you, Stefano DiMera would know that you can't do a DNA test on cut hair. He would know that you need five to ten full hairs with the bulbs intact for a maternity DNA test."

I lean in close enough to nuzzle her hair. "How would Stefano get those hairs?"

She bites her lower lip. She doesn't want to answer, yet she really, really does, because she loves the soap opera shit. This shouldn't be hot. But it is. "He'd find a way to get back into that salon spa area," she finally says.

"I thought cut hair doesn't work."

"It doesn't, but I combed Marvin's hair out, and a lot of hairs fall from simple combing. You lose up to a hundred hairs a day, and a comb tends to collect the ones that you've lost naturally but are still clinging on to your hair. Stefano would look for that comb." She's energized. Coming alive. "He'd hope the room and the styling tools haven't been cleaned."

"Let's do it," I say.

She turns to me now, gaze sharp. "You think the theory is bullshit."

I shrug. "What do I know? Let's get the hairs."

"Why the sudden change of heart?"

"Why not cover our bases?" I say. But really, I want more of her, any way I can get her.

"You need to send them to a lab," she says. "Gail has a lot of bells and whistles on this yacht, but I doubt she has a DNA testing lab onboard. And how awkward would it be to ask?"

"We're docking at St. Herve soon. All of these little islands have FedEx outposts."

She's intrigued. "You think this is gonna get me to not be mad at you for the list thing? Is that what's going on here? Because that is a no-go."

"All I'm saying is, why not cover all the bases?"

She doesn't want to love this idea, but she does. "Really?"

"Yeah. Let's rule this fake DNA thing out. I'm thinking Stefano would have done it yesterday. He would've trotted right up to that salon and searched it."

She licks her lips, and my cock is instantly hard. She's so hot when she's tempted. "On what pretext?"

I lower my voice. "Do soap opera villains need pretexts?"

"Soap opera villains always think of clever pretexts," she says.

"There's no need for a pretext if we just sneak into the salon."

Her eyes widen minutely. She wants this. And I want her. It's all wrong. And I can't stop.

"Right now. Let's go," I say.

"You're playing me."

"Don't you want to get the hairs tested? Nobody's watching us," I say. "This is our chance."

"You mean it?" She really wants me to mean it.

My heart bangs out of my chest, imagining getting her alone, away, all to myself. Us as a team again. "When I say a thing, I do it, kitten."

"Wow," she whispers. She's about to yield. It's delicious. She's delicious.

"You ready?" I say.

A slow smile spreads over her face. "The room is probably cleaned by now, but why not? It's worth a try," she says.

Chapter Fourteen

Rex

WE SLIP AWAY and cross through to the back of the ship, and up to the fourth level where there's a small lounge, and behind that, a weight room, a yoga room, and—at the very end of a corridor—the spa area.

We find the door unlocked and slip in. The main room is a beauty salon crossed with a jungle, hushed and quiet now except for the sound of water from unseen fountains.

I narrow my gaze at the strange glow from the rooms beyond. "Is this where they keep the ship's nuclear waste?" I whisper.

She puts on her playful annoyed face. "It's *salt lamps*. The massage rooms have salt lamps."

"Salt lamps," I say.

"They're good for you." She points at the partially open door. "Keep watch."

I go over and stand guard, keeping an eye on the hallway while she yanks open drawers and pulls out brushes and combs. I haven't snuck around like this since I was a kid back in South Boston. Though usually that was about self-preservation. About staying out of the way of gangs. Serious shit.

Drawers open and close. Utensils clink. Garbage pail lids clank softly. Finally there's a loud sigh, and I turn, struck again by how sexy she is, softly lit in the strange jungle-glow environment of the salon.

"The good news is that this is a full-service yacht where they clean things thoroughly after every use. The bad news…" She tosses a comb back into the drawer.

"Clean?"

She nods.

I wish suddenly that she'd found some hair, just because she so wanted it. We could've FedExed it to a lab. Useless waste of time as it would be, I want it for her. I go in now to where she's standing. "*Now* what would Stefano DiMera do?" I ask.

A sly smile. "You don't want to *know* what Stefano would do."

"Oh, I do." I slide a hand over the mass of hair that's caught up in her long ponytail, sliding it around so that it hangs over one shoulder.

Her breath quickens.

The energy between us runs thick and hot.

I slide a finger down the outside of her bare arm, shoulder to her wrist, slow and steady. "Tell me," I rasp. "Tell me what Stefano would do."

Her voice is barely a whisper. "Are you trying to distract me from the list? Is that what this is all about?"

"Kitten," I say, conscious of the heat of her skin, conscious of the fact that we're alone in this forbidden space where nobody will bother us. "I could think of far better ways than this to distract you from the list."

"Yeah, *now* you act interested in my theories. Now that I found the hate list."

Hoarsely, I say, "It's not a hate list."

She snorts, smoothing it over with humor, but the list wasn't funny. I hate that she found it. I hate that I wrote it. Why did I write it?

"So what next?" I slide my finger back up again, tracing a hot trail over her silky skin.

Her breath stutters.

The familiar tug in my groin intensifies.

"You're really on board with checking this thing out?" She looks up. Her gaze is dark, charged with lust. "Just to rule out the fake nephew possibility?"

I move closer to her, overwhelmed by my need for her and by the feeling that she wants me just as badly, in spite of everything.

Our chemistry runs thick and hot.

Her breath brushes my chin, my lips.

All available blood in my body rushes furiously southward, straight into my iron-hard cock—leaving my brain without sense.

That's the only explanation I can think of for my answer to her question of whether I'm on board with the fake nephew possibility. My very boneheaded answer.

"I don't know that I'd go so far as to call it a *possibility*," I say.

Her lips part, as if in shock. "Wait, what?" A furrow appears between her brows in the split second before she steps away. "Not a possibility? So what are you doing here, then?"

"Uh," I begin, regretting my words.

"What?" she asks. "You're just humoring me? Is that it? Humoring ol' bubble-headed Tabitha?"

"Well," I stammer, "maybe it's not *completely* impossible…"

"Not *completely* impossible? A UFO attack isn't completely impossible. Oh my god, you *are* just patronizing me! God, were you laughing at me the whole time?"

"I wasn't laughing at you," I say. "You have to admit, it's not the sanest idea ever—"

"Not the sanest? You *were* laughing at me. Like I'm this idiot? But then again, pathetically impoverished people with stupidly positive attitudes will believe most anything. How many ways can you be a complete asshole?"

"Tab—"

"Uhh!" She shoves me away. "You're such a pompous, self-obsessed hornbag."

"C'mon—"

"I don't need to be humored. I don't need to be patronized and made a fool of—"

"That's not what this is. I wanted to do something with you."

"You wanted to do something with me—yeah. I think I figured out that part."

"I didn't mean like that. It's something you're interested in. I care about what you're interested in—I do, and…" A flash of color in the corner of my eye halts my train of thought. My attention rivets to the far mirror just in time to see Marvin sneak up and flatten himself up against the hall wall outside the door.

Marvin. Hiding. Listening.

Spying on us.

What. The. Fuck.

My pulse races.

"What's wrong? Am I boring you now?" she demands.

I settle my hands onto her shoulders, giving her a significant look. "You could never bore me," I gust out as I maneuver her out of the sightline of the mirror—and Marvin—and push her against the wall.

Her eyes shine. "*This* is where you think this is going?"

Into her ear, I whisper, "Marvin's out there. Spying on us."

Saw him in the mirror." I point with a tip of my chin, watch her expression as she processes it. Blinking.

If I hadn't insulted her so deeply, she'd probably be a lot more excited by this strange new turn of events. And what is up with Marvin? Why would Marvin follow us? Why would he feel the need to watch us? Watching her, I get. But spying on us together?

She bites her bottom lip. I can practically see the gears turning in her head. Just what she needs—more fuel for her theory. She'd probably say he's worried we're onto him, and wants to see whether we're trying to find DNA.

But why *would* he follow us? Is he worried about us in some way?

I draw closer, lips grazing the shell of her ear. "Could he have seen you?" I whisper. "You know, while he was on the phone? Could he have figured out that you overheard?"

She frowns. Angry. I *was* patronizing her, but right now she needs to get over it.

"What do you think?" I add.

"He kept talking," she whispers back. "Why keep talking if he saw me?"

"Maybe he heard something and dismissed it," I whisper back, "but now he's wondering if it was something. Maybe he caught a flash of color and he's remembering back to what you wore. Or he thinks back and realizes that flash of chocolate could be your hair."

She seems to consider this. "Mmmm," she says under her breath. "It *is* true that my hair is a beautiful chocolaty brown."

"Be serious," I whisper. "Think back."

"He *did* seem to move his head to look up in my direction at one point," she mumbles softly. "I mean, I could only see the top of his head."

I cage her with my arms. "Why follow us here? I mean, the *salon?*" I breathe. That's the part that doesn't make sense. "Is he trying to find…proof we're fake? But it's not as if we're going to sneak in here to have a conversation about how fake our engagement is."

She whispers, "What could it be that my loving future husband just bullheadedly refuses to see? What could the reason be?"

I hear a soft scratching, like a watch rubbing lightly along a wall or a doorframe, there and gone. Is Marvin moving closer?

I put my lips to her ear. "Don't mess this up," I warn. "Act romantic."

Softly, she says, "I don't see my character going romantic in this scenario."

I level my gaze at Tabitha. "Do your job," I grumble.

She frowns.

"You're so hot when you're annoyed," I try, cajoling her into playing along. Also, it's true—she's hot when she's annoyed. She's hot all the time. I've never met a woman who's so fucking compelling, though that's not the right word, exactly. She drives me crazy, though that's not precisely it, either. "You know you are."

She rolls her eyes. She thinks I'm patronizing her again. I'm not. She's hot all the time. I've always felt it, I realize. All those Friday nights in my office.

"Kitten," I say in the commanding tone I use when I want my people to shape up. I whisper into her ear, "Marvin is out there listening. Play. Along. Play your role."

She does her one-eyed squint. "Mmmm. Do that again," she says.

I lean in, caging her with my arms. "Be more convincing," I whisper.

"Mmmm," she says. The *Mmmm* is more convincing, at least.

"You like that?" I rumble.

"Umm…*somewhat*," she says, more loudly.

I narrow my eyes. Lower my voice. "I think you love it. I can tell you love it."

"No, actually that does nothing for me," she says, eyes sparkling with mischief. "Try a different thing. Something less...mechanical."

I give her a stern look, and she bites her lip. Does she think that was a funny thing to say? I show her with my scowl that I do not think it was funny. I lean in, whisper into her ear, "Don't mess this up."

When I pull back, she has a dangerous light in her eyes. Breathily, she says, "Yes, Captain Sternpants."

I growl and put a finger to her lips. Marvin would've heard that one, too. *Captain Sternpants.* Great. He'll think that's her name for me now.

"Mmmm," she says, all sexy, but there's laughter in her eyes.

That scraping noise again. Is Marvin moving closer?

"Well," she says, grabbing my finger and pulling it away, speaking loudly enough for anyone to hear, "I have to level with you, honey—sometimes when you wear the squirrel outfit and want me to pet the tail? While you make those chittering noises? That's not working for me. I've been meaning to request that we don't do that particular role-play game anymore."

It takes a moment to process what she just said.

"I grant you it might be sexy to some people," she continues.

Quickly I slap my hand over her mouth. She's snorting silently beneath my hand. Her chest heaves, now—she's all-out laughing, or would be if I didn't have my hand there.

"Not funny," I grumble into her ear.

Her chest keeps convulsing. She clearly thinks it's hilarious. Her mouth is warm under my palm.

Again I growl. Just a growl.

She grabs one of my fingers and tears my hand from her mouth. "If you want to role-play, maybe something more conventional than squirrel and zookeeper? Might I suggest teacher and student—"

I clap my hand back over her mouth just in time. She's shaking with suppressed laughter.

"I'm glad you're entertaining yourself," I whisper, pressing her harder to the wall, lips warm under my palm.

She's still laughing.

"Stop," I whisper.

She doesn't stop.

Again I lean in, close to her ear. "What happens if I take away my hand? Will you keep laughing? Are you gonna be a problem?"

She nods her head yes. She'll keep laughing. I wouldn't expect anything less.

She's breathing hard, watching me with those goddamn laughing eyes. Fox brown. Rich like velvet. "Fuck," I hiss.

Her skin is warm under my harsh grip. Soft breaths heave in and out her nostrils.

I'm pressing her hard against the wall, hand mercilessly sealing her mouth.

And suddenly it's hot.

It's wrong that it's hot, me holding her captive like this, but goddamn, my cock has never been harder.

She gives me a smoldering look. She feels it, too.

"Are you gonna be a problem?" I rumble into her ear.

There's something new in her stare, now: Heat. Challenge. Lust, dark with need. She's never been hotter.

"Are you gonna be a problem if I take away my hand?" I ask again.

Her nostrils flare. Warm breath caresses my fingers.

"Well?" I grate out.

She nods. *Yes.* She'll be a problem if I take away my hand. She's going to be a problem. It's so Tabitha.

I should be angry, but I'm not. I never could be—not really.

I was anything but angry, all those Friday nights, just us in my office above the world. Anything but annoyed.

How did I get us so wrong?

Sitting there soaking in the closeness of her body, the feel of her bright spirit lighting the corners of my dark world. The way she'd tunnel her fingers into my hair, massaging my scalp; her careful *snip-snip-snip*; the way she'd brush my beard with the backs of her knuckles.

The friction of us—her bright chatter against the hard stone of my heart.

Fuck. This woman.

I breathe in her bright berry scent, let it surge through me. Fire licks up my skin.

Her gaze glows, bright with desire.

I want her so badly, I'm burning up.

"You and that smart mouth," I bite out.

And then I remember Marvin. Is he still out there? Because this isn't for Marvin. None of this is for Marvin.

"Not here," I whisper as I unseal her mouth. She looks surprised—maybe it's my raw tone. She likes everything to be fun and jokey with a bright surface, and I'm not playing—not anymore.

I pick her up and haul her right over my shoulder.

She lets out a small shriek as I carry her through the spa room, on through a darkened door, and into the massage area, dimly lit by the glowing globs of salt.

I kick the door closed and put her down on the table.

"Why, Rex!" she says in a husky tone. "The brutish thing is working for me."

The fingers of my free hand find the top button of her

bodice and flick it open. Then the next. My knuckles brush her chest as her dress falls open to me, skin igniting skin. I can barely think; I just need to be in her, deep and hard.

"Wow," she pants, grabbing the top of my belt and pulling me to her, fitting me flush against her. She wraps her legs around me and I give her what she wants, pressing into her hard, now, pressing my shaft in between her legs, right through the fabric of her cocktail dress.

"Come here," I rumble.

"Ngggg," she says.

Flames lick up my core. I'm kissing the side of her neck, yanking free the rest of the buttons.

"Look at you," I whisper, sliding my fingers around the edges of her bra, dark, hungry travelers encountering smooth, warm flesh.

"You think Marvin's still…"

"To hell with Marvin," I say, climbing up onto the table, looming over her, pushing her dress up, uncovering miles of sexy leg, and then stockings that end at her thigh, held up with straps. I go on to discover the barest wisp of a thong. "Good god," I groan.

She slides an appreciative hand over my chest. "What if he runs and tells—"

She trails off as I push her legs apart. I kiss the inside of her right thigh, then the inside of her left thigh, and then the damp scrap of fabric between. "Let him tell on us," I rumble into her core.

She squirms with pleasure, pulling me closer.

I grab her thighs and press them wide, feeling the energy thrum through her.

"Tabitha, Tabitha, Tabitha." I kiss her again, letting the scent of her arousal wash over me. "Need this."

She sucks in a sharp breath in response to my blunt statement. Tabitha is a bright, colorful fish who stays in the playful sunny surface water, mistrustful of things that run deeper.

I graze the edge of my teeth over her silk-clad folds, dizzy from the scent of her, from her strangled sounds of pleasure. Lost in her. I grab the pussy-protecting panel of her panties and yank it aside, baring her folds to the dim glow of the room.

I'm feeling out of control. I usually wouldn't be showing this to a woman. I usually wouldn't be feeling this for a woman.

Her hips rise, needy in the dim glow of the room.

I give her a lick and she gasps softly. "I want to make you feel good…" I tend to be a good dirty-talker, but I only want honesty now.

I lick her again.

Her whole body seems to undulate in response. A wave of feeling.

I nearly lose it right there.

I do her with merciless precision, so in tune with her. I can feel her in a way that's new for me. I flick my tongue over her needy bud as she devolves into a whimpering mess. She comes softly, all breathy whimpers.

Her orgasm stretches on until she's a sweaty, hard-breathing, chest-heaving confection of soft, warm curves, so Tabitha.

Usually I'm racing to be inside of a woman at this point, to give my cock the thing it most deeply desires in life—the sweet, sure plunge into a warm, wet pussy.

But I don't race to fuck her. That's not what this is about. I find myself sliding my hands over her hips. I can't believe how good she feels.

"What's up, dawg?" she jokes, keeping it light.

"Take it off," I rasp. "Off."

She grins and pulls her dress over her head, pulls off her bra, dramatic and jokey, but I'm not playing.

Her features look soft in the salt lamp's glow. Her breasts

are lush and full, nipples wide and dark with an in-your-face attitude, just like Tabitha. Nobody is like Tabitha.

The curls between her legs are damp, and I fall to kissing them. There's only her breath, her body, her quivering electric energy. I press my cheek to the soft pillow of her belly and splay my hands over her hips, holding her.

She shoves her hands into my hair, fingers grazing my scalp. The sweetness of her touch washes over me. It's so good, I have to close my eyes.

It's not about fucking her now. I just need her on a primal level. I need to be against her.

I move over her, drinking her with my lips, and then I turn my head and drink her with my cheek, letting my beard rasp across her skin.

She grabs my hair and pulls up my head now, looking me in the eyes. "Do I need to change your name to Captain Seri-ouspants? Captain Von Heartfelt-Dramapants?"

I growl and rise up out of her grip. I get off the table and I pull off my pants.

She reaches out and touches me. "Rex," she whispers. "If every cock looked like that, I might actually enjoy getting dick pics. I might frame them and hang them up on the wall."

I frown at the idea of other guys sending her dick pics. My fingers move to my shirt buttons, undoing them one after another.

"What are you doing?"

"Taking off my shirt."

"I thought you always fuck with your clothes on," she says.

"I usually do," I say, moving to another button. I need my skin to be against her skin. It's all I know.

"Then why are you unbuttoning it?" she asks. "How will you retain your crown as the world's ultimate control freak if you don't keep the shirt on?"

She's going for a light tone, but there's urgency in her

voice, like maybe she wants me to wake up out of this trance I've gotten into, to get back to my shallow player's moves, back to the safety of life's bright surface where everything is just a bubble from a pink wand.

"I want my shirt off, that's why," I say.

"Umm…serious much?" She sits up on the edge of the table, now, legs dangling over the side. She tries for one of her funny expressions, head cocked to the side. Slightly accusatory.

She's accusing me of breaking our rules by taking my shirt off. She wants me to bring the moves that I bring to my faceless lovers.

No fucking way.

I start on my cuffs. "It's different with us. Don't you feel it?" I say. My voice sounds rough, as though it's coming from somewhere new. It's unlike me to ask a question I don't know the answer to. *Don't you feel it?*

Does she?

"Earth to world-domination control freak," she tries.

"I need to feel you," I say.

She blinks, taking in my words. She glides a finger along my forearm. "Control freak, you're breaking up."

I muscle off the rest of my shirt, weary of the fucking buttons. Plastic pings on marble tile. "I don't care if I'm breaking up."

"Fuck," she gusts out, gazing at my chest. Her hands press a path over my heart, my muscles. Exploring me, hungrily, as if she can't stop herself.

I like that she can't stop herself from touching me.

"What are you doing, Rex?" she demands, angry.

She's angry at me for dragging her away from the jokes and the brightness, even as she responds to the pull of us.

"I want to feel you," I say. And then I fist her hair and take her mouth in a rough kiss.

"Mmm!" she hums, holding me off with humor even as she gives into the kiss.

I give everything to the kiss. No more games.

I can feel it when she changes.

Something in her softens, like her hard candy shell melting under the hot brand of my hands.

She makes a squeak of surrender, and that's it. She's responding with savage intensity—clinging to me, clawing at me. The rules are gone; there's just this need between us.

"Tabitha," I breathe.

She clamps her legs around me with a force that surprises me. Her fingers dig into my back, ferocious nails, fierce and hard, giving in.

There's no playful effervescence here—nothing to distract from the real girl, hungry and true.

It's everything. I kiss her. I lay her down on the massage table, consuming her.

"Tell me you have a condom," she grates. "Oh my god, tell me, please, please, please."

I roll over and grab my wallet from my pants pocket.

When I look back down, there's a rawness to her, like her heart's gone ragged.

She's never let me see that.

I slide on the condom with jerky movements. I get up on the table and crawl over her, panting. I shove apart her legs and position myself at her entrance.

"Please, Rex, please," she hisses. "Please, please, please."

"I got you." I press into her slowly. She's warm. Tight. Perfect. I groan out, blown away by how amazing she feels—and I'm barely in.

"More," she says.

I move into her velvet warmth, trying to hold back. "…don't want to hurt you."

"Just give me everything. Give me everything, Rex."

She lifts her hips, urging me in.

With that, all of my restraint goes offline. I dig my fingers into her hips, take her with one wicked thrust. She lets out a hiss of pleasure.

We're a blind, desperate tangle of hungry limbs.

I thrust into her, strong and sure, making certain to hit the spot she needs me to hit, quickly finding the rhythm she responds to.

Heat rushes through my veins.

Her groans of ecstasy fill my ears.

"Rex, Rex, Rex..." she rasps. I capture my name with a kiss. The feeling of her, needy and dark, it's almost too much.

I fuck her and kiss her. I press my forehead to hers, not wanting her to see my eyes. I'm not used to this level of intimacy.

"You're perfect," I hiss as I thrust into her.

Chapter Fifteen

Tabitha

LIKE A TRAITOR, my body arches up to meet his, to increase the intensity of us. Needing him and loving him, in spite of where that leads.

He's my terrifying new addiction, filling my ache, grinding against me deliciously. I pull him close as he thrusts into me.

His bare chest, all muscles and unforgiving contours and that harsh smattering of chest hair—something more that he shows only to me. I can't get enough of it, of him.

I press up to him, letting his chest rub roughly along my tender breasts. I want to feel his abrasion against my soul.

He slows, going more and more slowly until he stops.

His gaze invades mine.

My breath hitches. I can't look away—this is what he does to me. I raise a shaking hand to his beard. "Why did you stop?"

He doesn't reply. He's looking into me, piercing my defenses. He grabs my ass cheeks and grinds more slowly, circling against me now, watching me.

I'm trembling with pleasure.

His eyes crinkle. We know each other's minds now, and he knows he's making it good, but in my strange world right now, that is very, very bad.

He buries his growly, beautiful face in my neck. I tense against the pleasure of him wanting me, the bliss before the heartbreak.

He's moving on me slowly, like he wants to conjure an orgasm right up out of the electric space between us.

Which he definitely will if current trends hold.

"Rex," I say.

He says nothing. Him and his chest and his beard and his whole Rex way of being say nothing and everything.

"Rex, Rex, Rex," I chant. I'm acutely alive, but that's what they always say about people during a disaster.

The way he's making me feel is beyond anything I'd ever imagined, cutting his hair all those Friday nights, staring at the smooth hidden skin on the back of his neck, breathing in his spicy scent, listening to him bite out all of those speakerphone commands to unseen minions.

It's beyond anything I'd imagined even getting myself off in bed at night, his face in my mind's eye—my forbidden client.

Careful what you wish for.

He's dragging me deep.

I promise myself I'll stop with him after this. I'll shut the lid on this Pandora's box after.

He pushes himself up over me, gaze heavy on my face, my neck, my breasts.

I look down, and with a rush of pleasure, I notice that my breasts are pink from him. The pink is a badge of him on my skin. Maybe this is what makes him lose control, this badge of him on me, but he's sinking into me, shuddering into me, hard and fast and beasty.

"Yes," I gasp. He's fucking me with a primal force that makes my pussy ache, and I just want more.

Flesh slaps against flesh.

Heat blooms under my skin.

Pleasure coils up my body and finally explodes in my brain. The blaze behind my eyes matches the wild, orgasmic pleasure raging in my body.

He presses into me one final time; I can feel his cock pulsing inside me. He sucks in a breath, hot and sharp, lost like me.

His expression twists with agonized pleasure. Coal-dark eyelashes in a tight line.

He cries out and then collapses against me.

We're both panting.

All those months of crushing on him. The charged moments, the feeling of connection. I never thought it could be like this. The goodness of us together is dangerous.

It was just sex, I think. *It doesn't have to mean anything.*

A lie.

He props his head on his hand and gazes down at me with this baffled affection. He's looking at me like he never saw me before.

He's looking at me lovingly, but still in his surly Rex way.

Which just makes my heart swell more.

Mr. Hate list. Mr. Don't-date-a-woman-twice. This is who I choose to fall for.

"Don't look at me like that," I say.

"Like what?" he asks. "Like that wasn't incredible?"

"God! Stop talking." I push him off. "Stop ruining it."

"You know I'm right," he growls.

"You need to stop talking," I say, grabbing my bra. "That was fun, and now you're just so ruining it by taking it seriously." I clasp it with trembling fingers. Frightened. Hating my own cowardice.

"It was more than fun," he says.

"Whatever you say, Captain Von Heartfelt-Dramapants." I straighten my dress. "Also?" I say. "I can't believe you were letting me think you were into the DNA thing." I hit his arm.

"What?" he demands.

"What? I'll tell you what. You acting like you're going along with this whole thing to patronize me. Do you think that just because we had sex that I'm going to forget about that?"

He glares. He doesn't want to talk about Marvin.

"Magnificent as it is, your peen does not have mind-erasing powers," I add.

I can see right when he gives up on being serious with me —at least for the time being. He cocks his head. "It is magnificent," he says. "I hear it's the best possible dick pic."

I grin and hit his shoulder again. "Winning me over with hot sex doesn't work."

He looks thoughtful. "It was...*very* hot."

I give him a warning look. I'm not having it.

Into my ear, he rumbles, "Squirrel and zookeeper? I should put you over my knee right now."

I snort. "Sorry."

He says, "I don't give a shit what Marvin thinks. I don't care if he thinks I style myself as a sex-squirrel or a sex-penguin or a giant sex-clown with a big red nose."

"Did you really have to put that sex-clown image into my head?"

"Do I have to fuck it out of you?"

My pulse races. *Yes, please.*

He's right, of course. It was hot. So hot.

A little voice inside me says, *Soooo hot, and it will be even hotter next time!*

The little voice wants to know: *what's the harm of vacation sex? You're fake fiancés on a yacht for a few more days and then it's over. What's the harm?*

I like the little voice. When I eat one piece of English toffee and then stick the container way up high in the cupboard, it's that little voice that says, *why not get another piece? Just one more, and then you'll put it right back up there.*

"What?" Rex is watching me. "What are you thinking?"

"About English toffee," I say.

He frowns.

"Marvin was pretty interested in what we were up to, don't you think?" I say. "Can you deny the weirdness now?"

Rex brushes a strand of hair off my face. "I can't deny it," he says. "Why the hell is he following us around? Why follow us to this area? If he wants to eavesdrop on a business conversation, Clark and I are the ones who are running things. A man who's after a woman doesn't typically spy on her when she's with a guy. He wants to *be* the guy, not see me with you. If he wants a threesome or a cuckold thing, he comes in. Pretends he lost his way."

"That would've been a mood killer," I say.

"I don't like this," he rumbles. "Nothing makes sense."

I bite back a smile. Rex is such a control freak; of course he hates when things don't make sense. "You know my opinion," I tease. "He wanted to see if we were searching for hairs, realizing only too late that he didn't cover all of his bases and that his hair could still be in the salon. He never imagined in a million years that we'd figure him out, and he's *not* happy about it."

For once he doesn't act like the idea is ridiculous.

I touch my finger to his nose. "*Not* happy," I say again.

"It can't possibly be that. But…well, it'll be easy enough to rule out."

"Are you gonna rearrange his face like a marble cake?" I ask.

He looks down at me with that stern, hard look that gets lightning bolts flashing through my belly.

"I'm going to take a look in his room," he says. "I've been wanting to, anyway. I'll grab a few hairs while I'm there. Presumably he combs his own hair."

"Wait, what? You're on board with the fake nephew DNA thing?"

"On board is stretching it. I'm ninety-nine point nine percent sure that's not what's happening, but it's easy enough to rule out. I want to look in his room anyway."

My lips part in shock. He's serious?

"I don't like how little sense his actions make," he explains. "I don't like it."

I bite back a smile. I shouldn't love his annoyed tone so much, but I do. Especially when it's aimed at Marvin. "So… just bust into his room."

"Yacht locks are flimsy. It's why they have safes."

I find it interesting that he noticed the locks. Does he always notice things like that? I'm thinking of his whole history now; did his rough-and-tumble South Boston upbringing make him more attentive to security or is that his control-freak side talking?

"I'll go hang around on deck in a cabana or whatever tomorrow and wait until he's occupied and head in," he says, like it's nothing.

"Just bust right on in," I say.

"I think you love saying that," he says.

I do love saying it, but more, I love being with Rex—he makes me feel so weirdly happy and just alive. I love his determination and how strong and clear he is when he wants to solve a problem. This is the Rex I fell for over the past two years in his office—fierce and formidable and endlessly compelling.

And I love that he drank a pink drink for me, stupid and small as that was.

But I need to remember that he's not really on my side.

He's just stuck with me on a yacht and we have chemistry. Any guy would want to fuck.

Still, it feels a tiny bit like we're a team. I let myself imagine how it would be if he was really on my side, really mine.

It's a bad thing to want. If there's one thing I know, it's this: when you think somebody is yours, when you start thinking about the future with somebody, that's when you get destroyed.

Chapter Sixteen

Tabitha

CLARK IS WORKING AWAY on two phones and three computers the next day when Rex and I get back from an uneventful breakfast buffet session.

"I'm narrowing this down," Clark says, turning one of the monitors to where Rex can see it.

Rex bends down and lets out a string of profanities.

Clark is looking up at him. "Right?"

"Wydover," Rex growls.

"It's who you thought?" I ask. "Wydover is your business enemy, right?"

"Yeah, and he's been slowly and methodically dumping Bellcore all week."

"Wow," I say.

"What about connections to Marvin?" he asks Clark. "Anything turn up?"

"Not yet," Clark says. "Not surprising. Whatever's there,

they hid it well enough from Gail's people. *If* there's something there." Clark taps on more keys.

"What else?" Rex barks in his usual surly way, not worrying about niceties.

"Nothing. The PIs are chasing things down. Whatever *pull the trigger on Bellcore* means, still no clue."

"Damn," Rex says.

"Waiting game now."

"Sounds like cabana time," I say to Rex.

Clark snorts.

Rex turns to Clark. "You need me for anything?"

Clark furrows his brow, like that's a weird question. "Well, not specifically. Why?"

"Tabitha and I are going to sit in the cabana." He turns to me. "Go get ready."

Clark widens his eyes "You're going to sit in a cabana?"

"What? We need to watch Marvin. And this is our couples dynamic—I'm the brutish one, and she gets me to have fun, or what was it?" He turns to me.

"You're the brute who shows me his soft side and I'm the sassy fun one," I say.

He points at me. "That."

Clark furrows his brow. "So therefore you will sit in a *cabana*?" He looks over at me. I give him a big grin.

"I can run the algo team on my phone. Anyway, I want to keep an eye on Marvin," Rex says. "I want to get a look in his room."

"A look in his room," Clark says, and I find it interesting that he seemed way more surprised about the cabana thing.

"It's time. He's been following us," Rex says. "I want to know why."

A few moments later, Rex and I are heading onto the huge main deck in deck wear, which for me is my bikini, flip-flops, and an elegant black cover-up. For Rex it's trunks and a short-sleeved button-down shirt, yellow with a faded white print. His bare arms and legs shine in the sun, corded with muscles.

Stop being sexy, I think. *Stop, stop, stop!*

Marvin's nowhere, but Gail is at the coffee bar, and where Gail is, Marvin usually ends up. I wave to her, and she waves back. Rex gives her one of his rare and not entirely natural smiles. Grouchiness is his jam.

We choose the center cabana as the best place to keep an eye on the open-air dining space, the lounge couches, and the pool area. I settle into a plush lounger, perfectly shaded by the draped muslin that flaps lazily in the breeze.

Rex arranges his towel.

"You finally have the yachting vacation you always dreaded, huh?" I strip off my cover-up. I know exactly when his gaze settles on the ugly pair of scars that curl around on my hip. It's always been like that—knowing the moment people spot them. He wouldn't have seen them in the salt-lamp glow of the salon room, or when I wore a one-piece in the hot tub, but there's no hiding them with a bikini in the daylight. The scars on my legs have faded, but the hip ones are larger. I had a tattoo artist decorate them with tiny flowers—more to claim the scars than to cover them.

People usually don't say anything, but of course Rex isn't like other people.

"What happened?" he asks.

"Bike meets car," I say, trying to sound breezy. "I went right over the top of the car. My one time of flying and I don't even remember it." It's a well-worn line of mine that I use to lighten the mood when the talk of the accident rolls around.

Rex doesn't go for it. "Fuck," he says.

"It was their fault. Texting. Of course."

"Place in hell for those people," he grumbles.

"Right?" I settle into the lounger.

I can feel his gaze on me. "And that's when the mother-fucker left you. Your old fiancé."

I'm surprised for a moment...until I remember the duel of the breakup stories at dinner earlier in the trip. Rex didn't seem like he was listening, but he was. And he put my story together.

"Good riddance," I say. "I mean, if that's how he's gonna be?"

I'm smiling, but Rex isn't. Then again, Rex never smiles, not truly, but he's not even doing a fake smile.

"Really, it wasn't dramatic as all that," I say, because I don't like to be seen as the victim. The incident was important to me. It helped to teach me to never arrange my life to where a man can ruin everything. To never be my mother.

Rex could ruin things if I let him. It's what makes him so dangerous.

He turns on his side and reaches toward the scar—slowly, giving me time to stop him.

Like a fool, I don't.

His fingertip alights on one of the flowers. He traces the tiny petals. "Flowers growing out of the destruction. A blessing in disguise?"

"Yes," I say, enjoying how perceptive he is in spite of myself. "I wouldn't erase that incident from my life, even if I could. Your kitten is such a scrapper."

He traces another flower. This feels intimate—more inti-mate, even, than fucking. I want to make a joke to smooth out the seriousness of it all, but I can't think of one. It makes me feel nervous. Exposed.

Finding the fun and humor in things is a survival technique I hammered out as a child, like the way the cuteness of baby animals helps ensure they get fed, or how the white feathers on certain winter birds help camoflage them in the snow.

But here I am, letting him see me.

"People usually think the tattoo is there to cover up the scar," I say. The truth.

"People sometimes form opinions before they take the time to really look," he says.

Is he saying he underestimated me? It's kind of a compliment, and way too exciting. It's bad excitement. Dangerous excitement.

I feel frightened, suddenly—too close to the flame that burnt me, much as I crave the warmth.

"Gaspy-face," I say, ejecting his hand and grabbing some sunscreen. "Let those flowers serve as a metaphor for you, Rex. Maybe somehow, some way, you can turn the incredible hardship of having to sit in a cabana into a blessing in disguise, just like I did. This horrible hardship where you're not at your computer. It may not seem possible…"

I hold out the sunscreen for him. He shakes his head, because he's clothed and in the shade, but hopefully he's accepted my clear communication that he's strayed out of the bounds of our fake engagement vacation fling.

"Don't worry about me," he says. "I can run my massive and undeniably superior global empire from my phone. And I have the best investigators running down all things Bellcore before anybody can pull the trigger on anything."

"And if he is indeed a fake nephew," I tease, feeling our comfortable jokey banter get back on line. "Because if I'm right about that—"

"And I'm pretty sure you're not—"

"Ninety-nine-point-nine freaking percent!" I remind him.

He leans in, looking all sexy. "If you're right, then we don't need to prepare for the review at all."

"I'm so incredibly honored that you'll give me that tenth of a percent." I stand and adjust a flap of the cabana, feeling his eyes on me like a caress, taking in all of me, scar and all. Rex doesn't flinch from things. It's part of his jerky toolbox, and something I really like about him.

Slowly, I stretch out on the incredibly plush pool lounger so that the sunshine kisses my winter-sad belly, my thighs, my legs, but not my face and chest. My winter-sad skin soaks it in, practically undulating with pleasure.

"You'll be so shocked when he turns out to be a fake nephew," I tease.

Rex clicks away on his phone.

"Do you even know how to relax?" I ask after a while.

"Nope," he says.

"You should try."

He gives me one of his hard-ass glares and my pelvic muscles squeeze of their own accord. Like they have a mind of their own, and that mind is all about Rex. In a low voice, he says, "If you put a jasmine-scented cloth over my face, I'm gonna throw you in the pool."

I squirm with delight and keep poking the beast. "Try to empty your mind."

He goes back to his phone. "That's what stupid people do."

I grin. Such a jerk! "For the record, it's what smart people do. Relaxing the mind has been shown to have many benefits."

"That's a myth to make people feel better about being lazy," he says.

"Gasp!"

"You know, a simple gasp would be so much more efficient and accurate in communicating the concept of gasping," he says, clicking away.

"You know, saying things that remind me of the hate list is not an efficient way to get back into my good graces. I mean, if you think you're gonna ever get any of this action again." I sweep a hand above my bikini-clad self, up and then down.

"Oh, I think I will get some of that action again," he mumbles, and then he looks up, gray eyes sizzling over my skin.

"And I think it's going to be even better than the first time." With that, he goes back to his phone.

"Gasp," I say again. He's such an asshole! Yet I want to kiss him.

Clearly I need an intervention, possibly even a laboratory full of highly advanced interventionists armed with negative reinforcement techniques that have been proven to work on the toughest subjects. Maybe throw in one of those dog collars that sprays something yucky when I get within five feet of Rex O'Rourke and his scowly hotness? That would be good.

"So you never stop working," I say, fumbling back to a topic that will hopefully engage my powers of complex reasoning instead of my lizard brain. "Working too hard really isn't good for you, you know. I'm being serious, now."

"Work is good for you if you like it," he says. "It's important to keep moving forward and not let anybody get the better of you. If you're not getting ahead, you're being pummeled."

I straighten. "Seriously? That's what you actually think? Like you're being pummeled?"

"I'm not being pummeled. I'm the one who's getting ahead."

"So, kill or be killed."

"Exactly," he says.

"That's a grim way of looking at things. I don't see anybody trying to kill you right now."

"You're not looking hard enough."

"But, Rex, you have so much," I say. "Don't you feel like you've earned a vacation like all the rest of these people?"

"The people on this boat came up rich and connected, with safety nets under them. They take vacations. They don't earn them," he says. "Except maybe Gail. Maybe even Marvin in his way. And you earned one." He looks up over his sunglasses. "Though I might have to work you a little harder before I let you off."

I shudder down to my toes. "But surely you earned a vacation. I've seen you work like crazy for two years."

"Not happening." There's an edge to his voice that I haven't heard before.

"Why not?" Why is he so driven? I hate that he might work himself to death like Gail's late husband.

He studies my face, pondering the question. Or maybe pondering how much to tell me. "When you're not a Driscoll or a Vanderbilt or whatever, you have to fight a lot harder to keep what you won. When you started from where normal people start, you can't ever let go of the reins. You can't stop for a minute until you're the one controlling the game."

I watch the blue horizon, ratcheting up my assessment of how intense of a control freak this guy actually is. "Dude, as a billionaire you pretty much control everything already."

"Maybe if I can get Gail's accounts—*once* I get her accounts—I'll be in control of the market. In control of everything."

"Will you relax, then?" I ask, thinking about Clark's comments on how Rex is always moving the goalposts. "What good is success if you never get to relax and have fun?"

"Being awesome at business is fun. Winning is fun."

I reach over across the small space that separates our loungers and slide my finger over his whiskery cheek. It's sad that he doesn't feel like he can relax. "Why can't you take a vacation?"

"It's not me," he says.

"Why not?"

"You ask too many questions."

I press a finger to his lips. "You keep too many secrets." He wraps his meaty hand around my wrist and kisses the tip of my finger, eyes fixed on mine.

"Do you think you're gonna distract me?" I rasp.

"Yes." He kisses another finger.

"Because I'm stupid with an empty mind?"

"Quite the opposite." He kisses my next finger. "I think you always know what you're doing." Another finger. "I think there's always a lot going on in your mind." Pinky kiss. "And some of it's very dirty."

I yank away my hand. He's trying to change the subject. "Come on, be serious. You can never take a break?"

He raises his eyebrows, as if the answer is obvious, but I don't think it is. I think there's more, just like there's always been more to Rex. I remind myself this is just vacation sex—I can't get sucked in by him any more than I already am, but I can't help my curiosity.

"Your parents owned a bar. Didn't I read that somewhere?"

He reaches out and takes a strand of my hair between two fingers. This is one of his signature fake fiancé moves—winding a curl up around one finger, winding and winding. It's not right that he should have such a powerful effect on me. Around and around he winds the curl.

"I think you're trying to distract me," I say. "It won't work."

He keeps going, a hundred percent of his sexy gray gaze fixed on me. Slowly he begins to tug. Voice like velvety gravel, he asks, "What happens when I really pull your hair?"

"Uhh," I say, because it turns out that the strand of hair is basically a leash for my pussy. Somehow I get the wherewithal to bat away his hand, making him unwind his finger from my curl. "I'm asking for real."

"Yes, they owned a bar. We lived in the back of it. The back room."

"Just a room? For a family of three?"

"There was a loft."

"What kind of bar was it? A sports bar?"

"There was a TV, but it was no sports bar. It was the kind of bar that had a happy hour from nine to ten in the morning."

I frown. I've never heard of a bar that has a morning happy hour.

"Just to save you the math," he continues, "that equals a clientele of hard-core alcoholics, lots of fights, and a business with a lot of debt. I bought the thing and had it demolished when I made my first million."

"Oh," I say. "Really."

"It had to go."

"Did you put something better there?"

He sits up now and puts aside his phone. "No."

My pulse races. "You just wanted it gone?"

"Yes. And now it is. The benefits of being boss of the world cannot be overrated." I open my mouth to ask another question, but he swipes his thumb on my lower lip. "No more questions," he says.

"One more," I say.

In the grumbly voice that I so love, he asks, "Do you know what I do with girls like you?"

He's trying to distract me. "One more," I say.

He glowers. "Fine. One more."

I run through possible questions. Did he put in something new in its place? Where did his parents go? But only one feels important in a deep-down way.

"Did you watch?" I ask.

He looks at me strangely. "Nobody's ever asked me that."

I smile. Nobody ever asked it, and I'd bet he never told.

The silence stretches out so long, I think he won't give me an answer. But then he does—a lone word pronounced with extreme harshness: "*Yes.*"

Shivers go over me. I feel honored that he's told me this true thing. It makes me feel closer to him. Dangerously close.

"Don't worry, nobody was in it at the time," he adds. "Probably not even a mouse. Or hamster."

I nod. According to Google, Rex made his first big money

a decade ago. I imagine his thirty-year-old self standing in the shadows of some dead-end street, watching as his past gets smashed away.

"Was it everything you hoped?"

"Is that more than one question?"

"Fine." I give him a sassy look, because what am I doing? I'm trying to keep things light. This is a vacation fling—there's no place for deep, dark reveals. "And newsflash—there aren't other girls like me."

"No?"

"No. And you'd do well to remember that," I say haughtily.

And right then he smiles—a genuine, from-the-heart smile. I've seen his humorous smirk, his gotcha grin, his asshole face of superior pleasure in his own winning greatness, but a smile? Such a smile?

Rex's genuine smile is gorgeous. It lights everything inside me, makes me want to press my palms to his sexy, beardy cheeks and curl my legs around him and kiss him and eat him up.

It's like we're having this weird moment—a secret, beautiful moment just for us.

"Soooo…" I fumble back to the conversation, the last known area. "You don't believe me? That there aren't other girls like me?" I demand. "If you want a shot at a repeat performance of the salon, you'll need to show a little respect."

The smile lingers deliciously, and then, little by little, it fades. It fades into something dark and dangerous that I also very much like.

Low and grumbly, he says, "I know there aren't other girls like you."

"Uh-huh." I lie back down, determined to ignore him.

He makes me want things I shouldn't want.

He settles two warm fingers on my sun-drenched thigh and strokes them down toward my knee. He moves his fingers slowly—lazily, even—as if to say, here I am, touching you wherever.

This slow finger-stroke thing is something that he enjoys doing, which I also very much enjoy.

Slowly he trails his finger, down, down, down.

Rex's finger is an English country lord out on a walk of his lands, surveying all that he owns. Except way hotter—there will be no farming or cottage-building for Rex's finger. Rex's finger is interested only in dirty, dirty pleasure. His finger reverses course, heads away from my knee, back up into more tender lands, back up in the direction of my eager target.

"Definitely aren't other girls like you," he says.

My pulse kicks up. I was just fooling around when I gave him shit for that *girls like you* thing, but right now he's serious. The idea that I'm somehow different or special to him is a powerful drug, intoxicating and illicit. And dangerous. An overdose will kill me.

I sit up and nod at the bev area. "Gail looks like she's done with her serious convo." I stand, dislodging his finger. "And you know what I have? A comb and a baggie. For the DNA!" I grab my bag.

"Somebody's prepared."

I smile, enjoying the appreciation in his gaze. "At least one of us has to keep our eyes on the prize." I stand and pull my cover-up over myself and sling my little shoulder purse across my chest.

"Don't let Marvin see," he jokes.

"Right?" I spin around and head across the burnished brown deck, heart still pounding like mad.

Definitely aren't other girls like you.

It's a lie, of course. That line has been a lie from the beginning of time. Prince Charming doesn't truly want Cinderella for who she is—that's a dangerous fiction for girls to believe. Prince Charming only wants pretty Cinderella at the ball. He wants fun Cinderella. He doesn't care about washerwoman Cinderella and he certainly wouldn't go scouring the countryside for her. And if he did do that, once he finds her mopping floors, he'll be out of there so fast, on his way to find a new pretty girl to have fun with at the ball.

Gail's talking to a few people. The circle opens to let me in. One of the girls is showing Gail a YouTube clip on her phone. It's a humorous singing group, which is, admittedly, funny. We're laughing. The high school girls find other clips. People love showing Gail things. Gail has a way of making you feel special.

Gail asks them to show me one that I missed, and I act excited. I am, a little bit, but mostly I'm feeling weird, because I'm here for Gail's hair. I don't like fooling her, but if Marvin's a fake, she needs to know!

It would be so crazy if the fake nephew thing turned out to be true. There are a lot of other explanations, but what if? The man is up to something, that's for sure.

Gail's talking about tomorrow's breakfast now. I'm trying to find an excuse to comb her hair—I was thinking about doing a style suggestion, but now Gail's asking the girls if they want to be in a focus group.

"Somebody's doing a focus group?" I ask, studying her hair, still working on my excuse.

"Yeah, you," Gail says. "If you like."

"I am?" I ask.

"Maybe she doesn't want to reveal her idea," one of the girls says. "But we promise we won't steal it or tell about it."

"Ideas are a dime a dozen," Gail says. "Any idiot can work up an idea; it's the execution that makes the difference."

I grin. I love when she talks like that. "I'm not truly thinking about executing on it at this point," I say.

Gail wants to do it anyway. She's giving the girls just

enough to make them excited. They're practically begging for the chance to give their opinion.

"So are we on for the group?" Gail asks me, gaze warm. And I feel this crazy longing. It's not just the idea, it's having this older, wiser woman be interested in me and want to help me and to tell me things.

"I don't know…" I say. This focus group would be so perfect. If only I was really who I claim to be.

"It's never too early to gather information," Gail declares, because she cuts through the bullshit of everything. She points at the twins. "Ten? Right after breakfast?" They nod. The other cousins nod. Somebody's going to bring somebody else. It's happening—that's the power of Gail.

"Everyone likes to give their opinions," Gail observes once everybody's gone.

"I'm not seriously considering any of this," I warn.

"Yeah, I got that," Gail says in her blunt way, "but I can't drink mimosas and play croquet this whole time. Rather have something to sink my teeth into. Just for fun, okay?"

"I do have a few angles thought up," I admit. "I am curious about what they'd say."

She nods. If she's hurt I seem to be rejecting her overtures to mentor me and possibly invest, she's not showing it. "You need to talk about them? Work them out?"

I gaze up at the white flags flapping atop the hot tub deck, three stories above. "I want you to hear them fresh with everyone. I think that would be best."

She nods. "Good call."

"Okay," I say. "Now, something's bugging me." I pull out my comb. "May I?"

"What now?"

"Your part." I comb through her hair, acting like I'm restyling it, though she's doing a great job herself. "I promise I won't keep doing this," I confide.

"Nothing wrong with a perfectionist."

I nestle the comb into the plastic baggie hidden in my bag. "There. I think the wind undid it, that's all. You had it styled nicely."

"You got him relaxing," she says. I follow her gaze to where Rex is sitting. "First day he's been out here," she adds.

"I know. It's nice to see him finally doing vacation things," I say, and then I turn to her. "Can I ask you a question?"

"Shoot."

"Do you think people who came up with nothing have to work harder to maintain their position than somebody in an identical position who came up with money?"

"Coming up, they do," Gail says. "A man like Rex, he would've had to work twice as hard to get where he is. He would've been up against people with family connections, school connections, seed money. But there's more to life than work." She gives me her eagle eye. "You're good for him."

"I don't know about that," I say.

"He was a player for a long time," she says. "I've seen him at enough functions. Looking at other women even when he's with one. It's not happening now. It's as if he sees nobody else. Rex is a good man when he wants to be, and you keep him on his toes."

I nod, feeling my face blush with pleasure.

She points at her left hand. "He was smart."

For a second, I don't know what she's trying to communicate, then I realize she's pointing to her left finger. The ring finger. Our supposed engagement.

I hold out my hand, watch my ring sparkle in the light, hating myself on several levels at this point. I gaze over at him and catch his eye. He smiles and rises out of his chair. It's not his real smile, that rare smile he showed me in that moment of forgetting himself, but it's sexy all the same. "Guess his ears were burning," I say, beaming at him, and it's not part of the ruse.

Holding my gaze, he strolls over, all grace and power like a panther. The way he's watching me as he walks is just for show, but the feeling of him heading for me, having eyes only for me, it feels so real it aches.

I wonder for one foolish moment what it would be like to be the woman Gail thinks I am. The woman who's captured the heart of this beautiful, complex, secretive man. The woman who would get to work with Gail and make her mark in the fashion world.

He throws an arm around my shoulders and kisses the top of my head. "You two cooking up something over here?"

"A little something," Gail says.

I nestle myself into the nook of his arm. "An impromptu focus group for tomorrow after coffee," I say, hoping he doesn't hate that I'm walking down this road with Gail. It's not as if I could say no.

"A focus group," he says, expression carefully neutral.

"Never too early to gather data," Gail says as a few more people join us, including her oldest daughter, Wanda, and Wanda's preteen son. Wanda's son wants to know when the magician is coming, and Gail informs him that he'll arrive in an hour or so.

I'm shocked by this, because we're out in the middle of the ocean, after all. Where will this magician come from? "Arriving…how?" I finally say.

Somebody explains that he's coming by helicopter, and the boy suggests that if he were a real magician, he wouldn't need a helicopter, and the little group falls to discussing this in their casual, rich-person way, as if the remarkable thing is that a boy has suggested a magician might not really be magic and not that we are *on a yacht in the middle of the ocean and a magician will be flown in for us now.*

Rex makes an observation about the helipad, and the conversation winds on.

Rex has a commanding, charismatic presence; people pay extra attention to Rex when he speaks, seem almost to hang on his words. He's charming and handsome. He's also one of them—very solidly one of them. He thinks he's not one of them, thinks he has to work extra hard to keep up, but he is so clearly on their level. How does he not see it?

And does Rex really look at me differently than how he's looked at other dates? Hearing about that is so tempting—and exactly what I shouldn't want to hear.

For a crazy second, I wish that I could confide in Gail about this vacation-sex dilemma. She's so smart, I feel like she'd have good advice for me.

I'd confess how scary it is that I'm falling for him so hard. It would be one thing if he were treating it like a fun fling, but he has to go and act so serious, the way he did in the salon. Taking off his shirt. Acting like we're different, like we're real somehow. Maybe he believes it, but I know it can't be.

She puts her arm around her daughter, and this hit of jealousy heats my chest.

I look away. I never had somebody older and wiser to tell me things. There was just my dad, whose life's motto was, *what have you done for me lately?* And my mom in her dark little room watching TV in the haze of painkillers. Mom never had a lot of advice for me, but who could blame her? It was a battle just to get through the day.

A few more people come up, drawn by the spirited discussion, and that's when Marvin appears, his blond hair blazing brightly in the afternoon sun, expertly feathered around his sunglasses, pale freckles giving him a boyish look.

"Marvin enjoys magic acts," Gail says, smiling at him.

"This guy who's coming is one of the best," Marvin tells us, and then he goes on to describe one of the tricks the man can do. It involves chains and scarves.

Gail suggests we get front seats.

"Can't do it," Rex says. "No magicians."

Gail laughs in surprise. Everybody's laughing.

"Oh, come on. Not a little?" Gail asks.

"Nope," Rex says simply.

I blink. Nobody says no to Gail.

Except Rex, apparently.

She presses him, but he stays firm. "I don't do magicians," he says.

People are highly entertained. I shouldn't love it so much, but Rex is a thing to behold, being his impossible, contrarian self. And Gail seems to admire him all the more for it.

It's stunning to me. If there's any magic act happening now, it's how Rex takes what he wants and says no when he wants, owns his surliness.

He's being who he is instead of fawning over the queen. This is probably what he does in business—stands his ground with no apologies. A warm glow of pride fills my chest.

Gail turns to me. "Surely you'll be there."

I don't want to go. I don't like magicians, but more, this magician thing gives us a convenient window of time to search Marvin's room while he's publicly pinned down.

Rex takes my hand, as if to encourage me to leap with him. My heart starts to pound. I take a deep breath. "Here's the thing," I say with an enthusiastic smile. "I can't do magicians either!" I turn to Rex. "It's one of the things Rex and I bond over!"

Warmth crinkles his eyes. "That's right."

"That and not liking dill," I add.

"But Clark loves magicians," Rex says. "Clark'll be front and center with you all. It'll be a treat."

Marvin smiles.

We head back. "Clark can keep an eye on Marvin while we visit his room," Rex says.

"We're like Bonnie and Clyde," I say once we reach our level.

"In what way?"

"Just like, *we're not going to your goddamn magician show!*"

"You know Bonnie and Clyde were gunned down at the end," he says.

"But they kicked ass before that," I say.

"You did great," he says. "I thought you were going to cave there for a moment."

There's a minor lounge deck area at the back of the fourth level where our cabin is, and out past the railing, a school of flying fish is breaking the dark water, jumping pell-mell. "Look," I say, pointing.

Out of the corner of my eye, I see him turn to me. He's watching me instead of the fish. My pulse races.

"We *are* kicking ass," he says.

"Gail said that exact thing. Score!" I say, deliberately putting things back into the all-business category. When he doesn't reply, I turn, gripping the railing on either side over the rhythmic splash of the ocean that spreads endlessly behind me. "Sorry about the focus group. I know you don't want me spending extra time with people. I get that it's more room for error, but Gail really is sold on my idea, and it would've been weird to say no. I hope I'm not leading her on."

"I get it. Don't worry, she's not going to expect anything that you haven't overtly agreed to. Gail lives for this stuff, and she's a damn fine strategist. Working on your idea is like a fun puzzle to somebody like her. This focus group will be like free coaching. You'd be a fool not to take it."

"I really like her," I confess.

"She likes you," he says.

My chest swells with pride. "I know it's not like I can

partner up with her, you know…considering our fakery. Plus, I think she sees me as a more evolved businesswoman than I am."

"What do you mean? You're smart, effective, reliable, innovative. You know just how much to push. You can do anything you put your mind to," he says. "You got me to tolerate a head massage."

"You knew it was a head massage all along?"

"Kitten," he rumbles, sliding his hand over mine. My body comes alive in response to even that small touch. Rex is dangerous to me—there's no two ways about it.

"I'm enjoying this," he adds.

"Save it for the audience, Brando."

He moves around to face me, pressing his fingers onto my hips, sure and possessive. "I'm not playing."

"This whole thing is playing. It's the definition of playing. I'm playing the part of the fiancée. I'm literally wearing a costume. You remember how these aren't my regular clothes? Do you remember the sparkles that you so hate? I believe there was a list."

"Forget the list." Heat shivers up my spine as he leans in. "What happened in the salon…" He plants a kiss at the corner of my jaw, nose brushing my ear, tickling it, sending shivers over me. "Can you honestly tell me it wasn't the hottest sex of your life?"

"Vacation sex is often hot," I manage to say over the whooshing in my ears.

Chapter Seventeen

Rex

CLARK IS at the corner desk of our makeshift command center when we get in to the room.

"Anything new on the investigation?" I ask him.

"Not really."

I frown. Somebody out there is up to something. I need to know what it is.

Tabitha has a gleam in her eye that tugs on something deep inside of me. "Are you gonna tell him, or should I?"

"Tell me what?" Clark asks, still bent over the keyboard.

"Something about tonight," she says, now full-on grinning at me behind his back.

"One sec," he says, tapping a few keys. "Lemme finish this email."

She pantomimes being a magician pulling an endless scarf out of her sleeve.

I give her a frown that feels like a smile on my face, and she bites her lip. I love her happy. I might be getting addicted to it.

Clark finishes and spins around. "What?"

"Here's the thing," I say. "There's an after-dinner show tonight. A magician."

"Uh-huh," he says.

"And I'm afraid you're going to have to attend," I tell him.

He straightens. "What?"

"Attend...enthusiastically!" Tabitha adds, and then she does her dramatic wince. It's practically a full-body wince. "Sorry!"

"Enthusiastically? Why?" Clark rumbles.

"You love magicians. Like loooove them." She catches my eye, and I smile. Together we explain to Clark about his incredible love for all things magic.

"We need you to sit front and center and really enjoy the show," I say. "You'll also be watching Marvin, of course. And letting us know if he leaves at any point. We're gonna go into his place. I want a look around."

"And while we're there, we'll be grabbing DNA samples to send off to test," Tabitha adds.

"To test," Clark says.

"I already have Gail's," she says.

Clark turns to me. "You're not actually going to do this."

Tabitha puts her hands on her hips. "Rex gives the fake nephew theory a zero point zero one chance of viability. I'm going with more like fifty percent."

"Fifty now?" I say.

"Forty. But if you average it out between us, that's what?" she asks. "One in four?"

"Not how it works," Clark says.

"I'm gonna get ready for dinner." She disappears into her side of the suite.

I examine the monitor once we're alone, feeling Clark's inquiring gaze on me.

Clark has preliminary reports on Marvin up. Nothing

suspicious. I ask him a few questions and we run through the weekend data.

"Seems a bit much," Clark finally says. "The whole breaking and entering bit?"

I scroll through the latest numbers. "Some fiancés do strangely themed 5K races together, others wear matching outfits. We're pursuing a ridiculous theory."

"Not the aspect I was questioning," he says.

Breaking and entering is the least of my concerns. Growing up the way I did, going through locked doors was commonplace. I can't count the number of times my friends and I would slip into that random apartment lobby we had no business in late at night because the street was feeling wrong. Or let ourselves in the home of a school friend who'd probably let us in if they were there. Half of our neighborhood break-ins were stealing your shit back from whoever stole it in the first place. Locked doors didn't mean the same thing back then.

"So…what's going on?" he asks.

"We're having fun." It's the truth, and also a lie of omission.

"You don't like fun."

"I like fun with the right person," I say.

"You like fun with the *right person*," Clark repeats pointedly.

"Is it so hard to believe?"

"Yes. Yes, it is. You hate anything that's not work. Suddenly you're sitting in hot tubs and cabanas? Doing this detective thing? A room search? It's just…"

He trails off, but clearly he has more to say. "Spit it out," I say.

Clark leans back and crosses his legs. "It wasn't a hate list at all, was it?"

"No," I confess, thinking about how I'd anticipate the strange combustion of our Friday night haircutting sessions. How I'd yell at the housekeeper to have a nice suit teed up for

Friday. My annoyance when people were still in my office when our time rolled around.

My version of hell was always to be trapped with a woman after I'd had sex with her, but as I was lying there in the salon with her yesterday, my instincts to get away didn't kick in for once. For the first time in my life, I actually wanted to stay with a woman.

I go to the window. Being in a relationship looked like prison when I watched my parents fight in that dark little apartment behind the bar, all of that resentment and needy despair. I wanted nothing to do with it.

But I have this strange idea that Tabitha needing me would be a different experience. If Tabitha needed me, it would mean she was letting me in past her armor of fun. It would mean she was trusting me.

"What kind of list was it, then?" Clark asks.

"I don't know," I say.

"You've never been good at emotions," he observes.

A series of alerts announces that things are popping. We get to work. Time flies by.

The next time I look up, she's there in a black dress, her shoulders are squared, her thick chocolate curls caught up in a twist that makes her neck look long and elegant and insanely kissable.

She takes my breath away.

"Take a picture, it might last longer," she says.

"Maybe I will," I say.

"As long as it's not a mug shot!" She clutches her small bag to her chest, sparkly gold nails shining in the light. She looks hot in the dress, but her nails are my favorite part of her outfit —the one part that she herself chose.

I go to her, lower my voice to the tone she likes. "Nobody's getting mug shots."

She's happy that we're going to do this thing. It makes me happy.

Clark groans and excuses himself to change.

~

DINNER IS uneventful unless you count the pleasant undercurrent between Tabitha and me. The feeling of us having a secret. We're seated with distant cousins and the musicians, and Marvin doesn't try to sit with us this time.

Clark comes to join us after the dessert course. "A lot of people would charge extra for what you're about to make me do," he says.

Tabitha grins. "You'll have to give us the full report."

People are being rounded up. Gail comes by and asks again whether I'm sure about missing the magician. I make a joke out of my refusal. Gail acts put off, but I know she's not. People like Gail respect people who say no.

I stand and set an arm on Tabitha's shoulders. "Ready, kitten?"

Clark looks at me as if he barely recognizes me as we leave. I barely recognize myself. Usually I could get in a good four-hour block of work after dinner, but I'm running off with Tabitha on this crazy caper. Again.

I grab her hand as we head out. The sunset is a faint yellow ball drenching the horizon with glowing reds and oranges

"Can you believe that some people find this view a bore?" she says.

I adjust a strap on her dress. What I can't imagine is that I'm not taking this woman back to my room right now.

"Should we change clothes?" she asks.

"Why? You look fucking fantastic."

"You know what I mean."

"We're strolling into the wrong room for a few moments," I say. "Not paragliding into the Swiss Alps to rob a bank."

"Is that what you'd say if we got caught?" she asks. "Oops, we strolled into the wrong room?"

I push a strand of hair that escaped her updo behind her ear. "No. I'd say we meant to paraglide into the Swiss Alps."

Playfully she shoves at my arm. "Be serious! Do you have a thought about what we'd say if we got caught?"

"I'm not planning on us getting caught."

She looks up at me with a kind of trust in her eyes. She might not trust me on an emotional level, but I like that she knows she can count on me in at least this. "But what if? What would we say?"

"I'd figure something out."

"So you don't know?" she says.

"I never plan my responses ahead of time if that's what you're wondering." My phone goes off. It's Clark. He's one seat away from Marvin. He'll text if Marvin so much as sneezes. Though right now, he's just letting us know the magician has hit the stage. "Showtime."

"I can't believe we're actually doing this," she says.

Marvin's room is on the fourth level under the large family suites, way on the other side from where our room is. The level is accessible from two stairways, front and back. The front stairwell is visible from much of the recreational area. We'll be going up the back. I lead her around.

The walkway is empty. She squeezes my arm harder as we go. My credit card is already out before we reach Marvin's door. Quickly I work it into the crack. Her eyes rivet to what I'm doing. "Eep!" she whispers.

"Okay." I pause. "Are you going to be able to hold it together?"

"Hurry up!"

"Are you?" I ask.

"Yes!" The way she whisper-hisses it suggests maybe not. She clutches my other arm. "Except, oh my god! I can't believe we're actually doing this!"

"What happens on the soap operas?" I ask, to get her attention on something else.

She swallows, or more, gulps. "They get caught and there's a fistfight. Possibly somebody pulls a gun. Or somebody comes in while they're searching the room, and they hide under the bed. And then they hear a conversation they shouldn't hear while they're under there. Or they hear people having sex, and it's an illicit affair they shouldn't know about. But they can't tell, because then the people having the affair would know that they were in there."

"That's not what's going to happen here." I ease open the door, pull her in, and snick it shut.

She spins around.

"That was so…" Breathlessly she searches for just the word.

"It's not Fort Knox."

"Right there! That!" She's practically quivering with appre-hension.

I settle my hands onto her shoulders. "Breathe."

She sucks in a quick, sharp breath, then jerks it out.

"That was *not* the slow, calm breathing I was hoping for."

"Rex, I can't believe you're trying to get me to do calm breathing while we're illegally skulking around in Marvin's place about to be discovered at any moment!"

"We're not going to be discovered," I say. "Clark will alert me if Marvin comes back."

She nods excitedly.

I pull her to me and growl, "And I won't be hiding under a bed if somebody comes."

She lights up like she always does when I growl things

against her skin, and I want her more than anything. She's so keyed up right now, she'd probably get off with a touch.

I tear my attention from her and look around. "I'll take the bedroom, you take the bathroom. Sheets have been changed," I say. "Marvin's an everyday-maid-service type."

"Check around it anyway. Check out under the pillow, check the floor around the bedside table, wherever else…"

"I think I get the idea here, " I say. "I, too, have a head with hairs."

She heads to the bathroom.

I'm not finding hairs anywhere; the bedroom seems barren of all traces of human DNA. I'm surprised at how unhappy I am about this; I wanted this for her, and maybe even a little bit for me, too.

We're stopping at St. Herve tomorrow. I'd imagined us FedExing the hairs to my PI from there. Waiting for the results together. Not that I think anything will come of it; its more about the doing, the journey. I've never been an *it's about the journey* guy, but things are different with Tabitha.

I open the laptop on the desk, but it's password protected. I widen my search area to the chair next to the bed and to the desk, looking for things scribbled on notepads, anything. Eventually I head into the bathroom to see how Tabitha is doing.

I find her kneeling under the sink. "You okay down there?"

She backs out and stands. "The bad news: no hairs."

"Damn," I say.

A smile suddenly spreads across her face. She's sparkling. I'm practically feverish with the need to kiss her.

With a flourish, she lifts the baggie between us. "The good news: Toenails, anybody?"

I blink. "What?"

"Toenails."

"You have Marvin's toenails?"

She's beaming. "Yes. Because I'm magic."

"Toenails work for DNA?"

"Hell yeah." She stuffs the baggie into her clutch. "So if you're going to give out an award for the employee who executed the grossest job of the year, I feel that I personally should be up for it. I feel that I probably kicked ass on everybody in your entire organization in the Grossest Job Award category."

Something twists in my gut. I don't like that she sees herself as just an employee.

"Let's hightail it out of here," she says.

"Wait." I slide a palm over her cheek, needing to connect with her.

"What are you doing?" she asks.

I back her up to the sink. She sucks in a ragged breath. "What are you doing?"

"Kissing you." I take her lips in mine. She's sweet and warm and breathy.

"Oh my god, you're crazy," she says into the kiss, grabbing my dinner jacket lapels and as much fabric as she can fit into two fists and pulling me to her.

I rumble against her lips. I give her one last kiss, then I go to the door and crack it, listening, feeling her behind me, not quite touching me, but there—close, hot, and so fucking sweet.

When I'm sure nobody's coming, I pull her out and shut the door behind us. We head to the aft stairs we came up by.

"Easy," she says as we start down. "Too easy."

"Is that what they say in soap operas right before they're caught?" I ask.

"Yes." She steps off the last step onto the main deck and turns. "We did it."

I step down to her level. She's still wound up. I don't want this to end. It's fun with her. Everything is fun with her. That used to be my complaint about her; how did I ever see it as a problem?

I tuck a strand of hair behind her ear. "We did it," I say, remembering, with some embarrassment, what a jerk I was to her all of those Fridays of her showing up at eight in the evening when after-hours trading was over. Even insisting my appointment was Friday at eight in the evening was a dick move. But the way she'd launch into my office, upbeat and funny and utterly unflappable, you'd never know it.

Tabitha relates to the world like pink bubblegum, but deep down, she's pure steel.

"Feel like a cocktail?" I ask.

"Don't you have your precious Tokyo to attend to?"

"Tokyo can run without me."

The stars are out as we head over to the bar. She orders something called a Hot Pink Barbie that has coconut rum, vodka, Sprite, and three juices—orange, cranberry, and pineapple—with a cherry. I grab a scotch and we settle into the couch area.

She sighs contentedly, and suddenly I'm thinking about the supposedly funny stories she told at that first dinner. Her dad blowing off her birthday dinner, leaving her to sit alone at the TipTop on her twelfth birthday. That fiancé dumping her in her hospital bed. That thing about her messed-up mom.

"Did your dad really leave you alone on your birthday in a downtown Manhattan restaurant when you were twelve?"

"Who wants to know?" she asks.

"Come on. I'm curious," I say.

"Too bad you didn't do a proper questionnaire exchange," she says. "Or you would know the answer to that question."

"Tell me now."

"Too late."

"It's your birthday soon," I say.

"This is good." She swirls her drink. "I like to think that being in deck chairs conversing with drinks in our hands says, *nothing to see here, and we definitely weren't in rooms stealing toenails.*"

She doesn't want to talk about it. I let it go. For now. "Hot Pink Barbie," I say. "Is that your go-to cocktail?"

"One of them."

Without thinking about it, I'm adding the ingredients to the weekly instructions I give to my staff. I'm imagining her in my living room, the glow of dancing flames reflected in her gaze, on her cheeks.

"What?" she says.

"Coconut rum, Sprite, and three kinds of fruit juice. Not one. Not two. *Three*."

"Do you have an opinion you want to share with the class?"

"I grew up in a bar; I have an opinion on all alcoholic drinks. What it says about a specific person."

"So what does scotch without ice say?"

I look down at my drink. "Scotch is no nonsense. It's about taking a straight line between two points. A bit of a power drink."

"You definitely have the no-nonsense part nailed," she says.

"Not necessarily. I'm entertaining your soap opera theory."

"Entertaining might be a strong word for it," she says. "More like, jerkishly tolerating it."

I shrug, enjoying the way she isn't afraid to razz me.

"And Hot Pink Barbie?" she asks. "What does that say about me?"

"You're a unicorn."

She grins. "Come on. What if somebody walked into your parents' bar and ordered it?"

"It has three kinds of fruit juices and coconut rum and Sprite. That would never have happened. I think we maybe had one dusty old bottle of coconut rum in a dusty old corner. You wouldn't have made sense in there."

"What did your parents say when you demolished the place?"

"They were long gone. I couldn't break them out of there fast enough."

"You say it like it's a prison. Couldn't they have sold it?"

"You're like a dog with a bone, aren't you?" I say.

She slides nearer to me. "But couldn't they have? They owned it."

"No, the bar owned them," I say. "Not the other way around."

She reaches up and touches my cheek, runs a finger down the thickest part of my beard. It's something I always enjoyed, even when we were just client and hairdresser. "How does a place own people?" she asks.

A lot of people dig at my past, and it's usually about them. About satisfying their curiosity about why I'm an asshole, confirming a theory needed to wrap up a feature story in a neat bow. Tabitha's questioning feels different. Like she cares.

"They were in debt?" she guesses.

"Debt is a small word for it. They owed taxes, they owed back rent, they owed money lenders, they owed the neighborhood shakedown guys—too much ever to dig out or get free."

"Just no amount of money could free them?"

"No," I say. "It's hard to explain. It was the emotional entanglement, too," I say. "Their debt to each other, this spider's web of hate and blame and resentment. The worse things got, the more trapped they'd become. It was a dark, unhappy place they couldn't walk away from. I'd lie in bed at night listening to them fight, wishing I could give them the money to free them from that sad little place that reeked of alcohol and dreams gone to shit. And then I'd flatten it."

She's watching my eyes. "I'm sorry," she says.

"I'm not." The words emerge with a fierceness that surprises even me. "I've had a lot of teachers in my life, but none like that place. It taught me never to let myself be trapped or poor." I shift and pull her onto my lap. Holding her feels satisfying in a way I can't process.

She loops her arm around my neck. "Is it fake fiancée go time?" She's so careful to define our relationship as fake. Fake fiancée. Vacation fling. I've never been with a woman so eager to keep her distance from me.

"Not yet, kitten."

"You gave them something you'd wanted for them all your life. It's amazingly kind," she says.

"I needed to put them out of their misery."

"Did it work?" she asks. "Did they go their separate ways once you bailed them out?"

"Yeah. My mom went down to Florida and opened a flower shop. My dad's in a place in Jersey. Playing the ponies."

"You think they're happy now?"

"I found out last year that they still call each other and fight. Dad let it slip. There is no worldly reason they need to ever talk to each other again."

"That is kind of cute," she says.

"I don't like it," I say. "I wanted them to be free."

She watches me with that thoughtful fox-brown gaze. "Did it put *you* out of your misery? Getting that place behind you?"

I slide my thumb over her engagement ring. "No. I think that place got into my bones," I say, surprised, really, at my own admission. Have I ever admitted it, even to myself? "Maybe you never really escape the misery of the past. Maybe you just carry it as part of your load, like stones in a sack."

"Is that really how you see it, Rex? You collect stones in a sack, and then you die?"

Is that how I see it? I try to think of some proof that I have a nice life. All I can come up with is those Fridays with Tabitha. Giving Tabitha shit about her hair streaks and her Hello Kitty tattoo. Tabitha chattering on after I send people away. And then there's the fun of our Marvin caper. Kissing her on the plane. A day in a cabana.

"Maybe I need to start ordering Hot Pink Barbies," I say. "You think that'll do it? Or will people think I'm losing my edge?"

"Not to worry," she says. "You're a grouch and a tyrant. Triple threat on Wall Street. Hater of the pathetically impoverished and people who change the lyrics of love songs to be about their pets."

"I don't hate you," I gust out.

"I'm afraid I have it in writing."

"Tabitha—"

"Black and white, my friend."

"The list was never about hate," I say, pulling her closer.

"I don't know…H-A-T-E is a funny way of spelling *top ten awesomesauce features of the best women*." She's using her joking tone. The tone she uses to manage people, to disguise what's real.

I say, "Ten awesome features wouldn't scratch the surface of you."

"Well, there's one thing we can agree on," she says lightly.

I don't want her lightness—not while I'm telling her things I don't tell other people. "You have to stop talking about that list. You have to stop acting like this is nothing."

She presses a hand to my cheek. "Rex. Look, did you ever notice how, when Hollywood actors get cast to play a couple in a film, they sometimes end up together in real life? That is the power of pretending to be a couple when you're not. It's one of the biggest dangers of the fake fiancée thing. When you act *as if,* sometimes you buy your own illusion."

"It's not an illusion," I say.

Voices and laughter stream up from the deck below, signaling that the show is over. She leans in and whispers, "That's what the magician said."

"I'm not good at emotions," I say. "But then you came around, cracking through my haze of work like a kind of kryptonite…"

"Hold on, isn't kryptonite the thing that destroys all that's good for Superman?" She makes a playful face. "Dude."

"I didn't mean it like that."

She makes little devil horns with her fingers. "Kryptonite, bitches!"

"Stop it." I grab her hand. "I didn't mean it like that. More like, kryptonite for my tunnel vision of work…" But that's not right. She's under my skin. Something…

"Kidding!" She stands. "I'm heading back before I lose all my fake fiancée super strength."

I see Clark beelining toward us from the stairway, expression dark. *What now?* "This isn't over," I say.

"Did you get my texts?" Clark asks. "Have you seen?"

Eyes on her, I say, "No."

"What, did you turn your phone off?" Clark says. "ABCs are in full meltdown. Futures are going crazy. Rex—" He glances between us. "Sorry, this is important—"

"I was leaving," she says, and she heads off without so much as a fake fiancée kiss.

"I turned off my phone. Give me the worst."

≈

CLARK PUSHES AWAY A COFFEE MUG. We've been in full-on disaster management mode for two hours with the team— three guys in New York, a woman in Oakland, and Clark working to offset the effects of a meltdown on my precious Tokyo exchange, as Tabitha would call it. Really, I've been only half here. The other half is back on that deck chair.

Numbers run across the bottom of the screen. We're ninety percent back. Another tick upward and we've hit our goal.

"There it is," Cheryl in Oakland says.

"Yes." Clark claps once. "Anybody can run funds. The art is all in turning this shit around when it goes south."

Four out of four team members on the screen, and also that we can't get that new algo running soon enough. We would've headed off a lot of this hell if it had been in place. It's late on a Monday night; lord knows what plans they scuttled to help intervene. Even I have somewhere I would've rather been for once.

Cheryl gives me a quick update on her backend work, but my mind snaps to the sound of the shower shutting off in Tabitha's room. To the mental image of her warm and wet and naked, drops running down her long, sleek legs.

And to the echo of my idiotic words. Kryptonite? Why would I call her that? I couldn't have said something nice?

"Good job," Clark says to the team.

"Yeah, excellent work, guys," I say, feeling strangely emotional. "I really appreciate you. I don't say that enough."

Clark gives me a surprised look. It's not like me to congratulate people. I hire the best people and pay them ridiculous amounts, that's what I always say.

"You all gave up your night for me," I continue. "It means something."

My people are falling all over themselves to say that they're happy to do it, and it's nothing. They seem to love that I said it. One of the guys looks downright touched. Jesus, how little gratitude do I show to people?

Chapter Eighteen

Tabitha

I DRY MYSELF OFF, listening for the soft murmur of voices from the middle room.

I like when I can hear them working. I like being with other people, being in a group, feeling like I'm part of something, even if it's through that stupid door. Maybe it's a weakness, not wanting to be alone—sometimes I worry that it shows I'm not deep or something—but I can't help it. I'm not a solitary person; I'm a social person. I love people.

I pull on fresh panties, picking Rex's voice out of the group —it's not hard; Rex's voice is deep and velvety; confident and calm. I feel it inside me, some sort of sympathetic resonance.

I could listen to it forever.

I've been trying really hard not to think about Rex acting like the hate list might not be a hate list, but it secretly made me happy.

I pull on my PJs and grab my notebook where I've been writing down ideas for how to run the focus group. I really want it to go well. That's what I should concentrate on. I won't have access to Gail forever.

But a few minutes later, I'm thinking about Marvin's room. Rex was so cool about getting in—he got the lock open like such a pro. Where did he learn to open a lock like that? It was a little bit bad boy and a whole lot of competence porn.

And our kiss in there was the hottest thing ever. What if I hadn't pushed him away? Did he truly want to have sex in Marvin's room? I was tempted—I thought I might burst right out of my skin, just from him touching me. I didn't know things could be so hot.

And I believe he would've been able to handle it if we'd gotten caught. I feel like I can count on Rex for things. It's a new feeling.

And us rushing out of there like fun, sexy thieves in the night. It felt like it was us against the world, and I know he felt it, too.

And yes, we have chemistry—white-hot, blow-up-the-lab-in-a-raging-inferno combustible chemistry.

And he's unexpectedly deep in spite of that arrogant asshole surface.

But this can only ever be a fling. Because I know right down to my bones that when you think things with guys mean something, that's when you're in trouble.

That's how you end up all alone at the TipTop, crying in a party dress. Or lying in a hospital bed with a broken engagement and crater-holes in your soul. It's when you end up like my mom, alone with pills and pain.

Trusting a man with your heart is the fastest road to devastation.

I can't forget that Rex hates to be trapped in any way—he said so himself. His reason for wanting a fortune is specifically to never be trapped like his parents—who could've made hate lists about each other, no doubt.

I should've grabbed the list when I had the chance so that I could whip it out and study it when I'm having feelings for him —black-and-white proof of what a disaster we would be.

And women probably never say no to Rex. How much of his attraction to me is simply because he can't have me?

Still my traitorous heart beats like mad when his knock comes at my door.

"What?" I call out.

"I need to talk to you."

I clutch my notebook to my chest. "Can't this wait until tomorrow?" I'm stronger in the morning. More purpose-driven. Less hedonistic.

"It can't wait. You know it can't." His tone is full of emotion, and that makes the mushy part of me feel good. Devil kryptonite is liking the voice!

Get a grip, Tabitha!

He knocks again, just one time, though it's more like a slap, as though he slapped his hand against the door and left it there, pressing it, his heart breaking, and I have this mental image of going to the door and slapping my hand to it on the other side, and it'll be this romantic metaphor of two people from opposite worlds, never truly able to be together, except through massively hot vacation sex.

And then I pull my head out of my ass. "Your fake fiancée is officially closed for booty calls," I blurt out.

"This isn't that. I know you know it."

"Um…not really?"

"Tabitha," he growls. There's a beat of silence and then, more softly, he says, "Tabitha." He tried really hard to say my name gently the second time—I can tell. But I can still hear his grumpiness. I love the grumpiness.

I go and open the door.

His hair is mussed, gaze wild, pinned on me and me alone.

I have this sense of him as a beast in pain—a large mythical beast with an arrow in his flank, and he doesn't have a way to get it out, so he just stands there in pain. Needing something. So fucking beautiful.

And I love him.

"What?" I force myself to say.

"You feel like kryptonite," he says. "Because the feeling is strong. I didn't understand——"

"This is the clarification you felt you needed to make?" I say lightly, trying to get him to stop being serious.

"Have you ever been in a dark room and the light comes on?" he asks. "Or a strong flashlight switches on, and it feels harsh? Because it's so fucking bright after all of the darkness? Or when you're freezing," he says, "when warmth touches your skin, it feels like pain."

"You need to stop talking like this. Do you remember what I said about Hollywood actors? Brad Pitt and Angelina Jolie, anyone?"

"It feels real to me," he says.

I force myself to picture my mother, used and discarded. Devastated and addicted. That's what happens when you want a man more than he wants you. "I think you are sucking at the concept of vacation sex," I whisper.

He comes in and cups my face. He brushes a thumb over my cheek. The tenderness of the motion undoes me.

"When you're in darkness, or when you're cold, the senses register sudden warmth and light as pain," he continues. "But it really just means that you were without those things for too long."

He's holding my face like I'm the most precious thing ever. He thinks he wants me. He does want me.

For now.

"You're warmth and light," he says, "and I registered it as kryptonite."

"Dude," I say. "You're ruining our vacation sex."

He's about to say more—I can tell.

My pulse races. My will is crumbling. He needs to stop saying nice things. How do you get a man to stop saying things you love hearing?

I can think of one way only. I step back, fix him with a saucy smile, and whip off my nightshirt.

"What are you doing?" he rumbles.

I put my hands to my nipples, start tweaking them in the way I like.

He stills, transfixed in his surly Rex way.

"Mmm," I say, loving his dark gaze on me.

He balls his fists, inky brow furrowed. He hates that I'm doing this, yet he cannot resist. Eventually he relents. As if drawn by an otherworldly command, he comes to me. He cups my breasts while I'm doing my nipples, kissing one, then kissing the other.

"You're such a little witch," he grates. "Don't stop."

I don't stop—not until he yanks away one of my hands and presses his lips to my nipple, taking charge.

I hiss out a breath I didn't know I was holding. "Yesssss." I slide my hands over his broad back, grabbing handfuls of his shirt, pulling his shirt from his waistband.

"Take anything," he rasps.

I pull the shirt up over his torso. "How about this shirt? This shirt could be worth something on eBay."

He steps away and lets me pull his shirt clear over his head, chest rippling with muscle.

A hard light appears in his eyes. My pulse skitters in the split second before he pushes me back onto the bed with enough force that I bounce. Enough force that my mind melts a little.

He crawls over me, pawing at my pajama pants. He's a fucking sexy, wounded beast and I want him so bad I can't think.

"I've been imagining this all day," he says, stripping me. "Fuck, Tabitha." Hungrily, he takes my lips, then my neck. He's kissing my skin in slightly random soft places; I nearly orgasm just from that.

I roll over on top of him as he kicks off his shoes. I fall to exploring his body, all the private areas that are just him. He's endlessly perfect, endlessly delicious. I'm holding him and kissing him, and his hands are all over my ass.

And when he settles between my legs and pushes in, filling me perfectly, I groan like nobody's listening. We move like we're in each other's minds, reading each other, rolling around in perfect tune, as if we want the same things at the same time.

It's scary and it's exciting and it's utterly unstoppable.

Then he reaches between my legs, down between us, and he does my clit while he's inside of me, watching my eyes with that coal dark gaze, getting us both off together. It's the hottest thing, us watching each other while we come—scary and hot and like nothing else.

We're lying there afterwards, side by side, and he kisses me. "I wanna be new with you."

I press two fingers to his lips. "You know the number one way to ruin vacation sex?" I ask.

He glares at me. He doesn't like being silenced.

I say, "Acting like it's something else besides vacation sex."

He flips us over, pins me down. "Is this still about the hate list?"

"Another way to ruin vacation sex—talk about the hate list."

"Just answer me this—do you not believe my explanation for why I misconstrued my strong reaction to you, or do you simply not wish this thing between us to be anything more?"

"Oh my god," I say. "Talking about our relationship now. I'm getting out my bingo card."

"You're not fooling me," he says. "You feel it, too. I know I'm not wrong."

I sigh and close my eyes.

"Is that your *you're exasperating* sigh?" he asks.

"Maybe," I whisper, and I shift his arm to not be like a stone under my right shoulder, shift so that we fit perfectly together, willing him not to say anything more, because I love the feeling of being in his arms.

I want to confess everything to him. I feel like I could tell him anything right now, and I want to tell him that I'm scared —scared of my own powerful feelings for him. But I might as well give him a knife and let him know he's free to stab it into my heart at any time.

He seems to know that he's pushed it, or maybe he wants to stay like this as badly as I do, because he stops with the relationship talk.

"Okay," he whispers softly. "Okay, then."

I nestle deeper in.

Chapter Nineteen

Rex

I LINGER DISCREETLY at the breakfast bar, a ways away from where Tabitha is holding her Gail-enforced focus group.

I'm noodling on my phone, or at least that's what I'm pretending to do; I don't want to distract Tabitha or put her off her game by seeming to listen.

In truth, I'm listening with rapt attention. It's fascinating to see her pull honesty and information out of the seven women without them even realizing it—that's how good she is at making the whole thing feel like fun.

Running with such a light touch is smart; nothing ruins a focus group faster than when the people in it sense that you're deeply invested in the outcome. It's human nature to want to give the preferred answers, to please the person in charge.

She's posing a series of either/or questions to the group now. She's encouraging them to keep talking even when they have a problem with one of the choices. Serena especially seems to enjoy pointing out flaws in her plan, and Tabitha doesn't seem unhappy about it; rather, she encourages her, drawing her out with that indomitable sparkle, perfectly at ease.

The group is laughing. They don't see Tabitha's intelligence, her preparation. Except for Gail—Gail sees it. Gail chimes in from the sidelines now and then, but she trusts Tabitha, and Tabitha trusts her.

Tabitha had told me that she likes Gail, but now I see how much she likes Gail, how much she looks up to her. They've found a certain kinship. It makes sense; Tabitha's mother sounds like she checked out early; a woman like Gail taking an interest in Tabitha would mean everything. And none of Gail's daughters seem to have taken an interest in business.

They're perfect together.

Is this what Marvin senses? Does he feel threatened?

She throws out another idea, hidden in a volley of ideas like so many bright balls in the air, all fun and games.

I know it's an illusion—I can see right through her. She cares more deeply than most people realize.

~

THE YACHT DROPS anchor in the St. Herve harbor right on time that afternoon. A group of fifteen of us board a dinghy to the shore.

Gail stayed behind; so did Clark. Marvin, unfortunately, is along, and so is Serena.

We head out into the bay; the water sparkles like diamonds on a field of unearthly blue. Tabitha sits at the front of the boat, squinting out at the dead volcano in the middle of the island. I told her to dress up in something somewhat nice, wanting the excuse of a romantic dinner to be alone, but I wasn't prepared for the hotness of her in a cobalt-blue halter sundress.

She has a matching bag. That's where the package for our PI is. With the DNA samples. As soon as he gets them, he'll rush them to two separate DNA labs.

It's silly, really; I doubt even she thinks anything will come of it, but it's fun. It's play. At least for her it is; I have a more serious intent. Am I ripping a page out of Tabitha's book? Wrapping serious things in a layer of bright fun?

It wouldn't be the first thing I learned from her.

"Wish they'd step it up," I grumble over the hum of the motor.

"Don't we have until five?"

"That's according to website hours. A lot of businesses in these parts run on island time," I grumble.

"You hate when people don't hop to when you snap your fingers," she jokes.

"Then why am I hanging out with you?"

"We know why you're hanging out with me," she says.

Marvin is quizzing everybody on their plans for the island. The island has two villages, one on the east side and one on the west side. Eventually the question comes around to us. If Marvin's asking, I'm not telling. I slide an arm around Tabitha's shoulders and say, "It's a romantic surprise."

Tabitha beams at me.

"Where are *you* going?" I ask him.

"Winging it," he says.

I nod.

Tabitha catches my gaze. She thinks he's being suspicious, and she'll make a big deal out of it later.

Two of the women start talking about the focus group and Tabitha's ideas. They're excited.

"I'm sorry I wasn't there," Marvin says.

"Girls only," Tabitha says.

Marvin's tight smile doesn't quite reach his eyes. She kicks my foot.

We embark on the island. I buy her an orange Fanta in the little dockside shop while people sort themselves into taxis, including Marvin.

"Tell me that wasn't so weird!" she says when they're finally gone. "He wanted to know what everybody was doing, but he wouldn't say what he was doing."

"Maybe he wanted to see where the cool group was going?" The young cousins seem to have formed a cool group.

"He's onto us." she whispers. "The jig is up!"

"I think you're just teasing me now."

"Oh, yeah?" she says.

I hook my finger around the tie of her wraparound dress and pull her to me, wishing that we were alone. "I think it's a way you manage people. It's how you manage me." I lower my voice. "I think you have a fun strategy."

She tilts her head. "Is that so."

"I think it's how you manage life. You're a serious person with a fun strategy in life."

She looks surprised. "Oh yeah?"

"Yeah," I say.

"Well…" Instead of finishing her sentence, she taps the tip of my nose.

I grab her finger and close my teeth around it, as though I might bite it.

She squeals and yanks it away, very effectively using a fun strategy to end our discussion of how she's a serious person who uses a fun strategy.

In other words, proving my point.

We catch the next taxi. I direct the driver to the little village on the west side of the island, a few blocks from the FedEx place, just to humor her.

"Here?" the cabbie asks, slowing in front of one of the ubiquitous stands that sell random assortments of food and household goods. This particular one also marks the transition to little shacks separated by stretches of thick jungle foliage.

"Perfect," I say. I pay him, and we hop out. We pause in the shade at the side of the road that unfurls behind us like a brown ribbon into lush green jungle. To the other side is the road to the tourist hub. You can see people crowd around street vendors who've laid out their wares on blankets and small tables under colorful paper lanterns outside restaurants for the well-heeled tourists.

The FedEx station turns out to be just as modest as I'd imagined—more like a counter at the back of a dusty store that seems to specialize in bags of dried noodles, plantain bananas, and religious pictures in elaborate frames. We head to the back and stand at the counter under a beaten-up and decidedly unofficial-looking FedEx sign, and the clerk comes back and takes our package and our money for an overnight rush and throws it into a box. It goes out on Tuesdays and Thursdays, he tells us, then heads back up to the front.

She turns to me. "Today's Tuesday."

"I can't say I have a hundred percent faith in this process," I tell her. "We might not have the results until after we're back."

She nods without expression. Our two-week cruise ends on Saturday. Does she think about what happens when we're back?

"You're gonna be so shocked when the results come through," she says.

"Doubtful."

She smiles, and we head to the front. She pauses to browse the postcards, examining one of a baby wearing sunglasses. "I think I deserve an extra bonus once I crack this case wide open."

"I don't know that I'd call it a case," I say.

She picks out a postcard with a crab on it. There's a speech bubble where the crab is saying something about siestas. "I really want to assemble all of the passengers in the lounge and for you to make a speech about how one passenger among us is not who they say they are."

"Oh, I make the speech? How did I get such an honor?" I ask, sliding my finger under the strap of her sundress, unable to keep from touching her, wanting her. I plant a soft kiss on her shoulder.

"It feels right for you to do it instead of me."

"I see," I say. "And then afterward the lights go out and a shot rings out? And when we turn them back on, somebody's dead? Should I be the one to command that nobody may leave the yacht?"

"Yes, please." She adds a postcard of a white dog wearing a hat to her small stack. "This looks exactly like my friend's dog, Smuckers. Except Smuckers usually wears a bowtie."

"Who makes a dog wear a bow tie?"

"He loves it." She buys the cards, and then we head out to the dusty street and nearly bump into Marvin and Serena.

"You made it!" Marvin says, looking over at the store we just left. "Doing a little shopping?"

Tabitha pulls out her postcards. "Best. Selection. Ever," she tells him. "You should check it out."

Serena gives the store a disdainful look, but Marvin squints at the sign as though he's taking note of it. "Maybe I will."

"Let's go." I grab Tabitha's hand and lead her toward the small, dusty hub.

Tabitha looks backwards. "He's going in there," she says.

"You recommended it for postcards," I say.

"Should we double back and shadow him?"

"Now you're being silly. Come on."

"You're totally selective about which parts of this caper you take seriously," she says. "You don't think it's completely bizarre that Marvin was out there?"

"Nope." I keep walking. We head past the hub toward more modest shops and down to the place I found. The front is dusty and sad, half enclosed in iron bars, but I've done my research. Appearances can be deceiving.

"It says it's closed," she says hopefully.

"Not for us." I pull her inside. A young man with a white towel over his arm greets us and leads us out back into an enchanted dining area, a scattering of tables literally in the sand on a beach under a thatched roof.

Strings of brightly colored lights and shells and seaglass treasures are hung all around the place, the rhythmic surge of waves in and out of the turquoise blue bay sounding out just beyond.

Tabitha turns, taking it all in, speechless.

I'm soaking up the beauty of the place through her eyes. I have four more days with her, and it won't be enough.

Clark suggested one of two five-star restaurants on this island, but they were too stuffy for Tabitha. I reached out to the right people and stumbled upon this. Imaginative and beautiful and fancy-free, like her. I rented the entire thing out for the night. Clark doesn't know Tabitha the way I do.

"This is magical," she says finally. "How did you find it?"

"Grim relentlessness," I say.

She turns, secrets and fun in her smile.

There's one table set. The waiter brings a scotch and a Hot Pink Barbie. She puts her hands onto her hips, her tone accusing. "Did you call ahead?"

"Of course." I pull out a chair, and she sits. "And the best part…" I kick off my shoes.

She kicks off her shoes and wiggles her shiny polished toes in the soft, warm sand, and then, graceful as can be, she crosses her legs and takes a sip of her drink. "When you said best place, I imagined fancy. This is so much better."

I take the seat across from her. "Fancy is overrated."

"So overrated!" she says.

The waiter tells us the menu. There are only a few items, and they change every day. Everything, according to my sources, is excellent. We order several courses.

"So how many did you end up getting?" I nod at the small bag of postcards on the table.

"Ten. Check this one." She shows me one with a seahorse carrying a mailbag. "This is for my friend Noelle. She's a mail carrier." She shows me another one. She has an elaborate explanation for why she picked each one; most of them have to do with inside jokes or incidents with her friends, and each one is like a window into her life. She put an enormous amount of thought into her selections.

"Your friends are lucky," I say. "To have you in their lives."

"I'm lucky. We're like a family in that building," she says.

"You said you were worried about this building buyer? Kicking you all out? You really think that's going to happen?"

"I'm hoping it's just rumors. It would be devastating if we all had to move."

"Don't you ever imagine yourself creating a family and needing a bigger place?"

She gives me a breezy wave. "The whole settling down with a marriage and kids? Not for me."

"But the marriage thing *was* for you once, right? You said you were engaged—right out of college."

"Eons ago."

"And now you've sworn off relationships," I say. "What happened?"

She gives me a look. "If only you had the questionnaire…"

"Would that have been on there?"

"No. Also, I wouldn't say I've sworn off relationships," she says. "Friends with benefits is a relationship. Vacation fling, that's a relationship."

"Meaningless only?"

"Why are you acting surprised?" she asks. "Guys can do that and women can't? I have deep and meaningful relationships with my friends. Beyond that…asking for anything more…I've seen too much."

I want to say something that begins with *not all men,* but manage to stop myself. "Your fiancé left you when you were in the hospital with serious injuries. I can only imagine how awful that must have been."

She turns her gaze to the horizon. "I was half conscious when Jacob broke it off, so I suppose it's relative. It's possible being drugged up made it better."

"In the fucking hospital," I say.

"Well, it would've been worse if he'd wheeled me out just to break up with me."

"How about sticking by you?" I try to keep my anger at bay. I don't want to scare her.

She widens her eyes. "Right? Jerk."

I frown. She can make light of it—it's how she gets through things, I suppose, but I won't. "What the hell kind of man does that?"

She smiles as the waiter appears with a plate of calamari.

"I should tell you all my woes so you can do that growling-on-my-behalf thing," she says as soon as he leaves. "Because it's really working for me."

"He left you lying in a hospital bed."

"Okay, more growly feeling on that last one," she jokes, but it's too late—I'm a bloodhound on the scent, and I'm putting it all together. "What he did to you, it's the same thing your worthless dad did to your mother."

"Somebody's been paying attention," she says.

How could I not? I think. I'd give anything for that questionnaire now. I'd read a five-hundred-question questionnaire from her and never get bored.

She gazes out at the water. "It's not the same thing. Actually, it's the opposite. My worthless dad destroyed my mom; Jacob made me stronger. Dad and Jacob, the pair of them together, taught me an important lesson. They made me practically bulletproof. When the universe tells you two times that you have a tail, you'd better turn around and look."

"By which you might mean, men have a tail."

"I haven't officially checked you for a tail…" She props her foot on my knee, shoves at it playfully. "But the night is young."

"And that birthday. At the TipTop."

She tilts her head, impressed. "Yes, the tragic tale of the twelve-year-old girl crying at the TipTop, waiting alone for her dad, crushed party hat hidden in her lap. Nothing gets past you."

"And that's why you don't celebrate them. Another lesson learned?"

"Birthdays only suck if you build up expectations."

I cover her shin with my hands. "Expect the worst from guys? I don't call that bulletproof; I call it tragic."

"This from the man who famously won't date the same woman twice?" She grabs a piece of calamari.

"It's tragic. It's not right."

"Well, that's how I feel. Are you gonna kill the messenger?" she says. "Though I hear that's allowed."

My pulse thunders in my ears. "I don't want us to end, dammit."

Chapter Twenty

Tabitha

I RUB my fingertips together to get off the calamari crumbs, foot in his lap, pulse racing with dangerous hope.

He wants to keep our relationship going. It's exciting—heart-spinning-in-mad-circles exciting.

The waiter delivers what is probably the most delicious fish meal this side of Costa Rica. I try a bite, but I barely taste it. I want this so much.

"I don't see why we can't date after this, see where things lead," he says. "Certainly there's some middle ground between fake fiancés and a lifetime commitment of great and tragic proportions," he says, trying to keep the grumpy out of his voice.

It just makes me love him more. It reminds me that this man has the power to break my heart more violently and completely than Jacob ever did.

A lot of the charm of Jacob was about belonging some-where with somebody for once. Rex is light years beyond that

—every little thing about him gets my heart pounding. I wouldn't survive Rex dumping me, and how could this end any other way?

I say, "Dating won't work with us."

"Who says?" he asks.

"I do," I say. "And also, every article ever written about you."

"This is different," he says. "We're different."

I eat some more fish, surprised my digestive system is functioning when my stomach is in knots. I want to say yes.

"Tabitha," he says. His tone is raw. Real. "Tell me at least that you know we're different."

I set down my fork and look up at this gorgeous, temperamental man I've wanted for two years. I won't lie to him. Because I love him. "I know we're different," I say. "I know."

He straightens. "We can give it a chance, then. Take it slow. Baby steps."

My heart pounds nearly out of my chest.

"Right?" he says. "Why not?"

Because you have too much power over me, I think. *Because you'll never love me like I love you. Because I've seen this movie, and I know how this ends.* "Because we can't."

"That's not a reason," he says.

"It's my reason."

"That's a shitty reason. Give me one actual reason," he says. "Not a bullshit reason."

"This isn't a negotiation table," I say. "You can't huff and puff and blow my reason down."

He has his stormy look; he really wants to huff and puff—really, really badly. This is a man who is not used to the word no.

"Can we rewind and just be here in this beautiful place?" I say. "Stop worrying about the future?"

"Not until you tell me you'll keep an open mind," he says.

I look at him sadly.

"How about if we stop thinking about the future just for right now?"

He rumbles a little. I put my hand down on the table, on his side. "Fine." He takes it.

"Thank you," I say.

He squeezes my hand, frustrated and determined and achingly real. I'm going to miss him after this.

I'm going to miss his loyalty and his nearly imperceptible sense of humor. I'll miss the sharp intelligence in his gaze. I'll miss the way his scowl softens when he's feeling sentimental. The way the world lights up when he smiles his genuine smile, elusive as the dodo. I'll miss the way his annoyance makes me want to grab the scruff of his beard and kiss his face. I'll miss being able to do that.

"Was that too easy?" I say. "That felt a little easy."

"I'll stop worrying about it *today*," he says. "I won't stop knowing what I know—that this is more than some fling, and that you're letting assholes from your past dictate your future."

I give him a sassy look, because there's the surly Rex I know and love.

Things inch back to normal...almost. We try each other's food, and I tease him about his precious Tokyo team. He tells me about the people in his branch there.

This is how it would be, I think, heart squeezing painfully.

~

THE SUN IS SETTING when we get back to the spot on the pier where the dinghy is to pick us up.

Some of the people in our small party are drunk, some of them have large bags of purchases. Serena is drunk and has a large bag of stuff. People are comparing notes on the different sides of the island. A few have been to both. One side is determined to be better for shopping; one is better for eating and drinking.

We line up on the pier, waiting for the boatmen to help us into the dinghy, one by one. Marvin is at the head of the line. He looks back and gives me one of his weird *gotcha* smiles. Rex doesn't see it, but I do. I smile politely and look away. I have enough on my mind without Marvin being a freak.

But then I look back over at him. And I nearly keel into the water. Because he's clutching a cloth shopping bag with a picture of a parrot and "St. Herve" written in bright letters. And peeking up out the top of that bag is a large cardboard FedEx envelope, exactly like the one we sent. It's just an end, sticking up out of the bag, but the logo is right there for all to see.

"What?" Rex asks, looking at my face. I point with my eyes to Marvin's bag, but he's not seeing it, and then it's our turn to board.

Once on the boat, I grab his hand and guide him to a seat next to Marvin, putting Rex next to Marvin, because I need him to see.

Rex regards me quizzically, because usually I want to get away from Marvin.

Marvin sets the cloth bag with the FedEx envelope and a few touristy-looking things down next to his feet. When nobody's looking, I do laser eyes at Rex, and then at the envelope, nestled maddeningly in that cloth bag.

The edge of the envelope is still all you can see. You can't see the recipient or the sender. I'm praying for the bag to shift and for the side to billow out—just the tiniest bit of side billowing will afford a look.

"What?" he mouths.

The assistant boatman unties the ropes that lash the dinghy to the pier. Casually I put my arm around Rex and set my chin on his shoulder. I whisper, "Look down at Marvin's bag." And then I kiss him on the cheek to make it look natural, and also because I want to. Soon he'll be off limits. I won't be able to cut his hair anymore. It'll be for my own good.

The idea makes me ill.

I know exactly when Rex sees the envelope, just by the way his body changes. He looks over at me with a slight *what the fuck!* expression.

I bring my lips to his ear. "You think it's ours? You think he went in there and…"

A scowly shake of the head. A big no. "People get deliveries," he says in his low masculine rumble. "Della has a package, too." I look over and see a box next to her.

"But he didn't seem like he was planning on going in until he saw us," I whisper.

"You don't know that."

"And he smiled at me weird just now."

Rex has no comment. He doesn't believe me, but I know what I saw.

The boat pulls away from the pier, bouncing on the waves. We're both watching Marvin's bag, now. Personally, I'm hoping for a major boat bounce to shift it, or a crazy gust of wind. I just need to see the front of it.

I brush Rex's hair back from his ear. One of the cousins is laughing about something, telling a story that has everybody rapt.

It gives me an idea—I'll create a diversion and draw everybody to the back of the boat except the driver. If I can get people's attention on the shoreline, maybe Rex can jostle the side of the bag with his foot so that it reveals more of the envelope.

I lean in and tell him my plan.

Under his breath, he says, "This isn't an episode of *Scooby-Doo.*"

"Just follow my lead." Before he can stop me, I stand,

pointing at the cluster of palm trees on the receding shoreline. "Oh, wow!" I go to the back of the boat and grip the railing and lean out, as if it's so amazing. "Look! Do you see?" I'm pointing at nothing. "Under that tree? Is that…"

"What?" People are coming back to stand with me.

"What do you see?" Serena asks, glaring at the beach area.

"Is it a celeb?" Kitty asks.

"Whoa," I say breathlessly. Out the corner of my eye, I can see Marvin still sitting in his spot next to Rex.

"I don't see anything!" one of the cousins says. "What are we looking for?"

I haven't thought that far. I'm just hating that Marvin isn't moving. "So incredible!" I say.

"What?" another of them asks. They're all staring in the direction I'm pointing.

Maybe it was a stupid idea. Deflated, I say the first thing that comes to mind. "A squirrel."

A Driscoll cousin turns to me, baffled. "A squirrel?"

"Yeah," I say. "But now it's gone."

She furrows her brow. "A squirrel isn't that rare. They have them in the Caribbean."

I mumble something about an unusual color and head back to my seat, wishing I'd said monkey, at least. That would've been less weird.

Everybody's looking at me. "It seemed…like a unique breed or something?" Kitty asks.

"Yeah," I say. "Never mind."

Marvin regards me strangely. *What?* I think.

Luckily the boat guy chooses this time to scold the younger contingent for not wearing life vests.

"Really?" Rex whispers. "That's what you went with?"

"What?" I say.

"A squirrel? Why on earth would you choose squirrel?"

It's only then I remember our squirrel thing with the joke about sexy chittering from the salon. "Um…oops."

Rex scowls.

"I'm not good at inventing on the spot," I say.

"No, you're not, are you?"

I set my chin on his shoulder again and whisper, "Did you get a better look at the envelope?"

"How would I?" he replies under his breath.

I sigh. We ride the rest of the way in silence. Either Marvin picked up his own delivery, or he's smarter than we could ever have given him credit for, and he's tormenting us.

∼

CLARK IS CONCERNED when we get back to the room. "We can't find anything that's threatening Bellcore," he says. "I've been on the phone with Bob Bell nearly all day—he's made moves to prevent any possible sabotage or PR disaster. Our guys have been sniffing around behind his back and his team looks tight."

Rex scowls. "Keep looking."

"Will do," Clark says, gathering up his stuff to leave. "How was the island?"

Rex and I look at each other. That island was a lot of things.

Rex turns to me once he's gone. "A squirrel?"

"I'm sorry!" I try to look sorry, but really I'm biting my lip to keep from laughing because, what must Marvin think?

Rex backs me to the wall. "A squirrel?"

I snort.

He grabs my hands and kisses one of my knuckles, and then another one. He leans in near me, and into my ear he whispers, "I should put you over my knee and spank you for that."

My breath catches. "With your twittering tail?"

"What did you say?" he asks, and in a display of caveman awesomeness, he hoists me up yet again. I scream as he carries me through the computer area to his bedroom, where he throws me down on his bed and crawls over me. "Do you think it's funny?"

"No!" I protest.

"Liar!" he says. "You think it's funny."

"Maybe?"

He starts tickling me, and I'm laughing and screaming under him. Then I make him take off his shirt, and I roll on top of him and cling on to him like a barnacle, not that I'd say that out loud, because I'm getting the feeling that Rex is totally fed up with comparisons to the animal world.

But I'm a barnacle, gripping on to him tightly with my arms and legs, and I'm kissing him, and then I bite onto his lip.

He stills.

I let go and kiss him some more.

And then he's ripping off my clothes. His movements are frantic. Serious. We're not playing anymore.

I give in—I can't help it. I'm burning up, and he is, too—we match like that. I've never known I could match with a guy sexually like that. I didn't even know it was an option.

"Need you in me," I gust. "Please, let's do it."

Instead he looms over me, caging me with his strong arms, breath ragged.

He looks down at me, gaze intense. Unpolished. Real. "I won't give up. I don't care how long it takes."

"Heartfelt declarations." I reach up to his lips and press them together. "Definite *don't.*" I say.

He glares. He grabs my finger.

Playfully, I narrow my eyes, but inside I'm a wreck. I want to beg him to stop tempting me. Stop offering things that will break my heart.

Yes, I'm a coward. But I'm the one who was in that hospital bed after Jacob dumped me. I'm the one who was lying there, totally alone except for the beeping machines. And the nurses in the corner, whispering about me dying of a broken heart.

Rex says nothing more; he lets me keep my fingers on his beautiful lips. Slowly, holding my gaze, he moves his free hand —the free hand that's not supporting his weight—down to my thigh. One confident hand pushes my leg aside.

I can make him stop talking, but I can't make us stop connecting, and I can't stop the feeling between us—this feeling that is so huge, I can barely comprehend it.

He already has a condom on, because this is a man who takes care of things. He's watching me as he enters me. My heart stutters as he pushes into me, fills me.

He stills when he's fully seated inside of me. Gray eyes gazing into my soul.

He begins to move. Desperation fills my chest even as my body comes alive, as he gauges my reactions, stokes the feeling higher.

He's right there when I come. "I got you," he whispers. And when he comes, it's deep like an earthquake.

There's this raw feeling between us afterwards. Like everything between us is washed clean by a strange, beautiful rain. I curl up next to him in the bed one leg slung over his belly.

And I'm thinking dangerous things, like, *would a few more weeks of this hurt?*

And, *maybe he wouldn't break my heart too much.*

Chapter Twenty-One

Tabitha

WE EMERGE from the cabin at around seven in the morning. Rex was up at five, working away. I heard him discussing protective measures with Clark. He has a bad feeling about the Bellcore thing. Clark insists there was nothing to be found and so there must be nothing there, but Rex isn't so sure.

We grab coffees and watch the sunrise from the sixth-level deck. It's painted the eastern sky in pink—bright pink, deep pink, yellowy-pink, pale pink—all crazy pinks like a watercolor gone wild on the hugest canvas in the universe. Every east-facing surface of the yacht is bathed in a pink glow.

"Your color palette," Rex says to me.

"Definite DO!" I say, and then I lean onto his shoulder. I'm a sponge, soaking up every last bit of him.

We sit there for a while. I quiz Rex about Clark, and he describes how they've worked together over the years, with Clark being the one who's sensitive to people, while Rex is sensitive to markets. "Though economics is really just people in the end," Rex says.

I kind of love that he says that. It's so Rex. His job is a layer of numbers between him and people. I think that his scowls are a layer between him and people, too.

Eventually we head down to the main deck. We're sipping coffees at the cappuccino bar when I notice that Marvin is toting that FedEx envelope around with him—still in that same bag. I dig my fingers in Rex's arm and point at it with my eyes.

"It's probably nothing," he says to me.

"I'm having these visions of Marvin dumping hair and fingernails onto the breakfast table in front of Gail," I mumble. "How will we explain it?"

"Maybe we enjoy testing other people's DNA," he says.

"Right," I say casually. "Perhaps it is a hobby of ours."

"Maybe we're looking for long-lost cousins," Rex adds.

"Or maybe we're planning on doing an orgy later, and we want to make sure nobody here is a cousin of ours."

Rex snorts. "I'm sure it's a random delivery he picked up."

Apparently the moment of truth is at hand though, because Marvin is gathering everybody around the table where he's sitting with Gail. He stands up, holding the envelope with the air of a showman.

"Is he planning to make it disappear into his sleeve?" Rex grumbles.

"Or saw it in half?" I say.

But we fall silent as he begins to speak.

"The other day, Aunt Gail was talking about my mother, about the horseback riding lessons they used to take as children." He smiles at her. "She was talking about what a beautiful memory it was. And we were looking at pictures of them together riding horses around an obstacle course."

The way he's holding the envelope, you still can't see the

address. But then he flips it around and starts digging in it, and I breathe a sigh of relief.

Not ours.

My pulse ratchets down.

He turns to her. "It really has been so amazing to learn about my biological mother. Anyway, Gail told me how they would get a diamond horse pin for every year they were in riding school. And I remembered something…this box my adoptive mother had for me. The box contained school progress reports and trinkets, like my favorite polished agates, a few arrowheads, things like that. But in among the things there was a small pin. A girl's pin in a small blue box the size of a fifty-cent piece."

Gail gasps and turns to him.

"She called the little pin a family treasure," Marvin continues, "so I let it be in there, though it was a bit girlish for my tastes. All this time I thought it belonged to my adoptive family, but…" He pulls a small blue box out of the envelope and puts it in Gail's palm.

Gail closes her fingers around it, blinking fast, as if she's holding back tears.

"Open it," Marvin says.

Gail opens it. Her fingertips fly to her lips. "I lost mine," she says. "I can't believe Dana kept hers. It's so unlike her. I was the one who kept things, and she'd be the one to lose them. She never could find her keys."

"She didn't lose this," Marvin says. "She wanted to keep this. She wanted me to have it, and I want you to have it."

"Oh no," Gail says. "It was for you."

Marvin smiles and kneels next to Gail, pinning it onto her jacket. "I tried it on, but it didn't look right on a three-piece suit."

Gail sniffle-laughs; she looks so happy. There's all kinds of buzz around them suddenly as people get a look. Rex and I exchange sheepish glances. Eventually I take my turn at admiring the little pin. It's a filigree silver horse inside a circle. It has a blue jewel for the eye and pearls for the hooves. It looks very 1970s.

I grasp Gail's arm. "I'm so happy for you," I say, and I mean it—I really do.

Eventually, Rex and I drift over to the far side of the deck and lean over the railing, watching a freighter in the distance.

"Okay, it's a pretty random thing to be able to produce out of thin air," I say.

"It's very tiny and detailed," Rex says. "Not the kind of thing you can produce from a photo."

"No," I say. "Gail would know if it wasn't real."

"The nephew produces an heirloom," Rex says. "An actual hcirloom."

"I feel like a complete asshole," I confess. "All of my fake nephew intrigue. Our investigation. What was I thinking?"

"Yeah," he says. "I feel like an asshole, too."

"You do?" I turn to him. "I'm the one who thought of it."

"I got into it with you. Breaking and entering? I think we're both assholes."

Warmth blooms in my chest. We're a team, even in this. "Thanks for saying that."

He kisses the top of my head.

"Gail's relationship with Marvin makes her happy. I shouldn't have made light of it."

"You? Making light of something serious?" he teases. "So impossible to believe!"

"It's wrong," I say. "I don't take things seriously for myself, but I shouldn't do it with others."

Tenderly, he brushes the hair off my forehead. "I think you take things plenty seriously," he says. "I think not taking things seriously is the way you take things seriously."

"Not taking things seriously is how I take things seriously?" I say. "Mind blown."

"Don't bullshit me. You feel deeply. It's something I admire about you."

I try a smile and we fit our hands together.

"I really am glad Marvin's real—for her sake, I mean," I say. "He's obviously shady—Gail deserves better, but this relationship is important to her. It gives her solace about her sister."

"Gail won't be the first person to have a shady relative."

"Things don't have to make sense, do they?" I say. "Maybe that's the moral of this story. Sometimes the creepy guy really *is* up to something. And sometimes he is also really and truly the long-lost nephew."

"Yeah. And sometimes the bad guys win." He brings our joined hands to his lips and kisses my knuckles one after another. "Do things make sense in soap operas?" he asks.

"Definitely," I say. "Eventually."

"Like, happily ever after?"

"No, more in terms of karma. Horrible people eventually regret what they've done. Dark schemes bite the schemer in the ass. Secrets always get revealed. It takes a while, but karma always happens. And people who do good deeds without getting discouraged, even when life throws the worst at them, they come out ahead in the end."

He waits, listens. Like he knows there's more.

I say the rest. "And when bad things happen, it still turns out okay. The woman who gets burned and abandoned finds happiness. The man who abandons her is bitterly regretful. And her daughter wouldn't want to leave. The daughter would help the mother get over that addiction." My heart pounds. What am I doing?

"You were a kid." He looks me clear in the eye. "A little kid shouldn't be asked to save a parent. Not ever."

"Why do I still feel like the asshole, then?"

"Because things in real life don't make sense. But you're not the asshole in that drama, trust me," he says. "Who here is the asshole expert?"

I feel my lips curling into a smile.

"It was up to them to stand by you, not the other way around. And that motherfucker Jacob, too," he growls. "What the hell? Don't even get me started on what he did. A man doesn't do that."

I swallow. "Thank you for saying that."

"Don't thank me, it's just true," he says in his angry-on-my-behalf way that I love.

We're silent for a while. The waves splash against the hull. I like being quiet with him.

"What about the phone call?" I ask. "Should we tell her?"

He turns his gaze out to sea. I study the hard line of his jaw, waiting to see what he says. "The phone call alone without any evidence of wrongdoing doesn't feel like enough. Clark and I haven't been able to find anything amiss with Bellcore. If it turns out there was evidence of foul play, that's one thing, but there is a lot of nothing there. All we have is a guy talking in a suspicious way. And we don't know what the person on the other end was saying. Also, Gail's not an idiot."

"No," I agree. I only have a few more days of being around Gail, too. Of seeing the world through her eyes, of Gail seeing me as this real businesswoman who might actually be more than a visiting hairdresser.

"And Marvin's her people."

"I wish she was my people," I whisper.

"I know," he says, squeezing our joined hands together.

"You do?"

"Yeah," he says.

I'm flooded with affection that he knows, that he cares enough to see it—to see me. I breathe in his masculine scent feeling almost like I'm taking a last breath, storing the memory of him.

I wish *he* was my people.

But he'll get off this yacht and be sucked back into the cold, slushy world of Manhattan. I'll be back to being a hairdresser. There's no way it can be anything other than that.

Or maybe I'm just scared to want more than that. To deserve more than that.

Chapter Twenty-Two

Rex

I SLIDE a finger over the perfect silhouette of her hips.

"Mmm," she says, rolling over lazily with a satisfied, well-fucked look on her face. It connects to something deep in me. Putting that look on this woman's face, showing her how much I appreciate every inch of her body, is every bit as satisfying as any business victory.

More satisfying.

I lean over and kiss her shoulder.

I never bring women home, but I'm imagining Tabitha in my bed, on my couch. I'm imagining her sitting at my kitchen island, picking at food, or drinking something ridiculously frothy, making her half-wince face, one eye humorously closed.

I imagine learning more about her. Exploring every part of her. Learning the way her mind works, the ways her body works. Making her mine, little by little.

Three more days won't be enough. Three weeks or three

months or even three years won't be enough. That's what I know now.

I slide my finger up the back of her thigh, to the small crease right below her ass. "This is one of my favorite parts of you," I say. "Sexy and hidden. Overshadowed by the big fun of your gorgeous ass."

She turns in my arms. "I'm hearing you compare me to an ass in both parts of that metaphor…"

"My favorite ass."

She touches the tip of her finger to my nose. "Um, thank you?"

I grab her finger, bite the tip. She squeals.

That's when my phone starts pinging. I groan. It's Clark—he's one of the few who can get through on this setting. I reach over and grab it.

A moment later, my world starts careening.

I sit up.

"What is it?" she asks.

I stumble out to my office area, wake up the screens, and pull on some pants. My fingers fly to the keyboard. "Bellcore's in freefall."

She stands at the doorway, wrapped in a blanket. "That stock?"

"Yes. It's a bloodbath." There's still more room to fall and definitely another shoe to drop. I've already got the team unloading it, but we've taken a hit.

"What are you going to do?" she asks.

"Recover."

There's just the sound of me typing away. My spidey sense told me there would be trouble, but I thought we had time. I thought we had until their launch.

"Was it sabotage?" she asks. "Somebody doing something shady in the company like you thought?"

"No, the CEO himself was doing something shady in the company."

"Oh no!"

"It's Enron-big," I grumble, moving across the suite to unlock the door and let Clark in. He's on the phone. He sets an open laptop on the desk. The team's on, looking for leadership. The damage is bad. Deep.

It's come out that Bob Bell has mob connections. One of his device trials was falsified. A researcher was threatened. The information has thrown the entire product array into chaos. And being that they're the biggest players, the entire sector is spiraling, pulling down other firms. The market itself is affected.

"When did this hit the wire?" I ask Clark. "And where?"

"Thirty minutes ago. It came out somewhere obscure…"

And I wasn't paying attention. I had alerts set, but that doesn't work when your phone's on do-not-disturb. It's bad enough that the yacht has a slight delay compared to the light-ning-fast internet in the city.

"Damn!" I say when the numbers refresh. "What was I thinking?"

"Everybody missed it," Clark says. "Everybody is taking a bath. Except Wydover."

"Except Wydover," I say, staring at the graph. "He bet on this decline. He knew it was coming. He controlled the timing."

"That's the one you have Gail deep in," Tabitha observes.

"Yup," I grumble. "And the timing is probably just right to affect the review. Even though we're better than Wydover over time."

Tabitha hovers uncertainly around. "Maybe if I hadn't distracted you."

"Not your fault."

"If you hadn't been chasing down my weird theories—"

"Stop it. Wydover had a bombshell nobody imagined. And

he manipulated the timing of it expertly," I say, pulling up the Asia charts. "Actually, I played defense more than I would've if you hadn't heard what you heard. We'd be worse off if you hadn't heard that. But I'm a competitive motherfucker, and that's on me."

"Will Gail pull the account just on this?"

"She probably won't have a choice."

My tone is calm, but my head is spinning. Having Gail's account was about so much more than money.

And now my worst enemy will have everything I worked so hard for.

~

I EMERGE from the cabin five hours later to face the music. What Gail lost by having a fraction of her funds with us isn't going to bankrupt her, but it hurts.

Gail and Marvin are at a table under an umbrella, sharing a plate of mussels. Gail looks unhappy.

"How are you?" Marvin asks from behind Gail. His tone is concerned, but his expression is barely contained glee. My stomach curdles. He's so shady. Gail has to know it.

Small consolation. Like I said to Tabitha, Marvin is her people.

"Rex," Gail says, motioning at the third chair. I sit, and she gets right to it. "I like you, Rex. I always have," she says.

Her tone confirms what I suspected, that her hands are tied. I've lost the account to Wydover. The devastation of it is so huge, I almost can't process it.

"We need you to see around corners for us," Marvin says. "This drop is unacceptable."

I cross my legs. "Anybody can pick a horse," I say. "Not everybody can manage the cliffs and valleys over time." I turn to Gail. "You know how it works. You know how I work. I'm the one who brings you back from this kind of thing."

"I know," she says—regretfully.

Marvin sighs. "It's a different market than when you came up, Rex. You can't use brute instincts."

I grit my teeth. That's my reputation, even though my quant trading game is more robust than anyone's. Is this what Wydover has Marvin telling her?

Gail says, "If it were just me, that's one thing, but my board…we set parameters…"

Parameters designed to set me up for failure. Probably having to do with the time frame.

Marvin smirks. Acid churns in my gut. I ball my hand, itching for the exhilaration of my fist making contact with the bones of his face.

"I understand," I say.

"People's livelihoods rest on this decision," Marvin says. "We have to protect our people."

I swallow and address Gail. "I know that you have a lot of livelihoods riding on this."

And that's the real kicker. I'd do better for them than Wydover. I play by the rules out there, and he doesn't. Without cheating and exploiting connections, he's just nowhere near as good as I am. And it's not just about returns; stunts like this could cost a man his license, and that hurts clients like Gail.

Gail and the Driscoll image would really be hurt by being associated with a shady asset manager—far more than owning stock in a company that goes down.

If only I could prove that Wydover worked with Marvin. I'm thinking of my conversation with Tabitha. Real life doesn't make sense. Sometimes the bad guys win.

Maybe someday I'll find a way to prove what happened, but that's not my priority now. I have people to protect, too.

"I have to go back and manage my team," I say.

It's the truth, and I can see from Gail's expression she expected it. Sometimes you have to be on site with your team, in the office with the benefit of instantaneous communication.

"I'm sorry, I really am," she says.

"I want you to know that Tabitha and I enjoyed ourselves. I wouldn't have traded this time for the world," I tell her, and I'm being honest. "Thank you for inviting us." I stand. "I also want you to know, Rex Capital has three weeks left to shepherd your funds, and I'm going to do everything I can to restore the balance before the handover."

"It won't change anything," Marvin says.

I don't dignify his idiotic comment with a response. I don't need a reason to end things right for a client, and Gail knows it.

"There's a small airport on Fincher Island. We're in the vicinity. And of course my chopper is yours," she says. "And you tell that fiancée of yours to bring her business plan to me when she's ready."

"Thank you," I say.

"You're a good man," she says.

∿

THE PLANE RIDE back is an unending blur of bad news. The markets run on emotions every bit as much as they run on numbers, and things are feeling wild.

My people are in the saddle, but I need to be there at the front of this thing. I was serious about what I said to Gail—I smooth out the valleys, and this is a pretty dramatic valley for all of my clients. They trust me to protect and build their assets. I feel like Gail would've been happy to trust me too if she hadn't been steered into this thing by Marvin and Wydover. I'm sure they're working together.

I suppose it doesn't matter, now.

Tabitha's playing some kind of game on her phone on the party side of the plane.

It seems like ages ago that I was explaining the sides of the plane to her and suggesting that she stay on her side and not bother me. Now I'd do anything for her to sit next to me while I work. She wouldn't have to say anything; just her silent presence would mean a lot.

During a lull in the action, I go back there. She's wearing dark leggings and some sort of tunic thing, and she's stretched out on the couch.

"How's it going?" she asks.

"A lot of fires to put out," I say.

She nods. "How's Tokyo?"

I sit next to her. "Hanging in there." I settle a hand over her shin. "Looking forward to wearing bright colors again?"

"So forward," she says, voice low and dramatic.

I reach back and shove the pocket door closed. "It's not your fault. It really isn't."

"Thanks," she says, putting aside the phone. "So like, *can* you put out the fires?"

"No, but I can control the burn. I'll probably be at this for the next forty-eight hours."

She nods and turns her attention to the window. The sky is robin's-egg blue out there, but it's raining in the city.

"She loves your idea," I tell her. "She told me to have you send her your plan."

"I guess it's good to know she's that into it," Tabitha says sadly—sadly because she can't work with Gail. The fake fiancée lie would come out. It was bad enough that Clark committed me to that lie—it's not as if I'd be working day-to-day with Gail if I got her account; I probably wouldn't even see her more than once a year.

But a startup is an everyday thing, a close relationship. Two women shoulder to shoulder, sharing meals and late nights.

"You know, if we were dating, the fiancée thing wouldn't be such a lie," I say.

"Rex," she says. "The answer's the same."

"We have three more days on the contract," I remind her.

"We're off the yacht. This is the end of the vacation."

My heart thunders. "Only because it ended prematurely," I say.

"The contract specified until the end of the yacht trip."

"Screw the contract," I say. "I'm telling you I want to be in a relationship with you. I want to spend time with you. I want to wake up with you. I'm a lot of things, Tabitha, but I'm not a liar. I know you want it, too."

She looks at me sadly. "It just can't be."

"You don't know the future," I say.

"I know the past."

"The past has nothing to do with the future," I tell her.

She reaches up and touches the side of my beard, strokes the place she loves to touch. I shut my eyes, enjoying her touch, searching for the words to make this right.

There's a federally mandated disclaimer on earnings graphs that says *past performance is not a guarantee of future earnings.* People usually ignore it—the colorful graph showing brilliant returns always feels more real and compelling than the warning. Humans are hardwired to learn from the past. Often, literally, in the form of a flinch reaction.

That's what Tabitha has—a kind of flinch reaction. My heart rages with the knowledge.

I wrap my fingers around her wrist, make her keep her hand on my cheek. "Don't throw this away because of shitty guys in your past."

Clark comes back, phones in both hands. "Rex. You need to deal with this."

"Give us a minute," I growl. The pocket door slips back shut.

"You should go," she says.

"This is more important. *We* are more important."

"More important than finishing right with Gail? Making sure that the door to the account you've wanted all your life stays propped open, so when Wydover fails, you're the one she runs to?"

I'd told her my strategy on the helicopter. Doing the right thing. Staying the course. Hoping someday she comes back.

"More important than the business you've built your life around?" she asks. "The business that ensures that you'll never be trapped and miserable? More important than doing right by your people?"

"It's a false choice. I can do right by my people *and* be with you. I won't throw this away. You don't trust men—I get it—"

She pulls her hand from my grip. "Rex, look at me. Really look." Her eyes shine, but not with the usual mischief. "You have me dressed up in these clothes that aren't mine, playing your entrepreneurial-minded fiancée. The truth is, I'm just some girl who cuts your hair, and you're a guy who never wants to be limited or confined. And now we're going back to real life."

"Screw that. We can have one more date, one more dinner at least. What about that?" I say. "Give me one good reason we can't have one more date."

"Maybe I'm not brave," she says in a small voice. "Maybe a person only has so much bravery in life, and mine got used up."

My heart lurches. "I won't accept that."

"You don't have a choice," she says. "You saved me from losing my place. I'm so grateful. And in two months or whatever, I'll make my social media posts dovetail with yours for the breakup, just like we agreed." She pauses, then, "I loved us together," she adds. "Let it be an amazing memory."

I want to shake her and yell at her not to throw this away, but I can't bully her into dating me.

She shakes her head. She looks so sad.

I can make fortunes in my sleep, but I can't make Tabitha trust me. I can't make her give us a chance.

Chapter Twenty-Three

Tabitha

SECOND-GUESSING YOURSELF IS HELL.

Over the days following our return, Rex sends me texts that I shouldn't read and leaves me voice messages that I shouldn't listen to, but totally do.

He tells me about all of the little things that make him think of me through his days—a fun fact about jasmine in ancient Egypt, Clark's efforts to get him to smile more. He texts me a picture of actual Hello Kitty graffiti he noticed on a walk along the waterfront, which I kind of love, and then an image of a famous painting of an ocean horizon with the caption: *you know what I think about this!*

I force myself to delete them after I check them—especially the voicemails—it's too dangerous to keep them there. Unfortunately, there's no way to delete my heart, no way to stop myself from playing the memories of us together over and over.

I hate being a coward.

But I know what happens when you give a man the keys to your heart and happiness. Especially a confirmed playboy who hates being trapped.

I remind myself that men like him always want what they can't have. I remind myself that my refusal to date him is half of my charm. Maybe most of it.

I'm already miserable without him. It was only eleven days on that yacht.

Though that's not exactly right. It was two years of Fridays. Two years of saving up fun things to talk about with him. Of taking my time with his hair. The two of us sparring in our weird way in his lonely office above the city while everyone else in the world was doing Friday night stuff.

Two years of replaying his words in my mind the rest of the week. Picking out my best outfits—or more like, my most reaction-provoking outfits.

A few days later actual things start coming. He sends me a basket of mangoes, yogurt, and spiced nuts—that was the breakfast food I went crazy for on the yacht. Another day he sends a coffee mug with a cartoon of a maraschino cherry on it, with the words "best fruit ever!" underneath. Inside is a little necklace of a silver squirrel. I bring the mango and treats basket and mug to Noelle down the hall, but I tuck the neck-lace in the bottom drawer of my jewelry box.

He comes and sees me a week and a half after we get back. He buzzes from the entryway. I don't know why I answer—I should've just pretended I wasn't home, but I hit the intercom button, and it's him, just like I knew it would be. It's as if I felt him down there.

I tell him I'm coming down.

I head down through the lobby.

He's standing out there on the stoop in the cool spring air, scowly and gothic in a long, black coat, hair mussed. People rush up and down the sidewalk behind him. Horns blare up and down 45th. It's rush hour, but everything seems to still when we come face to face.

There are soft lines around his gray eyes—weariness, I think. "You look like you've been up for a week," I say.

He shoves his hands into his pockets, and I want to kiss him with everything in me.

"Two, actually," he says, and then his eyes crinkle with so much warmth, my heart nearly breaks. "It's good to see you."

"You, too," I say. It's not a lie.

He grins. "So did you give all of the boringly tedious yachting clothes to a needy but boringly tedious friend?"

I look down at my pink leggings and bright vintage Spice Girls shirt, also pink. "I gave them to a friend with a boringly tedious job with a boringly tedious dress code. She was very grateful."

"That works," he says.

I know I should cut this off, but I can't bring myself to yet. "How goes the battle?"

"Not so bad. You'll be happy to know that my precious Tokyo is coming through." He leans on the stone façade that surrounds the security door.

"Good for Tokyo." I'm happy for him.

"Come out for a cocktail," he says. "My car's around the corner."

Butterflies whirl in my belly. *A cocktail with Rex!* The butterflies want to go for it. They want to snuggle up next to him in a dark corner booth and share confessions and suck in his warm, spicy scent and kiss him. But then again, butterflies have brains the size of pinheads.

I close my eyes and force myself to remember my mom, broken and abandoned by Dad. To remember crying in that hospital bed, crying at the TipTop, like my own personal mantra of doom.

It's not that I think happy relationships can't exist, but this is the pattern of my family and my life; maybe it's even in my genes.

I say, "I came down so you could see my eyes when I tell you nothing's changed. So that you get that I meant it when I said we can't date."

He tips his head, giving me a playful look. "But you're also enjoying seeing me a little bit, right?"

I shake my head and look away. The sky is still bright with the last streaks of orange.

"Come out. It's just a cocktail."

"It never will be just a cocktail with us. Going out is how we kill what we had with a thousand bloody little cuts."

"And they say I'm dark and dramatic."

A smile tugs at my lips, but I purse them instead. "Rex. I'm asking you to respect my decision."

"I won't stop wanting you."

I suck in a deep breath. "I'm not going to answer the intercom again. I'm blocking your number. I won't take your gifts. Jada will sign for them and not tell me about them."

"I won't stop," he says. I'm not sure whether he means the gifts or about wanting to date.

I tell him goodbye. I make it sound final while my heart twists. I force myself to go into the lobby and march to the elevator and not watch him walk away.

I know I did the right thing, but sometimes late at night I wake up in my bed and think, *what if? What if I've made the biggest mistake of my life?*

Second-guessing yourself late at night is even worse hell.

On the upside, I have the bonus money that Rex deposited in my bank—the double bonus, thanks to the hate list—and several weeks left on my wrist-healing sabbatical from hair-cutting.

I make the time off count by throwing myself into the new business. I start working on a pop-up—the proof-of-concept run that Gail and I had brainstormed. I'd never think this big if it weren't for Gail.

I write up a business plan and start researching investors, but nobody will be like Gail. I miss her advice, her excitement.

Not half as much as I miss Rex. Life on that yacht, seen in the rearview mirror, looks more and more like a beautiful dream.

And there's this tiny voice growing louder and louder. It's wondering whether maybe that dream is worth taking a risk for. Maybe. Just maybe.

Sometimes I think it's the little voice that always wants me to have English toffee.

But sometimes I wonder if it's not the smartest, bravest part of me.

Chapter Twenty-Four

Rex

CLARK AND IVAN SIT in silence as the man in the thousand-dollar suit and the near-million-dollar watch shakes my hand. "My people will send details," the man says.

"Looking forward to it," I reply.

The three of us watch him stroll away from our booth, off through the plush, dimly lit space, past the well-heeled patrons mingling at the bar; it's nearly half a minute before they start giving me shit.

"Wasn't that Webster Schultz? Inviting you to his home for dinner?" Ivan says. "Does he realize you're just a townie who still eats with his hands?"

"Fuck off," I say.

"Somebody needs to tell him to hide his silverware *and* his daughters," Ivan says.

Clark laughs.

As my oldest friends, Clark and Ivan get to give me shit. Clark's been with me forever in business, and Ivan came up in the trenches with me. We were in the same boat coming to Manhattan—the wrong connections, the wrong education, the wrong clothes. I haven't seen him in the two weeks since the trip. It seems like a lifetime.

"Webster Schultz is wondering about your next play, but he doesn't quite want to tell you that," Clark notes, ever his perceptive self. "Magic Eight Ball says, you got your fuck-you power without landing Gail's account."

Like a lot of people, Webster Schultz took notice of how effectively I smoothed out the valley so many of us found ourselves in after the Bellcore disaster. I'll be handing Gail back her funds with a slight gain next week, which is quite a feat. It's not enough to keep her business out of Wydover's hands, unfortunately. Wydover still has it all wrapped up, thanks to his willingness to play dirty with Marvin's help—not that I can prove anything.

But what I can prove to Gail is that I'm a man she can rely on no matter what.

If only I could prove it to Tabitha.

I've been following her on Instagram. She's had her head down, true to her word, working tirelessly on her business. She's starting small, with a pop-up storefront. If she'd been able to accept Gail's investment and involvement, she'd be positioned to ten-X her efforts, but I have no doubt she'll do brilliantly without Gail.

"I haven't given up on Driscoll," I say. "Wydover will screw up, and she'll come back to me. It might be two years from now, it might be ten years from now, but I won't give up." I put up my hands, Tabitha style, as if to frame my words. "I am the fucking jaguar, waiting in the bush. I am the wind, whistling at Wydover's back when he's walking alone at night."

Ivan snorts.

"Challenges always have energized you," Clark says. "My money's on you."

I line up the beveled edge of my tumbler with the edge of the napkin.

"I want you to challenge your inability to master the extended metaphor," Ivan says. "Be the jaguar or the wind. You don't get to be both."

The instant he says that, my mind goes back to Tabitha yet again. Back to the way she'd count wrong when laying out reasons for things. The way she'd say there are three reasons for a thing but only come up with two, or she'd have four. And I'd give her such shit. How did I ever find her annoying?

"You're the jaguar, waiting in the bush, silently padding behind him when he walks alone at night," Ivan says. "How about that?"

"Whatever, Shakespeare."

"I like him as the *wind*," Clark says.

"Can we drop this?" I bite out.

"Somebody needs to get laid," Ivan says, angling his gaze at the table of three women nearby who have been looking over in our direction.

"I know, I saw them," I say. "Not interested, but you go ahead."

"The blonde in red?" Ivan presses. "She's just your type. Don't tell me you've already had her. You know that ridiculous one-fuck rule of yours is going to end up with you running out of eligible women, right?"

"I'm just not interested," I say.

Clark's eyeing me now.

"What's going on? Something's going on with you," Ivan says.

"Because I don't want to sleep with every supermodel on two legs?"

"Um, yeah?" Ivan says.

I shoot him a look. I was never that much of a manwhore, was I? But then, I suppose I was. Pre-yacht me seems like a different life, a different brain. The goals I had before feel empty. Devoid warmth. Meaning.

Part of me wishes I could rewind to a time where good returns and a faceless fuck were all I needed to be happy.

I sip my drink, savoring the burn. At least the burn feels like something real. "Anyway, I'm still technically engaged. No public dates until we break it off in three months."

"Doesn't have to be public," Ivan says.

"Not interested," I say, maybe too forcefully.

Clark's gaze sharpens. "Have you tried to talk to her?"

"Wait. Who?" Ivan says. "What'd I miss?"

Clark raises his brows.

"The woman I brought on the yacht," I say.

"Wait—the fake fiancée?" Ivan straightens. "I thought you picked her specifically because she was annoying and repugnant. Are you telling me you hit that?" Ivan's laughing. "A few days on the boat and you're banging the woman you chose specifically for her repugnant qualities? That's pathetic, man."

"There's nothing repugnant about her," I say. "Or annoying. I got it wrong."

My guys are watching me now. I have their attention.

"I got her wrong. All of it," I add.

Ivan is laughing. "Well, that's a hell of a thing to get wrong."

Clark gives him a warning look, shakes his head. Ivan, of course, ignores him.

"The *hairdresser*," Ivan says.

"You got something to say about hairdressers?"

Ivan holds up his hands.

"Have you tried to get in contact with her at all?" Clark asks.

I close my eyes. "Yes." I don't like to show vulnerability, even to my oldest friends. That's the culture I came up in, but maybe I just don't want to be alone with it anymore.

I order another round and I tell Ivan what an asshole I was, how I mocked the things Tabitha loves, ridiculed her theories, made a list of the characteristics of her that I thought I hated, and how it turns out I actually might love those things.

Clark chimes in, painting the scene when she saw the list. I tell Ivan how we ended up having an amazing connection, even after she discovered the list, but how she won't let it be more than a vacation fling. She refused my offer of a birthday dinner next week, a cocktail, a simple walk in the park.

"Guys have done nothing but let her down, and I'm asking her to trust the man who wrote the hate list?" I say. "No wonder she doesn't trust me."

"She wants to protect her heart," Clark says.

"Exactly," I say.

"But think about it," Clark says. "You don't have to protect your heart from somebody you don't care about. And I saw you two together. She had you sitting in hot tubs and cabanas and laughing and doing ridiculous shit during trading hours."

"During trading hours?" Ivan says. "New York trading hours? Jesus Christ."

"Even so, what does it matter?" I say. "She won't trust me."

"You're the turnaround king," Ivan says. "Turn it around. You say it's her birthday next week? Make her go out with you. Show her how it can be."

"Have you been listening?" I say. "She won't go out with me ever, and she definitely wouldn't go out with me on her birthday."

Ivan gets his Cheshire cat smile. "She'd go out with you on her birthday if she had to. If she had no choice." He pauses, sits back, crosses his legs. It's his legal checkmate attitude. "I helped you write the contract. In the three months after the yacht trip, she is bound by the terms to show up with you at up to three important public occasions or forfeit all monies.

Important occasion as defined by you. What could be more important than a birthday?"

"You're telling me to force her to go out with me on her birthday?"

"It's exactly what I'm telling you," Ivan says. "She could choose to say no and give back the money and face legal action, of course. She has to go. It gives you another chance to make your case."

"Wait, I'm not sure if that's a good idea," Clark says.

"If she won't see you, what do you have to lose?" Ivan says, playing the devil on my shoulder.

"Wait, are you considering it?" Clark says. "She'll be pissed."

"So get her an amazing gift," Ivan counters.

"Hmm," I say.

"Oh my god," Clark says. "You're considering it. Dude I can't think of any gift that would make her not pissed off to be forced into a date. You need to just keep asking."

"But that's not working," I say.

"Surely there's something she wants," Ivan says. "Something that would make her life better."

My gaze falls to my scotch. There's no way I can travel back in time and undo the fact that we lied right to Gail's face. However, there are other things Tabitha wants—like to know her building won't get demolished. It would mean everything if she knew that. I could give her security in the home she loves so much.

An idea slowly forms in my mind.

Chapter Twenty-Five

Tabitha

CLARK STANDS in the doorway looking unhappy. He's got a nice leather satchel in his hand. "Hey," he says. "How's it going?"

"You tell me," I say. "Was it stupid to have buzzed you up?" I thought Rex might be in trouble or something, but seeing the nervous look on Clark's face, I'm thinking I'm the one who's in trouble.

"It wouldn't have mattered," he says.

I motion him in. He sits on the couch in the place where he sat before this whole thing started and pulls a sheath of papers out of his satchel.

"A copy of the contract," he says. He turns to the second page and hands it to me. There's a section highlighted—it's the one requiring a minimum of three public post-yacht appearances deemed important occasions by Rex.

"The jig is up," I say. "Gail gave the account to somebody

else, so the pretense is null and void." I'm sort of proud of how legalistic I sound, what with my *null and void*. "She's not focused on us anymore. She doesn't have to believe the lie. I'm abiding by the no-public-dates-until-our-breakup thing, but that's all we need to do."

Our social media breakup announcement is scheduled just over two months out.

"Here's the thing," Clark says. "You signed a contract promising three joint appearances of Rex's choosing to take place after the yacht trip is over, and those appearances are not contingent on his getting the account."

"But the whole reason was to get the account. The reason is null and void," I say.

"I'm sorry, but that's not what the contract says. And Rex has identified an occasion. He'll be sending a car to pick you up on Friday at seven p.m. You'll be dining at the TipTop—"

"What?!" I say. "Oh, no. No way!" I hand the contract back. "There is zero chance in hell that I'm going to the TipTop for my birthday with Rex."

"Zero chance!" says Jada, who has materialized next to me.

Clark blinks nervously and turns to the end of the contract where yet another paragraph is highlighted, one that I initialed, showing that I understand that breaking the contract will result in my having to return all of the money and facing legal charges.

My blood goes cold.

"What?" Jada asks.

When I don't respond, she grabs the papers from my hand and reads the highlighted paragraph. "Oh, hellz no!"

"I'm sorry," Clark says.

"Does he want to punish me?" I say. "Because that's what this is! This is the worst possible thing he can ask."

"Tabby has birthday issues," Jada says. "You tell him that."

"He knows," I say.

"Uhhhhh," Jada says, giving Clark a million-watt glare, but this is a man who works with Rex. He's immune.

I only wish I was.

Chapter Twenty-Six

Rex

IT DOESN'T TAKE long to get the details of the sale of the building that Tabitha and her friends live in and find out who bought it.

The news couldn't be worse—it's Malcolm Blackberg, an Eastside-based entrepreneur who's notoriously private—and not private out of any kind of shyness, either, but rather an extreme dislike of people, according to rumor. And when he does come into contact with people, it apparently doesn't end well.

He doesn't see people or take meetings that he himself doesn't initiate, but that doesn't stop me from heading down to his office after his people said no to my people on the phone.

His office turns out to be a prewar fortress of a building on Central Park, six stories of stone with actual gargoyles on the top corners.

I bluster my way past a layer of receptionists, escalating and bribing my way from the first floor to the second floor and onward. Finally I reach the fifth floor where a team of hyper-efficient administrative assistants guard the executive elevator to the sixth floor, Malcolm's floor, like rabid dragons.

If I can't get to his elevator, I can't get to his floor.

I'd been prepared to pay far more than the building is worth—the man just bought it, after all, and if the rumors are true, that he's planning on flattening it, it means he's got something in the works, and that means cash outlays, probably to architects, lawyers, engineers, maybe even city zoning staff. I'm prepared to make it well worth his while.

I never expected I wouldn't be able to see him. The furthest I can get is to a woman named Gretchen, who seems to be a senior assistant to Malcolm. Gretchen sits in a corner office with an amazing view. She informs me that all buying and selling of real estate goes through her, but it's not helpful—she's not the decision maker; Malcolm is. She tells me that the building isn't for sale.

"Don't you think Mr. Blackberg would want to hear my offer?" I ask.

"No," she says. "He doesn't want to hear your offer."

I've come armed with homework. I know what he spent on the building, which is slightly more than its actual value. I take a piece of paper and write down a number that far exceeds what he paid just a matter of months ago. I slide it over. "Cash. This week. In exchange, Mr. Blackberg gives me the title free and clear."

"Do you not understand the concept of no?" she asks.

"Everybody has their price," I say.

"Mr. Blackberg won't sell. He has plans in place. That building is getting knocked down."

I take back the paper and write a higher number.

She shakes her head.

"Just take it to him," I say.

"I'm not in the habit of wasting Mr. Blackberg's time. This meeting is over."

I start laying bills on the desk. A nice little pile of money just for her. "I need to talk to him."

She sighs wearily.

"I'm not leaving. You may as well take it. I'm determined."

Her expression changes when I lay my last hundred on the desk. She dials the phone, puts it on speaker, and sets it on the desk.

"What?" comes the voice on the other end.

"I have a Rex O'Rourke here looking to buy 341 West Forty-fifth. He's willing to pay me a lot of money to let him in to see you with his offer of…" She picks up the paper and reads it off.

I lean in. "Mr. Blackberg, I'm offering you thirty percent more than the property is worth. Can we talk?"

"That building's not for sale."

I increase my offer.

"Why this building?" he says. "It's a piece of shit."

"A friend is extremely attached to that building," I say. "So that makes this your lucky day."

Laughter bellows over the intercom. "Now I'm the one doing you a favor. You're not buying that building. The answer is no. And trust me, no pussy is worth that amount of money."

"I want the building," I say simply.

There's a silence on his end. It was a forceful statement, possibly too forceful. This whole thing with Tabitha has me twisted in knots.

"I know who you are," Blackberg says. "And I know how you operate out there. Here's my message to you: If you try to exert financial pressure on me of any kind, I'll figure out who your *friend* is and I'll throw her out on the street with all of her shit so fast her head will spin. If you come at me in any way, I'll throw her out on her ass. And if you bribe my people again, I will throw her out on her ass for that, too." There's a click on the other end.

Gretchen pushes the pile of money back toward me with a smile.

"So should I take that as a maybe?" I say. "I heard maybe."

She doesn't find my comment funny. "He'll never change his mind. Especially not after this."

Of course I investigate Malcolm Blackberg. When a man doesn't want you to come at him, he usually has something he doesn't want you to find. I set my PI on it with instructions to dig around very discreetly for anything I can turn into leverage.

Every man has his price, and when he doesn't have a price, he has a vulnerability. It's Monday, and Tabitha's birthday is Friday.

Not a lot of time.

I imagine myself sitting down at the table and showing her a purchase agreement, telling her that she'll never have to worry about being evicted—not ever. I'll write up a contract guaranteeing it. Even if she refuses to speak to me ever again, her home is safe. She'll see that she can count on a man to come through with something.

My PI is still empty-handed on Wednesday. He warns me that going any deeper might alert Malcolm Blackberg.

Reluctantly, I admit defeat on the building and tell him to cut the investigation.

But I need something!

I make a new list—things Tabitha loves—and task a few of my own assistants to come up with alternative birthday presents. I can't go to her empty-handed. I won't.

As if to add insult to injury, Friday midnight is the deadline for my firm to relinquish all accounts associated with Driscoll. Will I lose the only two things I care about on the same day?

My assistants come to me Friday morning with their list of ideas. There's expensive sparkly jewelry, a paid mentorship from a fashion mogul, a custom hamster habitrail…all of it's bullshit except maybe the first-class trip for five to the Hello Kitty theme park, but even that feels like throwing money at her. Tabitha can't be bought.

For once I don't know what to do. The entire exercise of forcing her to go out for her birthday was based on having this building under contract, on being the guy who shows up for her with something so incredible that she has at least one happy birthday to remember.

Clark stops in with coffee. He thinks I should hire a marching band to march around outside her window and proclaim my affection.

I hate it. Nothing's right. Nothing's enough.

I tell myself that if I don't come up with something that will absolutely delight her by lunchtime, I'll let her out of the whole birthday fiasco. That's the thing she'd want most.

But it's after lunch and I still haven't found anything or brought myself to let her off the hook. Putting off the inevitable, I distractedly shuffle through the stack of mail one of my assistants deemed important enough to merit my attention. Few of these things will actually be worth my attention, but I'm procrastinating now, gut churning with dread.

I grab a FedEx envelope marked "confidential" and frown. What business do I have with a lab in Queens? Are they trying to sell me drug testing services or something? And why would this get through to me in the first place? I nearly throw it into the *figure-it-the-fuck-out!* pile, but something makes me pause.

It's the way it's addressed: "Rex O'Rourke Capital, Confidential, Attn: Rex O'Rourke," followed by my PI's name.

Are these Gail and Marvin's results? My PI would've had the results sent to me and probably duplicate results to himself.

I shut my eyes, remembering that day on the island when we sent off the package. Her little stack of postcards. Her delight at shoving her toes into the sand.

I think back further, to the salon, to that mischievous sparkle in her fox-brown eyes when Marvin appeared outside the salon door. The look we shared, and the way her breath sped with excitement and wonder, and how much of a brat she was with the squirrel bullshit, and how I had to fucking have her.

And for one small moment, she let down that jokey façade and let me see the real her—gritty and real and raw and wounded, and so alive.

God, I miss her.

I slide my finger over the address. The shadier Marvin acted, the more fun it was with her. Like we were a team.

I'm glad Gail never found out about our little game. Marvin's not a good person, but he's her family. I should've canceled the tests. I'd meant to before Bellcore blew up. Because what does it matter now?

Listlessly, I pull open the tab on the envelope and pull out the results, knowing what they'll say—Marvin is her nephew. He always was her nephew. He produced an heirloom. He looks like Gail.

But apparently I'll do anything to put off having to release Tabitha from going on a birthday date, so I pull out the report.

Written in stark letters, above the list of numbers and strange little charts, is "excluded" and "0.00015."

It takes a moment for my mind to make sense of what I'm looking at. I check it, and double-check it.

According to these results, Marvin is not a relative of Gail. Excluded as a relative.

My blood thunders.

I read the accompanying text, which only confirms my understanding.

Could it be a mistake? I get my PI on the phone. "I'm looking at these DNA results. But I'm not sure what to think about what I'm seeing."

"I was just going to call you," he says. "I got those this morning, too. I lit a fire under the other lab I used and that just came back negative. It's probably working its way through your mailroom. You were right. The guy's not who he says he is."

"You don't sound surprised," I say.

"Well, you cut off the investigation, but I had a few leads in progress, so I kept them cooking. None of it felt right."

"He produced an obscure family heirloom," I say. "I can't believe this DNA could possibly be accurate."

"No question it's accurate," my PI says.

"How do you account for the heirloom?"

"Are you sitting down?" he asks.

"Just tell me. You have reason to believe Marvin's a fraud other than this DNA?"

"We found out that Pete Wydover was involved with Gail's sister," he says.

"What?"

"Way back—it was after she left her family behind, but before she died. She stayed at the Wydover summer home in Martha's Vineyard some thirty years back."

"What?" I bark. "How did that not come out before?"

"Because you hire the best, my friend," my PI says. "Wydover and Gail's sister, Dana, had a short secret fling, it turns out. I'm guessing Dana stayed at his place and left a lot of her things there before traipsing off on her next adventure. That's probably how he got the heirloom. We traced her all over the place. We interviewed some of her friends from that time. She went hard-core vagabond after that. She did a lot of things, but she never had a kid."

"She knew Wydover," I say, putting it all together in my mind.

My PI explains that Pete Wydover was a rich kid who threw lots of parties, which I already knew. He not only dated Dana briefly, but he also knew Bob Bell of Bellcore, which is how he knew about Bellcore's shady, mobbed-up connections.

"How did nobody turn up these connections?" I say.

"Again," he says. "The best PI."

"Yeah, yeah, keep going," I say.

My PI tells me that Marvin and Wydover were both in Atlanta at the same time two years back. He learned through a highly illegal credit card trace that Wydover was a customer at a bar where Marvin was bartending the night of a Falcons game. He actually got security footage of them leaving the place together hours after bar time.

I'm reeling. "I can't believe it."

"Pretty fucking amazing if I do say so myself," he says. "I believe Wydover was sitting on those puzzle pieces for years—he trades in puzzle pieces just like you do, Rex. You guys are puzzle guys."

"Right," I say.

"So Wydover meets Marvin in Atlanta. This is two years ago," my PI says. "Wydover and Marvin get to talking, and he learns that Marvin was adopted. Wydover can see that Marvin looks enough like Gail to pass as a relative. He's been gunning for the Driscoll account just like you have been, and he decides to set Marvin up as a long-lost relative. Marvin gets a rich family—nothing he can inherit from, but the man was a bartender, right? It's gonna be a step up. Marvin enrolled in some finance courses at the local college two weeks later. He's taking the classes, Wydover is fixing the DNA shit, and suddenly this past fall, Gail has an instant nephew who has this econ knowledge. And sure, Gail's PI did a backgrounder on Marvin, but nothing like the scrutiny he'd get if he pretended to have Driscoll blood, right? Anyway, he turns up as Gail's relative and angles himself into the assets area. Marvin pushes for the review, and Wydover uses the bombshell about Bellcore to make the timing work."

"Back up. How did he manipulate the DNA results?" I ask.

"We're looking into hacks in the labs they used."

"DNA results are only as reliable as the weakest link in the chain," I say.

"Precisely. He was playing a very long game. He could've used the insight to make money in the market. Instead, he made money in the market and landed Gail's account." There's a pause. "What are you going to do?"

"Show Gail."

"She won't like that you tested her DNA. Why not feed this to a reporter?"

"Because that takes too long. Gail's contract with Wydover is about to go into effect. She'll want to know now."

"You think you can save the account?"

"I doubt it," I say, glancing at the time. "Gail hates any kind of deception. She probably won't want anything to do with either of us, but at least I keep Wydover from dragging Gail down with him."

"And it serves as a nice little warning to people who might think about trying to screw you out of accounts in the future."

"Doesn't it, though? How fast can you courier over the full report? I want everything you have on Wydover's association with Marvin and the sister."

"It's on its way."

I look at the clock. Well over three hours before I meet Tabitha. As far as birthday gifts go, the DNA results on Marvin aren't in the ballpark with my ensuring she'll never lose her beloved home, but she'll enjoy finding out that she was right all along, because busting Marvin was our thing—a project we worked on together, that we bonded over. Most of all, she'll be happy to know she saved Gail's ass. That's the kind of person she is. That will make her happy.

The courier is entering my building just as I'm leaving. I grab the report and head to my car, calling Gail en route.

"You don't have to do this personally," she says, meaning the transfer of her funds back to her. "There's no reason you need to be on site for this."

"I need to do it personally. I have something to show you."

∽

GAIL'S OFFICE is warm and colorful, with a gorgeous grandfather clock in the corner whose *tick-tick-tick* is the only sound I hear as I watch her study the DNA reports, mouth tight in a grim line.

"You had our DNA tested?" She finally looks up. "Without our knowledge?"

"Something didn't feel right," I say.

"You invaded our privacy?"

"Yes," I say simply.

She's angry. I knew she would be, but she deserves the truth. She sets the papers on her desk, slides them to the middle. "If this is true…"

I wait, watch her process it. She looks at the wall beside her with a glare so hot and hard, I'm shocked she doesn't blast a hole right through the plaster. Is that the side that Marvin's office is on? Is Marvin in the building? It's not even five yet.

She grabs her phone and sends a text, then tosses it down. "I don't know what I'm gonna do with you," she grumbles.

"You needed the facts," I say.

"Fucking right I did." There's a knock. "Come on in," she says.

"Something wrong?" Marvin asks, poking in his head. His gaze settles on me. "What're *you* doing here?"

"You ever see the inside of a prison cell, Marvin?" Gail asks.

Marvin comes in and shuts the door, frowning, looking between me and her. He's in a beautiful suit with a red tie. His blond hair is expertly tousled, but he doesn't have the sunglasses propped up on his head for once. "What is this?"

"Answer the question," she says. "Have you ever seen the inside of a prison cell?"

"No," Marvin says, stunned.

"You wanna?" she asks. "You wanna see one? You want to have the chance to decorate your own prison cell? Because fraud is a funny thing. Federal fraud, securities fraud, postal fraud. It's a very serious conviction. You can stretch those charges long and wide as the Mississippi."

Marvin frowns at me. "What bullshit has he been filling your head with?"

I take the opportunity to give him a big smile, wishing Tabitha were here. She'd be bursting at the seams with excitement. I know the exact smile she'd wear, or more, she'd be biting that lower lip, and there'd be a glow on her face.

I check the time on Gail's big ol' clock. Still early. I can still get to her with time to spare.

"Don't look at him, look at me," Gail says. "You're going to want to come clean to me."

"Are you threatening me?" Marvin asks.

She pushes the DNA test across the table.

Marvin picks up the sheet, studies it, brow furrowed. I'm already thinking about how I'll describe the moment. "You tested me?" He looks up at Gail. "What right…"

"I tested you," I say. "I did it."

"*You* did?" Marvin barks at me. "How did you get my DNA? That's an invasion of privacy. It's an *actionable* invasion—"

"Priorities, Marvin," Gail says. "Tell me your story or I call the cops."

A heavy hush settles over the room. I can see the gears going in Marvin's head.

I wait. This is the tricky part. Gail knows what he's done,

and she could send him to jail. But the publicity will damage the Driscoll brand, and Marvin knows it.

"What are you really going to do, though?" Marvin asks, clearly recognizing this as the game of chicken that it is. "Press charges? Put it in the papers? If I go down, you're going to look pretty gullible."

Gail folds her arms, cool as a cucumber. "I don't have to tell you what I'll do. That's the beauty of being in the position I'm currently in, and that's the danger of the position that you're in. I don't like the publicity, but then, it's just a matter of spin."

Marvin's expression is guarded. "You're bluffing. You won't jeopardize your beloved fucking brand just to get a confession from me. You'll be a laughingstock. Here's my thinking. I'll just walk out of here and let bygones be bygones," Marvin says. "We call it even. No harm, no foul."

Marvin's smart. Of course, he knows Gail well by now. He knows how she protects her company, her family.

"Will you take your chances with *me*?" I ask him coolly.

Warily, Marvin studies my face. "You're not that vengeful," he says. "You'd burn too many bridges. It would hurt the Driscoll brand. It's not who you are."

"You think it's not who I am?" I smile. "Let me ask you this —did you ever imagine that I'm the kind of man who knows how easily DNA results are manipulated? Did you ever imagine I could be the kind of man to break several laws to secretly obtain DNA samples from unwitting subjects and have them tested? Because apparently I might just be that kind of man. You don't think that level of vengeance is me?" I don't mention Tabitha's involvement. No way am I throwing her under the bus.

Marvin blinks. It really is outrageous—it's outrageous that I would've thought of the scheme, and it's outrageous to follow through on that testing.

I'm not that kind of man, of course.

Stefano DiMera from *Days of our Lives*, though, he is that kind of man.

I let my voice go silky. "How do you think I got your DNA material? I'll let you think about that a little." I smile. He has to know I broke into his cabin to get his DNA. That, too, is outrageous. It makes me look like an unhinged, calculating, vengeful villain.

Marvin goes a little ashen. He's not loving this.

I can feel Gail staring at me. She didn't think I was that kind of man, either. Which is, admittedly, not ideal. But I lost the chance to regain her business when I showed her the test.

Marvin snorts. "Fine, I'll tell you what happened…if you'll sign something that you won't press charges."

Gail crosses her arms. "How about you tell me everything and hope for my goodwill. Or don't."

Gail doesn't look at me, but she's highly aware of me. Gail and I have been going up against vipers in the negotiating room for years, and right now we're working together, an unreadable wall of intent, bearing down on Marvin's sorry ass.

In short, I'm the bad cop now. More like the crazy cop.

If Gail doesn't do something, will I? How reckless could I get?

I give Marvin the kind of crocodile smirk that I'd imagine Stefano DiMera would wear.

Finally Marvin crumbles. He tells all. He portrays himself as the victim of Wydover. Claims Wydover came to his bar where he worked and threatened him. He's probably lying about the threats, but the rest of his story matches what my PI worked out.

Gail eventually calls security. Marvin wants to leave on his own, but Gail makes him wait for the burly pair of guys to arrive. She tells him she doesn't want to see his face again. She doesn't want to hear his name again. She suggests Alaska.

I check the clock in the corner—one hour until our reservation. I text Tabitha, letting her know I could be running late.

If you get there first, sit tight—the surprise I have will be worth it, I promise!

"What do you have against Alaska?" I ask once Marvin's gone.

She's not in the mood for jokes. "So *are* you the kind of guy to break ten laws to secretly obtain DNA samples and have them tested?"

"Not really," I say. "It was…unusual for me."

"This whole thing is unbelievable," she says. "What possessed you…"

I swallow. "Have you ever watched *Days of our Lives*?" I ask her.

She folds her arms, eyes sparkling, and stares at me strangely. If I didn't lose her business with the DNA testing, I definitely have now.

"I need to be across town," I say.

"Wait. I have billions of dollars sitting in a reconciliation fund doing nothing, and you're going to leave and go across town?"

My pulse races as I make sense of her words. She's offering me the account? My blood races. The future I thought I'd lost begins to unfold in front of me. "What are you saying?" I ask.

"You put our house back in order nicely," she says. "Even though I was taking everything away and handing it over to Wydover, you did the right thing. Let's do this. I wanted you. I gave into his ridiculous review only because I assumed you'd win it."

"But what about all of the DNA business?"

"That snake was posing as my nephew. I'd say a little bit Stefano DiMera was called for, wouldn't you?" She winks. "But I have to say, you should've seen that Bellcore coming."

"I know. We've been analyzing it. Trying to learn from our

mistake on that." I still can't believe she's looking to work with me.

"You did the stand-up thing with my funds, and honestly, I won't have that money in reconciliation all weekend—I won't do it. You start the wheels on taking over our accounts right now and I'll get my board to sign off."

I can't believe it. I didn't expect it. I'm getting the account.

It's well into rush hour, but she wrests her board members out of wherever they were. I'm on my phone, fingers flying, pulling my team together.

I call Tabitha, but she doesn't answer. Is she showering? Getting ready for our date? I can't leave in the middle of this process, but I can't let her go sit alone at that restaurant—I won't take that chance. I call Clark over to Gail's tower. While she's updating her core group, I go down to the street-level entrance and wait for him.

"Don't you have to meet Tabitha for her birthday tonight?"

I tell him what happened and explain that if I manage everything right, we're getting every last cent of Gail's. We still have time. I might be a little late, but I'm thinking no more than twenty minutes.

"Doesn't she hate to be alone on her birthday?"

"This thing was our baby. She'll understand. And if this goes well, I'll walk in maybe ten minutes late, and she won't be alone, because you'll be there. Order a bottle of something bubbly. Tell her I have news she'll love."

I watch the car pull away, reminding myself that she and Clark are friendly, that she'll be happy to see him, and I'll be out the door soon—maybe I can wrap it all up and not even be late. I head up the elevator, imagining different ways to describe Marvin's face of shock. Tabitha will love the whole scene.

The idea of making her happy makes me happy.

The bonus check she'll be getting now that the account is

mine could buy her a nice condo. It's not the building, but it's security.

I get up there, and we get to work. Gail's board and her team come in, followed by my team.

We're surprisingly efficient. We hammer out new paperwork in no time. The lawyers take it to the next room, and we work on the next phase. I go back and forth between rooms, then settle in with Gail to figure out the operational stuff.

I look up at her grandfather clock at one point, and it's as if no time has passed at all.

I dive back in, energized. I'm going to nail this transition plan and get to Tabitha with time to spare. She's going to have a good experience on her birthday for once. And maybe she'll agree to another date after that. I built my empire with baby steps—maybe I can build her trust back the same way. Now that I got Gail's account, anything seems possible.

We're just starting to sign the first round of documents when Gail's phone buzzes. She glances at it and frowns, answers.

It's Clark. For me. She hands it over.

"Clark?"

"God, I thought you were in an accident somewhere," Clark says. "Why aren't you answering your phone?"

I check my pocket. Shit—I left my phone in one of the conference rooms.

"Do you know what time it is?" he asks.

I glance over at the grandfather clock in the corner. My blood freezes to ice as I realize that it hasn't changed. That it isn't ticking. I pull the phone away from my ear and see that it's ten thirty. I'm two-and-a-half hours late.

"Is Tabitha there?"

"I don't know anymore. She was, but I'm in the car. Her friends showed up at the restaurant, and let's just say it wasn't cool for me to stick around. I was not everybody's favorite person."

I stand, swearing under my breath. "But she's still there?"

"She was there when I left," Clark says. "She thought you were in the hospital or something. She was worried, Rex, but then I got hold of Adrian and she said you were holed up with Gail. She's pretty upset."

I mumble my thanks and hand Gail her phone, dazed.

"Problem?" she asks.

"I lost track of time." I look again at the grandfather clock.

"Oh, no—I hope you weren't relying on that old clock. It slows in the evening and peters out between eight and nine, depending on how hard it gets wound. Sentimental…"

I send somebody for my phone, send for a car, and start gathering my stuff. "We have the big stuff down," I say to her. I set up a proxy.

"Is everything okay?" Gail asks.

"I left Tabitha sitting and waiting," I say, trying to keep the emotion out of my voice. I grab my phone, and I'm out of there like a shot.

I roll through my messages in the elevator down and the car ride over. There are five from Tabitha, going from hopeful to angry. The last one came in at ten. It's one word, all caps:

SERIOUSLY?!!!!!!

There are even more from Clark. Warnings that I'm pushing it. That she's not going to sit and wait forever. That she's angry. There's nothing left to chat about. She's calling her friends.

I try her, but my call goes to voicemail. No surprise there.

I lean forward, telling the driver to hurry.

Chapter Twenty-Seven

Tabitha

LIZZIE AND WILLOW are the first to arrive. They shoo Clark out of there and make me move to the bar from my sad table for two.

"Honey!" Jada rushes up, fresh from dress rehearsal, and gives me a giant hug.

"Thank you for coming," I whisper. I drain the last of my Hot Pink Barbie.

She adjusts my party hat and looks down at my dress—a slinky pink number with a yellow cat heart-eyes emoji on the front done in sequins. "Too cute," she says.

"Thanks," I whisper. I felt so happy when I picked it out, imagining the look on Rex's face—the rise it would get out of him, the way he'd secretly love it, but act like he can't even.

"You're too cute for *him*," she says.

"Don't try to act like there's not mascara running down my cheeks," I say. "This is no time for pretty lies."

"Rex O'Rourke is a jerk!" Jada says. "How about that?"

"Better." I cross my arms and try to work up anger. I want to be angry. Anger is so much better than heartbreak.

"He blows you off on your birthday," she adds.

"Right?" I say. "Uhh."

"The motherfucker sent his friend instead of showing up?" Lizzie says. "What is that?"

"I can't even wrap my mind around that!" Jada says, taking off her coat. "He couldn't have designed a more horrible birthday if he tried!"

"I'm sorry, but I run a tech business," Willow says. "If I don't want to do business at eight at night, then I don't do business at eight at night. It's called being the boss. Same with my brother. If Theo doesn't want to be in the office at eight at night, he's not in the office."

"Did he offer any excuse at all?" Jada asks.

"He texted two hours ago." I show them my phone.

If you get there first, sit tight—the surprise I have will be worth it, I promise!

"Can you think of any surprise that makes this worth it?" Jada asks. "Because I can't."

"Hell no." I put my phone away. "Though he did send his assistant Clark to let me know that he might be ten minutes late." I make them all laugh with my description of Clark totally sweating bullets as ten minutes turned into twenty, then an hour. How Clark kept trying to text Rex under the table.

"Then we came and kicked Clark out," Lizzie says.

"And I blocked Rex's number," I say.

"Good riddance!" Jada says.

"Yeah, screw that!" Willow signals the bartender. "Another round of Hot Pink Barbies!"

Lizzie loops an arm around my shoulders. I love that my friends are here, but nothing will fix the hole in me. Nothing can undo the devastation of sitting there waiting while Clark made excuses for yet another man blowing me off on my birthday.

My heart hurts. If only he hadn't forced me to go out to the TipTop.

I need to recover from this, and I don't know how. I loved him. And the worst thing about it is that I still do.

"You deserve better," Lizzie says. "You're worth more than this. It's best he shows his true colors now, right?"

"No doubt!" Jada says. "He gave Tabitha a great present— the gift of knowledge—knowledge that he'll never be good enough for her."

I down my third Hot Pink Barbie. "Worst birthday present ever!"

Vicky arrives wearing a giant coat.

"Tabitha! Happy birthday! Also, that dress! You are killing me! But it makes your boobs look amazing." We kiss cheeks, and then the bulge in her coat starts squirming. "Crap. I didn't think we were staying." She pulls out a fluffy white dog.

"Oh my god, Smuckers has arrived!" I take him from her arms and pull his plump, warm body to my chest and push my face into his fur. Smuckers licks my arm, wiggling with excitement. I push my face into his fur, soaking in the pure love he has for people.

"I couldn't believe it when Lizzie called!" Vicky says. "Rex O'Rourke stood you up? Knowing you had a childhood birthday trauma at this restaurant and he stands you *up*?"

Noelle shows up—shy, sweet Noelle. She gives me a huge hug. "We're here for you," she says. "We're gonna make this your best birthday."

"Men are dogs," Jada puts in.

"Hey," Vicky says. "Poor Smuckers doesn't like that!"

"Losers," Jada says.

"Yeah," I agree half-heartedly.

They say people end up with guys like their fathers. Rex is very much like my father—a successful city guy who only cares about me when I'm useful to him. My dad enjoyed cute daughter Tabitha—the Tabitha that helped him get dates—but not the birthday girl who needed him to show up so badly.

Jacob was like that, too. He loved fun Tabitha. But hospital bed Tabitha? Not so much.

"It really is good to know these things up front," Vicky says as Henry comes up next to her. "It's good to have a warning."

"Right?" I laugh. "Side effects include realizing he doesn't give a shit and uncontrollable jaw-dropping shock when he ruins your birthday in the most stunning of ways, accompanied by severe self-recrimination for believing him!"

A server beelines over right then. "Dogs aren't allowed in here," she says to us. The server, however, doesn't understand the power of Smuckers; this server only knows that she has the overwhelming urge to pet him. Suddenly the entire floor staff is petting Smuckers, having fallen under his spell. "We never saw him, okay?" the server whispers.

Smuckers is the center of gravity now. I take a moment to breathe, to be alone with my thoughts. I'm honestly relieved. The spotlight was too much. I settle into an empty barstool, away from the cluster of people.

Noelle comes over and quietly tucks into the barstool next to me.

"Let's talk about something else besides me," I say. "Tell me something fun and funny."

She tells me about a crazy postal customer drama that would've never happened in her small hometown. Noelle is so shy and small-town-ish, it's fun to hear her tell her tales of a postal carrier in Manhattan. What she says actually isn't shocking if you've lived here—the entertaining part is how shocked she is. People say I'm brave, but she is, too.

And then she leans in. "Tabby, how are you doing?" she asks in her quiet way. "Tell me really."

"I was excited to see him," I confess. "In spite of the jerky way he made me come out, you know? When I was picking out my outfit, I felt happier than I did in a really long time. And I thought, maybe I can take a risk. Maybe he's worth the risk."

She nods, says nothing.

"I love him, Noelle, and I can't stop. I wanted to try. To stick my neck out one more time. But that's over."

"Are you sure you can't give him another chance?" she asks.

"Why should I? Give me one good reason."

"Because he's not Jacob. He's not your dad. Because you just told me this feels real."

"That's three reasons," I say quietly. Exactly the thing Rex would say. I wrap my arms around myself, wondering whether I'll ever not miss him.

Noelle settles a hand on my shoulder. "You are so fun and great, and you know we love you, but the fact is, life can't all be fun and sparkles. If it was worth risking a few hours ago, I think maybe it still is."

"Blowing me off on my birthday feels like a bridge too far," I say.

"What if he has an explanation?" she says.

"Maybe if he was in the emergency room. But he was at work. He didn't even call."

"Just think about it," she says.

"Can I think about gorillas on tiny bikes instead?" I say. "I'd so much rather think about gorillas on tiny bikes."

Noelle rolls her eyes. "Yes, okay. Just because it's your birthday."

Mia rushes in. "Happy birthday, babe!" She hugs me. "Max is out there with the car, come on! We're breaking you out of here!"

"We're leaving?" Jada asks, and then she downs the rest of her drink and comes over and downs my drink. I grab Noelle's arm, and we all leave.

And like a crazy person, I am thinking about it.

Chapter Twenty-Eight

Rex

I BURST into the TipTop and scan the place. She's nowhere to be seen.

What have I done? How could I have stood her up on her birthday of all days? I should've set an alarm. Five alarms.

I go up to the bartender and describe Tabitha. "Her friends might have come and gotten her," I say.

The bartender gives me a hard look. "*You're* the guy," she says in an accusatory tone.

"I am," I say. "Did they say where they were going?"

"No." She grabs a rag and wipes the bar.

I sink onto a stool, unsure what to do. I have everything I wanted. I shouldn't be this upset.

The bartender comes back over. She points at a booth near the panoramic window. There's a couple sitting on the same side, heads together, talking or maybe just snuggling.

"Those are friends of hers. You could ask them."

"Thanks," I say.

I head over. As I near, I notice the woman has a little white dog half inside her coat. And the man looks familiar. Have I met him?

"Hi, excuse me, are you friends of Tabitha Evans's?" I ask.

The man stands. "Rex O'Rourke. We finally meet." He extends his hand. "Henry Locke."

"Henry! A pleasure," I say. I've been on conference calls with Henry Locke of Locke Companies—they're a construction firm with their fingers in the real estate asset market. We've done deals on behalf of clients, but we've never met in person.

He introduces me to Vicky and Smuckers. Smuckers is far more happy to see me than Vicky is. He wiggles excitedly in her arms, trying to get to me. Vicky says hello unenthusiastically.

"I need to see her," I say to Vicky. "I need to apologize. You're probably aware that I screwed up hugely."

"Very aware," Vicky says.

"Do you know where she is?" I ask.

Vicky shakes her head. "I don't. And I don't know if I'd tell you if I did. Try calling her, asking her if she wants to see you."

"I can't get through."

"Well, if she doesn't want to see you, you have to respect that."

"If I could just explain," I say.

"There's not much to explain," Vicky says. "It's her birthday, and you contractually forced her to go to the scene of her worst birthday nightmare ever—*on* her birthday—and instead of showing up, you sent an employee of yours to sit with her. For over two hours. Why would you do that? Who *does* that?"

I wince. It doesn't sound very good when she says it like that, but it's what I did. "I know it looks bad. I didn't mean for it to go like that."

"Maybe you didn't mean for it to go like that, but that's how it went."

"I know," I say. "That's why I need to talk to her." There's this awkward silence where I stand there. I won't give up. I won't just walk off into the night.

Henry looks down at Vicky. "Maybe call Jada? You could call Jada and give Rex your phone and let him talk to her?"

"Seriously?"

"Jada knows Tabitha's state of mind," Henry continues. "Maybe Tabitha wants to hear him out?"

"Why would she?" Vicky asks.

"Because sometimes guys screw up," Henry says. "And sometimes they're very, very sorry for it." He looks at Vicky, and Vicky looks at him. There's this long moment of silence where they seem to be secretly communicating about something specific.

"It's different. He deliberately blew her off," Vicky protests.

"It wasn't deliberate," I say. "I need a chance to make this right. I need to find her."

Vicky sighs and pulls out her phone. "You can't make it right," she says. "I'm telling you, and Jada's going to tell you the same thing, but hey." She puts her phone to her ear. "Hey, yeah, hi, so we're still at the TipTop and Rex is here...yeah, I know..." She glares up at me. "He finally turned up...yup, standing right here and he wants to meet you guys out...or... wait...can you just tell him?"

She hands up her phone.

I take it, put it to my ear. "Hi, Jada," I say. "Is she okay?"

"Not exactly, Rex." Jada's voice sounds tinny. There's music in the background. "What you pulled tonight was so messed up. Were you trying to mess with her mind? It was cruel. Crazy cruel!"

I apologize, but Jada is livid. I tell her I want to speak with Tabitha.

"She doesn't want to speak with you. She never wants to speak with you again. She has made that clear numerous times, yet you keep coming at her. Does she have to take out a restraining order? Is that what will make you stop?"

"I need to explain."

"She told you she didn't want to see you, and then you made her go legally with your bullshit contract. And now...what?"

"Tell her..." I don't know what to say. *I love her* comes to mind.

Jada hangs up. The call is over. The silence on the line is deafening.

I hand the phone back to Vicky, shell-shocked. Could this really be it? I have everything I ever wanted—Gail's billions under management, the power to move markets.

And I couldn't care less. It's Tabitha I want. What was I thinking, allowing myself to be even five minutes late for her birthday? I should've been early, with balloons. One smile from her would've been worth all of the papers being shuffled around at Gail's office.

What have I done?

I head down to the street and get into my waiting car.

I shut the door and sit there in the hushed silence.

"Where to?" my driver asks.

"Give me a second," I say, feeling lost. Until I figure it out. Twenty minutes later I'm walking back into Gail's conference room. My lawyers are still in the same seats as when I walked out of here not an hour ago. It feels like a lifetime.

"I didn't expect to see you back," Gail says. "I thought you had to meet Tabitha."

"I did. I missed her."

Gail looks confused.

"Look, before we cement this deal, there's something I need you to know. A point of full disclosure."

Gail's confusion turns to wariness. "We're long past the disclosure stage."

"Give us a sec?" I tip my head at the door. The lawyers file out, giving us the room.

"I don't think I'm going to like this," she says.

"I need you to know, before we enter into anything, that Tabitha isn't really my fiancée."

Gail frowns. "I'm sorry," she says. "You two seemed so good together. So suited to each other. She...softened you."

Gail's right. Tabitha softened my hard edges. She took my hard, brittle heart and made it pliant and generous. She widened my world beyond the cold rat race I was so hell-bent on dominating. She unfroze my heart.

And now it's breaking.

My voice, when it comes out, sounds strange. "Tabitha never was my fiancée," I say. "It's true she was my hairdresser for years, but I forced her into playing the part of my fiancée on your yacht."

"What?" Gail's brow furrows. "She was never your fiancée?"

"We weren't even dating. It was because of the review—Clark and I didn't understand why you were conducting it; we figured you had reservations based on my playboy behavior and that article in the *Reporter*, so the plan was to bring a fiancée..."

"To make you look like you cleaned up your act?" she bites out. "You faked an engagement?"

I nod. She says it like it's the worst thing I could've done. She's not even close. I left Tabitha sitting alone on the most painful day of her life.

Gail's angry. "So that was all fake?"

My pulse races. This is really happening. I'm really throwing away this account. "We were never engaged," I say. "We'd never even dated."

She blinks in disbelief. "She seemed to care so deeply about you."

"I took advantage," I say. "And what I need you to know is that Tabitha is a good woman, an honest woman. She hated fooling you. But she was desperate—you don't know this, but she has a repetitive stress injury that makes it so that she can't cut hair for a while. She has no way to earn money, and she would've been homeless if she hadn't agreed to sign on to play the role. The plan was that we'd break it off later this spring."

Gail still seems totally shocked. "So she was nothing but your hairdresser."

I sink into a chair. She's so much more than that. She always was. But that's not what Gail is asking. "I made her pretend. I took advantage of her hardship."

Gail's silent for a long time. The account is lost, but Gail's relationship with Tabitha doesn't have to be.

"You know how I feel about trust," Gail says. "I need to trust the people I do business with. This changes everything."

"I know."

She folds her arms over her chest. "Why the hell are you telling me this right now? I don't understand. Don't get me wrong, I'm glad you did, but I would never have known."

"Because Tabitha is the one you should be working with," I say. "Her time with you meant everything to her."

"Well, she has a funny way of showing it," Gail says. "I let her know on many occasions how much I want to work with her. Her idea has merit and she's the person to run with it and I wanted to run with her. I wanted to get my hands into that business. But she keeps refusing me."

"It's because she felt guilty about building a partnership and working closely with you while having this engagement lie going. She signed a confidentiality agreement, and her word is good. She would never break it."

"But you're breaking it. You're telling me now."

"I'm trying to do the right thing for her for once. You were more than a potential investor to her, Gail. She looks up to you in every way. And she's not the dishonest person here—I am. If anything, she was my victim."

My heart pounds. I'm letting go of the account I worked so hard to get all of these years but the idea of Tabitha having a shot at her dream feels worth it. They say when you leave a relationship, you should leave that person better off than when you found them. That's the one thing I want, now.

"I can't go through with this." She motions at the table where the papers aren't yet filed. "Our partnership. This doesn't work."

"I understand," I say.

Gail stares out the window, thoughtful. Then she grabs a scrap of paper and scribbles something. "Fine. Go and give this to Tabitha. I need her to show up at Sydmore's tomorrow at one. That's my private cell right there. Have her call if she can't make it, but we've waited long enough to get this thing started and we have a lot of work to do. You tell her I'm glad this nonsense is past. She has no choice but to work with me now."

"You might have to tell her yourself. She's not talking to me. She doesn't ever want to see me again."

She extends the card to me. "You find a way to get this number to her."

"I want to respect her space."

"Figure it out," Gail says. "Figure it out."

Chapter Twenty-Nine

Tabitha

WE THANK the Lyft driver and climb out onto the sidewalk—Jada, Mia, Max, Kelsey, Noelle, and Antonio, and me. It's two in the morning, and we have big plans to listen to Prince and dance in Kelsey's apartment.

We're heading toward our building entrance. Antonio's gone ahead; he's waiting for us under the door canopy, slumped against the wall, voguing extreme boredom, like we're all taking too long.

I'm nearly there when Jada clutches my arm. "No way!" she whispers.

I look where she's looking.

It's Rex. Coming down the walk.

Our gazes collide. My pulse kicks up.

He speeds up, his long legs eating up the distance between us, long coat flapping open behind him. His face is somber, gaze stormy, dark hair mussed. I hate that he's here, yet there's nobody I want to see more.

"I just need a second," he says. "It's important."

"We really *are* going to get that restraining order," Jada says to him, pulling me more tightly to her side.

My friends gather around me, flanking me. "How many times do you think you can fool her?" Jada says.

"It really is important," Rex repeats.

Antonio steps up to Rex. "This guy giving you trouble?"

"He's not," I say. "Go on in. I'll see what he has."

"If he just has something to give you, he can give it to you in front of us," Mia says.

"It's fine," I say.

If warning glares could kill, Rex would be dead on the sidewalk seven times over, because that's what all of my friends are giving him—major warning glances as they back off toward the door. Mia literally points to her eyes with two fingers, and then points at him. She'll be watching from the window. They all will be. They file in, and the door shuts.

"I am so sorry. I know sorry isn't enough," Rex says.

"How could you?" I gust out.

"I lost track of time. I know that's not a good enough excuse. Today of all days you deserve so much better."

"You left me sitting there."

"I know," he says, straightening. His eyes are a translucent gray in the streetlight. He looks how I feel—sad. Tired.

"So why are you here, then?" I ask. "I'm glad about what happened. It was like the universe reminding me, this is how it works. This is what happens."

"Don't say that," he says, "it's not how it works. It should never be how it works."

Do better, I'm thinking. *Please do better.* Instead, I say, "I had a fun birthday anyway, so—"

He steps forward. I can feel his heat. His mouth opens and closes like he wants to say a million things.

I should turn and leave, but somehow I can't. And it's my

birthday; I can stand here with the man I love for a few more moments, right? Pretend like things might be okay?

"This is for you." He holds out a scrap of paper.

I take it. It's a phone number and the words: *Sydmore's Café,* 1 p.m., Saturday.

I look up. "You're looking for a do-over here?"

"It's not from me, it's from Gail. It's her private line. She wants you to meet her at Sydmore's tomorrow for a working lunch. She wants to do your business, Tabitha. Invest. Be your mentor."

"You know I can't work with her, Rex. Not with the fake fiancée thing hanging out there. That's not me."

"Gail *knows*," he says. "I told her all about it. I told her how I pushed you into posing as my fiancée, that you really had no choice because of your wrist injury. I told her how much you hated lying to her, how uncomfortable you were with it."

"I don't understand," I say. "Why would you rat on yourself? I thought you were going to try to get her account in the future. You were going to fight for it and all of that."

"Well, funny story," he says. "Long story. This came today." He reaches in his breast pocket and pulls out some folded sheets of paper. "I thought you'd enjoy seeing these," he says, removing the paperclip and handing them over.

I blink. The name of some lab is in the upper right-hand corner. The page is entitled "Avuncular DNA Report." There are three columns. At the top of the first column are the words "mother" and "not tested." The middle column says "child" and "John Doe." The third column says "alleged aunt" and "Jane Doe." John Doe and Jane Doe columns are full of numbers.

"I don't understand," I say.

"John Doe is Marvin. Jane Doe is Gail." Rex points to the blue box at the bottom, just above some signatures, where it says, "0.00015%." He says, "That's the probability of their being related."

"Whoa!" I stare up at him. "He's not her nephew?"

He shakes his head.

I'm in shock. I look back down at the sheet. "What the hell?"

"It's real. My guy ran a redundant test that tells the same story." He takes the papers and shows me another sheet full of numbers from another lab with the same general results.

Maybe I'm emotionally overwrought—that's the only explanation I can think of for the fact that I'm just laughing. "Marvin's a fake nephew."

"Apparently they hacked the lab Gail used."

I clutch them to my chest. "Oh my god!"

He shoves his hands in his pocket. "Right?"

"Did you show Gail?"

"So, yes." Rex tells me the whole story—him racing over there to beat the deadline for the turnover. The details about Wydover, and how his PI traced him to Marvin. He tells me how Gail called Marvin into her office, and best of all, he describes Marvin's reactions in precise and extremely satisfying detail.

"If it weren't for you meddling kids!" I say. "Did Marvin say that? Please tell me that he did!"

Rex's lip quirks at my *Scooby-Doo* reference. And for a second, it's like everything's good with us, until I remember where we are.

I take a breath. "Did she give you the account back? Surely Gail can see that you were the one she should've gone with all the time. You were the one she wanted."

"You know how she feels about liars," Rex says.

"But you saved her ass!" I say.

Rex shakes his head.

"Wait." My mind whirls. "You lost the account because you told her about our fakery."

"She doesn't like deception. I don't either. It was the right thing to do."

"But you didn't have to." My heart pounds. "She never even cared about the article or your playboy thing—the whole review was because of Marvin. You could've had it all, but you told her. Wait." I stare down at the little card. "You told her in order to get this, didn't you?"

"She's very interested in throwing all kinds of money at you. It's a good sign. This could be big."

"Rex. You threw away the account you always wanted?"

"Getting the account I always wanted with trickery was always the wrong thing," he says.

"But…"

"It's just another account," he says over my protests. "She thinks your idea's worthwhile. She wouldn't waste her time otherwise. You know that, right?"

I clutch the little card so hard, it's a miracle I'm not ripping it. "No more pathetically impoverished. Maybe."

He smiles sadly.

"Sorry, it's just…this is amazing. I didn't mean to bring up the hate list," I say.

"Don't call it that. It wasn't hate," he says. "Clark always tells me I'm shit at feelings. You have no idea how right he is. Because the way you've been barging into my thoughts the past two years, I was too dense to know what that meant. The way I'd turn over the things you say in my mind, over and over from one Friday to the next. The image of how fucking beautiful you are and the way you blazed into my dim reality, I didn't know."

"Rex," I say.

"No, listen," he says. That little furrow forms between his eyebrows as he continues. "The way I'd obsess about you so much that I could barely enjoy being with other women, I didn't know how to process it. You made me feel emotions I didn't have a name for, and the feelings were so fucking strong, Tabitha, so strong that I thought they had to be hate, because what other feeling could disrupt my life? What other feeling could take over my mind, or make my heart race in the middle of the night? What else?"

Cars and shouts and sirens and other late-night sounds fade into the background. There's just Rex. I swallow back the dryness in my mouth.

"All of those fierce, furious feelings…" His voice sounds hoarse. "That was the opposite of hate and I didn't know."

I clutch the paper. My pulse whooshes in my ears. "I—"

"Please." He puts up a hand. "Let me finish. It was love, Tabitha. Your ridiculous soap operas and bubbly personality and sparkles and Hello Kitty shit and all that, those were things I love about you. I won't stop loving you."

I blink, at a loss.

"Also, that couples dynamic you decided on for us?" he continues. "Me as the alpha who shows his soft side only to you? It's wrong. I'm the fuckup and the bully who's not used to having other people to care for, who didn't know his own heart until it was too late. I'm the guy who will do anything for you. The guy who'll spend as long as it takes to make this up to you and never give up. And you don't have to do anything back. You don't have to be fun. You just have to be you. That's enough. Because I'm the guy who'll always love you no matter what."

My throat is so clogged I can't speak. Did he say he loves me?

"I get it," he says. "I don't deserve another chance, but I'm not done. I don't expect you to say anything now, but I'm not going to stop trying. Okay?"

He comes to me and he kisses my forehead. The feeling of

it whooshes through my heart. Before I know what's happening, he's walking off into the night, black coat flying after him.

Cold air hits my lips and tongue. That's the only way I know I'm standing there slack-jawed.

Mouth just hanging open.

Rex gave up his most precious business goal for me.

He loves me.

"Rex!" I call after him. "Wait."

He stops. He turns.

"That thing you just said."

"Yeah?"

I swallow. "It might be a bit long for a couples dynamic," I say.

I start toward him. I can't read his expression, but I feel him. I always have.

"How about this— you're the alpha who shows me his soft side." I stop in front of him and smooth his lapels, cool from the night air. "And I'm the girl who's been burned a lot, but she'll risk her heart for you." I look up. "Because she knows you. And she loves you. She always has."

"Kitten." He cradles my cheeks in his hands. "What?"

"I love you," I say. "I always have."

He sucks in a breath, palms warm on my cheeks. "Heart face."

I go up on my toes and kiss him. "Heart face isn't a thing," I say into the kiss. "But I love you anyway."

Epilogue

Six months later
Tabitha

I'M LEANING on the polished oak railing of Gail's yacht, looking out at the vast ocean stretching for miles around. The water is a deep shade of cobalt blue, with just the tips of the waves dancing and sparkling in the dazzling sunlight.

Rex comes up behind me and wraps his arms around me. I've been here for a couple days, working with Gail to get ready for our huge influencer party celebrating the launch of ten flagship storefronts across seven cities.

He came in by helicopter late last night. We have a huge suite up on the fifth level this time around. It's the prettiest thing I've ever seen.

Rex has spent the early morning directing his empire from a cabana.

"Things going good?" I ask him.

He sets his chin on top of my head. "Very good."

We fit together in every way now. I never knew it could be like this.

Back in the city, I have my own office in Gail's tower, but after hours I usually head to Rex's building and we work together, sharing ideas and insights while the rest of the city heads home. I used to think he was way too much of a workaholic, but now I get what it feels like to be passionate about a project.

Sundays, however, are strictly us-days. At first Rex got twitchy from not working for a whole day, but now it's natural. We read the paper in bed. We head out to the park with Mike, the rescue dog we adopted—Mike's a big pit bull mix who's as sweet as taffy, even when Seymour runs free on Rex's living room floor.

We love going out to the farmers market. Rex has gotten into cooking, of all things, and okay, the way he does it is a bit intense—he's competitive and perfectionistic, and he even has his own signature dish, but we laugh about it. And then we hang out on his deck overlooking the park and feast.

Seymour and I stay at his sprawling and palatial condo more often than not. I'll be moving in soon, but that doesn't mean I'll lose connection with my girl squad.

Quite the opposite—Gail and I are opening a style storefront right down the block from our building, right on 9th Avenue—next to the Cookie Madness where everybody hangs out. Needless to say, I see my friends from the building just as much as I ever did.

"Oh, the monotony," Rex says, as the waves turn up their dazzle-factor.

"Such monotony," I agree. "Can you even?"

"So did Jada have any news?" he asks, settling in next to me at the railing.

By *news* he means news about the wrecking ball. I just got off the phone with Jada. There have been rumors that

Malcolm Blackberg is sending out eviction notices soon, and that the wrecking balls will be moving in. People are freaking.

"Okay, I don't even know where to start," I say. "You remember Noelle? Sweet, shy, plain little mail carrier?"

"Who never rode in an elevator until the age of twenty-seven?" he asks.

I snort. Rex has been fixated on that detail ever since Noelle confessed it when a bunch of us were out.

A waiter comes over with mimosas for us. We take them and clink glasses.

"So get this—Noelle got in to see that jackass this week," I tell him, taking a sip. "Face to face. To plead for the building."

"Wait, what?" He turns to me. "She got in to see Malcolm Blackberg?"

"Yes, the girl who never rode an elevator actually got in to see the big bad wolf."

Rex narrows his eyes. "How? Do you know how hard I tried to get in there? Henry Locke was trying, too. Two billionaires tried to get to him."

"Apparently she wore her letter carrier uniform. But here's the crazy part," I say. "I don't even know whether to believe it —somehow Malcolm Blackberg's people mistook her for his new court-ordered executive sensitivity coach or something like that. And Noelle just went with it."

"What?" Rex nearly spits out his drink. "That little girl is impersonating Blackberg's executive coach?"

"That's what Jada said. Is that even a thing?" I ask. "Court-ordered executive coach?"

"People are always hauling Blackberg into court," he says. "I could see a judge ordering some kind of training for him. The man's a psycho. But Noelle? No way," he says.

"Jada says they've barely heard from her ever since. Maybe Jada misunderstood. Maybe I misunderstood."

"Maybe your mind is still melted from this morning," Rex says.

My face goes completely beet red just in time for one of the party planners to appear and show me images of the way they're doing the tables in the dining room.

"I love these glittery willow frond things. Can you have more of them? I just want these centerpieces so crazy bright."

"Agreed," Gail says, walking up. She's in her signature black, her thick round glasses contrasting with the snowy white of her hair. "Unexpected shine, that's our brand."

The planner nods and walks off.

"I feel like we're ready," I say to Gail. Working with her has been a dream. She's more than a partner—she's become a friend.

"Ahead of schedule," Gail says, settling in next to Rex, putting Rex in the middle of us. "Rex, nice to see you."

"Likewise, Gail," he says.

"Tell me," she says, squinting at him. "You think they'll throw the book at Wydover?"

"They got one of his own guys to turn state's witness," Rex says. "The man kept records. There's no way Wydover doesn't do time. He'll take a deal, but it won't be pretty."

"I dodged a bullet," she says.

"Good for all of us to have a man like that go down," Rex says. We don't mention Marvin. Marvin seems to have gone into hiding, which is probably for the best. Wanda heard he's working handyman odd jobs down in Albuquerque under a fake name.

"You been watching what my in-house guys have been doing with our portfolio?" she asks Rex in her usual point-blank style.

Rex gives a half shrug. "Well…" he says. "I'm out there, so you know."

"Yeah, I know. You're being diplomatic. I bet you've got thoughts."

I stiffen. Rex has a lot of thoughts about the team Gail chose. Namely, that they suck.

"I always have thoughts," Rex says.

"That's something I've always liked about you," she says. "And I'm gonna be honest with you here—I don't like the numbers I'm getting."

Rex nods. He says nothing.

"I don't like being played. I won't work with people who think they can play me," she says. "But I do like a man who tries to make things right."

Rex is silent, listening. My heart is pounding. I've been planting seeds with Gail about Rex. I bite my lip.

"You came to me instead of letting things implode on their own," Gail says. "You could've let me twist and then picked up the pieces, but you didn't do that. And now I see what's on Tabitha's finger."

"What is on my finger? Oh, look!" I hold up the diamond ring Rex gave to me. He proposed to me at our fake favorite sushi restaurant, Sushi of Gari, which is now one of our real favorite restaurants. The ring is crazy sparkly, and I never get sick of looking at it.

Gail smiles her crafty smile. "Looks like you're fiancés after all. So what do you say?" she asks him. "You want to take over my funds?"

"Gail," he says, "I'd be honored."

"Well, thank goodness." She clasps his hand. "Let's get that ball rolling." He looks over her shoulder and catches my eye. Later, he'll playfully accuse me of planting seeds with her. And I'll tell him that of course I planted seeds with her. And we'll wrestle on the bed, and I'll threaten him with a jasmine-scented face cloth. And things will turn dirty from there.

But for now, I'm biting my lip, and he's watching me bite my lip, and then he comes to me and pulls me close.

Gail is looking out over the horizon. "Look, look!" She points. "Do you see?"

We squint out at shimmery water. Suddenly, without warning, a large black whale tail breaks the bright surface, surging up with the cool strength of something that's been there all along, ancient and forever.

I put my head on Rex's shoulder and sigh.

~ *The End* ~

Acknowledgments

I'm so lucky to have so many talented and generous badasses in my life to help me find my way through the long and sometimes foggy maze of authoring. You guys!

In chronological order, I owe massive gratitude to Joanna Chambers, who cares about themes and journeys and will never let me get away with a just a boring alphahole dom sex scene. Thank you for helping me see this dynamic with clarity. And writerly sorceress Molly O'Keefe, you helped me keep going forward and helped me see Tabitha in an achingly new way, and tirelessly helped me nail the important moment of their couples dance in the salon.

Elizabeth Jarrett Andrew, Marcia Peck, Mark Powell, and Terri Whitman, you brought so many new ideas and artistic nuances to this manuscript, I can't even count them. Most important, you helped me to find the perspective that I needed. Your ideas on how to make things work, how to create better Clark moments and better Rex and Tabitha interactions were golden! And also, Tabitha would've never gotten to see the whales without you! You are the best!

Thanks also to Sadye Scott-Hainchek of Fussy Librarian—

you bring such art and care to the proof/copyedit process, and Judy Zweifel—you are so professional and thorough and thoughtful about the tiniest comma!

And Courtenay Bennett, you found so many little flubs, and you also brought a true artist's eye to how things might be tweaked for better reading. So amazing. And thank you to Joan Lai and Shelley Charlton for reaching out with late-breaking catches. This book is truly the product of a village of people I adore!

Cover love, as always, goes out to Michele Catalano! You are so beyond talented! And to Wander Aguiar for the photography. Major props also to Melissa Gaston—I can't believe how lucky I am to have you in my corner. And the social butterfly gang – Kelley Beckham, Brooke Nowiski, Shannon Passmore and everyone else there – thank you for being such smart, generous helpers. And Nina Grinstead, you are just my total rock star wizard of everything and such a sweet friend.

I'm so grateful to my blogger friends, Instagram book lover peeps, Goodreads reviewers, and other reviewer pals who take the time to read and review these books. It's a creative labor of love that you do, and I appreciate what you write more than I can say.

I'm also so grateful to my fun-loving and creative ARC gang—you have generous spirits, you really do, and it just means the world when you embrace my characters and take the time to read and review my books and then to usher them into the world. Writing is waaaay more fun when I picture you guys reading my books! (which…umm…I frequently do!)

And big love to my Fabulous Gang! You are always there with kind words and fun comments and fresh takes when I need them. Your generosity and your enthusiasm feed my soul.

And finally, thank you to all of you readers out there for buying and reading my books. It's just everything. Heart eyes to you all!

Also by Annika Martin

Stand-alone romantic comedy (read in any order)

Most Eligible Billionaire

The Billionaire's Wake-up-call Girl

Breaking The Billionaire's Rules

The Billionaire's Fake Fiancée

Return Billionaire to Sender

Just Not That Into Billionaires

∾

Find a complete list of books and audiobooks at www.annikamartinbooks.com

About the Author

Annika Martin is a New York Times bestselling author who sometimes writes as RITA®-award-winning Carolyn Crane. She lives in Minneapolis with her husband; in her spare time she enjoys taking pictures of her cats, consuming boatloads of chocolate suckers, and tending her wild, bee-friendly garden.

newsletter:
http://annikamartinbooks.com/newletter

Facebook:
www.facebook.com/AnnikaMartinBooks

Instagram:
instagram.com/annikamartinauthor

website:
www.annikamartinbooks.com

email:
annika@annikamartinbooks.com

Lightning Source UK Ltd.
Milton Keynes UK
UKHW020653281022
411251UK00016B/1108

9 781944 736156